WALKING THE DOG

ELIZABETH SWADOS

WALKING THE DOG

A NOVEL

With an afterword by Gloria Steinem

THE FEMINIST PRESS
AT THE CITY UNIVERSITY OF NEW YORK
NEW YORK CITY

Published in 2016 by the Feminist Press
at the City University of New York
The Graduate Center
365 Fifth Avenue, Suite 5406
New York, NY 10016

feministpress.org

First Feminist Press edition 2016

 This book is supported in part by an award from the National Endowment for the Arts.

 This book was made possible thanks to a grant from New York State Council on the Arts with the support of Governor Andrew Cuomo and the New York State Legislature.

First printing June 2016

Cover design and text design by Suki Boynton

Names: Swados, Elizabeth, author.
Title: Walking the dog : a novel / Elizabeth Swados.
Description: New York : Feminist Press, 2016.
Identifiers: LCCN 2015048949| ISBN 9781558619210 (softcover) | ISBN 9781558619227 (ebook)
Subjects: LCSH: Self-realization in women—Fiction. | Mothers and daughters—Fiction. | Parent and adult child—Fiction. | Ex-convicts—Fiction. | BISAC: FICTION / Coming of Age. | FICTION / Contemporary Women. | PETS / Dogs / General.
Classification: LCC PS3569.W17 W35 2016 | DDC 813/.54--dc23
LC record available at https://lccn.loc.gov/2015048949

This book is dedicated to

Judith Ginsberg
Rebecca Keren
Richard Sadowsky

and to Roz.

WALKING THE DOG

I'm not used to walking on grounds without fences. I don't know what to do with the four corners of open space. And to look up and not see a watchtower? The sky seems infinite and looming. Like it could swallow you. I understand the concept of crating a puppy. Back at Clayton I always used them for training. The dogs knew where freedom began and ended. Life was clear and squared in. There were the bars on the walls. There was the gated door. The door stayed closed unless I opened it. There was the space in the corner where the crate fit, and when a dog was let out, he knew exactly how much space he had to walk. What would my dogs have done with a wide-open road with no gates? Puppies running without boundaries. They might run and run until they exhausted themselves. They might've gone so far from the starting place that they wouldn't know what it meant to return. The vastness of space might fool them too. They could go just a tiny distance and yet feel as if they'd arrived at some gigantic different location. Lost. Afraid. The puppies need their crates.

First, you have to get used to the basic concept of living. And practice the small, safe, familiar moves. You come and go through the recognizable door, hearing the recognizable click both ways. And then, one day, you nose your way onto the sidewalk or grass. But even then there's a leash holding you. The freedom is exhilarating. The disappearance of gates is terrifying. If you're lucky, when you go too far the owner pulls you back. Or if you're too shy to move, you have an owner to tempt you out of your corner with treats. These first few months out of prison, I could have used one of those retractable leashes. And a treat or two.

THE EARLY DAYS OF FREEDOM

A few days ago I fell down a full flight of stairs inside a loft building on Wooster Street. I was yanked by three Yorkies, each one
no bigger than a spare rib: Larry, Moe, and Curly, after the Three
Stooges (though Curly is a girl). Their owner, Mr. Arthur, was
an overweight, slightly alcoholic lawyer on the verge of losing
his job due to downsizing. He had the judgmental snideness
of the mean category of drunk. He'd recently separated from
his wife, and they had joint custody of the three hairbrush-like
dogs. My job was to deliver them from the lawyer's loft to his
wife's apartment above Taste of India on Bleecker Street and
vice versa. This was because the two weren't speaking to each
other. Whenever they had something to communicate, they'd
tuck a note under one of the dogs' collars. One note said, *I'm
not renewing the fucking fire insurance.* (Of course I read them.)
My favorite missive so far: *If you can get your dick out of your
assistant's vagina, your son might appreciate a call.* One day I may
write a note of my own and fold it under Larry or Moe's collar.
Something like, *I've planted a bomb under the bonsai tree and it's
going to blow now.* Just to see what it might do. Normally this
was an easy twice-a-week job, not like dragging Doorbell, the
giant bullmastiff, around a long block. But when I took the fall
I was a bit shaken. I couldn't stop. I couldn't go into bandaging

or a cast. It brought on the horrors. What if I'd broken a limb? There'd be no one to sit with me in the ER while I waited for the X-ray. The complexities of freedom were continually being revealed to me. Every day I discovered another way in which I had to catch up.

CLAYTON

I got this job at PetPals through the warden at Clayton Correctional. She was a five-foot cowgirl named Jen Lee. Her voice was a cross between Huddie Ledbetter and Tom Waits. Her chopped gray hair made her seem very butch, though everyone knew she had a husband at one time, and a couple of grown kids could be seen driving in and out of the warden's house when they visited. Jen Lee tried to come off like the new progressive style of warden. She'd have a regular game of dominoes with a group of guards and walk the grounds unarmed. She'd take her strolls up the hill to the ivy-covered houses where the honor prisoners lived (the ones with years of no demerits and plenty of school credits). Then she'd turn toward the big gravel hill and follow the path toward the main facilities. She'd stop at the flat, one-floor "special detention" house for the girls who were just too mean to live with anyone else. Jen Lee liked to spend time with those snakes. She didn't take their shit.

Anyway, back in 2008, she called me into her office. She sat in her long upholstered chair, her toes barely touching the floor. "I got a letter from one of our graduates," she said. (She calls the ones who get out "graduates.") She rolled back and forth and sideways in her dark chair, enjoying the ride. "Yeah, one of our girls, Lucinda—you don't know her—is starting a dog walking service with her useless junkie of a boyfriend. She's a bit of a nutcase, but so are you. And maybe her business has a chance in this bloodsucking economy. She's looking for girls from the Dogs for the Blind program. If you get parole, I'll get you her number!"

I didn't answer her.

I wasn't prepared to dive into a real skilled job. But I didn't challenge authority for no reason. I'd learned the technique from my dogs. Seeming obedience, but instant readiness. "You wanna get outta here, don't you?" Jen Lee asked. She could see the bargaining going on in my brain. "Aren't you doing the good girl thing now? Sewing up your prom dress?" She was suspicious. She grabbed a swizzle stick from a round container of them on her desk and started chewing. She started spitting plastic shards into the air. "I'm going to recommend you to Lucinda," she said, "regardless." This was a typical way of her demonstrating her compassionate and liberal sadism. She knew I had PTSD and a pocketbook full of other troubles that could end me up, like so many others, back in the slammer less than a year after parole.

Unlike most of the women at Clayton, I hadn't lived each hour waiting for the morning I'd get out. I guess I'd become somewhat Zen. Or passive. Or suicidal. They said that when you got out of the hospital after a long sickness, the first day you're home pictures, scenes, and faces from the entire stay would flash before your eyes. I didn't know what would happen when my body hit air. Would I fly or incinerate? Jen Lee just watched my brain negotiate between *stay* or *go*. "Everyone's afraid," she said. It's a hell of a thing to contemplate life starting all over at the age of forty-three. After over twenty-five years of being locked up, how do I untie the strings of knots my life got tied into? Jen Lee dripped her chewed-up swizzle stick into the trash, dug out another, and chewed.

"It's like being born," she told me. "Only you're aware of it. All that life coming at you. When you've been in a dark room, one blast of light can blind you."

Jen Lee started searching through her desk. It was covered with dog-eared files, Post-its, and memos. There were key chains and handwritten letters and drawings from different prisoners' kids. She dug down deep in a file drawer and pulled out a pair of ugly, bright-yellow wraparound sunglasses.

"Here," she said.

I winced, lowered my eyes, and shifted uncomfortably. The color was aggressively phony and the shapes of each eye minutely different enough from the other to distort the wearer's face into a glaring inquisitor.

"These'll make the sun less bright for a few months." Then she turned back to stern lady warden. "But you gotta keep up with all your therapies, Carleen. The world can't adjust its colors and shapes for a loony tune. You're gonna have to live in all those waiting rooms when you leave here."

"Absolutely," I lied. What was she talking about? I carried a life sentence. I wasn't getting parole.

LADIES WHO LUNCH

Sarabeth's was one of those brunch places for ladies who were the opposite of an ex-con. It looked as if Laura Ashley had designed it for the interior of a dollhouse. There were lace embroideries around every quilted, flowered pillow. You could catch a waft at different times of brown sugar, ginger, cinnamon, or molasses. I felt like I forgot my bonnet. My daughter had chosen this place ostensibly because it was near where she resided with her father, stepsiblings, and stepmother in their town house—yes, town house. I'd never seen this proof of Leonard's success because I was considered unhealthy, perhaps contagious, to the family unit. And despite my nature, I'd cooled it with the stalking. Anything I did got me in twice the trouble of anyone else. Convict karma. My daughter had two stepbrothers, aged eight and six. I'd never known their names.

Her name used to be Pony. I named her that in the prison hospital with the hopes that she'd gallop through life, mane in the wind, unobstructed by fences, halters, bridles, and saddles. Last year, the year I got out, I received an anonymous note saying she had changed her name to Batya Shulamit. Batya was the princess who rescued Moses from the bulrushes. She explained this to me in impeccable square penmanship on graph paper: *I hope I will be able to act as bravely*

and selflessly as Batya did toward her fellow man. "Fellow."
"Man." She didn't seem to be a feminist, at least linguisti-
cally. This was her only direct communication with me since
she'd been born. I knew that Leonard, her father, had moved
toward a new bond with his Jewish past. Perhaps it coincided
with his thinning hair or soft belly. I didn't know. To be fair,
perhaps it had helped him recover the belief in humanity that
I'd destroyed. The new family belonged to a synagogue where
the rabbi was called by his first name and where, during Shab-
bat, the congregants would dance and sing in the aisles as if
participating in *The Pirates of Penzance*. I could never visual-
ize Batya dipping and bobbing in any aisles. Apart from strict
ballet lessons, my savior of Moses didn't seem to possess the
free dancing spirit of the Hasidim on Purim. Perhaps the loss
of me weighted down her feet. I knew all this because, as I
said, I stalked her from time to time. Never for dangerous
reasons. I didn't even know if I was curious. By the way, in
her note, she'd informed me that she would not explain the
second name, "Shulamit," until she decided I deserved the
honor. I liked that. Judge Judy of the Upper East Side.

I'd arrived fifteen minutes early to Sarabeth's to observe her
entrance. This was the first time in the four months I'd been
out that she'd agreed to meet me. I'd taken the luxury of showing up first. On her first and only visit to see me inside Clayton
Prison, she had to wait for me in the dim and dark "family"
room with its card tables and folding chairs. Neither of us
benefited from my arrival in coveralls and shackles at the feet,
waist, and ankles. Perhaps that was why she only came once,
looked at me, turned around, screamed at the top of her lungs,
and left. She was four at the time and already prissy as hell. She
never wrote me or sent me bad drawings.

That day at Sarabeth's she was wearing lilac overalls. Her

white blouse had a round collar and the buttons were plastic yellow flowers. Her innocent apparel made me nervous. She had waist-length, straight red hair—the color of strawberries and red oranges. Her cheeks were chubby, but a lean young girl was emerging from the square awkwardness. Her brown eyes looked down. I always looked down or to the side, too. She was unabashedly shy, my biblical geisha girl. Her hair was held back in a headband. It was shiny and lit with a rainbow of cheap colors. For some reason, this accentuated my anxiety. She was Alice in Wonderland without the pursed lips or the flirtatious petulance. Her skin was pale and clear except for the tremendous blushing which rose onto her neck when the hostess noticed her. She had an overbite and a train track of braces. She tried to cover the hardware with her upper lip. This made her look like she was constantly thinking. She'd just turned eleven and was only on the verge of puberty. She carried her unhappy body along as if it were a second person. She didn't know why she'd made the decision to meet me. She'd already given back the one gift I'd tried to present her, a notebook with a horse sketched on the cover. I'd heard she loved to write. She was clear with me: "You don't deserve to give me presents."

My red-haired Alice, my gentile-looking Batya Shulamit, delicately dipped into the bentwood chair directly across from me. Her taste in clothes worried me. Already somewhat grandmotherly. And so proper. Her posture was severe and upright. Maybe she was trying to hold herself together. "I mustn't stay long," she said with a formality that made me want to bash Leonard's teeth in. Didn't he ever tickle her?

"Of course," I said with the instant agreeableness of one who's up shit creek already, just trying to hold on and get her to see me again.

"I have a tutorial for my bat mitzvah."

The waiter, an anorexic out-of-work actor, interrupted my impassioned exchange with this creature who happened to be my daughter. We both ordered tea and miniature pumpkin muffins. I couldn't stand either. At least tea took time to boil. That should buy me a few extra minutes with her.

"You have a tutor?" I asked dumbly.

"Yes," she said, bored with me and the conversation. "We study Aramaic and Torah. She is helping me prepare my portion and my Haftorah."

"You like her?" I asked, obviously the stupidest choice of questions when I could've inquired after Aramaic, Torah portions, or Haftorah. But alas. Batya Shulamit leaned her squarish little chest forward a bit.

"I love her," she said, with no small amount of venom toward the nontutor across from her.

"She looks like an ancient Moroccan Berber queen and she's been to Israel and she sings and has written a musical about Rachel and Leah. She is also in the Folksbiene Yiddish Theater Company and leads a spin class on the Upper West Side where Chelsea Clinton has been known to go."

"Why is that important?" I asked. I genuinely wanted to know and hoped it would open up many roads of conversation.

Batya took her pink backpack off her chair, folded her napkin, and tapped her lips. I'd desecrated the teachings of the twelve fathers.

"*What* has *that* got to do with *anything*?" Her face was flushed. Could a preteen have a stroke? She was clearly pissed.

"I didn't mean to offend you," I replied.

She stood up with great purpose.

"This isn't working out," she said.

"I'm sorry. I wasn't making fun." I was shocked at how I was begging the little snit. "Let me try again."

"Perhaps," she said. "But not at this moment." She deftly took a five-dollar bill from her backpack and dropped it on the table.

"That should be approximately half," she said. "I'm leaving. Elisheva will be at the house."

Elisheva? Had I busted out of the pen and landed in Ancient Egypt?

"Please," I said.

"Another time, perhaps." My daughter was a step from the table. "There will be no goodbye handshakes or kisses." I watched her leave. She walked quickly through the restaurant as if she were Audrey Hepburn and had just been slapped.

"Steal a fucking teddy bear," I said under my breath.

BEYONCÉ AND ARETHA

The keys hung off the loop of my jeans and pulled the frayed-denim waist down. I liked the weight of the metal even though it reminded me of all those guards at Clayton and how you'd immediately tense up when you heard the jinglejangle. Transformers: Those cars that'd turn into angular robot monsters. Those Japanese warriors that'd turn into humanoid steel gargoyles with superpowered weapons and glowing eyes. A somewhat appropriate description of a guard if you were left alone with him.

I hadn't bought a chain to put the keys around my neck, nor had I bought one of those little Velcro dyke packs to snap around my waist. It felt appropriate to have my jeans falling down. The heavier the weight, the greater measure of my success. It meant they're giving me more dogs. My fat-faced junkie boss said the clients were "in affirmation with your style. Don't fuck up." Then he nodded out. His woman Lucinda, who was locked up for being his mule, seemed to be staying clean, but she was snotty to me because I was requested by more dog owners than she was. I guess it was because I took the time to play with each dog and, in some cases, I did training. I wasn't required to do this. We were supposed to just do the walk, dump, and pee patrol, but New York dogs . . . they have such weird lives. Everyone should have two dogs, not just one. The potential isolation of eight hours alone while the owner's at work gave me an ache. I would've liked to keep them with me all day, to hold them and protect their innocence.

There was this very tall, somewhat Finnish or Danish, fashionable chick named Tess who ran the Foundation for Zambo Sneakers. An oxymoron. Zambo made over-the-top running shoes, and their profits could've run a third world country. Of course, they used children in Thailand, Cambodia, and Vietnam to make the sneakers for two cents an hour in sweatshops that'd make the Triangle Shirtwaist Factory sound like a luxury corporate office building. Tess traveled the world planning rock concerts with Bono and the like to raise money to feed the kids her corporation starved. She had no concept of the paradox. She was home three weeks or so out of every month, and Edward, her handy man and lover, would sleep there when she was gone. I'd walk Beyoncé and Aretha, her Afghan hounds, two times a day—sometimes three if she was "really stuck" at one of those openings at a Soho gallery for painters who specialized in squares or dots. Zambo made sneakers that would go with evening gowns and could cost up to $1,800 a pair. Tess's Afghan hounds were as beautiful and superficial as Zambo sneakers. So was Tess. She truly loved her "poo poos," and paid me thirty dollars extra under the table to brush the shit out of them once a week. They were spectacular looking—a combination of couture runway models and George Lucas planetary hookers—but I don't know what category of brains they were made with. After a month of bribing them with steak tartar, they started to delicately bounce to me when I called. But sitting or lying down was so beyond them one would compare it to a dyslexic child taking a math SAT. If I commanded "sit," they'd cock their coiffed heads. "What?" Never mind.

I eventually figured out how to reach them. They now walked absolutely by my side as if I were a pimp. They did the same for Tess which, when she wore her knee-length Humphrey Bogart leather trench coat, high-heeled matching boots, and Burberry subtle but multicolored woven scarf, made her look like a casual full-page shot in an expensive Italian fashion magazine. Pedestrians slowed down when they saw the combination, as if she was famous but they couldn't place her. Tess had no desire to be famous. When we occasionally crossed paths, she'd talk about a Prada boutique that was miraculously opening in Croatia or the banquet they'd held at the Intercontinental Hotel in Abu Dhabi for the new roller coaster they were building there. Then she'd switch to the horror of clitoridectomies and tell me that Zambo would hold a benefit fashion show to send doctors to those barbaric countries that cut off "labias" so the doctors could restore sexual pleasure. In the midst of all this, Beyoncé and Aretha lay, bored as teenage girls, on Tess's giant shabby-chic couches as she downed a half bottle of Vitamin Water Zero and rushed out.

Afghan hounds may not be as stupid as I think they are. They could just be vain and cold. I am a big-boned ex-con in jeans and a sweatshirt. Beyoncé and Aretha would pull slightly away from each of my thighs as if they didn't want to be seen with me. This could've been my imagination since I was the one who didn't want to be seen with me. But with Tess they were as coordinated, light-footed, and fluffy as back up singers to Diana Ross. One credit I had to give those two drag queens (don't Afghans remind you of drag queens?): they'd always walk calmly and balanced. They'd never favor one side or the other or throw their extremely tall Finnish mistress off-balance in her fashionable high heels. This was important because she only had one leg. She'd lost the left to cancer when she was eighteen. Luckily she was a runner, skier, skater, and athletic goddess type, so physical therapy was, though not easy, able to give her the gift of a walk that didn't click or limp. She also had a prosthesis that was designed by scientists in Israel to give maximum flexibility and strength.

I knew all of this because one day I picked up Beyoncé and Aretha an hour early—prearranged—but Tess had forgotten. I rang the doorbell, announced myself, and simply opened the lock as I always did, and there was Tess, in a Beverly Hills Hotel–type bathrobe, hopping around her stainless steel and glass kitchen. Beyoncé and Aretha didn't bother to greet me. They never did. But Tess let out one little cry and froze in place like a flamingo on her gorgeous, smooth, muscled right leg. I probably should've backed out, but I was mesmerized.

"Oh, I forgot. I forgot," she said with her alto voice, which had an indecipherable accent of some sort. "You're here for my honeys," she said.

"I'm sorry—we'd scheduled for . . . " My apology was awkward and not very caring. I'd seen a lot worse.

Tess immediately regained her composure. She'd obviously been through the trauma of hundreds of cocktail parties and could ace any surprise attack.

"This . . . ," she said, pointing to the stump hidden by the robe, "is my most profound secret." Her dramatics were almost convincing. "Now you have possession of my two precious doll-dolls and my life's lie. You mustn't tell a soul. Some demon will blackmail me and I'll lose my position at Zambo."

"Listen, Tess," I said. I almost stood at attention. "I'm an ex-con. I'm on parole. I'm just trying to pay for my room at the halfway house, eat, and keep out of that life. I really don't give a shit about what the other dog owners or walkers know or don't know. I just want to get all your dogs home on time, hopefully having defecated in a way that proves they're healthy, and come back on time the next day to fulfill my duties as their play partner, trainer, or exercise supervisor. This is the first conversation you and I have had in the five months that I've been walking Beyoncé and Aretha, and it stays on the inside."

"That's right. You were in jail," Tess perked up as if comforted. "This must be all trivial bullshit to you."

"Not losing a leg," I said. "But gossip couldn't be less important."

She slipped her stump into a flesh-colored contraption that gave the appearance of half a mannequin's leg and half science-fiction creature.

"Well, I shall live in terror of you for the rest of my life," she said cheerfully. "You can blackmail me, kidnap me, and steal my leg, or sell my story to the *Enquirer* for extra cash. I could also have you murdered. But I don't know any assassins. Do you? Being an ex-convict and all?"

Stupid as an Afghan, I thought. "Don't you think I should take Beyoncé and Aretha out?" I asked her. I hooked up my reality TV stars to their halters as they reluctantly abandoned their separate chairs, took their time stretching their long legs, and slunk to my side like sullen teenagers. "Queens," I said under my breath. They rewarded me with swishes of their tails.

"This didn't happen," Tess said.

"It certainly didn't," I replied.

I don't even know if it did.

TIKKUN OLAM

Before Clayton my prisons changed locations and descriptions. First came a nameless Federal House of Detention. I don't remember much except being shocked into a state of white blindness. Knowing percussion as I did, I pounded away my fear on the metal bars. A couple of the other women newly transferred from court slapped my shoulders to stop me. I've always been crazy about metal. Metal. The slam of the metal doors. The keys in the locks. Again and again. Door after door. The keys in the calloused hands of the cops. My hands drummed on the bars like they were rusty marimbas. One guard slammed my hand with a baton to get me to stop. I think she broke some fingers. I didn't feel pain but it became harder to hold brushes. I still can't quite bend my fingers the whole way. I have so many breaks and cuts that have healed in weird ways, Tim Burton would want to sculpt me for a pietà.

I was welcomed into the circus cage with other tigers yet to be tamed. I got kicked around by the guards pretty badly because there'd been cops hurt by my crimes. But there was an upside. The other newbies left me alone out of some perverse respect. All the women from the city corners to the psycho farmlands were testing each other out, choosing up territories, and making profitable but perilous relationships. I wasn't aware of these unspoken bargains.

But I miraculously encountered an ugly but lifesaving angel right at the top. She reached out with a *"Tikkun olam,"* meaning a gift of good for no reason. The fat-assed, pale redheaded lady at Federal admissions took an extra amount of time, for God knows why, going over my papers despite all the cursing and shoving. (Everyone was in such a nervous hurry to end up nowhere.) This lady gave me a once over. She was maybe thirty-six with small green eyes, a pug nose, and a goldfish mouth; she had chubby pink fingers and bitten nails.

"We're changing your name," she growled between little yellow teeth.

I think I shook my head. My hair was dyed into white and gray and purple stripes, and fell past my waist. It was a wild animal shake, a crystal meth growl—the last remnants of a deluded terrorist. The pig was stealing my identity.

"Ester Rosenthal ain't gonna go down too well in these cells. They'll kill you within a day and a half for crucifying their Lord. Everyone goes for the Jews first. They think they smell hidden money. Jews are the devil. The whole tail and horns stuff. Save your ass. I'm changing your name. Carleen Kepper. Say it."

"Carleen Kepper," I repeated dumbly. Then, in a sweeping motion, she grabbed a pair of scissors and roughly cut my hair. I was scared of the blades so I didn't fight back. Nor did I fight when I heard the buzz of the shaver, and, yes, she shaved all of it off. I was bald with messy patches. The other women whistled and whooped. So my long hair and beatnik youth disappeared with my famous name. Maybe the spitting and pickpocketing I'd endured until now would cease. She snapped another picture of me.

"That's you from now on." She handed me PJs, a toothbrush, an airline-sized toothpaste, and an ID card that read "Carleen Kepper #231-B" with that driver's license picture she'd taken. I looked like a possessed character out of a Stephen King novel. Carleen Kepper—excommunicated from her tribe. Why had this gnome from *Peer Gynt* saved me? Maybe a Jew had done a mitzvah for her. Maybe she could see I was barely eighteen.

SERVING TIME

Time is not my friend. I've been bashed around so much my brain is a broken chandelier. I can't remember the year of processing or my trial, but maybe I will. In the meantime I stand here.

The name of my first "home" (maximum security prison) was Powell Federal Prison, and it was in Ohio. Even though my real name continued to dominate the papers, I no longer looked anything like what was being broadcast all over TV, and prison populations change frequently, so those who recognized me were mostly gone before they made a commotion. I'd also found a temporary life-saving vocation: drawing. I drew perfect caricatures of anyone who wanted them on the recreation room wall. Every night the guards made me wash off the ink from the Sharpies I stole from so-called art therapy. Every day I started again. My knuckles bled for weeks. But it was worth it when for some reason I was in focus again and my picture and real name showed up in USA Today and Time. Girlfriends had varying reactions to my fame. They shouted out names like "Kik van Kike" or "Jewcunt" or "Jewdy Doody." Nothing too lethal.

They tossed my cell, too. Was I hiding money? They searched every part of my body. But those clichés were accompanied by others: Would I write love letters to their men? Cyrano de Rosenthal. Could I help them with their speeches for parole boards? What did I know about criminal law? And then it died down, and I didn't give a damn about what the Nazis said or did. I preferred setting up illegal profit-making schemes with the guards—dope, cigarettes, food—but sometimes I cheated them out of percentages just to feel the baton against my flesh or the crack of a Taser. When I was in the mood I started fist-fights in the cafeteria so I could spend a few days in solitary. Once they put me there for three months for punching the penitentiary doctor when he said he thought he felt a lump in my perfectly smooth breast. In those first years my engine was driven by blind rage. I was positive the government had laid cruel and unusual punishment on me. I screamed my "legal right to speak out." I hadn't been at the scene of my notorious crime. (Though I'd planned it and a bunch of others). I'd been around the corner. I wasn't holding a weapon. There was one on the seat next to me. I certainly hadn't hit the cop that broke his neck and made him a paraplegic for the rest of his life. And I had nothing, *nothing* to do with the killing of the others. I lived inside a tornado of accusations, self-righteous demands, and terrified madness. I was also probably wildly manic since serious bipolar illness runs in the family.

I think there's maybe ten prisons out of thousands and thousands that separate the mentally ill from the psychopaths or criminals. Powell wasn't one of them. The population was a mixture of bad chemistry and fully developed, devious, vengeful personalities.

DOORBELL

I sat on a green wooden bench under the giant cherry tree at the Mercer-Houston Dog Run (for which I have the key). Doorbell, one of the great loves of my life, lay protectively on my feet. I think Tina and Jerry Gilligan named him Doorbell out of some misguided notion that he would guard their door and let them know when the enemy was approaching. But Doorbell would instead gurgle and snort, and had the mellow disposition of a pothead. The dog felt it was his duty to greet all humankind with several slam-bams of his tail and a slurp from a tongue the size of a ham. A typical response to Doorbell would be to back up and say, "Yes, hello sweetheart. No, no kisses. Yes, I'm happy to see you, too. Don't jump on me or I'll fall on my ass, Doorbell." But, undeterred, he'd slobber, lick, jump up, slam his bottom back and forth in a kind of tribal welcome ritual. I dreaded calling him from the opposite end of the dog run because I knew he'd gallop full speed toward me, only to screech to a stop by jamming his enormous head into my belly. What was it Bob Marley used to say? *Ja man. Could you be love?*

Tina and Jerry were among my first clients, because Hubb, owner of PetPals, in his junkie wisdom, figured a big-boned woman ex-con would be strong enough to handle 170 pounds of pure, ecstatic agitation. Or he imagined I'd quit on sight. Or get killed. Tina and Jerry were also among the first few who were willing to engage a woman with my record. Other potential clients would hide their jewelry. One client hid an antique butter knife in the pocket of his Adidas running shorts. You'd be surprised how many people want background checks for plumbers, carpenters, and other menial types these days. On the street I was always vigilant to pick up dog shit in a baggy lest a camera hidden in a lamppost catch the misdemeanor— therefore violating my parole.

Tina and Jerry were very upfront with me. They recognized me right away, and Jerry said, "Just don't use Doorbell as a hostage for any of your causes. We're just middle-class with a mediocre life. We can barely afford health insurance."

"My cause right now," I said, "is reentry." Jen Lee taught us that the months after release would be dangerous, as if a con were an astronaut in a suit rocketing back and forth between weightlessness and the earth's gravity. She said it'd be the most dangerous time. Just like that space shuttle that slowly disintegrated after reentry, tumbling toward its final landing. There was a period for each con where old met new and prison life crashed into freedom. You could fall apart if you didn't balance the weights. It was like a war between past and present. Better to keep your head down and move real slow.

Lucinda and Hubb owned and ran the business, but they insisted that clients interview their individual walkers. When Tina and Jerry first interviewed me, Tina, who does PR work for a toy-store franchise, probed. "I don't get why you're doing this job," she said. She was sleek and speedy like many thirtyish female executives. "Why don't you crunch out an outline and write a zillion-dollar book about your life. I know some agents, a few editors."

"I'm not really allowed to," I said. There were all kinds of legal footnotes about what one could and couldn't say. Anyway, I'm a mother with a kid. I'd rather not have her read about my past exploits.

I always got agitated from talking too much anyway. In prison you learned to keep details to yourself. I still hadn't learned the rhythms of civilian interaction.

"Some night we'll have you for dinner and you'll tell us everything," Tina said.

"It'd make a great children's book," Jerry said. "Tina can pitch it to the three-and-under crowd."

"Oh, shut up," she said. They seemed to like each other. Jerry was tall and stocky, balding, with a clean-shaven, reddish face and long sideburns. He was a freelance art director for a variety of books, but restless with his work. Things were slow for him, and if Hubb wasn't counting every penny I brought in, I would've lowered Doorbell's rate. Hell, I would've walked him for free. Tina and Jerry were the only people who weren't the least bit nervous with me. And I took pleasure in the picture that Doorbell and I made. A scarred-up, tattooed woman strolling casually on West Broadway pulling a bull on a chain.

I used dried-chicken treats for bribery, and we walked at different speeds. I think Doorbell understood me. When we went to the Mercer-Houston Dog Run, he'd complete his mountain of business immediately so I could drag myself to one of the benches right away. He'd lay on my feet for the required fifty minutes. We'd just sit and share dreams. Chewing tennis balls and other dogs weren't in his repertoire. Love was his primary trick. I needed that kind of overpowering, inconvenient passion that had nothing to do with sex. Doorbell also kept me safe. There's a walk or a scent or some mysterious aura that comes along with having spent years in prison. Homeless guys and blue-collar workers could smell it. Especially guys who'd done time themselves. I'm not particularly attractive these days, but I used to be, in an ethnic, curly-haired—what Leonard used to say was "biblical"—way.

"Hey chickie chickie chickie."

"You got some stuff, woman?"

"I know where you come from. I know where you're headed."

"You wanna rough me up, woman?"

"You're a lonely lady, bitch."

Guys don't usually harass a woman in her forties with such abandon. I knew it was my past lingering around me like a cloud. Sometimes a construction worker would give me a little push, or a drunk hanging on a stoop would try and trip me. I kept the ever-present rage under control. No fights. No verbal altercations to draw attention. I couldn't blow parole. I couldn't blow parole. Life would be over. But when I was on the street with Doorbell, it was as quiet as a chapel. If a guy even sneered, showed a gold tooth, or made a gesture behind my back, a dangerous rumbling would circle around my whole body. Doorbell's massive belly moved like a geyser at Yellowstone up through the folds of flesh in his throat and a kind of growl spit out from his floppy but impressive mouth. His brown eyes got a shade darker, and even I didn't want to mess with him.

"Just jokin', ma'am."

"Hi, puppy."

"That's a *big* animal."

"Holy shit, keep that monster away."

"What's that kind of dog called anyway?"

Silence or a radical change of tone. Doorbell wasn't so much my physical protector as guardian of whatever dignity I had left. When we were in the chair at Tina and Jerry's, half his tongue would happily drop out and his massive tail did its flip-flop furry helicopter routine. Like, *I played that one good, didn't I, Carleen?* and I'd give him a treat. Once a really determined schizophrenic who was invoking presidents came straight at me with a metal pipe. Doorbell pulled back his lips, and for the first and only time he exposed his killer teeth. The guy found a car to pound instead of me, but in the process I noticed Doorbell's teeth were covered with plaque and his gums were irritated red. I had to talk to Jerry and Tina about taking him to the vet to get his teeth cleaned, even though they'd have to put him under and I hated that. When the plaque builds up like that he could get a gum infection, which could cause all kinds of ear and throat trouble. A clot could even appear in his neck. Huge dogs don't necessarily have great immune systems. Every part of their creature is working full steam to keep the fast, huge muscles and heart going. That's why they don't usually live as long as the middle or little ones. After that, I bought a large dog toothbrush and began an excavation process once a day, on my own.

TRYING NOT TO GO BACKWARD

Once my old cellmate at Clayton, DeLisa, who was back for a "second tour," called me from the payphone. "Might as well come back, honey. You never leave here, no how. Every siren out there is comin' for you. Every shout you hear is to jump into line. And locks, man you hear a *click,* baby, or a *clank,* and you know you in for the night. Worst of all, that so-called freedom comes with you looking out the side of your eyes all the time. You don't know who the enemy is—except it's everyone. I didn't feel safe eatin' Sunday at Gram's with the kids whispering 'killer killer killer' behind my back. There's no second chances, Carleen; it's better to be back here. It's all nightmare incorporated on the outside designed to make you think you goin' somewhere that's a hallucination. Life gotta be the familiar. For girls like us there's no direction but back."

I thought about DeLisa as I sat in the family courtroom. Tina helped me pick out a fitted shirtwaist dress. "Respectable, but casual," she said. "An honest-looking outfit." I was changing sizes as fast as mood. Navy blue seemed an inoffensive color. Subdued, but not morose or dangerous. No jewelry. And my long white, black, and gray mane was woven into some modest but chic braid. We dyed out the purple. Definitely not hippie or leftist. I was already soaked with sweat. The room changed from a square to a rectangle to a looming diagonal shape. There was a loud swooshing in my ears. And the pressure behind my eyes felt like I was going to have a seizure. I told myself that it was just a courtroom, years after the crime. This wasn't the murder trial. I shouldn't have been experiencing post-traumatic stress. There wasn't shouting. No cameras flashing. My hands weren't tied behind my back. I wasn't aching from the sprained and broken bones on my hands and face. I told myself that it was a different time. I wasn't going back. The judge wouldn't be Republican Harold Forger, whose hatred of me glared off his bifocals and onto the TV camera lenses of 1984 and 85. The jury wouldn't nail me with their curious, disgusted stares. I was falling backward in time. When it came to the murders, I asked myself again why I chose to go to trial alone instead of joining the others. They got off so much better than I did. I was the denim-dressed ringleader. But I didn't kill anybody. I was miles away. I couldn't stop the voices in my head. The images. The voices were laughing and condemning me. I bit my lower lip hard so the pain would get me out of this classic attack of the PBS special on PTSD. Commercials sang along in my head in single harmonies, warnings for the drugs for depression and bipolar disease. Side effects: lack of sleep, nausea, death. But then Leonard arrived with his lawyer, and an icy hit of reality instantly cleared my brain. I was jarringly in the 2000s and the utterly different present tense. I remembered that I was the one who had called this particular hearing. The bearded, pudgy, Orthodox legal-aid lawyer seated next to me was named Harry and had been my mediocre champion since the murder trials however many years ago.

"This is profoundly hopeless so early," he sighed at me. "Carleen, you don't have a prayer. Not even one of mine. I don't know why you're doing this."

"Because I do things," I said. "I do them out of order. I'm not a linear person."

Leonard was in his customary Brooks Brothers costume, accompanied by his wife of the last ten years—blond, sleek, Nordic. The two of them looked like a PTA meeting: wealthy, concerned parents. I tried to catch Leonard's glance because sometime ago—maybe it was when his darling Olympics wife came along—he began to hate me with such venom it resonated like someone hitting the inside of a piano with a shovel. In the beginning he'd been more forgiving, or let's call it tolerant. But then he forbade Pony to visit me or communicate, and blackmailed me into ceasing all attempts to get in touch with her. He said he would lie if he had to and would make my life more miserable in prison than I could ever know. I was so ill and confused at the time that I believed him. Truth was, he had no connections. I was the one who could make his life a legal carnival. But I'd lost my power and dignity and was dragged too raw to remember any of the truth.

Leonard Salin's lawyer was a woman better dressed than all of us. A chic suit, light brown suede heels. Her nails were done in what I'd learned is called a French manicure. Leonard's wife's white-blond hair was cut in a $300 faux hawk, but the lawyer had the real look: a shiny pageboy that flipped efficiently, but not too stylishly, when she moved her head. It was like one of those perky Revlon ads where the hair seemed to be manipulated by puppeteers. The lawyer was thin but not starving, and obviously ran or lifted barbells or kickboxed with oversized trainers. My God, I was speeding. Why was I nervous about a hopeless case? Calm. Repeat. Repeat. Repeat. I was going to file a petition every six months until I wore them down. In the fog that was my mental state I heard Harry address the judge.

" . . . remarkable recommendations from the warden herself

at Clayton . . . consistent on-time visits to her parole officer, no demerits at her halfway house, a steady job, a continuation in her pursuit of a master's degree, volunteer work in Kenmoor's Veterans Hospital . . . "

The list was true enough, if useless. I was just trying to get permission to see Pony once a month, even supervised, instead of living in this childless Siberian isolation to which I'd been condemned. Leonard wanted me not to exist. He had total custody as well as an order of protection. I wasn't allowed within three hundred yards of my daughter. He got very busy in the legal end of things when he found out I was about to be paroled. In some ways I agreed with him. No one knew how I'd turn out. But he couldn't believe I would lay a grain of harm on a little girl. And even in mischief I wouldn't dare try to get her to break laws or put herself in danger. I didn't even want to talk to her about my past. I was in search of potential.

I barely listened to Leonard's lawyer as she recreated the heinous nature of my crimes. I knew her shtick by heart: Drugs manufacture. The juvenile felonies. The mobster gang I put together in college. Miko, my psychopathic dead boyfriend. The robberies. Shootings. Death. Your basic light airplane reading. And then there's the early violent years at Powell Penitentiary. My drug use. My tendency toward confrontation. The "low life" quality of my employment. The dilapidated halfway house on the Lower East Side. My empty social life. My various and conflicting psychological diagnoses. How easy it would be for me to slip backward into a criminal way of life. Dealing drugs. Small thefts. What could I possibly give this sensitive, vulnerable little girl but confusion and pain?

I heard the blur, the variations of what I knew she'd say, the new conjugations, adjectives, and adverbs. I looked over at Leonard. He looked like a man watching a forest fire eat his house. He punctuated each point with his chin. He was still a very handsome man to my taste. Curly, gray-black hair. A large but straight nose. Thin lips. Clean shaven. His long, thin fingers folded on the table were playing a nervous game of "here's the church, here's the steeple." He was an expert carver, and I remembered that after our first date I discovered raw-oak statues of couples in romantic positions that spelled out "MORE" in the bathroom. Somehow he had transformed from a kind, slightly spineless hypocrite into a grown-up, rigid, two-faced bastard. But hey, he builds playgrounds all over the world and makes these magical toys for a living that he sells at some fancy toy store called Leonard's Land—sounds like the father of the year. I on the other hand . . .

During the recess I stayed alone at the plaintiff's table. I took a bag of M&Ms from my purse, poured a handful into my palm, and wolfed them down like heart medication. The smooth cover of the candy gave me a nice sugar hit, and the chocolate soothed me.

The judge was restating the heinous travelogue of my life when Leonard's perky lawyer interrupted her. The hair-shampoo actress noted in a nasal voice that she had an essential piece of evidence that she wanted to introduce. The judge said it was too late, but she'd listen anyway. Ah, the American justice system. The evidence was a note, and the lawyer had Leonard stand and read it out loud.

"To the members of this courtroom," he read in a gravelly Brooklyn voice. "I have spent one extended luncheon at a restaurant called Sarabeth's with my birth mother, Carleen Kepper née Ester Rosenthal." (*Née*. Where'd she get that word, and didn't any one of her coaches tell her she was using it wrong?) The letter went on.

"She was rather cold to me, and we had absolutely nothing

to talk about. I found her to be unkempt, shifty, and we shared little mutually. I was not hungry in her presence.

"She didn't scare me as my father warned me she might, but I don't see any reason for her and I to continue attempts to reconcile. I've seen her only once since birth, and I don't remember anything except the ugliness of the prison. I have love and support all around me and don't need her to have a meaningful life. Therefore, I personally recommend that she not be granted any sort of visitation rights. Sincerely, Batya Shulamit Salin."

It felt like the inside of my head exploded. I was afraid I'd had a stroke. I wanted to leap across the table like the Incredible Hulk and tear Leonard, his wife, and their lawyer to shreds. Then I was fine. My wishes to reconcile with the chubby, red-haired eleven-year-old dissolved. I'd never have her as my friend in middle school, and I'd be sure to kick mud on her jersey during soccer. I'd steal her iPod and fill it with filthy rap and death metal before I returned it. I'd knock into her in the cafeteria line and outside her ritzy Dalton school. I'd plant a joint in her pink backpack and tell the security guard she was carrying drugs. What a priss. Where did she get that *tone*? From *Masterpiece Theatre*? I wanted out. No more petitions. There wasn't one atom of nice in that girl. Something had been implanted in her by Tea Party parental substitutes.

"Carleen," I heard Harry cough. "Stand up. The judge is speaking to you." I stood up though I didn't know if it was required.

"Carleen Kepper," the judge said. "I want to impress upon you that I have, for a long time, been aware of your ground-breaking works with theater, art, and animals at Clayton Penitentiary. I admire your choice not to act out tabloid-oriented or pedantic, publicity grabbing behavior of any kind on your reentry, but to slowly and carefully find your way back into the world. Nonetheless, you have only been paroled for eleven months, and we, the court, would like to observe your behavior for several more months before we allow you to spend time with an underage girl who has never known you as her mother. The court is concerned with relapses in drug-induced behavior and your, shall we say, somewhat notorious wildness of character. We therefore deny the petition to see your daughter, supervised or unsupervised, and we warn you to stay at the allotted distance. You obviously have maternal instincts, so we would hope you respect her loving, secure, growth-oriented surroundings. That is my judgment for now, but I encourage you to return in eight to ten months and see where we stand."

Harry stood next to me and nudged my elbow.

"It's not news," he said. "It's not like a headline that gave us a shock in the gut. "

"One other matter," the judge said. The smug goings-on at the victory table paused.

"The contents of the daughter's letter stinks of coaching."

"She wrote it entirely on her own," the lawyer said proudly.

"But I doubt she volunteered to write it," the judge snapped.

Silence from the winners of the gold trophy.

"We involved in family law find it tasteless and destructive for one parent to denigrate another. It makes for a sick kid. Leonard Salin, you got what you wanted, but your daughter has been taught to despise a woman who has paid her debt to society. I will take this kind of smearing and brainwashing into account the next time we meet."

I glanced at Leonard peripherally. His shiny face had turned gray and sullen.

"There are extenuating circumstances," the lawyer said, "that we did not go into here. We've simply been protecting the girl from undue influence."

What? What? Voices screamed in my head. What circum-stances? What bare-naked scarred part of my past didn't they put in their freak show? Nothing came to me. Curiosity. What could they have against me the next time? Then the relief washed through me. There wouldn't be a next time. Life was bad enough without Wendy from Peter Pan or fucking sweet-faced spoiled Annie. I didn't need a prepubescent Jane Aus-ten character to call my "daughter." My ovaries didn't ache. My breasts didn't leak milk. My memory had just canceled the preceding hour as if I were in a video game. Inner mechanisms bleeped onto the exact present. I had forty minutes to get myself to Pookie or he'd trash his owner's place. I pulled myself up, didn't thank pudgy Harry, and took off for Barrow Street by foot. It took every ounce of inner strength not to deliver a full jujitsu kick onto Leonard's back. I needed a cigarette.

POOKIE THE TERROR

Pookie was a giant pitch-black standard poodle who lived in a ritzy, old town house with two gay men, Ralph and Evan. People who read *The New Yorker* often say that owners look like their dogs or that dogs reflect the character of the owner or blah blah blah. But Ralph, Evan, and Pookie either disproved the theory or were the exception to a folkloric truth. The two gentlemen were in their late thirties; both were quiet, despite wonderful and vicious senses of humor. Ralph was short, thin, and delicate. He combed his blond, thinning hair back, wore large horn-rimmed glasses and vests, and had a collection of wing-tip shoes. He was a world expert on French antique furniture. I couldn't think of anything more boring. His clientele were mail-order buyers and sellers, shop owners, collectors (why collect such shit?), musicians, and historians. Authors and filmmakers consulted him for authenticity, and auction houses brought him in to evaluate and price tables, chairs, armoires, beds with canopies, banquet dining tables, and who gives a fuck. I didn't have a clue as to how Ralph gained his expertise or recognition, but everything in their town house was a precious antique. Ralph had become very rich from this worthless profession. He knew I felt contempt for his life's work and would simply lift an eyebrow and say, "As opposed to your essential contribution to the cessation of starvation in third world countries."

He and Evan had been together twelve years. Evan was a dark twin of Ralph: Small. Delicate. With a slight potbelly and hairy arms. He drew maps of anything from the Alps to the ancient city of Pompeii for junior high and high school textbooks. He did travel manuals in Fodor's guidebooks and minutely detailed sketches of essential tourist spots all over the world. His precise lines depicting back roads, delicate waves of hills, miniature snow-capped mountains, and American battlefields could be considered great art, but he scoffed when I admired one of his sketches. "Technical blueprints, Carleen. Technical blueprints. One day when you've washed up from the dog feces, Ralph and I will take you to the Met and remind you of what real art is. The first canvases we'll visit will be yours."

Evan didn't have to work. The town house was part of an inheritance. He had considerable sums of family money, but the obsessive concentration on miniworlds kept him from lapsing into paralyzing depressions. He had been in analysis his whole life and was on a regimen of antidepressants that competed with Ralph's generic diet of vitamins, minerals, herbs, and supplements. They both did tai chi, when Ralph wasn't morose, and took walks by their country estate in Connecticut, where they spent their weekends entertaining wealthy, intellectual dinner guests who, in turn, invited them to exactly the same kind of parties. They lived for each other's love, though they bickered constantly and would often go several days not speaking to each other. They were two halves of some exotic gourd-like vegetable. They didn't trust me with their valuables, but felt pride that they used me nonetheless. Besides, I was saving them from their dog—with whom they had a sadomasochistic relationship.

Pookie was a disaster. They had decided to buy a dog when they had the flue in the downstairs living room cleaned out. "Aesthetically, we thought a large dog lying by the fire would complete a sort of queer tableau," said Ralph. So they googled virtually every top breeder in the country and found a litter sired by ChauncyArgumentPeedbornHorseJumpyFlower (I'm making this up), some first-prize Westminster stud, and EtholRoundbridgeBridgewaterSlamot, an equally regarded bitch. Ralph and Evan ordered the largest puppy by mail. I don't know why two such retiring, delicate men settled on a big black poodle, but it appealed to the imaginary portrait they saw of themselves, photographed by Annie Leibovitz (an acquaintance but not a friend), by their fireplace. They nicknamed the puppy Pookie, after Evelyn Murkten, an elderly society lady whom they often entertained at their town house and with whom they attended various society parties and art openings. Evelyn, a frilly, rich widow, was known as Pookie to her close friends. She spent her days reading nineteenth-century romance novels and writing checks for hospital wings for children with craniofacial disorders. She died at age eighty-seven from surgical complications, having broken a hip after a bad fall.

Standard poodles are fantastic specimens. They were bred for bird hunting so they're not as hoity-toity as the dog shows would have us believe. There's no real scientific proof, but I think each color comes with a specific personality. White poodles are somewhat aloof and arrogant and often win at dog shows. Red to champagne poodles are of a looser class. They're friendlier, more athletic, and often solitary, and take to a single human love, remaining loyal and otherwise sloppy. Brown standards tend to be obsessive. One brown I used to walk would do nothing but chase a ball, bring it back, chase a ball, bring it back, chase a ball, bring it back—for hours. At home they can be found parked by the front door in an absolutely erect sit waiting for God knows what. They are the only standard to go after other dogs in the street. This is called *fear aggression* and is almost impossible to train out of them. I had a client who broke her wrist when her dog, St. Luke, went after a tiny little shih tzu on the sidewalk and pulled her over. But the browns are affectionate and have a quality to their eyes that seems deep, ancient, and wide. I could stare into St. Luke's eyes forever, and he'd peer right back at me as if he knew exactly why my life turned out the way it had. I know that's bullshit.

Black standards are the manic clowns of the bunch, skinny nonstop seekers of joy. Outside, they are capable of jumping higher than almost any breed, and they will jump for a ball, a Frisbee, or nothing at all. When they are particularly gleeful they zoom around in circles chasing nothing but wind. They'll practically take your arm off rushing for pigeons. They demand constant, unequivocal love and will leap into your lap as if they were toy versions of themselves and are insulted when ordered to get off. They learn their commands instantly, but not because they are particularly smart. They're more like teenage boys who joined the army too soon and will do any discipline just to prove they can do it. They should be circus dogs. They live to love but have no particular loyalty to master or mistress. If you don't hold on to them, they'll jump up on an elderly woman with osteoporosis and hump her thick stockings until her seams pull apart. In other words, most black standard poodles are exhausting and best matched with adolescent boys diagnosed with Asperger's syndrome.

Although their love is bottomless, it is also petulant and vengeful. If you leave them alone they'll chew on your furniture and shoes, eat your glasses, and even open your drawers and toss your clothes around the apartment. They rip the covers off furniture, digging deep enough to get to the foam and shredding it, or they go after the down comforter and toss feathers around like a girls' sleepover. The only way to cure these heartbreakers is to lock them up in a heavily barred crate. Then they will howl and bark until the neighbors call 911 or have you kicked out of your building. They are joyous, first-rate rodeo clowns in the country, but unless you live by a huge dog park in the city and have three to six free hours a day, a black standard poodle, in my opinion, is not an ideal choice.

Evan and Ralph were, therefore, mad. They had no idea that by acquiring Pookie they'd invited Satan into their home. Neither man was particularly athletic (they sailed in the summer and skied the intermediate slope at Aspen in the winter). There'd never been such a mismatch in the history of man and dog. And yet, despite ripped maps of the Andes, a chewed-up dressing table from 1897, pulverized throw pillows, demolished inherited dishes, curried mayonnaise spilled on an ancient Persian rug, a broken wrist (Evan's), a cracked set of dentures (Ralph's secret), two sprained ankles (both of them), and chaos at the most intellectual of dinner parties, these two fruits adored her. They'd lie down on I-95 to stop traffic for her. They researched highly sophisticated diets that might calm her nerves and read advice on how to train her from monks. They paid for collars and harnesses to prevent collisions and knockdowns. They bought her the Hilton of crates made from a substance that was guaranteed not to contain mercury. They called and looked up every dog walking service in Manhattan as if they were the CIA. They didn't even consider PetPals, but heard of me because Ralph happened to be appraising a canopy bed for Tess and immediately noticed how well her fluffy Afghans were behaving. She raved about me, so they called me directly on my new, cheap cell issued and monitored by Hubb. PetPals had a strict rule that all clients must come through them, and walkers weren't allowed to take on separate clients. You could get fired for "insubordation," as it's written and misspelled in the employee handbook. But the second I heard Ralph's classical, somewhat-affected baritone, I sensed he and Hubb might not hit it off—especially if Hubb was doing crack that day and called Ralph a fag or doubled the rate because Ralph sounded rich. Hubb wasn't the quintessential businessman. It's a wonder he and Lucinda kept going so long. Attached to each other's missteps, they skimmed money off the collective tips and scheduled clients at the wrong time. They used a beat-up yearly calendar of half-naked female fly fishermen as their schedule. But they had great walkers.

On my first day, Ralph and Evan's town house was tidy but musty from all those French antiques. There was no sign that any monster lurked nearby. I heard squealing and scratching from a room in the back of the rather large house. Ralph and Evan led me past closed doors painted a perfect eggshell color with blue trim. At the end of a long hallway was an identical door, but it had a crack in it. I could hear persistent scratching. Whines alternated with indignant soprano barks.

We opened the door to find what it must be like when a surgeon opens a patient who's been eating the heads of Barbic dolls. There were over fifty toys torn to shreds. Stuffing was everywhere. Soaked newspapers covered the floors. The immaculate powder-blue walls had been scratched down to the sheet rock. A huge pitch-black nuclear missile barreled at Evan, knocked him over, and began kissing him all over.

"Daddy loves you too," Evan said breathlessly.

Ralph ducked into the demolished room, knelt, and Pookie got on his back and humped.

"No no no, sweetie," he said severely. "I'm gay."

Then Pookie the psychotic show dog turned on me, leaped, and put her paws on my shoulders as if she had chosen to do the cha-cha. She had rich, joyous, crazy brown eyes. In a flash I pushed her paws down, chucked her under the chin, and said, "*Sit.*" She obeyed. Ralph and Evan gasped in unison.

"You can't live like this," I told them. "She's the mad aunt hidden in your attic. She's going to destroy your house and set you on fire when you're in your pajamas. Let me place her with a good family in the country."

"No, you don't understand," Roger wheezed. "She's our Shango, our Coyote, our Crow, our Trickster from the mountains."

"You're going to have to explain that to me," I said. "I'm not up on the classics." Evan sat on the floor cross-legged as Pookie leapt around her room, stopping every now and then to knock him over, wash him with kisses, and take off again.

"Here we are," Ralph said, his back leaning tight against the door. "Two small-boned, highly intellectual gay men. Our lives are full of culture, acquaintances, travel, even love. But we've never had any trouble, not really. We've never had to conquer a diabolical force greater than ourselves."

"We've never even been audited," Evan said.

"She's so profoundly animal and raw. She's so unpredictable and passionate."

"I spend hours just watching her," said Ralph.

"But we can't live with her like this. We know that. I mean we're realists," Evan said in an exhausted voice.

"However, to give her up," Evan sighed, "is to admit defeat. To lose the one wild thing in our lives."

"Why don't you go on one of those National Geographic safaris or boot camp vacations?" I replied.

I could sense that they were prickly, impatient, and I was the messenger of devastation.

"You've got to train her," Ralph begged. "We'll pay double."

"Okay," I said, thinking how craziness on the outside feels so much like craziness in prison.

"What do you plan to do?" Ralph asked suspiciously, as if he envisioned electrodes and hypodermic needles.

First, I cleaned their apartment. Cleaning a place is how I introduce myself to it. I sanded the expensive, now-scratched-up parquet floor. I introduced the worried men to Nature's Miracle, known for getting rid of secret dog smells so they won't piss where they have before. It felt so good to be scrubbing until my hands were raw. The only reason I didn't take cleaning-lady jobs when I got paroled was because I fold clothes and bedding and towels like shit. I can never get a corner to exactly match another, or there's always a lump in the pants seam even if I think I've got it creased and smoothed out.

Ralph and Evan were intimidated but grateful for me. Pookie tried, at first, to win me over by prancing wherever I'd just scrubbed the floor, leaving dirty, wet paw prints. She leaned over and licked my face and tried humping my back, all while Ralph and Evan giggled at her antics. I completely ignored her. She was one of the sleekest, most gorgeous poodles I'd ever seen, but she'd taken advantage of those two sweet, dotty men and she couldn't be allowed to do that. In the weeks that followed I walked her on a chain collar, locked her in her crate except when it was playtime, and gave her a treat or a toy when she shut up.

At first it was all *La Traviata* and *La Bohème* with wails, moans, and silent suffering. She'd turn her back whenever one of us walked in the room. I know Evan and Ralph considered firing me more than once, but fundamentally, they were relieved. Sometimes, bored with her own divaness and phony sorrow, she'd scratch politely on her double-locked crate. I'd let her out, and she'd approach one of the men and press her head against his leg. They were not allowed to kneel down to their queen—she was nearly taller than them as it was and I didn't want her getting off on her height. Poodles are indeed smart, and Pookie the socialite caught on quickly that, as long as I was around, her reign was over, or at least diminished. But she didn't hate me. We ladies have an understanding. And I let her run like an antelope free of it all at least once a day in any unsupervised park I could find.

A LETTER TO BATYA SHULAMIT

Dear Batya Shulamit,

You probably will never see this because Leonard will be censoring your mail. He'll take a glimpse at my hand-writing and know right away. I don't own a computer yet, but even if I did, no one would let me have your email. Since I was an artist I still like the feel of pen on paper. It's almost like eating spaghetti, swimming, or pulling long fingernails through sand. I know I sound stupid. My letters from prison were much less ootchy-kootchy than this, but they always came back unopened. If I was the daughter of a convict I'd be curious about her life and I'd search for the letters full of apologies and sorrow.

I'm writing to tell you I looked up your names in the dictionary, and they are well thought out choices. It was brave for the Pharaoh's daughter to rescue a Jewish baby from the river. Is your second name connected to the Queen of Sheba? That beautiful black woman who shows up in the Song of Songs? You know all the answers but you can't reach me. When I was involved in my research Batya appeared to me in a kind of brick red and Shulamit in Caribbean blue. I have a condition where I see num-bers and letters in colors. Not that you'd give a shit. I'm

*just trying to do what psychologists call "relate." I wish
Leonard would let you read this so we could begin to take
down the monster image of me just a little. Our lunch
turned into two dinosaurs ripping each other to shreds
over a pat of strawberry butter. But disasters can be fun.
Sometimes they are amusing. I'm including a sketch of a
horse flying through an open field. It represents your name
in the abstract. Ask Leonard to explain it some time. It's
my dream of freedom. For me. For you. For all of us tied up
in our bodies even a little. (It's probably worth a fortune,
this drawing. Sell it if you don't want it and put the cash
toward Smith or whatever those tight-asses have in mind
for you.) That's all for now, I'm scared to say.*

Carleen

THE HELL OF POWELL

I learned just as much at Powell in Ohio than I did at the somewhat more "liberal" Clayton Correctional in upstate New York. When you're basically an upper middle class white woman from the Upper West Side, no matter what you do you can't fathom what continual physical violence, even the threat of it, can do to your senses. In every cell I was placed in the "sisters" tested me constantly. I didn't fall into an easy category. I hadn't murdered anyone directly one-on-one, but I was notorious for organizing a lighthearted event in which three people were shot dead. Two of them cops. So, was I a featherweight or ripe convict-leader material? The Royals (I liked to think of them as the Amazon Queens of the prison) made absolutely sure I got the initiation that was coming to me. These women at the top reminded me of the prints of judges seated at a table in their wavy pure white wigs that you see in Hogarth lithographs. (Look up Hogarth. He's nasty.) The Royals of Powell were so pierced and tattooed you couldn't tell them apart— aside from black, white, and Latina—and they were often stabbing each other as much as the "newbies," as a new con is called for at least two years. The Royals were fifteen or so women who achieved their status either through time, black market prowess, or fighting ability. In some ways the hierarchy seemed arbitrary, but they ruled with unquestioned tyranny. Their initiations were ruthless and planned out with detail and expertise. A newbie was often the recipient of four or five beatings a day, was awakened with kicking and screaming every hour, was slowly starved or poisoned, and—this was mandatory—newbies were sent to solitary, escorted by the most corrupt guards. These guards at Powell were encouraged to rape newbies. Some got gifts for originality or cruelty. The only way to avoid initiations was to find an appropriate protector-husband-wife. This was a person who'd earned the respect or fear of the Royals by outdoing them in their own sadism and schemes.

I had my share of abuse. When they found out I was a painter, they first made me draw. But then they burned my drawings and broke both my hands—all the fingers on my hand one-by-one, like the Pinochet soldiers did to the famous singer-guitarist Victor Jara during the Chilean coup d'état. It took weeks to heal, but I did excruciating exercises all the time to regain the nimbleness that would allow me to paint. This had some effect on the Royals, but not much. Punishments were doled out for any breaking of the Royals' rules, and they made up their rules as they went along. Women got beaten for chewing gum without asking. Royals raped women with bottles and batons. It was worse begging for help from the hapless guards. Most guards reported to the Royals, and any fool who took the side of the newbies found herself like a blues song, "Broken and Bruised." I tried to be cool. I knew not to complain, but it didn't help much. Nonetheless, I held up. I've always had a wall-like resistance to anyone who abuses power. I wish I could say it was moral. But it seems instinctive—animal. So whatever the Royals laid on me, I took. And I came back. And took it again. This resilience had a twofold effect. A clique within the powerful dynasty began to put together an elaborate hit on me. But I also managed to earn the respect of the strangest and most demented prisoner in maximum security. Her name was Fits, a six-foot-three Viking who wore undershirts and sweatpants, and had fists the size of bowling balls. Plus, she was epileptic, or psychotic, and once every couple of months she'd have a seizure where she shook and struck out like a cartoon creature zapped by an electric wire (thus, her nickname). It would take three or four male guards to hold her down. I think they had to shoot her with a quart of Thorazine to keep her from becoming the Hulk. She was slow, but far from stupid. She simply had impulse-control problems and the strength of a grizzly bear. She'd been in solitary so many times she had permanent red stripes—like a zebra—from crashing into the bars. She had scars on her head from trying to butt the metal doors. Her arms were misshapen from how many times she'd broken them. But she stood tall.

She was in for four or five life sentences. The story went that on the outside a couple street boys made fun of her on a basketball court in her suburban town as she kept missing baskets. The more they mocked Fits the more she kept missing baskets. I will never know the true details (few of us ever do on the inside), but my impression is that Fits went into some kind of standing, abominable snowman seizure. They found half of a pickup game with their necks broken and Fits sound asleep on the gravel. She didn't resist. She took on a kind of blankness that people interpreted as retardation. I think it was more likely her chemistry or wiring. She came from a poor farm family where the mother had run off, so no one had ever cared enough to try to get her medicated. They just called what she had the "devil twitches." The defense claimed that the boys attacked Fits, even though she couldn't remember.

I was going through a nonstop Ferris wheel of hell at Powell's—everything from getting beat up, to finding shit in my bed, to getting stabbed with needles, razors, and tacks. My broken fingers made it hard to fight back. That's probably a good thing, because if I had blown up in my usual way I'd be dead. Every now and then I think it might be useful to be alive. But back then, given that everyone on the outside had completely disowned me, I was prime for just doing a cannonball off the top tier of cells and ending up like a jellyfish on the filthy plywood floor. I was ready. But then Fits, in her quiet bear, spaceman manner, took on the job of becoming my husband.

PRISON WIFE

One nameless day Fits ducked into my cell (she was taller than the gate) and sat on the bed next to me. I thought, This is it, and a shiver of simultaneous terror and relief went through me. I waited to be murdered at Powell like I waited for Fits's seizures. My unconscious knew an attack was inevitable. I knew she'd crumble me like soft rock. But she kept her huge hands in fists on her lap.

"You have a mark on you," she grunted. "They want to wear you down. I saw some of the boys back home do it to a dog. They like to watch you go slow. You've got that mark. They'll bring you back to life and start all over again. It's nothing personal. Just an activity. But you haven't done anything to deserve it. And you don't complain and you don't fight back and that pisses off the Royals. They see you as conceited. And everybody gossips, says you're rich. Is that the truth?"

" . . . Yes, from my art . . . ," I answered. I was still shaking in fear.

"And it got all famous when you got busted."

"Yeah, it did," I admitted; no need to explain that my work had been selling since I was a kid. "But I'm here like everyone else."

"Here's the thing. I'm not some big lug with a heart of gold.

I don't believe in justice, neither. I don't kill just for fun like the Royals, but I'm not leaving, so there's no reason to behave. You have something I want. That's how we work here. Barter."

The idea of having sex with Fits nauseated me despite how many times I had been raped. I decided to take apart my bed and find a sharp edge and dig away at my wrists until I bled to death. I was beyond pain.

"I like art," Fits was saying. "I'm crazy about it. Loved those paintings of the kids with huge eyes. I had a picture of Elvis painted on black velvet in my room at home. Whenever I could lift a book of paintings from a street fair or whatnot I did that too. Lifted myself a book of Picasso. Weighed a ton. Thought for sure I'd get busted."

Picasso is a misogynist pig crook, but I wasn't about to say it.

"He's a little bent in the head," said Fits, "but it was okay, like cartoons."

I was beginning to think the Royals had drugged my lunch. Then I thought, No, that's condescending. The con in me was curious about Frankenstein's monster as a cultural connoisseur.

"I can teach you about art," I said meekly. Fits's knuckles went white. I winced.

"I don't want to know nothing from an art school," Fits said. She pulled out a thick, sweaty, eight-by-ten-inch sketchbook she'd been sitting on. The pages were empty.

"Once a week you make me a book of pictures and I become your man. You don't have to fuck me. Just make me books."

I felt the urge to scream with laughter. Like the orangutans in a cheap circus or chimps I'd seen on PBS. My fingers were barely healed. I didn't know if I could hold a brush. This hell called Powell had made me numb. I had no pictures, textures, or sounds of color speaking in my brain. I was deaf. I was blind. I'd been murdered over and over again. How could I make books for this woman? She didn't understand that my artwork had been the only source of what had been good in my life, and I no longer had life. How could I do one page, much less a book a week? I began sweating as if the room were radiating bright red. Fits didn't notice.

"No one will touch you if I'm your man. I have the supreme juju here. Even if I'm in solitary no one acts against me. They think I'm only half human." She grinned like a cartoon wolf.

I took the sketchbook. It was thick. A month's worth of sketches. It would take six to fill it with watercolors or pastels.

"One a week?" I asked.

"Both sides," Fits answered. "I got connections. I can get colored pencils, charcoal, watercolors, acrylic oils, scissors, glue, oil paints, brushes—any shit you want. I've got connections for every kind of speed too. Otherwise I need you straight. I hate those phony hallucinogenic-type, rock-and-roll pictures."

"What if you don't like the pictures?" I could barely ask.

"All I care is if it's real art. You make me all kinds. All styles. You got to really do it though. You can't fake me. You doodle or make fun of my bargain, I'll leave you cold. I'll set the Royals on you with a nod of the head."

I clutched the pad.

"What if the Royals fuck with my stuff?"

"No one will. Everyone thinks I'm possessed. I carry the souls of demons people haven't even heard of."

Fits stood up. She was so tall. She made me think of a giant in a Yiddish folktale. The Golem.

"Okay," I gasped.

She had condemned me to death, second degree.

A LIFE OF LISTS

One hundred pages of a book to fill. My paintings were more primitive than in the years before because of the stiffness in my fingers, but they were real and displayed technical skill and a knowledge of styles. So maybe she won't set the wolves on me, I thought. I wasn't filling up white squares anymore. I was washing off splotches of blood with color, pictures, and satanic prayers.

1. My stalker
2. My intimate friend
3. My boss
4. My third world slave
5. The mocking sneer
6. The welcoming grin
7. Arms out, palms reach
8. A slap across the jaw
9. The starter gun
10. The old pillow
11. The possibility
12. The impossibilities

13. Memories in sepia

14. Plans in blue and white

15. The threat

16. The salvation

17. The humiliation

18. The redemption from

19. Imaginary torture

20. The silent rape

21. The electric guitar solo

22. The starter pistol

23. The too-tall wall

24. The stairs upward

25. My enemy, my enemy

26. My enemy, my enemy

27. My angel

28. The blank page as the brushes fall
    from swollen hands

As a newbie, I was assigned to the bathrooms and garbage disposals. I lifted heavy loads by day and painted in a secret space Fits set up for me at night. I heard weeping and cries of pain coming from all directions, as if I was in a sports stadium after a coup.

At 6:00 a.m. breakfast I saw the other newbies beat to shit, with swollen lips, black eyes, and slashes on their limbs. They could barely sit down. I didn't have any of that, but my fingers bent in weird directions and the lack of circulation turned them purple and blue.

HALFWAY HOUSE

Upon my release, I lived in a halfway house off First Street. It was near the projects and the river. The architecture was like a 1960s ghetto elementary school transformed into an apartment building. The floors were chipped wood and old tile. There was a common dining room that gave off that grimy atmosphere of a school cafeteria that wasn't funded anymore. I had a roommate, Seña Ramos, whom I could tolerate. The room wasn't huge, but we didn't crash into each other. I liked that the ceiling was high and we actually had a regular rectangular window. I could see identical, ugly brown housing projects and hints of the FDR. I knew the river, and it ached me with its brown emptiness or comforted me when there were freighters. Seña Ramos was Latina and Catholic and into Santeria, that mystical magical shit. And she had erected a tin altar with magazine shots of Jesus glued to cardboard and Virgin Mary plastic statues wearing costume jewelry. She had about twenty "Santos," like Barbie dolls in biblical outfits. I worried the candles and incense would burn the place down. And I was exhausted because her strange chanting at night triggered nightmares of incidents I didn't even know were in my brain. But there were advantages, too. Every week Seña scrubbed the whole place with this special soap one of her fellow worshippers got in Hartford. It was supposed to keep devils away. To me it smelled like plain old Ajax or Clorox—but what the hell, we had the cleanest place in the facility.

Seña had been there a year longer than me so she got overnight and weekend passes to see her kids and parents. She used to be the head of a lesbian gang in the South Bronx, and they managed to do a lot of damage to other gangs of the same type. I think she shot at a bunch of preteens in her old life and carried heroin around the city for a Latino don. She also managed to have three kids in the midst of that. It's hard for me to imagine a five-foot Latina with a Tony Orlando haircut, black jeans, spikes, and pierced everything walking around with a baby sticking out of her totally boy-figure six pack. But what do I know? She'd been in and out of jail since she was ten. I knew she'd slashed a few enemies, even lately. She described knives in the way an entitled, knowledgeable gourmet could talk about a special, rare delicacy. She was nice to me though, and brought me back rice, beans, pork intestines—whatever she'd been eating when she went home. Her hair fell in long curls, and she had dark eyes. We stayed up nights exchanging prison stories, though hers were very different than mine since she had been a member of her version of the Royals at a prison on the border of Pennsylvania. She talked to me about the boyfriends she was accumulating in her transformative, straight life. Most beat her, and she'd scratch back with her long, squared purple fingernails. (She had a job as a cleaning lady at a beauty salon and got discounted manicures.) This was freedom.

I had a 10:00 p.m. curfew and orders to check in with Ramone or Francine, the guards, anytime I went anywhere, even if it was just to work. I went to my parole officer once a week, Joe Kasakowski. He was a police officer and a "counselor." I don't know how he got the job since he didn't seem like the social-work type to me. In fact, that's why I liked him. Maybe next to Tina and the dogs, he's what you might call a friend. He looked like a retired cop with a red-and-gray crew cut, strong upper body, and beer belly, but he wore Kmart blue jeans with old sneakers and his shirt collar always stayed open despite his tie. At first he was uncomfortable with me, but last visit he offered me an orange Tic Tac.

"Bad news about the kid," he said.

"Yeah, well, I expected it."

"But Harry said it got pretty rough."

"Rough? What's rough at this point?"

"Listen, big shot. Moms want their kids. It's biological, right? But you can't go near yours. Don't be thinking about revenge or popping something to ease the pain. You going to meetings?"

"No."

"It's a condition under your parole. Don't fuck with me, Carleen."

"I hardly have time, Joe, and I'm not the 'Hi group, I'm Carleen and I'm a narcotic ax murderer' type."

"Who'd you kill with an ax?" Joe smiled. His teeth were small and surprisingly white.

"No one yet," I shrugged. I was down, no doubt about it.

"Yeah, well, go to the meetings. They're not the worst things in the world. And I got those weekly forms with the boxes I gotta check. It looks better."

"At least I don't lie," I offered.

"That's the truth about you," Joe said. "How's the job?"

"Saving my sanity."

"I wish Doreen didn't have that fucking cat. It gives me hives and I want a chow chow."

"Why a chow?" I asked.

"They look like lions and have black tongues," Joe explained.

"They can be vicious if not trained right," I said.

"Same as you," Joe nodded at me.

"I'm mellowing," I said. "Life's not much to fight for these days."

"You taking your meds?" Joe asked.

"Like a trooper."

Joe put on his cop voice. "That's a no-compromise issue."

"I know that, Joe. I'm not deluded. I'm aware of what could happen without them."

"You're a good girl, Carleen," Joe said. "As crazy as they come, but good. Me and Harry think you got a raw deal—you know that. Every step along the way. But neither of us can help you if you screw up."

"My boss is a junkie," I said. "That's hard."

"I'm aware of that," Joe said. "But if we bust him, there's a whole thing behind the scenes that's gonna go down. They'll blame you. Anyways, it's a job."

"Drugs are around me all the time," I reminded him.

"Life is around you all the time, kid."

"How profound."

"Fuck you." Joe smiled.

I got up and shook hands. Joe blushed.

"You know, Carleen. I've wanted to ask you this from the get-go . . . "

"Shoot," I said, praying to God he wasn't going to hit on me.

He was already uncomfortable. "You could've bought yourself out of this shit parole. I mean, expensive shrink, ankle bracelets at home uptown. Maybe find some classier job. Why're you playin' the low-class routine?" His whole head turned beet red. "That was a joke." He coughed.

"You don't get it, Joe. This is exactly where I had to end up.

No one's about to give me a thing. And if I hung out with any of my old world, I'd be a pet—a sightseeing tour. I've been on this side longer than the other. I don't want to be anybody's piece of art anymore."

"Well, someone's looking for you," Joe teased. I froze.

"Yeah, some business type called here. We're checking him out."

"I can't imagine who it is," I replied.

Joe sighed. He only half believed me.

"Well, next week then. Don't self-destruct, Carleen. I'm not sure, but I think you got something worth saving inside. Don't break one rule. And go to those fucking meetings."

"Yes, your highness," I answered.

"Maybe you'll draw me a picture sometime," he joked.

"No, never," I answered truthfully. "I'll train your chow."

I paused.

"Listen, Joe," I looked back. "Write a letter to family court. Tell them you're my parole officer and you think I got screwed."

Joe shrugged. "As if it could make any difference at this stage."

A PARTY WITH POOKIE

Ralph and Evan decided they should cook a dinner in honor of my continuing success with Pookie, the poodle shark. They had complimented each other's "gourmet expertise" innumerable times, and insisted they conjure up food for me that would be "healthy and delectable." I didn't want to go. I desperately didn't want to go.

"Wear a black shift," Tina told me. "Gay men love moody, mysterious women." My stomach was tight as a fist when we went to Ann Taylor to purchase the costume. It's hard to clothe women my size. The laundry sisters at Clayton were always cursing me about it. But Tina and I found a black fake-silk garment that was supposed to be floor-length, but came to my calves. I had black flats to replace my sneakers.

Roger and Evan's town house was weird at night. The antique lamps, tables, sofas, and portraits took on faces in the dim light and made me antsy. I was relieved to see Pookie, who walked calmly to me and sat—as I had taught her—and then bounded, leapt, and licked me all over when I gave her a treat. We're working on calmer reactions.

Dinner was unbearable. The table was set with an old cloth like from *Arsenic and Old Lace*. The china had ugly purple intertwining flowers painted on it. There was actually a candelabra, and the thing that really scared me was that there were forks and spoons of different sizes laid out next to each other, which meant there'd be a bunch of unrecognizable courses. I sweat with anxiety. Evan was in the large kitchen singing while he cooked and this creeped me out, too. I sat on one of the velvet sofas and Pookie lay at my feet. Ralph was dressed in a T-shirt and creased navy jeans. His sneakers were brand-new white.

"You look ravishing, Carleen," he said. "Like the Russian poetess Anna Akhmatova. May I offer you a drink?"

Yes, a bottle of bourbon.

"No," I replied. At that time I only communicated with humans using three or four words at a time. Unless I was working or explaining a technique, I preferred monosyllables. To frame coherent sentences outside of the halfway house that didn't have to do with dog training was excruciating.

"Come look, Evan. She's stunning," Ralph said. Evan peeked his head out of the sour-smelling kitchen.

"She could've danced with Nureyev," he sang.

My hands were ice. I couldn't feel my feet. Pookie sensed my dread and put her head on my lap. I knew I was never going to make it to that table. I was a cardboard character in Clue. And, for such a seasoned liar, I couldn't figure out how to escape.

"Guys," I called out. "Guys."

They lined up happily in front of me like two prep school boys.

"You went to so much trouble"—I was cracking with nerves—"but I can't do this. Too soon. Too soon."

"Oh, darling," Evan said empathetically. "Shall I just grill you some chicken? We can eat our French repast tomorrow."

"No problem," said Ralph. "We live for leftovers."

"I have to go," I said. "I'm so sorry. This is too soon."

"Phobias," Evan said quietly. "You must have a truckload after being locked up all that time."

"Go," Ralph said, helping me up somewhat clumsily. "Go—but do have McDonald's or something. Eat!"

I stopped at their carved wooden door, which was now swirling like a pool in the spa. I turned to them. They didn't seem angry, but I had to ask.

"Will you still let me work with Pookie?" I asked.

"Oh, darling," said Ralph. He went to hug me, and I backed up against the door. "We've put you in our will. You're Pookie's guardian. Now go. We'll try again in six months and eat in the kitchen." I tore the hell out of there not even stopping to pet my student.

ANOTHER LETTER TO MADAME BATYA

Dear Batya Shulamit,

I don't know if Leonard will give you this letter. I don't know if I should describe every bit and detail of all my crimes and swear I'm trying to make up for them, or the opposite—never mention what happened long ago so you can look at me with a beginner's mind. I don't know what you know or what you don't know. I don't know what your room looks like or what posters you have hanging up. Do you take piano lessons or play soccer? Do you even have a favorite color? Are you anything like me at all? Do you dance in your room? Maybe we could try again. Maybe you can meet me in Battery Park when I'm walking Snuzzle. Snuzzle is really amazing. He's a rescue dog. Sloppy, silly, but that's a disguise. Like a wise Fellini clown. I think he's got shepherd and pug and Portuguese water dog in him. He's not too big so he's not scary. He could be compared to a Dr. Seuss character. The thing about Snuzzle is that he has a way of learning bizarre tricks. I mean, he shakes hands and all that, but he high fives too. And he break-dances. He rolls around on his back and freezes in a pose. Also, when you say pow! he falls down dead. And the best of all is that if you're sitting, he jumps on your lap and crosses his legs exactly like you do and talks. He doesn't say words, but he really imitates human cadence. His parents, a math teacher named Phil and a woman who manages a bunch of gyms, Linda, want me to take him on David Letterman. Their ambitions are useless. Snuzzles only does his tricks for me, and, according to the rules of my parole, I'm not allowed to make any public appearances. So as a part of my community service, another rule of my parole, I take him to children's wards at hospitals and old-age homes. He's always a hit. He stands on his hind legs and claps for himself. His owners think I'm going to steal him so they've hired a limousine to take us around with a guard as a driver. Snuzzles passes out with his head on my lap and snores like your father used to do. Imagine a bunch of hippopotamuses bathing in an African river. They sound just like that. You should buy this LP of wild animal sounds that a composer recorded in Kenya and Botswana. I used to love to paint to it.

"Shit," I said out loud. "This is lame." But I signed it anyway.

With love,
    Carleen Kepper

I shoved the letter in an envelope and put a stamp on it. I walked by a mailbox and dropped it in.

"Fuck you, Leonard," I mumbled.

A few days later I was in my room trying to get interested in reading again. I was on the third page and couldn't even remember the name of the book. My cell phone rang and I picked it up, hoping it was Hubb or a new client. But it was Harry.

"I got a call from Leonard's lawyer," he said. I went tense in my throat. Maybe there's a change.

"He says Leonard insists you stop sending letters or he's going to consider it harassment."

I didn't answer.

"He'll call your parole officer and then put in a formal complaint with the DA."

I hung up the phone. What the hell? Maybe I should just kill Leonard. I thought of spending the rest of my life at Clayton and found the option not so bad. But I had to hammer it into my head that hardly any judges picked homes for criminals on the basis of what would be convenient for them. It could've been Powell or worse. I tried to understand Leonard's cruelty. It was his idea to get married. Years later he thought I conned him into making a baby so I'd have an easier sentence. Not true. I knew a lot about cruelty. The cruelty of the games of gangs against newbies. The cruelty of initiation. Of rape. Of wrecking property. Tearing down a person's pride piece by piece. I even knew the cruelty of murdering innocent people. But Leonard was beyond me. No one gains anything by making me crazier than I already am.

THROUGH THE LOOKING GLASS

I was a millionaire by the time I was ten or maybe twelve. I gave my parents full control because money meant nothing to me. I wasn't autistic and didn't have Asperger's, but something in my brain caused me to dedicate hours each day to filling white squares with color, shape, textures, shades, lines, and on and on and on. The white squares went quickly from "Baby's Sketch Pad" to real canvas. I wasn't an idiot savant either—my room was extraordinarily clean and I had fine table manners. I did have a tendency to walk away in the middle of a conversation, but that was because I had a white square to fill. Adults, rather than be offended by this, found it "fascinating."

I was popular in grammar school partly because I was famous, primarily because of my pranks. I hung out with kids who later in life probably ended up as nerds or greasers. My little gang worked well despite occasional fistfights and nasty name-calling on the playground. I remained aloof. If they started fighting I just abandoned the whole gang and went off to paint. I don't remember exactly what we did. Time is not my friend, and I've been beaten to shit so many times I'm like a boxer who has to learn jabs and hooks and footing from scratch every time. I still have recollection of a few choice events though. Some neurologists have requested that I take some tests. They're flabbergasted that I remember so much after so many beatings. I can't explain it to them. Except that no assholes are going to steal my life from me. Even in the form of memory.

1. The time we let all the frogs out from biology class before the chloroform routine started to sink in. It was a class of twenty, and it was a hip-hop hopping festival. They showed up in such divergent locations: gym class, the English teacher's desk, and on someone's Salisbury steak in the cafeteria.

2. Once, I brought my parents' bottle of vodka in and, not only did we get drunk, but we carefully spiked the juice of the first graders. It was wild to see what six-year-olds did when they were smashed, although a bunch of them did throw up. I poured a bit into the teacher's thermos so she couldn't control the twenty-five waving, giggling, vomiting, sobbing, dancing drunks.

3. Clogging all the toilets with dog food so it looked like shit.

4. The time I made dinosaur costumes and about twelve of us invaded the school, "ate" composition books and papers, covered the security guards with glue, destroyed the copy machine, and ate all the food that was being prepared. We also used that day to kidnap any "cool" kid who'd disparaged us and wound them up in duct tape.

I think I was expelled a few times before my parents decided I would be better educated at home with a select group of extremely intelligent tutors who also specialized in "singular" or "different" children. The smart ones gave up on me and just let me paint while they read out loud or played roaring boom boxes.

My father was a leading ophthalmologist. He specialized in research and treatment of diseases of the retina. He was a quiet man, often amused, and was fascinated from a clinical point of view by the content of my painting. He was too busy and laid-back to worry about my minidelinquencies, and figured it just came with my exceptionally odd talent. He often sat in the doorway of the basement they'd converted into a studio and worked on his papers as I slashed and rubbed and stroked away. We never tried to talk to each other. I often felt like a favorite specimen, or a pet.

My mother was a dyed-blond Jewish lady who was a sort of elegant drag queen. She didn't have to work, but she was smart, and got herself on the boards of directors of many organizations:

1. Children with messed-up faces

2. Tiny theaters in Brooklyn

3. Reversing clitoridectomies in the Congo

4. A kibbutz in Israel that made vegan clothes

5. The Museum of Modern Art

6. Self-Esteem for Secretaries and Clerks

7. The Feminist Jewish Historical Society

8. The National Yiddish Theatre Folksbiene

9. Shakespeare Association of America

10. The International Food and Housing Organizations

11. The Bronx Zoo

12. The National Center for Homeless Education

13. The Amputee Coalition

My mother wasn't superficial. She had several phones and old-style computers and lived at her desk when she was home. She went to meetings constantly. She genuinely wanted to make a better world. From what I could gather she was hard-working, über-efficient, and in great demand. She and my father attended benefits and chic private dinners. She was slightly cold, a borderline alcoholic, but not an unhappy woman. She just didn't particularly like me. I don't think that she or my father cared one way or another about having children. It was just that I turned out so messy and noisy. She was miffed.

My notoriety embarrassed her. Both she and my father refused to pose with me for *People, Art International,* or *Vanity Fair.* It was always me—dwarfed by a large man's shirt, looking as if someone had smudged a multicolored palate across my face and hair—my paintings, and one or two famous collectors. Not private views of a prodigy's homelife. The one valuable task my mother did do was audition, in her woozy, brusque way, the most important dealers in the country, and she chose a man, Rico da Silva, who, through my adolescence, respected my artwork, got me into the best galleries, found rich but tasteful collectors, and timed my one "woman" shows so they would be huge events. I don't think he was a bad man. In fact, I think he was dismayed that my general communications with him were shrugs. He left me alone to do what my chemically colored brain commanded. He also made me, and himself, a fortune. Not everyone liked my style—some despised it. I started out as a baby phenomenon, but I endured. Collectors streamed in and out of my studio for years. My mother took offense to my messy appearance and my refusal to let her contribute any of my money to her worthy causes.

"It just sits there," she'd say. She was scary in her own way and guilt provoking, so one day I wrote a note to my very honest business manager and told him to break into one of my trusts and write her a check for thousands of dollars.

When she received the check she quietly descended the steep stairs down to my studio and worked her way through the messy floor to stand next to me. She put her hand on my head. I was too wet with paint to hug.

"Thanking you is not enough for this," she said. "You know I won't spend a penny on myself." She smelled of Scotch and hand lotion.

"You'll do what's righteous," I replied in a somewhat-sarcastic teenage voice. She cautiously leaned forward to see if she could kiss my cheek without getting paint on her. I pulled away. She let out a quiet, husky laugh-cry. She stayed where she was with her arms folded. She looked exactly as if she was doing an imitation of one person staring intently at another. But no one was staring back.

"Let me introduce myself," she snapped. "I'm your mother. We both occupy this house."

"We walk through each other," I said, "like poltergeists." I noticed for the first time that her eyes were a very unusual green with brown flecks and rims. Like a swamp. I didn't know what I'd have to do to capture that color. She walked unevenly toward the steps.

"Where'd you come from?" she asked the universe.

"And where am I going?" I replied.

My parents never understood my vision or hunger or technique because they were workaholics in their own right.

Although unimpressed by my success, they were flabber-gasted by my arrest, and I don't think they had the emotional equipment to deal with the tsunami that accompanied my conviction. As if they were each an ancient Egyptian clay vase, so thin that if one crack appeared thousands of years of history would shatter. Years of pretense and pretending would be revealed to show ugly emotions and secret perver-sions. I don't know what they were so afraid of, but nothing in their behavior changed. They gave no quotes. They wouldn't speak about me. The glacier stayed as it had always been. They never visited, wrote, or saw me again. Something in my house caused great distances, nonexistences, and a desperate need to deal with the color white.

EARNING COURAGE

I'm forbidden from driving or even taking any mode of public transportation out of the city limits, but Joe Kasakowski got me a special pass so that Tina can drive me every two weeks to Ossining to visit Charlie. Charlie is the cop who got paralyzed during the robbery, which was part of my crime. Miko hit him on the head with a club three times, half blinding him and severing enough nerves in Charlie's neck to render his legs unusable and his left arm quite weak. Charlie was married to Saundra, and for a while she was this washed-out blond who stood by him after he'd been attacked by us, the Terrartists. There were articles in *People*, interviews on *The Today Show*. They even made a special home for him with ramps and various gadgets on some TV show where they build new homes for the disadvantaged. Charlie and Saundra wrote a book, *Love Moves Us*, referring to Charlie's paralytic state and how that would never come between them. Also how he dealt with his two partners being killed. Two or three years after the incident, Saundra moved to South Beach, Florida, to try her hand at designing bathing suits, and she met up with a condo management executive named Zak. She divorced Charlie and married Zak. The divorce was really ugly. Saundra claimed that she was Charlie's slave all those years without so much as a thank you.

She washed his clothes, prepared his meals, took him to shit, showered him, endured his PTSD. He even tried to run her over with his wheelchair. They were in their early thirties, and she wanted a life other than as an uncompensated nurse. She didn't mention sex. Charlie sold his TV home and had to go live in a retired cop home in Ossining for the poor and injured with no insurance or back-up. I went out to the place as soon as I was allowed to because I wanted to tell Charlie I had nothing to do with the murders, not directly, and I'd legally sanction Rico da Silva to sell a couple of my paintings if he wanted his house back. (I lied to myself and others about my ignorance of my financial state. But in reality, I did this because it was much easier for me to pretend it didn't exist and not complicate things. I wanted to be the simple stroke of a brush. Acknowledging my wealth opened the door to a kind of morality and guilt for life's actions that could overtake my art.)

That first day Tina drove me to the gate, but she didn't go in because cripples freaked her out—nothing, absolutely nothing, bad had ever happened to her, and she was afraid if she got too close to someone with cancer or who'd had a stroke, she'd catch it out of God's revenge for her having had such an easy life. Doorbell drove up with us. He took up the whole back seat of the car and chewed on a stinking piece of rawhide the size of a softball.

"I'm going antique shopping," Tina said to me. "I saw a bunch of shacks in the area. Doorbell and I will look for a stream. I'll come by in an hour when you're finished with whoever it is you're visiting—I don't want to know. Don't tell me."

She let me off at the gate, and I had to hike almost a half mile up a gravel road surrounded by a dark arch of forest trees. It all opened up into a facility made up of low brick houses in a semicircular shape like a British boarding school. There were guys on crutches swinging around and wheelchair sports. Some quadruple amputee was reading a book up on a post, and he turned the pages with a stick he held in his mouth like a large toothpick. That freaked me out. This was a place where soldiers who'd gone to Iraq or Afghanistan went too. Images of legs and arms started making circles behind my eyes as if someone were juggling them.

I wobbled up to the desk. I was a bit faint. There was a small, chubby woman with white curly hair and thick glasses that magnified her eyes and made her look demented. She was filing already stubby nails, but seemed chipper and not the least bored.

"I'm here to see Charlie Timms," I said.

"Does he know you're coming?" the lady rasped. She didn't look up at me. She'd hit a cuticle.

"No," I said.

Then she focused her revolving planet eyes on me and smiled. She had huge gray teeth that made her look like a sweet-natured donkey.

"Oh, that's the best," she squealed. "They love surprises, you know. You have to leave your bag up here with me and get it on the way out. If you've brought him a gift I have to inspect it." She transferred from sweet and roly-poly to memorized and efficient.

"Yeah, well, I heard he likes cashews." I extracted my gift box of cashews from my bag and gave it to her. She grabbed a sharp letter opener, ripped the plastic, took the lid off the box, and started to rummage around the various sections of cashews— the plain ones, the salted ones, the chocolate-covered ones. Then she patted the mess down with her chubby little palm to make it look neat and stuck the cardboard top unevenly back on.

"Sorry, but this is a police and military facility," she said in her Auntie Em voice. "These kids understand. Not that we haven't had complaints. But if you're blown to pieces what's the use of being blown to pieces again?"

"Absolutely," I replied quickly. I was too nervous to get into it. "Charlie Timms," I repeated.

"I'll call him and you can meet him in the visitors' lounge."

The visitors' lounge wasn't so different from where we watched TV at Clayton once you reached Level 3 privileges. The difference was that the lounge had large flat-screen TVs, a ping-pong table, a pool table, a table hockey game, and a wall of noisy pinball machines. But the men weren't crowded around any of the toys. Small groups were scattered about as if they were trying out machines for the first time. I could see through wide glass windows that there was a gym across the hall where men were lined up for weights, heavy boxing bags, and cardio machines, as well as various ropes and chains that looked more like torture equipment than rehabilitation devices. Laughter, shouts, grunts, and wails of pain were slightly muffled by the windows.

A man with white John F. Kennedy hair, a soft, clean-shaven face, and a black patch over one eye zoomed toward me in one of those small, manual athletic wheelchairs. His upper body was thick with muscles. His chest and arms were covered with tattoos. He could've been a world-famous wrestler. His withered legs were covered by black nylon running pants with white stripes. Suddenly, he came to a dead stop about six feet away from me. Then he squinted and appeared confused. Stupidly, I tried to close the distance and hand him the cashews. He didn't take his teary dark brown eye off me.

"How'd you know I like nuts?" he asked as he took the gift. His voice had a raspy, choked sound. I couldn't remember if Miko had injured his windpipe in their fighting match.

"Research," I said.

"Who are you?" he asked. "My memory's not what it was."

I didn't say anything. The noises in the rec room took on the silence of a cue in a movie score. The man's face began to turn red. I could see the outline of a long white scar from his forehead to his jaw.

"I'm Carleen Kepper," I answered.

"That wasn't your name before though, was it?" he pushed. His voice was definitely impaired.

"No," I replied.

"It was some kike name, right? Some Jew bitch name. Some high-class Jew bitch name."

"Ester Rosenthal," I whispered.

"That's right—I saw on TV somewhere. You got out? They actually fucking let you out?"

He threw the large box of cashews at me. The nuts stung like rubber bullets. He tore at the cardboard lid with his good hand. He tore it to little pieces.

"Eat it," he rasped. "Eat your goddamn guilty bribe. Eat the paper of your fucking parole and the paper you wipe your shit with too."

I didn't move away despite the fact that his next move might've been to try to run me down. A cleaning lady descended on the mess of nuts with a hand broom. A male nurse stood ready to push me away.

"I was miles away when my partner attacked you and shot your friends. It wasn't supposed to happen that way—"

"I know where you were," Charlie spit. "And it don't make a piss of difference. Unless you're here to give me a blow job, get the fuck out."

The veins on Charlie's neck and forehead were sticking out. His good eye was bright red. The nurse had some kind of syringe ready. I registered the helplessness of this brutalized man. I registered it deeply.

"I'm pathetic!" I shouted. All the witnesses look surprised. "Pull down your pants! Good. Yes. I'll give you a blow job. I'll lick your asshole. I don't know why the fuck I'm here. I just thought you'd want some money."

The nurse moved closer to me and a woman in a purple cable-knit sweater had now joined the small crowd. She held on to a notebook nervously. Charlie spit in my face. He missed and hit my hair. Then he went quiet. I saw what was left of a smile. He was an exhausted man. But not dead inside. I was glad to see that.

"I go over the money shit with that dealer and accountant every couple years," he said in a singsong voice. "I know you Jews think money takes care of all burdens, but it don't suck bullets from flesh or get people breathing."

"Fuck your pride," I said. I shook but couldn't control my mouth. "You don't have to forgive anyone. I don't expect to do an Oprah show. I could just help make you more comfortable."

Charlie blasted his wheelchair right into me. He'd caught everyone by surprise. I thought my legs were broken because he rammed me so hard.

"Get the fuck outta here. I got friends here. I got brotherhood here. I'm gonna die here and it's fine. I'm more alive than you'll ever be. You stupid rich girl—fucking *gang leader*. Where're your 'Terrartists'?"

"Mostly dead," I whispered.

Charlie Timms smiled. "Are you gonna suck my dick or not?"

"If you want," I said, acting bored.

I went painfully to my knees and reached for his pants. Everyone else got very busy pulling me off of him.

"Next time," he said. "I can't believe you're out. Who kills cops and gets parole?"

"I got lucky in a bunch of ways," I said.

"You ever sleep at night?" he asked.

"I do," I said. But I wanted to say that my days were darker than his nights.

"I hope you got dyke AIDS," Charlie said. "Die slow, like me. Have death say good morning every day. Have sores that never heal . . . like me."

He did an expert wheelie with his chair and rolled back to the gym. The male nurse, woman in purple, and a few patients stared silently at me. I limped straight for the door. I slowly crossed the lawn and saw Tina's car chugging at the gate. He hadn't broken any bones. I'd just have black-and-blue marks for weeks.

"How was it?" Tina asked. There was an ugly antique bedside table wedged in the back seat. I twisted around it. Doorbell had taken over the front and I didn't want to order him to move.

"Not bad," I replied.

BOMBAST

I have a new dog named Bombast. She's a scrappy Brussels griffon. The kind with the pushed-in face who always look offended. "I'm giving her to you because she's ugly," Hubb told me. This was his version of being affectionate. But if I said, "No uglier than you," like some of his "bros" might, he'd tell me to have some respect, or, depending on how much Adderall and meth he'd ingested, he might fire me. He'd fired me twice already for insubordination and trying to steal clients from the company behind his back. Then he'd call me on my cell and act as if nothing had happened. He'd drone out my schedule and order me to get my ass over to the office to pick up keys. Hubb wasn't a bad guy for an ex-con junkie. When he was straight, he ran a good business. When he was high, schedules went into chaos and he'd take out one of his guns and aim it at Lucinda and whoever happened to be in the office. When Hubb was in those states Lucinda would quietly fix the damage. First she'd opiate him with Percocet or OxyContin. If she was out of that, she'd shoot him with smack. (I hated watching that.) Then, when he was calm, Lucinda and I would each make a few apologetic phone calls—"His cousin died," etc.—and post a tidy, new, rearranged schedule. Lucinda was wary of me and generally cold, but no one spent enough time around the incredibly messy office to get in any serious long-term trouble. I had a long way to go, but I was the best trainer, and some people asked for me out of curiosity once they heard I worked there. "Didn't you know you was famous?" Hubb said. "I'd charge extra, like for a limo instead of an SUV." He was almost proud of my reputation.

Bombast was high-strung and prickly. His expression—*Why am I here in this life?*—was comical and truly full of angst. I walked him around the West Village where he barked and challenged every dog that passed by us. Then he'd pee, having scared himself to death. His owner, Kao, was a Brazilian flight attendant whose trainer had recently quit to go to law school. From what I understand, Bombast was deeply traumatized by this. At home he'd pace the floors of Kao's small one-bedroom apartment. Then he'd jump on Kao's lap and snuggle deep in. Any sound had Bombast jump nearly to the ceiling and dash from wall to wall—a mini, psychotic medieval knight who chased imaginary mice and dragons.

I took Bombast to my first Narcotics Anonymous meeting on Perry Street. I was trying to untangle him. He'd gotten his frizzy hair all wound up in his leash after zooming in circles after a bunch of sparrows. I noticed a bunch of ragged hip-looking folks of all ages descending into the basement of the church across the street. It dawned on me that I hadn't kept my promise to my parole officer about going to meetings and didn't have much time left. I stuffed Bombast into my straw tote bag and followed the faithful down some steep stone stairs. The room had a low ceiling, stone walls, and neon lights. The floor was covered with cheap linoleum, and each fold-up chair was different and more beat-up than the next. There was a podium that was as light and insubstantial as a music stand. A lonely crooked table in the back balanced an overused boilerplate, teakettle, and coffee machine, and some hardened sugar cookies were spread out unevenly on paper plates. If you weren't depressed to begin with, this would do the job. About ten people were smoking, which had me worried for Bombast. I stayed by the door so he'd have the benefit of the church's musty air. Bombast was happiest in my tote bag since he traveled frequently with Kao in a similar one made by the airline. I could hear him snoring.

The meeting was very crowded, long, and useless. I didn't introduce myself or say I was an addict. Because I'm not, actually. Drugs were part of the recipe that brought me down, or (shall we say) sped up my tachometer, but I never needed them; they were useful for escaping beatings, other forms of initiation, corporal punishments, and occasional torture sessions.

Afraid Bombast was going to yelp during the serenity prayer, I backed out quietly, but not before I recognized a face that made my heart go into my throat. He was completely shaved—egghead chic—and he wore red-rimmed sunglasses. He was still a towering presence, but he'd developed a softness, a slight belly under his Hawaiian shirt and typical Persian pants. He saw me. His mouth literally dropped open. I dashed out of there, but I could hear him following me. "Ester! Ester!" I wasn't ready. I couldn't go near that part of my life.

It was David Sessions. He was a popular painter of massive canvases. One in whom I truly believed. And he had respected me, too. We'd been best friends. In college we pulled obscene and dangerous pranks on each other. We slept on the floor of each other's studios dead drunk while the other was going through the torture of finishing a work. Images and colors and shapes inspired screaming fights. We hiked together and made up songs that bitched about the Guggenheim and MoMA. He made up an opera about a painting he hated and how he ass-kissed collectors. Together we wept over the mastery of painters we adored. We were creative soul mates. He was gay, but before I met Leonard, as far as we were concerned, we were husband and wife without sexual parts. Like Barbie and Ken. These memories stabbed me. It was like pouring lava onto bare skin. "Ester! Ester!" I could live with misery, but a joyous reunion would be like slowly cutting into a vein with a dull razor. Take it away.

David had moved to Denmark months before the whole Terrartist series unfolded. His paintings had the textures of ash and mud, as if he'd lived in volcanoes at the beginning of time. He brought the life of the earth to a canvas. And yet he was a totally bitchy, highly cultured, Harvard Phi Beta Kappa PhD—a massively tall, pink-faced, chubby queen who wore Persian pants and kimonos. He drank at least two bottles of wine a day and often rolled on the base of his paintings in coal-miner overalls. I could never figure out where he found the uniforms.

After the robbery and murders I never heard from him again. He had been my mentor, my only friend in the art world, my "queer people." And I never heard from him.

I rushed upstairs to Kao's apartment. My hands shook and I had trouble with the keys. Kao was there so he opened the door. I laid the tote bag with Bombast on his dining room table. I made my way to the bathroom. I don't know for how long I vomited. I thought I'd turned myself inside out. I saw blood.

"Carleen. Carleen!" Kao kept kicking the door. "Should I be calling 911?"

"No, no," I coughed. "Food poisoning."

When I finally exited the bathroom Kao gently wiped my face with a damp paper towel.

"I was scared," he said.

"I'm sorry." I barely had a voice. "I gypped you fifteen minutes."

"You're devastatingly sick."

"Please don't tell Hubb," I begged him. "I'll make up the time." Completely unwanted tears covered my face.

"I don't know what you ate." Kao had kind green eyes. They reflected pity and fear. He was trying to believe me, but he probably thought I was stoned.

"Where's Bombast?" I panicked.

"Tsch, tsch, tsch," Kao chided gently. "He is still asleep in your bag."

I took a deep breath, a remnant of one of the hundreds of varieties of mood-management classes I'd taken for criminals or the mentally ill.

"You can keep that bag if he likes it so much," I said. "Just please don't fire me." I was trying not to sound whiny.

"No." Kao smiled. "The airline—they keep designing new ones and give me one every week."

"Oh man," I said. "I've got to get to my next client. Thank you. I'm so sorry. Thanks. I'm mortified."

Kao picked Bombast out of the bag. The little dog growled and went to nip his master.

"Ow," Kao laughed. "Is that the way to treat Papa?"

I stood in Kao's doorway and held the door. I took another prescribed breath.

"Will you let me still walk him?" I kept asking owners that question. It had to stop.

"Carleen," Kao said. "You're sick! You take good care. Bombast would rip anyone else to some shredded rag doll. Please be here tomorrow morning. I have an 8:00 a.m. to Bogotá."

I ran down Kao's steps without a clue as to what had possessed me. I did a quick check of the street to make sure David wasn't looking for me. I hustled because I had to be at Walker and Broadway to pick up a couple of dull brown labs named Tika and Jaka. No problems. Got their leashes on, walked them a few blocks—bim bam business done—then walked them home.

One of David Sessions's sculptures kept appearing in my brain. It was a huge boulder, crafted and shaped to look like an unconquerable peak. On the side was a small, smooth stone made of red clay or cement painted with earth tones. The stone was on the side of the boulder halfway up. There was a sense of movement with the stone where you knew it was carrying itself up and that once it reached the top it would plummet to the gravel surrounding the sculpture. *Sisyphus* was on permanent display in the garden at Storm King. David had said that when the stone reached the bottom, if it didn't shatter, it would begin its assent up the same stern rocky face again. It was dedicated to me. I was Sisyphus.

THE ART OF TORTURE AT POWELL

Fits was worse than any dealer I'd ever had. I'm talking art dealers. Dope dealers are a whole other conversation. But art dealers not only push artists to fill canvases of art so they can put them on the market or fill a show, they also cajole, guilt-trip, and manipulate. They set up competitions between their "children" that mirror dysfunctional family dynamics. They give emotional uplifts and then turn their backs seconds later. At the time, I was too young and never cared about what most adults said, but I know now that dealers' "families" are like cults. The backrooms of galleries have the smell and pain of sweatshops in the early 1900s. Fits upped the ante.

The sketchbooks she gave me were one hundred pages long, and every week I was to fill both sides of each page by 5:00 p.m. Sunday. She told me if I fucked up deadlines "there were no excuses unless my hands were chopped off." She had a few former slaves clear a space in the back of the sewing room and took care of the guards so I didn't have to do overtime for chores. My situation might sound like an easy exchange, but to render one hundred complete pieces of art per week is close to impossible. The labor alone pushed me to the brink of mono or Epstein-Barr.

As a very young painter, my technique or my style or whatever you call it had involved thick layers of paint into which I stuck objects like stones, watchworks, or dollhouse furniture. And, while the paint was wet, I'd take charcoal, pastel, and marker and draw pictures deep into the thick paint, scratching unpredictable drawings onto the canvas. The drawings inside the globs of paint could be ultrarealistic, cartoon, or abstract depending on the mood of my inner story. I could copy any style, period, palette, and yet somehow I twisted it so it came out as my own. I liked to make rituals, pageants, parties, and events. They were thick, sticky movies with no specific theme except my invented holiday. Themes went from tea parties to lynching. My "collage" technique, as many stupid critics called it, was unique because it "seemed to take place in colored waves of ocean, sand dunes, parking lots, piles of snow, etc., etc., etc." I simply referred to it as "stuff jabbed into gobs of paint," but I was able to do very complicated line drawings and portraits inside the layers of paint that took weeks to dry. It gave me a toddler-like joy to pile on a mass of paint and then draw straight through it like a straw through pudding. These pieces made me so merry I would walk around the house pounding on furniture like I was imitating a member of a child's Lionel Hampton band. But the sensual high of swimming through my paintings and jabbing sharp pens through the paint's gooey, soft texture must've been similar to what video games did later for boys, filled with guns, rockets, knives, and killing. I was an assassin—my paintings were violent even if the collage depicted an eighteenth-century family. My mother never took me to doctors or psychologists because I didn't exhibit pain or conflict and therefore was simply "spoiled and unclean."

Years later at Powell I couldn't do any collages for Fits. I knew that the pages would stick together if I used that much paint, and the sketchbooks were too small. So after the initial terror wore off I made a pact with myself that I'd simply attempt to fulfill her demands. If I failed, she'd leave me like a wounded bird for the vultures. If I filled her pages, the beaks that would eventually rip me to shreds would at least be filed down or aimed at other prey. I was doomed, but I'd fight it off as long as possible.

Art became a game of survival in a jungle, like one of those ever-advancing video games where poisonous creatures, bottomless holes, and excellent killers—equipped with bows and arrows, poison darts, spears, AK47s, laser beams, and nuclear missiles—lie in wait to bring down one person: me. I was still paranoid about the Royals, who still growled and clicked at me when I passed them. The other inmates jabbed or tripped me without being noticed. One guard kept saying, "It won't be long now," and I wanted to ask, "What? *What?*" I got so stressed by my deadlines and veiled warnings that I dared to ask Fits for some Xanax. At first she said, "Yer too young," (I was twenty-two), but then she reluctantly doled out a few a day. "As long as it don't affect your artistry," she warned me. Soon I was eating handfuls just so my hands wouldn't shake.

The first book wasn't hard. I was adrenalized and battered into a place where I could draw every style of comic book character, classic nudes, and variations or copies of all the great artists you're required to do in school. Monet was mixed with Kandinsky. Stan Mack with Seurat. I didn't hand in the book early because I didn't want her to think I was being careless. She wasn't the type to come check on me either. She'd get what she ordered or not.

When I handed Fits the first book, I was shaking as hard as the first time I heard the metal gates of Powell slam behind me. Fits was tall, formidable, and zombielike. A golem made from sand and stale dough. She was expressionless with me. That was it. She was a Midwestern Frankenstein's monster and I'd become her hunchback slave. If my life didn't depend on it, this would be a Mel Brooks movie. The absurdity of the situation made me want to snort with laughter, growl, scream in frustration, weep as if I were five years old. Fits didn't seem to register my emotional buffet. Her stillness was so eerie. She held out her hand. I gave her the book. She walked off. An hour later she was back. I was lying on my cot in a fetal position, praying for irrelevant and impossible things. This is it, I thought. I'm dead.

"You didn't sign any of them," Fits said in her wooden voice.

"You didn't tell me to." I tried to sound somewhat robotic.

"Now I am telling you," she said. "Sign every page and return the book within the afternoon."

She marched off again.

Blindly, I signed each page, not even examining my artwork. I had to finish this first job. That was it.

No one knew how Fits lived or what her cell looked like. She was mysterious. Rumors abounded. There was a sheet hanging over the bars like a shower curtain and she never invited anyone in. She didn't eat with us at mealtimes and someone said she was allowed to cook her own meals. She'd been at Powell for years, and there were many rumors about her besides the basketball kids. She'd killed a woman who mocked her expressionless way of talking—tore out her tongue. She was at Powell because she murdered her entire family at Thanksgiving and then served them turkey. The only reason she wasn't on death row was because she'd quietly kill all her executioners before they got her. She showered alone deep into the night and hummed a weird little song, but no one dared laugh. Someone claimed to have seen Fits's naked body and said she had no tattoos but was covered with scars from stabbings and burns on every inch of her skin. A human quilt. She never had visitors. Once a month she sent a letter to an aunt in Ohio. The aunt sent her packages the guards didn't dare inspect. Inmates spread the word that Fits's seizures conjured powerful juju whose electricity could kill you if you touched her. She was an animal. She ate flesh. Everyone claimed Fits was for sure a transsexual. The stories were ferocious and intense. But she'd been here long enough to earn an absolutely unique place in the criminal hierarchy. Even the Royals and the stone-hard lifers were not certain who she was or what she'd done.

One thing was clear though—you did not provoke Fits. She'd never strike right away, but her revenge would come when you least expected it. She shoved a lifer into a giant clothes dryer two years after the woman stabbed her with a shank. She slit the throat of a guard six months after he started raping a nineteen-year-old newbie. Her motives were impossible to discern. Sometimes revenge or justice. Once the Royals tried a meticulous mass attack on her, but she swatted the twenty women down like flies with her gigantic hands.

This was my husband, my guardian, my dealer, and my collector. I said to myself that she wasn't attracted to me. She just liked art. It was probably the most insane relationship of my life, but the most clear. She didn't abuse it.

Week after week I produced books for Fits. My eyes began to blur. My fingers were badly blistered and cramped, but on the whole it was great for discipline. I was in a medieval apprenticeship. But there were weeks when my mind was blank, and I had to create images and textures out of raw emotions. Those were some of the most interesting abstracts. Once I had an easy week and decided to draw all the members of my family, from my mom and dad to aunts and cousins and second cousins to their cleaning ladies and gardener. I had a good time, and resorted to an easy boardwalk caricature technique

I'd used at family Hanukkah parties or for a charity drive for some cause my mother was into. For once my hands weren't cramped because the technique I'd used was barely more than sketches filled in with watercolor. I handed in the book to Fits, but late that night I woke to find my roommate cowering in the corner and Fits standing over my bed. She began to beat me with the notebook, the metal spirals digging into my skin.

"I'll not accept this," she said in her calm voice. "I do not consider carnival tricks art. This is an insult. Fix it immediately."

I stumbled into my "studio" in the laundry room half-stoned because I lived on Klonopin or Xanax. I could barely stay awake. I took each caricature and filled it in with real por-traiture. Then I took a fountain pen and wrote names, stories, recipes, diagrams—anything I could remember—over sec-tions of each picture in different prints and styles of font. Fits sat on a stool the entire time smoking thin Nat Sherman cigars. I worked until reveille and in every break during the morn-ing and afternoon laundry shifts. I managed to accomplish in hours what would usually take the whole week. When the last page was done Fits grabbed the notebook from my blistered hands and said, "That's better." She walked out of the laundry room, and I could see her disappear into the steam.

Sometimes I think my time at Powell was a hallucination. They keep telling me, but I can't remember how many years I was locked up there. I don't know how many notebooks I filled. But my scarred arthritic hands are evidence of the truth. And I know exactly where the notebooks are now. I know how to get them, though I wouldn't dream of doing so. In another stage of my recovery or insanity I'll get on a plane and retrieve the boxes filled with the results of Fits's regime.

THE ASSIGNMENT

The halfway house was a sorority of damaged women with hope. It was fascinating to watch who was crawling out of her individual hole and who couldn't summon the energy or will to do anything but get sent back. Seña found a permanent position at a Korean beauty salon and specialized in nail designs. She offered to get me a job, but my hands weren't made for such miniature, delicate work. I was bereft when she got her release.

I was sitting in my room trying to concentrate on a book about dog grooming. I figured if I was a fully equipped walker, one of those multitudes of new places that had sprung up might hire me. Doggy Day Care seemed to be a new enterprise that had come about because most families had both parents working: holding down two jobs in technology, fashion, design, architecture, law, publishing, medicine—with odd hours, no lunch break, and too much socializing for proper dog care. People were opening coffee shops and boutique clothing stores. Everyone was working hard. Holding on to the edge of the recession like a cliff. People were impelled to travel more. New York could only be the base from which they spread their products and expertise to smaller brand-name satellites. The economy had imposed a kind of vocational ADD.

But certain businesses flourished, and the Doggy Day Care grooming enterprise seemed to be one. I thought maybe I could get away from Hubb and land a position at Dogs' Love, Pet House, Best Pets, Puppy Palace, Darling Dogs, or some other disgustingly named enterprise. A steady paycheck might ease my anxiety and I could stop popping the pills I was downing like Tic Tacs.

I was reading about the undercoat of certain breeds when a scratchy voice called out, "Kepper—visitor." I froze. I'd learned to expect the worst: A phony story about my conduct. A drug test. A trip to the lawyer's office. The news of a death. A false occupation. A wrongful identification in a major crime. I'd seen it all happen. Once you'd been an outsider from the day-to-day world, you were never safe—freedom had a chip attached to it.

But when I snuck into the visitors' area (check out the enemy before they gain sight of you), I saw a stunning princess in her late twenties. She was tall and thin. Her black hair hung straight and shiny to her waist. The color of her skin was white and clean like a model in a soap commercial. She wore a simple black dress that went to her calves and fit her, not too baggy, but not so tight that you could call her sexy. Her face was the most striking thing about her. She had a beak for a nose, but it was birdlike—stunning. Full lips with light, tasteful lipstick and large brown eyes, almost almond in shape, lined with kohl. She was wealthy and radiant and most definitely Jewish.

She had an easy confidence. If I were a girl in a halfway house being stared down by women resembling truck drivers and whores, I'd twitch or bite a nail. But she stood serene. I knew immediately that she was Pony's tutor, and the only thing that stopped me from going straight back to my room was that she was wearing cowboy boots. Shiny. Expensive.

But still cowboy boots. So she clearly wasn't a total rabbi's emissary. I was ashamed because I was wearing a long-sleeved T-shirt with two huge flannel shirts on top and baggy, ripped jeans and motorcycle boots. It was one of my dog walking outfits. My hair was still black with white and gray stripes. It was thick and long and hung all over my face to hide my scars and identity. I hated her. Nonetheless, I feigned disinterest and walked toward her.

"Hey," I said.

She jumped a little, which relaxed me, but when her beautiful eyes inspected me, they immediately took everything in. I knew I came off like a hardened, bitchy, sarcastic con. I saw pain in her eyes, not pity.

"I'm Elisheva," she said. "Batya Shulamit's tutor."

"I figured that out," I said.

"I thought we should meet." She held out a long, smooth white hand. I realized how rough and arthritic my own hands were, particularly my right. I'd creamed them and repeated grueling exercise after grueling exercise to maintain a wounded painter's grace. Not the product of a spa, but I held out what I perceived was still a strong woman's hand anyway. The shake was short, but she didn't seem to be fearful of catching leprosy.

I led her to the back of the visitors' room. Luckily, no one was watching reruns of *Wheel of Fortune* or *American Idol*. The TV was on, but no sound came from it. Harriet, a small white imp with a bleached crew cut, was curled in one of the torn vinyl Salvation Army love seats. She'd been a crack addict and mule for her boyfriend, a bass player in what they'd called an "alternative rock" band. I liked the term but wasn't sure I recognized the style. One of my first purchases upon release had been an old-time clock radio to make sure I'd always be up and know what to wear for walking the dog. I didn't listen to music. The young voices and their passion tore into me, and reminded me of the emotional fire that had been stomped out. I devoured the news. I always had. I needed to know who was who and what they believed, what the usual never-changing white men owned, and destroyed, in the name of what morals and dreams.

Harriet stayed in her chair a sufficient amount of time and then dashed out. We have unspoken rules for situations like these, and she knew I'd pay her back later with a candy bar or cigarettes. I was afraid for this immaculately groomed girl. Lice. Fleas. Bedbugs. But I led her to the donated leather couch and sat away from her. Now she seemed a bit more on edge, but covered it very well by feigning interest in the mossy, drab visitors' lounge.

"I don't know your purpose," I said.

"I've been trying to figure out what to tell you."

"Yeah"—I could've said yes—"I get it, Ms. Tutor. You could get fired."

"Fired isn't half of it," she spoke quickly now, more like a teenager. "If Leonard ever found out I came here, he wouldn't just fire me. He'd call B'nai Shalom, which is where I get most of these gigs, and tell them I was not to be trusted and shouldn't be allowed to tutor their kids anymore. And he'd spread the word down the jeweled JCC train track and all my recommendations would dry up."

I was weary, barely curious as to why she'd come to meet me. She was not some uptight yeshiva girl with ugly hair and a floor-length knit skirt, but I didn't want to waste hope just because she didn't fit the stereotype.

"I know your name is that of a Jewess."

"Well, Beth is what half the people in my life call me. Elisheva is the Jewish translation. I prefer to be called Elisheva."

I sighed, "Elisheva."

She looked down at her hands and breathed deeply as if she'd learned the exercise in drama class to gain equilibrium. I now knew a similar technique, but for me it just brought so much emptiness that I was filled with an ache.

Finally Elisheva spoke.

"Do you know what tikkun olam is?" she asked.

Now's the pitch, I thought. I was about to lean back on the musty couch, close my eyes, and wave her away when I caught a glimpse of her eyes. There was nothing preachy about them. She was asking me a question.

"Yeah," I said, bored.

Elisheva sensed my wave of hostility. She moved away an inch. She became less of a teenager and transformed a little more into the ancient, serene woman I'd seen at the door.

"Look," she said, "I'm not here to 'Jew' you." She flipped her mane to the side as if worried I might hit her. "I didn't talk to anybody," she whispered. "I swear, no one. I'm totally on my own."

"I believe you," I said. She had the touch of the dramatic about her.

"But I must admit, in full disclosure, that I've read everything—absolutely everything—I could read about you." Her confession was a bit noble.

"I didn't think after the arrest there'd be much to read." I was beginning to feel a little paranoid. Stalked by a yeshiva student.

"Oh my God, you don't know? There's over a hundred listings on Google alone and page after page after page of blog entries. Not just on your art. But on the ethics of your prison term. And then there's that Powell jail where you almost got killed. Dozens of blog posts on the justice system. They may close down the women's facility."

I closed my eyes. My arthritis was knotting up from sitting too long. My knees and wrists especially.

"Tikkun olam," I reminded her.

"I'm sorry," she said. "This is a very difficult trip for me."

White girl problems, I thought. In the pen anything less than a double suicide is a white girl problem.

"I think Batya Shulamit needs to know you," Elisheva said.

"She wants nothing to do with me. And she's guarded like Princess Diana," I snapped.

Elisheva stood her ground. "She's eleven. She's brilliant. She's a deeply spiritual soul. But she doesn't know what the fuck she wants."

I was beginning to like this Elisheva.

I stood up.

"Look," I said. "I have dogs to walk. I can't ever be late. I have to take off in about five minutes. You can't walk with me because one of Leonard's secret agents might see you. But I appreciate your concern or whatever it is."

She stood up quickly, stopping me from running off.

"There's a practicality to this," she said. "She has a list of questions about your crimes she wants you to answer before she decides what to do next."

"I thought she wanted to black me out," I replied.

"Something changed. I don't know what," Elisheva explained. "I'm not her shrink. I'm her Hebrew teacher. And I'm preparing her for her bat mitzvah. Once in a while, she lets down that proper lady pose and acts like an eleven-year-old. She's brilliant when she's not snubbing all mankind. She writes beautifully too. Fantasy. Science fiction. Her English teacher wants to enter one of her stories in a Scholastic writing contest, but she refused. She's not really a happy girl."

Something like guilt poured over the plaster of paris carving I lived in. I was a George Segal statue. I was white and hard. There was no sky above me. But a wisp of a cloud blew by, and an unrecognizable feeling rushed through me.

"She asked me to give you an assignment," Elisheva said, looking away from me.

"She wants you to write down everything about your criminal life, from the start of the first crime to the last. She wants to know everything you did without any excuses or long explanations. She'd like you to number them. Make a list."

I laughed for the first time in weeks.

"That's cold," I answered.

"She needs to know your interpretation of events. All she knows is what's on the Internet and what Leonard explained to her. Leonard has encouraged her to forget you. In fact, he's pretty much ordered her to. He's a mensch, but weird when it comes to you."

Elisheva suddenly became all business.

"Here's our plan. You write your list in English. I will translate your list into Hebrew, and she can read your answers from my translations. I will try to be as accurate as possible and then burn the English so no one ever knows."

"Sounds like you've been watching a lot of CSI," I said.

"This was entirely Batya Shulamit's idea. She said it would also help her modern Hebrew. She wants to go to Israel on that Birthright fellowship."

I was suddenly back in Clayton again. Doing bizarre assignments to work through my brain damage and save my life. I hadn't blocked out the past, but I didn't want to visit it in alphabetical order.

"She asks that you tell the absolute truth."

This irked me.

"Tell Batya Shoodoopbeedoo that I was savagely beaten—

no don't tell her that. Tell her that sometimes I can't remember facts exactly as they are. Not after twenty-five years. No one can."

"She could. She has a photographic memory."

"But she wasn't in New England twenty-five years ago, and she wasn't a witness."

Tikkun olam.

"Let me think about it," I hesitated.

Tears brimmed in Elisheva's perfectly lined eyes. I was shocked. I felt badly about messing up her makeup.

"This isn't going like you thought?" I asked.

She sniffed. Another breakdown of the Queen of Sheba's perfect face.

"I come from Jewish tradition, family is the core of life and motivation. I thought you'd jump at the idea to communicate with Batya Shulamit because she's your birth daughter and meeting her last time was so terrible. I thought a healing could begin. I risked my career for it."

She paused.

"No, I'm sorry for mentioning my career. Good deeds should be done for the deeds themselves. The Talmud says the breaking of a word or a promise is acceptable if the outcome of the untruth brings true grace to all parties involved."

I smiled at her. I didn't know what the fuck she was talking about.

"You're one beautiful, complicated young woman," I said. "Do you have a boyfriend?"

She rolled her eyes.

"Too many. If you only knew. According to my parents, I should have finished rabbinical school by now and be married and on my way to a second son."

"They sound as unrealistic as you and what's her name."

Elisheva grinned. "You're teasing me. I haven't found the husband of my dreams. I've found sections lodged in separate guys, but that's about it."

"It's good you're picky," I said. "When you refer to Pony's unhappiness . . . what are you talking about?" I stopped myself. "No, never mind. No more. No more talk." I closed the subject. I put my crone's hand over her smooth white one. "I'll think about it."

"What do I tell her?" Elisheva seemed genuinely distressed. She slipped her hand from beneath mine and ran her manicured fingers through her perfectly shiny, brushed mane.

"Tell her you couldn't find me," I said.

"I don't lie," Elisheva said simply and unpretentiously.

"Yes, you do," I replied lightly. "I'm sure you lie to a number of the young yarmulkes waiting in line to make you their bride."

Her eyes flicked with surprise.

She turned so red I thought she'd faint. But she also smirked, then shrugged.

"What is this? The CIA?" she asked.

"You just don't have to be so Jewish and pedantic around me," I replied. "We've covered the brilliant religious student scenes of this story. We know Judaism is for some reason awesome. Go tell Pony whatever you want, leaving out the savagely beaten part, and tell her I'll think about it. A list of my crimes could get into someone's hands and wreck this rather fragile parole."

"I think we're in tune," said Elisheva. "You know, you're not so different from other women. Your life could start now."

"Save me the *Grey's Anatomy* or that one with Sally Fields and her dull, useless family. Goodbye, Elisheva."

She blushed again. "Please, she's your daughter."

I turned my neck so I didn't have to watch her pained exit. I didn't appreciate the complications she'd just presented me. I was too deeply tired to sort through this new information, these new challenges.

I rushed to get to the duplex in Tribeca to pick up Curly, Larry, and Moe, the toothpicks with fur. I could never be late. Mrs. Arthur, who was at least fifteen years younger than me, was very strict about time. She felt it was "a matter of respect." I once read the letter tucked away in Larry's collar from her that Mr. Arthur's "constant last-minute arrivals proved, without question, that he didn't love who she was or what she stood for." I wanted to show her I loved her tips, so I always came early.

For some reason the Yorkies were delirious to see me. It was almost impossible to get them hooked up because they were jumping and punk dancing all around me. "Order in the court," I shouted at them. I could see that my tone scared Mrs. Arthur. She'd had a lot of facework done and had only three expressions, but this was not one I'd seen. Right now she was stuck in a skeletal smile.

Curly, Larry, and Moe quieted down. They knew they'd taken it too far, and I hooked them up and headed for the door.

"Please, in the future try not to raise your voice," Mrs. Arthur said primly. "I believe in positive-reinforcement training."

Oh, please, I couldn't lose this job. Couldn't lose it. Couldn't lose it.

"I'm *so* sorry if I scared you, ma'am," I said. "It's kind of a joke the four of us have when they go bonkers."

"Yes, well, they do tend to go *bonkers*," she twitched. "Maybe if I raised my voice a bit, several aspects of my life would resolve themselves." She let out a dramatic sigh.

White girl problems.

I walked the usual route through Tribeca to get them to Mr. Arthur's apartment on Hudson Street, where they would spend the next forty-eight hours, exactly, until it was time to return them to Stretch Face. I was conjuring up Pony's list in my mind. I knew I could probably lie or censor, but that wouldn't be a good beginning. I decided to list all the crimes, leave out my promiscuity, go light on the drugs, and really play down the violence, especially toward the end. I could see a good reason to not fulfill her request. What if her Talmudic righteous lifestyle was a phase and she turned brat punk on me? Then she might admire what I had done and try to imitate the Terrartists. God no. I didn't want that. On the other hand, this list was a step toward real communication, though I wasn't sure if I cared enough anymore. I was in my plaster of paris personage, and the most important concern was not to let the hard veneer chip or soften. Or to want it to. This legal way of holding myself together was new.

God, I missed drugs.

I missed the high, but the various substances and chemical recipes even more. I missed the frantic business, the bargains, the enterprise, the danger, and the relief when a delivery happened as planned. My brain was still finding how to think in the "real" world. Not every mood was a buyout or a payoff. Acting for the sake of getting through the day itself was new. Plus I was still on the edge of illness. I would be weak for a long time. Caution and patience. Those were the watchwords of my recovery. I didn't think that smoking or snorting would get me back to jail, but the habit could increase at an alarming rate. It was my need to do wrong. I wasn't proud of myself. I was fighting off the need for thrills. I pretended I was meditation itself. A thing of blankness. A white square. God, it was hard.

LARRY, MOE, CURLY, AND DAVID

Out on the street, I sensed someone was following me. In prison you get used to eyes all over your body. I didn't speed up or slow down. I walked until I got to the corner of Varick and Walker and stopped dead, executing a perfect turn without touching. If I struck a stranger, my life would be over.

"What the fuck do you want?" I shouted. Curly, Larry, and Moe went berserk and ran in circles on their leashes. They tangled me and my stalker together and yipped until my eardrums vibrated.

"Whoa," the person said. He was very tall. "Let's not do *Charlie's Angels*. I don't even jog."

David was wearing a pink-and-brown Hawaiian shirt and beige Persian pants. His bald head was lost in sunlight. I couldn't see his face.

"No," I ordered him. "No."

"Come on, Essie, what's with you?"

I shoved him, but he was two hundred pounds of solid weight.

"Go away," I said.

"Stop the Frances Farmer routine. Eventually you have to see me," David said. "I miss you."

"No!" I shouted. I'd become a raging toddler. Curly, Larry,

and Moe were yelping and growling at David. They looked ridiculous in their bows and braids and pigtails, in their T-shirts, going at him like Dobermans. I yanked at them and they flew into the air.

"Order in the court!" I yelled. They piped down immediately. I realized how absurd it all looked. I almost laughed. "Please," I said to David. "My name is Carleen now. I have a job, which as ridiculous as it seems has really strict rules. I've only been out seven or eight months and I'm trying to build back a life, whatever the crap that means. I'm not who I was. I'm not who I am."

"We could have tea," David said helplessly. "Sit in sullen silence. You could come to my studio in Dumbo and crouch in a corner and snarl. I don't care."

"I absolutely can't be late," I hissed at him. "You're making me late." I began to run toward Hudson, practically dragging the little dogs after me. "Fuck," I said. I leaned down to pick them up.

David put his large, long arms around me. "Essie. Carleen. Whoever you are. I want this beautiful monster back in my life." I pushed him off. I started to run again. I knew he always wore flip-flops, so he'd be helpless. Halfway down the block the extraordinary pain in my legs lightened to a bearable ache. I was going faster, and actually enjoying the speed. When I got to the condo at Hudson I didn't look behind me. My legs hurt. I gently let the terriers down and went for the key to the condo. Before I did, I remembered the note tucked in Larry's collar and couldn't resist. I took it out and read:

You motherfucker. The sink backed up and I had to call the plumber. I'm not paying for it myself. You owe me $123.56. I've changed my checking account number so you can't *direct deposit it. Send a check in the mail.* Today. *I'll see you in therapy.*

I wondered why he couldn't just hand her the check in therapy. White people problems. And I was one of the afflicted white people. I tucked the note back in and opened the door. Mr. Arthur was sitting at his kitchen table reading *The New Yorker*. He was a pudgy man, balding, with rimless spectacles and thin lips. He wore a vest, a half-unbuttoned white shirt, and striped pajama bottoms. He stood up instantly when we walked in.

"My babies are here," he said in a high voice. "My babies, my boodoos, my *biddle biddles*." Curly, Larry, and Moe went into their terrier insanity routine, jumping on him, kissing him. He lay down flat and they crawled all over him.

"Treats, treats. Treats, treats," he squeaked and tossed them tiny kibble bones from a jar. I liked him much better than I liked Mrs. Arthur, and wondered why he didn't just divorce her.

"Oh, hello, Carleen," he said. He slicked down his hair with his hands. "I'm home today. Have a touch of a bug or something. My body aches, my throat feels like it has speckles. You ever have that?"

"Yeah," I said. "It's probably just a cold coming on."

"Probably the stress. Such stress right now. I hope it's not leukemia or something. It couldn't be AIDS. I'm HIV negative. But my head is pounding. I have a tendency toward migraines. Tumors run in my family, too. I could barely get out of bed this morning."

"I could come by and do a five o'clock walk," I offered.

"Oh, never," he said. "Never, never, never," he said to the dogs. "They're my only sanity. It looks like the partners are downsizing the law firm and I may be one of the first to go.

They say I just haven't been carrying my weight. It's hard getting corporate clients these days. I'm not going to be able to support two homes. Really bad timing if I lose my health insurance and have lymphoma or lupus. It's the speckles on the throat and tongue, and I have some hives on the bottom of my feet. Did you ever hear of that?"

"Probably just the flu," I said. "Sleep. You'll be fine."

"Brunhilde the witch doesn't know I'm losing my job. She's going to kill me, Carleen. Stab me with her sterling-silver, engraved, wedding-gift steak knives."

Mr. Arthur tried to cough, but there was nothing there. He unraveled the note.

"Hmm, the sink got plugged," Mr. Arthur mumbled, and then tried to cough again. He leaned over his dogs.

"Who are my pooches? Who are my babies? Who are Daddy's *dadadas*?"

"I've got to go to my next job," I said.

"So have you ever had these speckles in the throat?"

"Not personally."

"Oh, Carleen, I meant to tell you. There was an article in *The New Yorker* a few months ago about how many more police dogs there are in the city right now. You know, sniffing and guarding and lunging. It's fascinating. I'm sure you can bring it up on your computer."

"Thanks, Mr. Arthur," I said. I didn't want to tell him I didn't own a computer.

My next dog was a perfectly normal boxer whose name was Socks. White markings decorated his feet, thus the name. White markings cover a bunch of dogs' feet, and a lot of them are named Socks. I wonder if you put them all in a playground and called out, "Come, Socks!" what it would look like. Probably beautiful, like a herd of antelope in the Serengeti. Or a military formation marching forward, like at Clayton when they'd order us in our gray jumpsuits to "Line up!" We could have as many as eight lineups a day—running from wherever we were and whatever we were doing so they could count us. They were forever counting us. And like a mob of dogs with white paws named Socks, we came when we were called.

THE LAST DAYS OF POWELL

Three or four years into my apprenticeship with Fits came the catastrophe that transported me to the next chapter of this "No, I am not lying" story. We were in lineup and the guards kept us for longer than usual. Then, in one of the rows far down from me, voices exploded in fast talk, shouts, and laughter. The guards ran down to the scene and used their sticks to bat away what seemed like a crowd of witches bent over giant stinking cauldrons.

"Yo' wife is havin' an exorcism," a con shouted at me. I ran to where the commotion was. Fits was on the floor writhing and kicking. Her mouth foamed and I knew I had to get to her tongue. I didn't remember why, but I knew it was the tongue. The women parted when I arrived, as is the unspoken custom, and I told a bunch of them to hold her down. It must've taken ten women. I had paintbrushes in my pocket and I pulled one out. Somehow I pried Fits's mouth open and stuck the paint-brush in her mouth. She bit through it. I shoved in two more and then reached in and grabbed her tongue to keep her from swallowing it. She was choking and her yellow-white skin had taken on a tinge of blue. I cleared out the mucus and spit from her throat and she began to cough hoarsely.

She was breathing clearly again. She'd also shit herself. The guards took the women back to their cells. By now the nurse was there and she seemed utterly disgusted. Fits was sound asleep and filling the halls with a loud, unhealthy snore. "Clean her up," ordered the nurse, "and I'll have the guards take her to the infirmary." I did as I was told. I felt a rush—not of pity but of a sickening sadness. I think it was sadness. I experienced it while watching National Geographic or Discovery when they showed footage of a lethal animal being humiliated or conquered. Inside my head I saw a rhino falling to its knees.

I was asleep that night when I felt her in the room. She preferred waking me up to interrupting my work. "Get out," she said to my cellmate. "Go take a shower."

My tiny, silent shadow took off without hesitation.

"Don't sit up," Fits said. "Keep lying down. Far away from me." I was afraid as usual, but not repulsed by what I'd had to wipe up that afternoon. "I just have a question."

"Fine," I said into my pillow.

There was a silence.

"Did I urinate and defecate on myself this afternoon?"

"Yes," I said. "It was a bad seizure."

"And who cleaned it up?"

"I did." I was tense, waiting for a blow or for her to yank my head back by my hair.

"Did the others see?" Fits asked.

"Some." I'd never lie to her.

"Did they laugh?"

"Some," I repeated.

"And the others?"

"They were being dragged back to their cells."

"I'm having a problem figuring out whose eye to throw this lye in," she said calmly. "Not yours."

"Fits," I said.

"Yes."

"If I may . . . " My heart was pounding.

"Speak," she said.

"I don't understand the logic of the lye," I uttered softly. Silence again.

"To wipe out what they've seen," she replied.

"They'll still remember."

"This will teach them not to laugh."

"There's no telling what the warden will do to you if you blind a bunch of basically innocent women." I clenched my teeth. "It would be stupid to give up your freedom here. You'll be in solitary for life."

"I'll have restored my dignity," she proclaimed.

"You haven't lost it," I told her.

"How do you know? You're property. Not human. My slave. Powell doesn't make your rules. I do."

"That's the first time I've ever heard you lie," I said. I was in one of my carefree suicidal highs. Taunting my mother. "I know you feel humiliated."

Fits sat down at the foot of my bed and the whole bunk practically tipped over. She caught it with her massive shoulders and swore something under her breath in a language I'd never heard before. She managed to settle in and sat on the edge of the cot hunched over like a caricature of a prehistoric man.

"There is an address I will give you," Fits said. "It is of my aunt, Ms. Rue Franzheldt in Ohio. This is news to you, but after I'm finished with your books, I wrap each one in plastic and send it to her. She doesn't open them. She brought me up and trusts me. She puts the books in specially treated boxes so the pages will not yellow or fray. If and when you get out of prison you may go and retrieve your work. My aunt has a picture of you and will identify your face."

I was exhausted. Perhaps Fits's seizure had caused momentary dementia.

"I'll be much older, Fits," I sighed. "I'm not getting out."

She ignored me. "She also has your fingerprints and DNA."

"Very CIA," I said.

"You joke. But you will not be so flip always. And you will want your books back."

I stayed silent. The idea seemed ludicrous to me. Fits's small button eyes were shining like the living dead in the horror film they showed at Powell every month or so for recreation.

"Now I will lock you in the laundry room and chain you up so that no one will mistakenly blame you for my act of cleansing."

She pulled my collar and dragged me. I kicked and screamed as would be expected, but the guards barely looked up. This all felt preordained. Like an oracle in a Greek myth. I was giddy. I wanted to say, "Hey Fits, after all this time and hundreds of books, did you like any of it? Did you have any favorites? Did it matter? Is art a reason to live? Does art define life? Bee bob a do dad a la lalala life goes on!"

She threw me in my studio and double locked all the doors to the laundry. She chained me over and over to an iron pole. My back felt crushed with pain. I could barely move. "Fits," I tried, "In a week no one will care."

"You know nothing about convict time," she said gently. "Certain events go down like in Homer." She walked out the door toward the rows and rows of cells. I never saw her again.

Stories in prisons can be brutally true or they can be beyond true, crossing a character or speech into myth. When you're part of the prison culture, belief can be fatal. You go along with stories to stay sane, to share oxygen, to avoid the deterioration that comes with loneliness.

I've never heard the same version of what happened twice. I only heard much later that she threw industrial-strength lye in the faces of ten to fifteen women before the guards brought in an officer to shoot her down. Some stories put the number up to thirty, and that ten of them are blind now. Some lost their lips and noses. Other versions say that she only got to seven women before the gangs brought out the hidden shanks and knives. The details of her scarred skin, bleeding eyeballs, hair that hissed and disappeared, seemed to be essential to every version. The gunshot bullet in Fits's head was a minor detail. The story usually ends with a mob of women stomping on her, punching and pulling her until she was completely crushed and mutilated. Garbage.

But they weren't finished, and this I know for a fact. About fifteen of them got the keys to the laundry room, ripped the doors open, and came after me. It's proof of Fits's skewed thinking that she thought her legacy would keep me safe. The survivors, the ones who witnessed their partners and loved ones burned and mutilated, unchained and beat me nearly to death. My only luck was that they didn't pour acid on me and that the bone fragments inside my body didn't pierce my lungs or heart. But the enraged mob took turns and carefully and viciously acted out their vengeance one by one, and caused a myriad of internal injuries. They set all my paints and a half-finished book on fire and left me to die in the smoke and flames. At least I think that's what happened. What I remember is the doors opening and prehistoric, primal animals stampeding toward me. Their faces were like the kind of masks they make for those new zombie movies, dripping and ugly, teeth sharp as knives and eyes of coal. Arms that were metallic and bodies made of construction buildings. That's what I remember. That's all I've ever remembered.

I woke up in a dingy hospital weeks later covered with gauze and plaster. I was attached to chains and pulleys like a tortured acrobat. A blue tube was stuck down my throat and breathed for me. I remember asking if I was paralyzed, and some nurse shrugged and said she didn't know what I was saying. I was in excruciating pain and they were not generous with morphine. I think I remember the warden (whom I'd only seen at assemblies) and a woman in a purple sweater dress with glasses halfway down her nose seated beside me. Her face was Christian, stern, and unfriendly. The warden leaned forward and he stank of cigars and Old Spice. I remember a collage of words—*seedy* and *gangland* and *New Jersey private detective* and *Italian fascist* and *Latin assassins*—singing chaos in musical comedy–style in my head. I knew things about this warden. Everyone did. The rumors came to life in my head. Didn't he sell drugs and rifles? Didn't he blackmail the guards who brought in shipments of drugs and rape the newbies of his choice? Didn't he pay off the Royals with booze, drugs, and cigarettes, and offer free family visits to coerce the other inmates into order? Where did I get that from? I thought I heard him say, "We can't have our most famous patient battered by a bunch of sick hooligans." I laughed at the word *hooligans*. I choked. I tried to spit at the hypocritical tyrant. The woman leaned over me and tried to look me in the eye. I wanted morphine, not earnest glances of truth.

"We're going to transfer you to a facility more suitable to your temperament and the level of your crime," she said. "The handling of all this has been reprehensible."

"Absolutely," the warden nervously agreed.

I giggled. It felt like every nerve in my bones was attached to an electric circuit and I'd just set it off.

"God," I moaned. "Oh God."

There was some commotion, a hypodermic in my hip, and a quick rush of the soothing warmth. A mother's liquid hand.

"Women have been working on your behalf this entire time. Don't you know that?" the purple lady said. "It took something this catastrophic to allow access to you and the conditions of your imprisonment. A woman's federal committee has been set up to investigate Powell." So the purple Christian lady turned out to be on my side.

"And we will cooperate fully," the warden said, too quickly. He had tickets somewhere soon. The woman leaned far forward into my face.

She whispered, "Your sisters are behind you."

Oh no, I thought to myself. A feminist. I passed out.

I stayed in one hospital or another for close to six months. I think I kept lapsing in and out of comas. Then they pulled the blue tube out and loaded me into a helicopter and transferred me to a military facility. They'd decided it looked good to transport me to a facility that was equipped to treat the extent of my injuries in the most effective ways. I thought the helicopter was a freight train and I was a bum in the thirties drunkenly traveling everywhere and nowhere. Then I thought it was a cattle car and I was locked in a crowded, stinking train to Auschwitz. I think I tried to warn the EMTs about the gas chambers that awaited us. My pain was so intense that it affected my temperature and heartbeat. One doctor put together a combination of drugs that was as interesting as the shrooms I'd ingested hungrily and the crack and meth that took the place of my meals and became a large part of my destruction in college. Wrapped up like a mummy or burn victim, I hallucinated constantly, and my moods skyrocketed and then fell out from under me. Much of the time I didn't know who I was. I was a creature who lay absolutely still and watched the movies in my head. When I regained motion in my arms I tried to strangle myself. Ridiculous. Not because I was depressed. I was bored.

The nurses in the first hospital had encountered me writhing, filthy with paint and covered with my own feces. I must've seemed like a mad animal. I couldn't speak so they had no sense of my personality. Also, despite my broken bones, I was put in restraints and under twenty-four-hour guard. During that extremely fuzzy period when I was close to dying, no one but medical staff was allowed near me. My parents were contacted, but they'd long ago publicly disowned me. The daughter they'd once had wasn't a terrorist or a murderer. Too sick to register any kind of loneliness, I regained my ability to think. I didn't understand why I was being kept in such isolation.

Later I realized they were playing out some phony investigation as to whether I'd conspired with Fits to attack those women. Stories were going around that could get the federal government investigated or sued. No one could prove any kind of theory that I was a conspirator. The warden had his own story. He claimed that Fits had been out to get the Royals and me, and he'd had to use physical force to stop the growing riot. Pepper spray, Tasers, and clubs were used to break up the gang warfare. Afterward, there wasn't enough staff to help all the injured, and four women died. It was all lies and sadism. Misogynous. Powell and its hospital were put under investigation, and, if I lived, I'd be the perfect type to testify. So, various government agencies took over my medical treatment, which kept changing. Some higher authority wanted me to live. The prison system desperately wanted me to die. I had too many doctors, a complicated diagnosis, medicines that fogged me out or caused geysers of rage in my head. The ambivalent attempts to heal me almost resulted in death several times.

Even as bones and surgeries began to heal, I'd suffered brain damage and had to have rigorous physical and neurological therapy to relearn to function, just so I could live in another maximum security prison. That prospect didn't motivate me. I took on the affect of a near-catatonic survivor walking through an eternal Hiroshima. At the military hospital, the physical therapists were much more enthusiastic about vets and fallen athletes than an ex-terrorist convict. Elite army officials and politicians showed up now and then for photo ops with the vets. That's when the nurses avoided me and the phys-ed workers administered subtle pinches on my blisters, as well as yanks on my hair, and covered up their shoves and kicks. The guards assigned to me intensified their disapproval of my anti-American actions and they put on a show of extreme dedication. I was the changeling. I lived in a ward of medieval torture: Pulls. Pushes. Stretches. Crunches. Lifts. Drops. Weights. Walkers. Treadmills. The worst was when I had to grab solid metal balls with my hands and squeeze. I conjured up Clint Eastwood in my imagination, gritted my teeth, and vowed to quietly return and kill my torturers after I was released.

After the military hospital, I think I was transferred to another government-run rehabilitation center for vets who couldn't afford medical care. I still wasn't popular but I was less openly despised.

Eventually my vocabulary increased, and I tried to do crossword puzzles to build my brain muscles. But that was not my world. Different guys gave me comic books. Sometimes I could make out the words, but more importantly, I noticed that the colors of the graphics were getting brighter. I especially liked the Japanese manga stuff. Those guys made art out of their trash. And the *Bazapps!* and *Kazangs!* and *Blangs!* and *Kapows!* took on animation, bright hues. I could hear the words like drums.

The rehabilitation center stank. It was raw. And it grew freezing when they tried to use cold air to blow out the stink. They also posted a guard near me to make sure I didn't mess with everyone's machines or try to turn the ward against the doctors. I was a terrorist after all, even if I couldn't move. I could be faking at any time. My guards were always the tiny or skinny types and they deeply resented being assigned to me. It was considered a punishment.

Two or three months later the doctors said I could function well enough to be transferred to the hospital at the Clayton Correctional Institution for Women in upstate New York. I would be hospitalized and guarded, but I didn't know if I was going there for my stiff and stitched body or to begin a conventional lifetime in prison.

MY CRIMES

I often took Pookie, the manic black poodle, on the path along the Hudson from Twenty-Third to Battery Park. There were several wide-open spaces of grass beside the concrete where, when I let her off the leash, she could zip into her circus leaps and runs. It was illegal but Pookie needed it. Pookie was a certified maniac. Her favorite act was to run in circles until she wore herself out or seemed to realize that there was no purpose in her running beyond receiving a treat.

It was a fall day and I'd been out eight or ten months. I think. (My memory will never get seasons or events in order. Especially when it comes to dates.) But I remember this autumn because it was the first time I'd received a full day and dinner pass, and I especially remember the day because I'd decided to write Pony's list down for her. I hadn't done it right away. My reluctance was legitimate. An account of my crimes on paper was tantamount to many more confessions than I'd already given. And, with my luck, there was no telling what someone would do if they got their hands on it. Elisheva had visited me a couple more times and was quite convincing about Pony's solitary nature and the precocious spiritual way in which she perceived the events of her life. But, then again, Elisheva also worked for Leonard, and he could get to me through this unique, subtle spy. More evidence to keep me from ever getting to know Pony. He was obviously still angry enough. I couldn't figure out why he desperately needed me to disappear. He'd always been the gentle, forgiving type, with a Jewish Afro and steamed-up glasses.

There was an old boat called the *Queen Mary* by the pier on the way toward Battery Park, and I used to camp out there after Pookie's runs. I could hike in the shadows by what was once a wood bar, sit on a stool, and close my eyes to the different rhythms of the Hudson. I was insanely paranoid about jeopardizing my parole, but at the same time I hadn't tempted the fates since I'd left prison, and minor dangers like loitering were like miniscule hits of cocaine. Every now and then I just had to do something wrong. I was a crook by nature.

The interior of the old fishing boat was made of metal and wood. The benches had cracks in them, but the boat smelled as if it was still used. Maybe for tourists or an occasional fishing trip. I didn't want to get caught by the parks department, but I didn't want to take this enormous step of writing to Pony in my room or even on a park bench. Life was only theater to me. No deeper. When I was not dizzy or blank I made my own sets wherever I went. Space. Background. Color. Sound. I even had special routes that I felt were appropriate for each of my dogs.

My list of crimes. I spent a long time diddling back and forth between whether I should use numbers for the list or A-B-C. But I figured if I went beyond twenty-six I'd have to get into the AA-, BB-type category, and I knew I'd start making mistakes because it was tiny details like those that were hampered by my brain damage. Numbers weren't so hot either, but I'd just have to keep checking back to see if I'd repeated or skipped some digit. I was stalling. Where to begin. Pony wanted a complete list of my crimes. But I couldn't just lay them out for her without context. On the other hand, if I constructed what might seem like a short bio, I wasn't following orders. I thought this might displease my obsessive eleven-year-old or cause difficulties for her translator.

MY CRIMES LIST FOR PONY

A super-secret document for Batya Shulamit
by Carleen Kepper, once known as Ester Rosenthal.

1. At ten years old I was discovered as a prodigy painter and sculptor. By eleven I had a painting in the Biennial at the Guggenheim and was part of a group show at MoMA. At the Guggenheim reception I stole a key chain from the gift shop. No one found out.

2. I was taken out of school and taught by tutors up to six hours every day. My painting master was Luciano Brodeney. He tried to be very harsh with me but was a great teacher. He never used art school language. He just gave me tools and toys. He started with basic brushes with boring names and shapes like angular, bright, fan, filbert, flat, hake, high liner, mop, one stroke, oval wash, quill, round, sash, script, and square wash. He told me that some were used for precise strokes, lines, and curves; some for short strokes and thick and heavy color; some for smoothing and blending; and on and on. I didn't like the new brushes, and I didn't care what they were used for. I switched back to my teacher's old out-of-shape brushes from his palettes and bottles of turpentine. He found this very amusing and thanked me. After that we didn't talk much. We painted. Once or twice he got in front of me and stroked a huge *X* across my painting. This made me laugh, and I painted around the huge X and wrote

all over it in different categories. I never did the same to him because I knew there were boundaries even I couldn't cross.

3. One day he asked me if I liked animals, and I said I'd never thought about it. He told me that the best brushes were made from animal hair and maybe we'd get some guns and go hunting and make brushes out of our victims. He told me that brushes were made from badger hair, camel hair, hog bristle, mongoose hair, ox hair, pony hair, squirrel hair, hair from animals we didn't know the names of, and synthetic hair like on Barbie dolls or wigs. We never did go hunting, but my parents gave him the money to go to a taxidermist where we picked up most of the animals and I got to make my own brushes. I stole a very stiff frog and a garter snake, but the taxidermist didn't mention it because we'd bought so much.

   I probably shouldn't go on about this art teacher because he has nothing to do with my crime, but he did come up with an ingenious method for teaching me the color wheel. My color wheel was far more complex than the standard blue, red, green, yellow, etc. My teacher included rings within rings of combinations like naphthol red light, quinacridone magenta, phthalo blue, vat orange 1, peppermint green. He included in the wheel earth tones like burnt sienna, red oxide, and raw umber. Of course there was zinc white, but also titanium white and yellow ocher. I'd seen, heard, and tested hundreds of colors my whole life, but he gave them names. He transformed his giant color wheel into a dartboard. If I wanted to combine colors, first I had to hit their names on the dartboard and then I had to mix together the corresponding paint on a palette.

Through imaginative games and tricks Luciano Brodeney managed to instill a solid technique into my raw talents. We also painted the side of a small barn together because he could tell I would need more than just the crafts and techniques of the artist. I learned how to use a wire brush, putty knife, glazing compound, spackling paste, long hand brush, scrub brush, sandpaper and blocks, a caulking gun, tubes of caulk, masking tape, roller trays and grit, drop cloths, and much more. This work really enhanced my sculpting, and I did enjoy visiting hardware stores and, particularly, stealing keys that had not yet been cut into the shapes for peoples' locks. Once I got caught by a humorless, college-age clerk and he threatened to call the police. I told him to go ahead because I was curious to see what would happen. I remained cool and passive while he called me a bitch. But I walked out of the store with ten brass keys, and he did nothing.

After a year, Luciano Brodeney told my parents he'd taught me all he could and that I was as knowledgeable as any thirty-year-old. He also said he really didn't like children and had had enough. He needed to get rid of me before I destroyed his creativity. What a truly great man. We never said goodbye. I didn't admire his artwork particularly, but a clay wall shifts inside me when I see his face in my head. Sometimes when I touch a certain brush I hear his low voice and light accent in the bristles.

4. The *New York Times* did a magazine cover story on me

when I was twelve. My paintings were being sold for over a hundred thousand dollars. I met Andy Warhol. He was an empty-headed, sadistic, exploitative freak. (What's that in Hebrew? Elisheva, sorry, I don't know if you can translate that. You might just have to improvise!) When I visited the Factory I stole a bar of soap from the bathroom. Because it was Andy Warhol, the soap was part of an exhibit of wrapped Ivory soaps from floor to ceiling. I toppled the towers. He invited me back and told me I could destroy any of his art that I wanted, but once it was allowed it lost its wonder.

5. Anything I stole I stuck in my paintings because very early on I liked using collage technique. I visited many antique boutiques with my mother and her friends, and lifted a couple brooches, earrings, and simple bracelets.

6. My mother "needed her own space" and thought that art for art's sake was "elitist and egotistical." All the "artsy people" didn't mix with her political and charitable volunteers. But it was essential that she appeared to be a deep, self-sacrificing mother, so she hired me a dealer with a large gallery to get the paintings and crowds out of our house. I barely talked to anyone but Rico da Silva, the very rich Rico da Silva whose accent I thought was phony. Supposedly, his gallery was the most la-di-da gallery for famous living painters and sculptors. I don't know who the dealer was for dead painters. I would've preferred that. Just to confuse buyers. A man who was an Oliver Sacks–type guy said to let me be and watch how I developed. No one knew I was practicing pickpocketing at parties and setting

business cards on fire in my room. My mother once tried to talk to me, saying, "There's a world out there. You were named for a queen who saved her people. You should at least teach poor children how to paint." I rocked back on my heels and replied, "Mother, I would be a judgmental teacher. I don't like children." She waited for more, but that's all I said. She really didn't like me.

7. My father, all in favor of my idiosyncrasies, still thought I should have whiffs of a normal childhood. Therefore he sent me on one of those cross-country packaged teen trips. I was a rich artsy celebrity, but I had no friends my age. I could barely converse or even make eye contact. I didn't mind. I took a suitcase of sketchbooks. I made sketches and pastels of the countryside, mountains, and canyons that seemed to transform me far more than the stories of what movies had been shot next to what red mountains. The best part for me was discovering that I could shoplift from every souvenir shop from Jamestown to Disneyland. It was in my blood. My collection was eclectic, and I experienced a kind of physical rush whenever I laid out my loot on a hotel bed. I stole five-dollar Mickey Mouse key chains and $300 arrowheads from the Four Corners. No one told on me because I was so slick, no kids could really see what I was doing. The few sharp ones who suspected me I either bribed or intimidated. Or I taught them how. I also touched each of the ancient Indian relics behind the ropes in national parks. I wanted to feel in my fingers the work

of ancient iron tools and clay from the old Indian red earth. This wasn't criminal. I wouldn't allow a scratch to hurt those primitive masterpieces, but I did get caught once or twice and got kicked out at almost every exhibit.

8. My private works, inspired by my booty of cross-country art, were abstract spirit lands: capes with stolen beads, feathers, buffalo and deer hide drowned and dried out, lizards from early floods. The collection was bought by a Chinese toy company that manufactured baby dolls that wet themselves. Made in China. I liked that. I made a million dollars or so. The Chinese donated my original sketches to various appropriate museums, but I wouldn't let them take certain treasures out of New York for more than three months at a time. I treasured my collection of key chains, feathers, miniatures, and bracelets. I must've stolen over two hundred souvenirs and stuck them in my paintings. When the paintings went on exhibit at Luciano's gallery in New York I went every day for two months to play with the hidden souvenirs, which was unusual for me, but I've always liked "things."

9. At sixteen I stopped painting. I just stopped. The art world speculated that my "prodigious output" (over two hundred paintings and twenty-five sculptures) had burned me out. Art magazines speculated that perhaps I was an "idiot savant," I had Asperger's, I was a dilettante, or, like Mozart, I was "burned out" or "dying." But after three months I went to college and started painting again. This was the uneven rhythm

of my brain. No explanation. Much speculation. No change. More paintings. More sculptures.

10. I was compared a great deal to Mozart. I read many books on him and listened to his music. I found him too frilly and without syncopation. I got sleepy every time his music was played for me. And every time an adult sociologist compared us I let out as weird of a laugh as possible. I never made a conscious effort to alienate adult sociologists. I didn't care enough. But like with shoplifting, any action that put me on the edge gave me a spark and filled the white squares in my brain.

11. By sixteen I really had become a burden. My parents were relieved that I chose to skip the last year of high school and move on. I think they were very tired of me, and I wasn't exactly titillating to have around. I was incommunicative to the point of comatose. But any college would have me: Harvard. RISD. Caltech School of Visual Arts. I was good for PR, boards of directors, alumni, but I adamantly chose a tiny liberal arts college in New Hampshire with a good art faculty but no visual arts major.

12. I rode horses and learned to ski my freshman year. I also met a handsome townie named Miko, who was my first friend and boyfriend. He was over six feet five, and lean. I think he was part Polynesian because his skin was dark and smooth and his eyes weren't slits but had an oval, heavy-lidded look (maybe because he was stoned). As an artist I saw him as a perfectly created human specimen. (I will not mention sex because you

are eleven and Elisheva says you are not interested. But, except in certain circumstances, it is not something to disapprove or be afraid of.) Miko knew nothing about art, barely read papers, and didn't know who I was. He taught me to ride motorcycles very fast, and, more importantly, how to polish, screw, weld, hammer, and fit every bit of every kind of screw, bolt, and wire together to make an engine. Miko was blown away by the fact that in a week I'd memorized terms like ignition switch, rear brake pedal, and reservoir tank. His townie friends made fun of his "baby girlfriend," but they shut up when I could slam together an engine faster than any of the guys. I relished the shapes of the tiny parts and the feel of the metals in my fingers and fists. Some parts needed welding or the use of heavy wrenches, but I grew strong. Although not original, each engine was a work of art, and I developed a deep respect for mechanics and engineers. More so than I had for most sculptors. I was convinced I loved him, and I did everything he promised would be an adventure for us. In the past I'd never wanted a thing from the money I made. Not clothing. Not houses. Not even traveling. All I wanted to do was paint. After I met Miko though, I bought a BMW 650, a Norton 75, and a Harley Davidson that I destroyed and rebuilt so it could have the fastest zero-to-sixty revs of any motorcycle on or off the market.

13. Miko asked what the point was of building fast motorcycles if there wasn't any reason to run them. I suggested races, but for some reason neither he nor I was interested in that. (This is important.)

14. When I started painting again in college, I only painted motorcycles and very strange people riding on them. I also met your father Leonard Salin during that time, and he and I played on jungle gyms he was constructing for an architecture class. I want to tell you straight out that he had nothing to do with anything illegal. That's what made him so boring to me. But Leonard, as you probably know by now, could be a lot of fun. He took me to trapeze school and helped me shape goofy zombies out of Play-Doh. I liked how much he was in love with me. Together we built a wild playground of unexpected shapes and won a large fellowship.

MY TESTIMONY FOR PONY

The splashing of the Hudson against the boat had begun to annoy me. The motion made me slightly sick. Or maybe it was the memories. The alarm went off on my watch. It was time to take Pookie home. Evan was a stickler about time. I was frustrated and agitated. I hated what I'd written for Pony's list. I didn't want to brag about all that shoplifting, but I was following her rules. What a bad influence! But I relished a good shoplift the way people picked a good-looking table for blackjack. It was the sleight of a hand, of close-up touching, grabbing, and then hiding. I probably would've done it even now if it wasn't for my terror of getting caught and violating even one grain of my parole. I reexamined my testimony for Pony. Why had I gone on and on about the motorcycles? I was furious with myself. I was avoiding exactly what she'd requested. The details of the crimes. And what was I supposed to reveal about her straight-laced father? What did she know about him? I felt completely blocked. Perhaps I wasn't ready. I couldn't face it. I contemplated taking out the cigarette lighter that was a gift from one of my sisters at Clayton and setting the notebook on fire. A minor act of arson might relieve the pressure in my brain. But Mr. Jiminy Cricket on my shoulder told me Uncle Walt wanted me to be a good girl. Otherwise

I'd be back in the solitary-confinement castle with Mr. Ratshit and Ms. Clogged Toilet Drain. I kept the list in one piece and took off with bouncing, twirling Pookie. I tried running with her once more, but the hour of sitting in the boat had stiffened my joints and pain slowed me down. Nothing was right. Nothing was really progressing. I was in a tornado of self-pity. But I dropped the poodle off exactly on time. I'd learned punctuality and discipline at Clayton. Twelve years in that prison gave me tools for living in a civilized society where you did the right thing because of threats, not choice. But those lessons had taken forever, and I was very wobbly about it all on my way back into the real world. When a mood hit I got the urge to rob a bodega or smash some gallery or boutique so I could get my rush. Time and again I had to remind myself that they might not send me back to Clayton. I could end up at another Powell. And, in that case, I might as well shoot myself in the head.

I knew I should go to an NA meeting, but I called Tina and Jeremy instead and shyly asked if I could get a "Doorbell Fix." I rarely, if almost never, asked anyone for anything, but Doorbell was my shaman, my healer, and Tina and Jeremy were always so busy with their thriving, computer-driven business that they were grateful if their sweet monster of a dog got extra attention. It was an easy walk. Doorbell and I both took advantage of being slow and big. When I was with Doorbell my motivation for staying clean was this mastiff, who clearly had a god's soul inside him (if there was any god). He seemed to understand that I needed to take him into those neighborhoods where peril and hatred abounded. I had to have a touch of familiarity. I wasn't ready yet for the other world. Then we'd walk out of the inferno and I'd find a patch in Prospect or Battery or Central Park and we'd lie down and I'd lean my head on the soft folds of his massive neck and weep.

THE EARLY YEARS OF CLAYTON

My first weeks at Clayton were spent in the prison hospital. I was still injured and ill. The huge change in my life also induced repeated incidents of post-traumatic stress. I went bonkers quite a bit. I didn't want to eat or sleep. I refused to speak. I lunged at anyone who made a sudden move at me. The other occupants in my ward either told me to shut up or cheered me on. Some of them were there for illnesses like pneumonia, the flu, or AIDS. There were several who had bad injuries from knife fights or knockouts from batons. They, like me, were in restraints. They were women of all ages, and although the ward was clean I could smell a very old inmate a few beds down who was dying. In my mind's dark state, I was sure that would be me.

My bad behavior calmed down because no one engaged with me and the doctor didn't flinch when I tried to punch him. Several nurses had to talk to me while taking my blood pressure and temperature. I was treated like a wild animal they were absolutely certain they'd tame. My early months were filled with nightmares of Miko, Powell, Fits, forests with lynched convicts hanging off trees, canvases on fire, rapes by prehistoric creatures, nuns in a cabal putting up stakes for burning Jews, dead dogs, my breasts turning into guns, sharing dark holes of solitary confinement, watching gang members bleed to death, me drowning in their blood, being forced to jump off cliffs, voices and faces condemning me, being tangled in crippling wire sculptures, suffocating under a pile of guns, my father stabbing himself with one of my brushes, my mother turning her back. My sleep forced every fear out of me. It made me frozen and terrorized in my waking hours. When I woke, terror transposed into rage, and I felt as if I were capable of ripping my sheets and strangling the nurses. Smashing my bed against the wall and demolishing the drywall. I could've probably killed someone with the sheer strength that came from my anger at my life. I also fell victim to many seizures where I'd shake and pound the floor. When I came to, I thought of Fits and exploded into an emotional maelstrom. In the beginning I was given strong shots that just knocked me out—little by little the strength of the drugs lessened and my horrors were muted, foggy. The ever-present guard was removed from my bedside and replaced by rotating officers who covered the whole unit, not just me. The lessening of constant scrutiny took some pressure off me, and when I began to sit and then walk I wasn't overcome with paranoia. My uneven steps began to grow stronger. They told me I could start physical therapy again as soon as I started to behave.

A tall, reedy woman with whitish-red hair pulled up a chair next to my bed. She introduced herself as Sister Jean. She was a gruff old nun and told me, "If you'd get this vow of silence over, we could get going a lot faster." She said she used to hate it when she was in the convent because it prevented her from cursing out the Mother Superior and the upright phonies. The spiritual hypocrites always said that God was going to punish her for her lack of complete devotion. She wondered how they knew the extent of her devotion. "Did they have a meter?" The asshole nuns, she said, also talked a lot about God keeping accounts. She didn't think that there was an accounting firm called God & Son. Jesus didn't punish, she told me. Human beings who were liars did so in his name. And God, by the way, was too busy to be an accountant. Sister Jean gave the impression that Clayton was certainly different from Powell, but I didn't trust what might be hope in myself. And I smelled a bit of a con artist in her tough-lady, unholy-holy routine. This Jean could be softening me up for any sort of scam. But one day she told me to "cut the shit." That I was suffering from PTSD and it was scary and disorienting, but I wasn't helping things one bit with my "Marcel Marceau routine." I liked that. Several days later a nurse brought me dinner and I said thank you. I didn't even know I'd said it. It just slipped out. She didn't make a big deal out of it at the time, but the next day Sister Jean said, "I hear you have manners."

"I'm not a monster when I'm not treated like one," I replied.

"That's true of most of us," she said. "Even the real monsters, and you certainly are not one of those."

"What's going to happen to me?" I asked, though I barely had a voice from lack of practice.

"We're going to keep you here for a while longer," Sister Jean explained. "Just to make sure you've thoroughly abandoned the Mike Tyson imitation you were enjoying when you first arrived. You haven't tried to knock anybody out for quite a while, and that's much more manageable. Then you will be released and forced to go through the formal admissions policy to Clayton: paperwork, uniform, etc. You will meet with the warden and most likely be assigned to the maximum-security unit until we can put you into your program toward personal and spiritual rehabilitation."

Sister Jean must've seen my eyes cloud over. She leaned toward me—brave woman—but I had no desire to push against my restraints.

"This isn't Powell, Carleen," she said with the first note of sympathy I'd heard in her voice. "God knows it's a far fall from heaven, but it's not Powell."

She was right about maximum security. It was located in a separate building surrounded by its own high wire fence. My cell had no bars, only a heavy metal door with several locks. The room was entirely bare except for a cot, a bench for clothes, a sink, and a toilet. The walls were painted a strange, very light yellow. The floor was stone, and there was a tiny skylight high in the ceiling. There was no way to reach it no matter how you angled the bed, but at least complete darkness wasn't part of the punishment. Sometimes I was overcome with fantasies of either squeezing through that window to freedom or hanging from it to finish my confused existence. I still couldn't eat much because of the damage that had been done to my stomach, but the guards opened up the door all the way to bring me my meals and didn't slip them through the "doggie door." They were under strict rules not to curse or mock me despite the fact I'd "killed two of their own." But you could tell time was on hold until I regained my strength. Every meal was soft and mashed up as if I were a toddler and even included two bottles of Ensure. Most of it stayed down, and I didn't experience the same cramps I had been living with for months. That the bosses at Clayton were trying to get me healthy made me extremely anxious. I kept thinking of the witch in Hansel and Gretel. Fattening me up so they could eat me. The real madness came from the fact that in maximum security I was allowed to do nothing. Often I sat on my bed for a whole day and concentrated on the wall across from me.

Either because of the isolation or my unhealed brain, my time spent staring at the wall was like the vision quests of the Native Americans who would look at the "magical" clay and stone walls and see the legends of their forefathers. I didn't connect with my great-great uncle Breslov in Lithuania, but I saw visions of my paintings. My brush strokes moved according to my moods. Rips in the canvas from when I'd stabbed an unsatisfactory painting in a crazed tantrum. I saw New Hampshire right before dusk and the engines of tractors and trucks. I saw the individual faces of my "posse." I didn't know what had happened to any of them. My little collegiate posse and I were like a 1940s mob doing trivial crimes for fun. It was almost a thesis project. But then, when it oxidized into a poison, I got the whole rap. The fucking wusses said they were blackmailed or threatened. Face by face like a slide show of their mug shots. And I watched reruns of pranks and crimes. The bigger ones. The catastrophic event. I saw Leonard's face. And David Sessions. Miko rode by on a Kawasaki. I saw his thin muscular body, his hairless dark skin, and the henna patterns I painted on his back. Dreams and memories became confused. I didn't see my parents. I hadn't seen them since college. I saw an enormous poster on the wall where my mother publicly requested if she could legally "divorce me." My parents pulled out their eyes. When I hallucinated them, their eyes were all white.

My wall was the biggest TV I'd ever seen, but I had no control over programs or channels. I also didn't learn anything about who I was or why I'd done what I'd done. I missed Leonard, but only fleeting commercials of him flashed by. I wanted to roll in paint. I wanted to feel grease on my hand. My life was going dry. My skin was cracking. I stayed very still. The only visuals and physical sensations that were real were my daily two-hour trips to physical therapy. Strangers in white outfits set me on thinly covered hardwood tables. The equipment wasn't state of the art, and the pain was so excruciating I became feral. They shackled me to bend and unbend my legs, to twist my knees. They belted me down when I was to lift weights. They ordered me to walk on ramps and treadmills. A guard sat with a rifle pointed at me the entire time. I saw torturers dressed in white and variations of uniform shapes. It was the twilight zone. I contemplated refusing to move so they would beat me. I dreamed of running off so a guard would shoot me in the back, but then I remembered the crisp and somewhat dykey Sister Jean. I didn't have any reason to trust her, but I considered wanting to.

After weeks or months, more guards arrived. They shackled my wrists, but not my feet, and led me to a brick building that looked like a headmaster's cottage at a second-rate prep school. There was no sign on the metal door that was surrounded by light red bricks and some pitiful ivy.

I was led into a large room. The decor seemed to have been bought and designed by the Salvation Army. There must've been fifteen chairs, all different styles, for impromptu meetings. Couches. Love seats. Lamps of different shapes and brightness. The walls were covered with artwork obviously done by inmates over the years. I didn't judge it. There were diplomas and state certificates. Loads of files lay in straight lines on mismatching rugs, most likely also woven by convicts. I liked the chaos. It was like being inside an engine. Futuristic. There was an enormous desk that took up practically a quarter of the room. Papers and photographs were strewn on a thick, ugly mahogany table. There were four phones, plus a thick cell phone. Stuffed animals sat on the desk. They were not in good condition. The buffalo was missing its nose—a black button lay on the desk in front of it. The teddy bear had an ear torn off. Dogs? Grandchildren? I couldn't tell. The walls, unlike my present home, were all lined with stuffed bookshelves. The books looked like they had come originally from a second-hand store. There was a framed piece of paper with rows and rows of extremely neat handwriting. The title read "Clayton Prisoners' Constitution."

The unthreatening eccentricity of the place was offset by the presence of two guards in ranger hats and police uniforms. Guns in holsters rested on thin hips and bullets decorated their belts. They also carried mace, pepper spray, and heavy batons. I wasn't put off by this. I figured the warden met with convicted murderers every day (myself included)—she didn't shit around. I saw that Sister Jean was lodged in one of the ugly chairs with her feet up and tucked under her. I tried to suppress a feeling of pure hatred.

The warden was barely five feet tall and a bit chubby, but she wore a tight uniform so I could tell she was very strong. She didn't tell the guards to remove my shackles, but held out her hand.

"I'm Warden Jen Lee," she said to me. Her voice was that of a heavy smoker, raspy and phlegmy. "But the women call me Jen if they choose."

"I choose Warden Lee," I said with attitude. I didn't take her hand. First name or not, she would probably Taser me as well as anyone.

"Sit down," the warden ordered. "Sister Jean tells me you've made some progress."

"I don't know what that means, Warden. I've been isolated for three weeks," I said.

"Nine days, but one does lose track of time." She sat down, nearly disappearing behind the desk.

She read from a folder. "You're less violent, your health's vastly improved, and you're not such a shit."

I laughed out loud.

"Oh yes I am," I said.

"Don't think so, Carleen. You're separating the present from the past," Sister Jean said. "You're less of a paranoid freak and you define, to some extent, who is on your side."

"How do you know?" I asked. "I've been in that chicken coop."

"We have spies," said the warden. She smiled, but it was grim. "Don't be mistaken. At this stage the team I've assigned to you knows what's important to know. This isn't *Mission: Impossible*, but Clayton has acquired sophisticated surveillance and every guard hands in a written report at the end of each day. If you spit in your soup, we know."

Sister Jean pulled out a Parliament and lit it. "We've decided you're ready to join the general population to begin serving the federal government's official sentence. This is the hardest part, babe. No extremes. No madness. Just day after day. *Day after day*. We all find out who you are."

I was practically dragged through the admitting procedure. I once again filled out reams of documents. I was checked for head lice, bedbugs, strep, crabs. Angry guards shoved three grayish-blue shirts at me with "Clayton," my number, and my section on them. I was given underpants, drawstring pants, and hideously ugly sneakers somewhere between Keds and Converse. Their sickly green color made me think there'd been a mistake at some manufacturers and they donated the trash to Clayton.

I was basically thrown into a cell in the maximum-security building with three other women. It was a two-person cell. The women were black, and the thought of them ganging up on me and repeating Powell's racial dramas almost made me crack my nose against a bar so I could go back to the hospital. But these were lifers, older than I was, and one of them was being extradited to Kentucky the next day to go to some designated death-row habitation. She was asleep on one of the three mattresses they'd arranged on the floor. She held a Bible like a stuffed bear. The other two women didn't seem particularly sympathetic to her and were already bored with me. They spoke only in monosyllables as they pointed out exactly where they'd decided to store my possessions and where I could sleep and sit. I said only yes and thank you. They didn't even tell me their names and only spoke to me when they wanted me to move to a corner of the cell or push ahead of me at the sink. I accepted my junior role without resistance, but it was weird that they never spoke to me. After the third one was taken away the next morning, they relaxed because there was more room. I had no choice but to listen to laughter, growls, gossip, non sequiturs about other women on the floor, letters and news from outside, opinions about movie stars, food, and the personalities of various guards, teachers, and doctors. I stayed safe by keeping my mouth shut and basically waiting on my roommates.

I wasn't particularly lonely. This was a good place for a cautious kind of healing. I ached all the time, but there were less of those stabbing, sharp pains. I worked, opened and closed my hands constantly, and began to actually miss painting. Aside from that, I had few other feelings.

My chores were handed to me by the woman known as the captain of floor eight (where I was). She didn't call me by my name, but "hey you" seemed to suffice. Of course, being a newbie, I got the bathrooms, showers, garbage, sweeping, mopping, and dishwashing. I worked from 4:00 a.m. until lights out at 10:00 p.m., and this satisfied my cloudy brain. No one talked to me—not even a hello. I was only ordered around. Even a "this looks like shit, do it again" seemed like pleasant enough conversation. What made me nervous was that 85 percent of the women were black, and I was waiting—in the showers, the cafeteria, the kitchen—for the punishment for my height and my race. I'd heard a couple women whisper "honky bitch" when I got in their way, but the verbal or physical onslaught didn't come.

One night I got back from preparing the dishes for breakfast at about 9:30 p.m. My cellmates were awake and both of them had their eyes on me. One was heavyset and moved with labored breath. She used an inhaler quite frequently. She wore a pink-and-white checked housecoat with Clayton pajamas underneath. Tufts of her dyed black hair were covered in pink sponge rollers that she used every night. She was sitting on her cot, a three-month-old *People Magazine* on her lap. The other woman straightened her short hair with a product that made her bangs hang over gloomy brown eyes that could be seen through the cracks. She wore a Clayton T-shirt and pajama bottoms. She was thin and muscular, and I thought she could be capable of real trouble.

My mattress was rolled up against the wall as per their instructions. At night I rolled it out between their cots to go to sleep. I wasn't allowed to change clothes until morning if they were in bed or asleep so I tried to brush my teeth and do a wash in the kitchen sink each night if the staff let me.

I rolled out my mattress and the heavyset cellmate pointed to a clear part of her mattress.

"Sit," she wheezed.

"Yeah, sit," said the other.

I sat.

"You been a really good girl," the fat one said.

"Better than we ever thought," commented the other.

"So we're going to tell you our names. Mine's Rolanda and she's Sue."

Of course I'd known their names from the first day since they used them with each other all the time, but I solemnly nodded my head.

"Don't pretend you don't know," Sue snapped at me. "We're just saying you can talk to us out loud now. Conversation like."

"I appreciate that," I said. "I'm not being sarcastic or anything, but should I tell you mine?"

"Your name is Carleen Kepper, and you was some Jew name before that," Sue said. "Which we're not interested in."

"You been doin' real good," wheezed Rolanda.

"And we want you to keep it up," Sue chimed in.

"Floor eight is pleased with your behavior," Rolanda announced. "Now you can start to live at Clayton."

"Can you tell me what that means?" I asked politely.

"No one will bother you unless you slack off, pick a fight, or become a white Aryan."

"No way," I promised. "No white Aryan stuff."

"And don't think we're your buddy just cause we talkin' to you. You still have your place and nothin' higher."

"Friendship is an earned medal," Sue said. "Friendship is a proved, long-form, algebraic truth. Friendship is a mountain climb in an ice storm. You go up inch by inch together," she added. "That's from one of my poems."

"Sue's in the stand-up poetry class," Rolanda said. "We killed people but we're not stupid. Isn't that right?"

"If you don't know the circumstances you can't speculate on the motive," Sue explained. "In fact some very high IQs have ended lives."

"Don't answer us 'cause we're not really interested in your opinions."

"I'm not very interesting," I heard myself saying.

"We don't care about that either," Rolanda said. "You sleep and shit here, but you're not our friend."

"We're not even each other's friends yet." Sue gestured between her and Rolanda.

"Two years and working it out," Rolanda nodded.

"Friendship inside is a marriage," Sue said. "Anyways, we got you a clean mattress."

"We were worried about that stinky piece of shit you been sleepin' on. Lice. Bedbugs. Even maggots if someone died on it."

"Don't thank us," Sue said. "That's not our etiquette."

CAUGHT

One afternoon I was summoned back to the PetPals office. Hubbs and Lucinda had rescued two pit bulls, Gunner and AK, from the South Bronx. Despite Hubbs's habit and Lucinda's sometimes insufferable bossiness, I admired them for this. They'd both come from the streets, but were completely against dog fighting. They'd lost a lot of friends for their opinions and made enemies by summoning cops to break up the fights. This was one of the reasons they'd set up the office in Soho and, in the beginning, I guess they paid for their rent with drug money. I never got any clear stories from them about their beginnings. Although I was curious, I figured it was better that I didn't know.

Gunner and AK were all muscle. Gunner was brown with white markings and AK (short for AK47) was pure white. They were gorgeous specimens, and I identified with them because they were covered with scars. They'd both been nearly dead when Hubbs and Lucinda adopted them. Hubbs spent all his free hours training the hate out of them. If provoked, they still attacked, and I muzzled them on the street. A mistaken signal, unexpected crash, or bad smell from another dog could set them off. I'd seen Gunner lose control in the office and even Hubbs had to kick him with his combat boot to keep the dog from leaping for his throat. Afterward, Hubbs would hold him and rock him, explaining that "that kind of shit just isn't cool, man." Except for very, very few incidents, they had obedient, loving natures, and as Hubbs said, "They didn't do this to themselves, criminals did." I was another kind of criminal, so Hubbs figured we were a good match. I always walked them to Brooklyn and worked them hard near the bridge where there were abandoned lots and future construction sites. They chased soccer balls and jumped through hoops, and I'd throw old pillows up in the air for them to demolish. I took Lucinda's bike with an engine and revved it up in the lots and had them chase me. I always made sure no one was anywhere in sight and I put the muzzles on quickly if even a car passed and slowed down to see what we were doing. I never got attacked by either of them and thought of them as my brothers. I think, next to Hubbs, they felt the most protective and loyal to me.

I was always given the difficult dogs, so I rarely saw a golden retriever or Lab except at dog runs. I missed a simple walk. A dog on a leash sniffing now and then, wagging his golden tail as he looked back with brown eyes for approval. I missed anything simple and easy in my life. I also knew I'd be consistently scared, confused, and guilty until I finished Pony's list, so during my free hours or during meal breaks, I snuck down into what I now considered my boat, and letter by letter, word by word, tried to eke out what was the real part of the story. Here's more of it:

CONTINUING MY
CRIMES LIST FOR PONY

15. As I said, I met Leonard Salin in college. We mostly played with toys and games. He was tall and very thin, with dark curly brown hair and a mustache. The thing I liked about him was that he always wore shorts, even

in winter. He was studying architecture because he wanted to build creative revolutionary toys, games, and playgrounds. He could be kind and goofy. He was also unpredictably moody and sensitive. Sometimes he drank a few glasses of wine to calm his fears.

16. My clique of artsy-type students was nothing special. There were five of us: a composer, a French horn player, a painter/sculptor, a novelist, and a kid who was a critic and knew thousands of facts about art and literature even if he didn't do anything. Leonard was not a member.

17. Miko also had no interest in my college life. He was gradually becoming irritably hostile and intolerant. He had begun the downward road from pot to cocaine to meth. In the beginning I refused to do anything beyond pot. I loved to paint when I was stoned, but I always had to redo details the next day, so I didn't trust it.

18. Nonetheless, my clique began to experiment with cocaine and took to creating "site specific" and "spontaneous art" in the woods, in supermarkets, and in rivers. We celebrated holidays that didn't exist, staged parades and marches for causes that we made up.

19. We were rich, spoiled brats. We easily got bored. I remained dedicated to pranks and assignments and private experiments, so all I was losing was sleep. Leonard didn't know about the clique or our progressive art forms. He could be very full of himself and only came out of his cloud when he chose to. He barely noticed when I was on one drug or another. His addiction was to me. I didn't know if he really loved

me, or if he was in love with being in love with me. He built a tree house for us with ropes, ladders, and swings. He said it was our love nest. But he was so into its construction I began to think he'd forgotten who he was building it for.

20. Miko gave me my first taste of meth. How could I give him up? I was immortal, a muse, an angel. I had power over colors, shapes, and sounds. The colors that had always guided my life exploded in dimensions and intensities.

21. My whole clique started indulging in more drugs and different varieties. But the pranks and performance art were losing their thrill. I still shoplifted and it gave me a nice twinge. Perhaps stealing might provide the rush we all needed. I suggested that we become criminals. I put myself in charge of planning the robberies, but I didn't have a clue how to do more than slip a costume necklace into my pocket. I asked Miko for advice. He'd served time twice for crimes related to drugs. He thought I was a riot.

22. I lied to Leonard. About everything. About my whereabouts. About my posse. About Miko. About drugs. About booze (I loved vodka). He was suspicious and hurt. Like I said, his own mood swings could be spectacular and we'd clash at times. The two of us were a trapeze act swinging back and forth. We somehow seemed to meet in midair. Grabbing on to one another, we could spend whole nights passionately discovering incoherent philosophies of the postmoderns or simply staring at each other. One night, Leonard decided we should get married. I accepted Leonard's

proposal without pause. It fit in perfectly with the pranks, drugs, and confusing fantasies of crimes. As for time, there was only now.

23. I also started using the tree house as a hideaway home base for my pathetic crime schemes. I demanded my clique come up with a name. Our writer came up with "the Terrartists." Stoned, the pun seemed brilliant, as did every plan and idea. And so we began our secret criminal lives. Simultaneously, Miko was learning to make crystal meth in a farm twenty miles or so from the school. I didn't know anything about it, didn't even know what crystal meth was, but I vaguely noticed that his personality was a bit unpredictable, and, at times, deep back in my throat, I was intimidated.

24. The Beginning: I set out my rules. The Terrartists would never rob anyone for money. We were robbing for the sake of doing it and the thrill, not the money. After all, most of us came from wealthy or middle-class backgrounds. We'd start in small groups and knock off some convenience stores in small towns. Just to get the knack of demanding or grabbing objects. We'd steal ridiculous things like batteries, Pez dispensers, adult diapers—sardonic, amusing, sophomoric crime. We decided to get in shape in case we needed to make a run for it, and jogged together for an hour each dawn. We did push-ups and sit-ups, arm wrestled, and bought expensive boxing gear. Since we were all artists we didn't get very strong and gave up very fast. But for me, it was a pleasure. It was almost as if I had friends. This was as close as I was going to get to being a normal college student. We never talked about our

personal lives or families. Nor did we share feelings. We were so stoned most of the time I doubt any of us were carrying on the same conversation.

25. In the midst of the Terrartists planning and training, Leonard and I drove to New York City, got to City Hall, got a license, and got married by a judge in a blue suit and red striped shirt. Just like that. And then we stayed at the Ritz and ordered room service. It was a rich white kids night and we had no fear of the consequences. Annulment and divorce were as easy as birth control. Before bed we went to a Mexican restaurant, got drunk on margaritas, and zoomed back and forth on the Taconic State Parkway in Leonard's Mustang, taking the curves as fast as we dared. When I drove, Leonard was terrified. I think our honeymoon was spent vomiting somewhere near Tarrytown. When we got back to college we were both dizzy, weak, and laughing. We were happy. We decided to postpone a formal announcement until finals were over, though. He didn't want any distractions from his finals.

26. After my marriage, the Terrartists held a meeting at the tree house and I laid out the plan for our first big robbery. I could feel the thrill rushing through my veins (or maybe it was just the drugs). One kid had a paper due and another had a concert so it was hard to nail down an exact date. Finally we found a Friday that was completely free. I had been scouting and came upon a somewhat-isolated clothing boutique on a street near a community college outside Amherst, Massachusetts (land of the WASPs). There was a church on one side of it and a framing shop on the other. Across the street

was a large mall, but I'd made sure its parking lot was a mile away so no large groups would hear or see.

27. I told Miko that I'd married Leonard. For about five seconds he didn't say anything. Then he asked if it was going to make any difference. I said of course not. He laughed. I told him about our plan for the Terrartists' first heist, and he agreed it was a good beginners' scheme. He taught me the art of switching cars. We also researched back roads just in case there was a problem on Route 7-A. Miko was a patient teacher. He thought my foray into crime was a joke. But he also said, "You're going to be an awesome criminal." I thought I loved him when he was teaching me to be bad, but it must've been the meth.

28. I was the driver. I was always the driver. The reasons for this were simple. I was most likely to be recognized. Secondly, and more importantly, I knew the most about cars and had been trained by my lover to take curves at high speeds. Back roads in New England are nothing but steep curves and hills. Here was the plan:

   a) Two kids stayed at school (with much protest) to create our alibis.
   b) One kid waited in the first car, an old Volvo, seven miles outside of Amherst.
   c) I waited in the second car ten miles, and in an unexpected direction, from him. My car was a Buick, but it had a redesigned high-voltage racing engine. I'm telling you it could fly.
   d) The female poet would commit the robbery (it was a women's store).

e) After dropping the robbers off at school, I was in charge of getting across the border and hiding the loot.

29. Miko wanted to supply us with guns. But I said absolutely not. There might be an elderly saleswoman and I didn't want to be responsible for a stroke or a heart attack. Miko wasn't amused and said he wasn't sure he wanted to be associated with "rich preppies who played cops and robbers." He said we were bound to get caught. That we'd probably get off because of our rich parents' lawyers. He'd been a little moody since my marriage and I teased him about it. He dropped his stern attitude and said we should just paint some water guns, which we did. When Miko pushed me too much about the guns, I reminded myself what Leonard always said to calm me down: "Remember what the caterpillar said to Alice: Keep your temper." We wore extra-large gray hoodies and goggles.

30. The first heist was perfection. I was focused on the thrill not the items. The clothes weren't close to our style, so I told the poet to steal only coat hangers. She bagged about fifty hangers and off we went. It was a thrill speeding from car to car even though no one was chasing us. I careened on the corners the way Miko had taught me to and because of the coke I'd snorted, I was fearless.

31. I incorporated the hangers into a large sculpture made out of bent steel from abandoned cars. It wasn't like any piece of art I'd made before, and I wished I could display it. The energy of the heist gave my sculpture shape; angular objects hung like mobiles attached to mobiles. One night I went to the woods to grab a look

at my sculpture and I laughed. I had the sense that it could be my Dorian Gray. I'd be Ester on the outside—eccentric, charming, spacey, dedicated—but in the woods I'd keep welding and soldering and gluing objects I'd lifted onto the sculpture, which would grow monstrous and moldy, and would be lined with snakes and demented chipmunks.

32. Leonard knew nothing of this part of my life. As far as he was concerned, I was working on a massive show for a new gallery in New York. We'd discussed getting our marriage annulled, but avoided doing it. There was a genuine connection between us. However, on both our parts, the connection was based on only a fraction of the whole. We held together, steady and kind. He stayed stable. I lied with virtuosity. He got a three-month fellowship to Denmark, Sweden, and Finland, where some master carpenter was creating jungle gyms, mazes, and vehicles for children. This master was supposed to be one of a kind. And when he got back, Leonard wanted to spend a couple months at Epcot Center in Orlando so he could see how Disney did its magic. I think he stole a lot of original ideas and techniques during his fellowships. Leonard was ambitious and politically correct, but didn't sparkle in the imagination department. This really bothered him, so he pretended other architects' creations had occurred to him before and they just got them out to the public first.

33. The new, famous, hip painter David Sessions came to our college to do a residency. He was going through this period of painting huge, huge canvases, and our college cleaned out a barn for him, bought him all his

materials, and promised anonymity. David Sessions was a real one as far as I was concerned, so I felt excited and humbled to have him around. We hit it off immediately. He was a fan of my work, especially the collages and Bauhaus motorcycles. He found my sculpture in the woods to be very frightening, secretive, but, yes, up to my other work. He encouraged me to show it, but I adamantly refused, lest some evidence accidentally get revealed. We were brother and sister and our painting was love. I didn't trust him, but he had the least faults of anyone I knew. And I worshipped his technique. His backgrounds taught me as much as the fully completed paintings themselves. I became one of his assistants and often would show up stoned. "I didn't know you were a druggie," he'd say to me.

"I'm not," I'd reply. "I'm just trying it out to see if it adds anything to my biography."

"Just don't Jackson Pollock on us. It's been done with the car thing and it'll only up your sales for a year at most."

When I wasn't biking with Miko or planning heists with my friends, I helped David stretch canvases. I loved the feeling of pulling a canvas over a frame, the pain of it getting tighter and tighter. I was making an enormous drumhead. I just loved the labor and the groaning sounds that went into the collective birth. David always said that painters are engineers and mechanics. All the good ones are messy, greasy boys and girls who have muscles and crave dust, grime, and dirt.

34. My criminal life developed slowly and steadily at the same time. I mapped out jobs that were far away from one another and would look as if they'd been done by crooks with different personalities and motives. Here is the list:

1) 205 bottles of nail polish from Kim Soh Nail and Waxing—Vermont
2) 68 true crime books from Mr. Mystery's Bookstore—Massachusetts
3) 12 Priest, Nurse, Police, and Fireman uniforms from Buckles, Inc.—Rhode Island
4) 72 wigs and hats from Moskowitz's, an orthodox family factory—New York
5) 100 boxes from a FedEx office—Maine

The wig heist was really the climax. We each tried on tons of them at the tree house, drunk on vodka and beer and me blasted on coke. We loved being a posse and, like any addicts, longed to find new ways to commit more significant, dangerous crimes.

35. Miko and I had become closer since Leonard was away on his fellowship. My drug use increased, and pictures, tableaus, and images jumped out at me in 3-D. Miko became an ancient god to me. It was his black hair that hung to his waist. His muscles were defined so strongly under his tight black jeans, white undershirts, and black vests. His scuffed motorcycle boots had just the right flamenco heels. He was involved with the secret crystal-meth lab deep in the woods and was making money. For once I wasn't paying for all the motorcycles and cars, and my respect for him grew. In exchange I dealt for him on campus. Or rather I deliv-

ered and collected the cash. I also experimented quite a bit. The biggest effect it had on me was that objects and sensations took precedence over human beings.

36. I tried to work in David Sessions's warehouse during my straight hours. Besides stretching canvases, I mixed pots of paint as big as the Egyptian vases at the Met. Putting together colors was like cooking for a villain. He and I would stand over a pot for as much as two hours, adding a touch of yellow or taking out red by adding a spoonful of black. We talked over the formulas. He was obsessive. No detail was too small. The first painting I took part in must have been fifteen feet long. I treasured using house paint rollers and walking barefoot over the canvas as we spread the base. We talked about our childhoods, Leonard, the men in his life, as well as art, music, the cross-country trip, police procedural TV shows, fashion, and politics. He became a real friend as well as a mentor. But I didn't reveal a hint about my posse or our antics. I didn't know what his reaction would be and we both took stock in being the best of ourselves for each other.

37. Since I financed the whole criminal operation, it was up to me to propose the next step. Something more dangerous. More high stakes than college pranks. Miko said that I might find hijacking to be a real high. I'd learn to run cars and trucks to a dead stop or off the road. We'd force the drivers to leave their vehicles. But then we wouldn't take anything. Miko was in a "loving Ester" mode so he taught me some techniques he'd used on vans and trucks that delivered jewelry or cash to store owners. I wanted our first hit to be a Pepperidge Farm cookie truck.

38. Miko told me if I bought a van he would teach me how to push it off the road with my Buick. So I did. A VW camper. Miko and I practiced for hours in the abandoned countryside with the van and the Buick. The exercises were like the bumper cars at an amusement park. With all the drugs I'd taken, I had no concept that innocent people might be driving the van. I just knew that all this practice was leading up to a monumental Ike and Tina Turner–style crime and we had to perfect our act each step along the way. Miko had done a bunch of hijackings, and he'd never rolled over or crashed into a tree. No one in the other cars got hurt either. He swore on it. (He lied.)

39. This was the mode of hijacking:

   a) I'd be in the head car and run the van or truck to the shoulder of the road. I tried hard to avoid bad accidents.

   b) Miko would be in the next car with two of the Terrartists.

   c) One would stay back in a bar or store to be good for our alibi.

   d) Once I got the van or truck stopped I'd zoom ahead to a designated location (about twenty miles away) and wait.

   e) The others would descend on the crippled vehicle to scare the drivers or take some loot (I gave in on this).

   f) Then they'd disappear in three different directions toward our meeting place. This way I figured that if a cop got alerted and started chasing us, he wouldn't have a clue about which one of us to follow.

40. Our Heists:

1) Pepperidge Farm cookies (I got my revenge).
2) A whole truck of Chef Boyardee canned spaghetti and ravioli.
3) CARE organizations' boxes of toys for poor who-evers (I felt a bad about this).
4) We did agree: a shipment of the new Fryes. Every-one took at least five pairs.

41. The drugs were draining my sense of humor, and I had an edgy nervousness in my body. During practice I liked scaring the drivers, but I was always careful not to do them serious harm. Miko mocked me and said that I'd never know what it was really like until there was genuine danger. When the stakes were real. He was the one who found out there was a shipment of Cartier jewelry going through southern New Hampshire in about two weeks and we should "do" the truck. He'd take the jewelry and fence it. The gold would make us a fortune. His constant proximity to crystal meth had brought on a kind of grandiosity that I found hard to counter. I asked the others and they were all for it. They were put off by me having too much power. They preferred Miko because he was risky, dangerous, beautiful, and scary—a "real criminal" who probably knew more about what we were doing than any of us.

42. My creativity was shot to hell. The only real work I did was in David Sessions's warehouse. He'd never admit it, but I painted about five of his most popular giant canvases. It doesn't reflect on his talent. All his other stuff was brilliant, too. I didn't judge his integrity. I was grateful for the opportunity to lose what guilt I was feeling in oceans of color and texture. He also said

he'd give me credit if they were taken by a collector or museum. He never did. However, he did care about my deterioration. He always had fresh fruit and yogurt around when I arrived, and I could see him staring at me when he thought I was preoccupied with a mixture of hues. "Darling," he said to me on several occasions in various ways, "you seem to be involved in some opium den or, less romantic, let's say a filthy crack house. Don't go down the tubes. It's so unattractive—a washed-up genius. Boring if you ask me. All those circles under your eyes, cracked lips, that look on your face as if you're playing an understudy in Dawn of the Dead. Really, it doesn't suit an upper-class Jewish girl from Central Park West."

43. Leonard called me almost daily from wherever he was in Denmark. He had his suspicions, too. I was rarely home when he called, or was sound asleep. "If you're going anywhere near Miko, I'm annulling our marriage as soon as I get back." For some reason, this bothered me. I liked the state of being married, though I did nothing to respect it. Leonard seemed to miss me, and it was an odd emotional transaction because I tended to forget about him for long periods of time.

   a) I smoked several pipes of meth before the Cartier heist. The Terrartists were scared shitless and the fear jazzed them. I found the truck cruising on a back road toward I-95 and began my excellent bumping and pushing. Miko was in the car with me, shouting when to brake, steer, accelerate, and bump. His approach wasn't delicate. I ended up pushing the Cartier truck over the shoulder and it flipped onto its side. Miko got out and I sped forward to our designated meeting spot near Lenox, Massachusetts. I thought about the truck on its side and saw the violence repeated in my head in slow motion. No one could get hurt, I reminded myself. Anyway, I'd been reading some of David's philosophy books and there was this writer, Timothy Oldsmar, who claimed that physical pain was the key to finding our connection to our primal animal. He was a performance artist who hung himself from hooks in Soho. Part of me thought his claims were bullshit. But, on the other hand, David Sessions often said he wished to capture the human experience on his canvases in its most extreme (he could talk pretentiously too). He had a series of watercolors called *Adrenaline 1–15* and I could see physical pain in every one of them. I cramped up and I knew it wasn't philosophical—it was guilt. I thought, How did I go from lifting Statue of Liberty pins to throwing fellow humans off the road? But the thought left before it was finished.

b) Miko found a fence and each of us got about five thousand dollars. I knew he kept much more off the top, but he was a criminal, so I expected him to screw us. There was another shipment of gold and diamonds passing through Troy, New York, a couple weeks later. Troy was a connection to the New York State Thruway toward the city. This company was a multimillion-dollar jewelry legend called Wolfmanns. They leased necklaces and bracelets to movie stars and society ladies.

Very few sales were less than six figures. They didn't have a store in Manhattan, but rather a town house where the jewelry was on display. Then, if a wealthy lady or gentleman was interested in a purchase, they brought it to your home for private appraisal. The van for this treasured jewelry was more elaborate than the others we'd hit. The driver and his assistant carried keys to boxes in which the pieces were kept. Miko used some of his connections and found a way to have duplicates of the keys made. He'd moved up in the crime world with the meth business and was being courted by some kind of Russian mafia group or a South American cartel. He exaggerated, confused the details, and simply didn't care. But he and I were both doing more meth, which made us impulsive and quick-tempered. I had bronchitis from smoking too much, and there were voices in my brain singing cheap pop songs.

44. Meanwhile, the other Terrartists held a meeting behind my back and decided Miko and I were going too far, were too into drugs, and that they wanted their normal college lives back. One of the practice Cartier drivers smashed up Miko's arm and that freaked them out. They realized they were way past pulling pranks, and the buzz was gone. They didn't like me much anymore either because all I did was strategize and give them orders. One by one they pulled out. I didn't care and wished them well, but Miko got paranoid. He said if even one of them became a snitch we'd be ruined. He took it upon himself to hold a meeting and warn

my gang of artists that if any one of them ever talked, even to each other, about what we'd been doing the past two years, he'd make sure that not just one, but all of them and all their families would be kidnapped, tortured, or killed. The five of them were flabbergasted, and I remember the silence in the room. I could feel it. A black hole. I remember nodding off in a corner and thinking to myself that Miko was sounding very *Godfather II*–ish, and I found it ridiculous and sexy. I knew we had nothing to worry about. They were all headed for graduate school, teaching, orchestras, or publishing. What would be the purpose of sending themselves to jail? Then Miko laughed, hugged each one of them, and gave them an envelope with some cash. The atmosphere was eerie.

45. A week before the major Wolfmanns heist, Leonard returned to the States. A young, growing architectural firm was impressed by his proposals and wanted an interview for building experimental playgrounds. He demanded to see me though I claimed to be on deadline—I never had deadlines—and was down with the flu and looked horrible. After much back and forth, I agreed to meet him in New York City. I washed my hair, found a clean smock, and drove the BMW on the Taconic so at least I'd have the pleasure of its curves.

Our meeting was evasive. It was next to impossible for me to get through the day without meth, and wherever we went—Bully's Deli, the Empire Hotel—I excused myself to go to the ladies' room to at least sustain myself with a snort of coke (though that was no comparison). Leonard didn't comment on the obvious fact that I'd lost nearly twenty pounds, and I didn't say anything about his frizzy hair tied back in a ponytail and Van Dyke beard. He wore a suit and tie and I looked like his rebellious daughter. We tried to talk at the restaurant.

"How's the painting going?" he asked stiffly.

"Harrowing," I replied.

"Are you trying something new?"

"I'm always trying something new," I snapped, and sighed. "I'm sorry," I said.

He smiled meekly and looked distant.

I changed the subject.

"So, did you get lots of new ideas?" I asked.

"I've always had the ideas." He was annoyed. "I'm learning how to craft them."

"This is a nonconversation," I stated.

"We've always been this way," he replied. Which wasn't true. We'd never been any way. I didn't know this person.

"David Sessions is in residence," Leonard said. "Do you like him?"

"Adore him," I said.

There was silence.

"He's gay," I added quietly.

"I know," Leonard said.

There was another long silence.

"What's really going on with you?" Leonard asked. But there didn't seem to be a real passion behind the question. More like fear.

"Just what I've said. What about you? I have a strong instinct that there's a six-foot, blond Danish woman in your life." I paused. "And furthermore, I think this is a very strange meal. I don't think either of us is saying one word of truth."

Leonard tapped the tabletop with his long fingers and averted his eyes.

"But I would like some apple pie," I went on. "And you want a divorce or an annulment. The Torn Tuba."

Leonard smiled. "The ketubah. We never had one." He leaned his long frame toward me. His eyes looked sad behind his horn-rimmed glasses.

"Essie," he started.

"Wait I . . . I have to go to the bathroom. Hold that life-changing sentence."

I practically ran to the ladies' room and fell into a stall. I sobbed and heaved. I pulled myself together, checked to see if anyone was around, took a pipe from my purse, and lit up. Immediately the universe came into perspective. I returned to Leonard.

"You were saying . . . "

"I don't want to do the legal thing yet," he said. His voice was a little fuzzy. "I really like you as my wife. I know you're fucking around with Miko. I've talked to him."

"You what?"

"I called him to find you. I asked him if he'd killed you yet. He said he was working on it."

"You didn't have any right to do that." I was furious.

"I'm your husband. I like being your husband. I'm going to move back here so you don't go down the rabbit hole. Look."

He laid out some brochures. I took a quick glance. Payne Whitney, Hazelden, McLean's—hospitals.

"You need to get clean," he said. "You're a full-fledged junkie now."

I stood up from the table.

"I'm divorcing you," I said.

Tears made marks on Leonard's cheeks. "You don't have time," he said.

"What do you mean by that?"

"I mean you'll lose the energy. You won't bother. You're insane on coke and meth. I'm coming back and setting you straight."

"What makes you think you can do that?" I was about to walk off.

"I'm your husband, your hero," Leonard smiled.

He was nuts.

"Do me a favor and finish out your fellowship, and when you've made a jungle gym that even God can't duplicate, come home and we'll discuss this. But in the meantime—fuck you."

"Remember what the caterpillar said to Alice," he shouted from the distance. But it was too late.

I walked out of Bully's. I drove to New Hampshire at eighty miles an hour, daring a cop to stop me. I made record time.

"Why didn't you tell me you were talking to Leonard?" I screamed at Miko.

Miko shrugged and smiled.

"He's a jerk. But he's got a good nerdy sense of humor." Miko lit a reefer and sighed in deeply. "Don't worry, I didn't tell him important stuff. It's just boyfriends jousting and I'm so ahead."

46. The dinner with Leonard and the follow-up with Miko left me paranoid and restless. I decided to escape into my studies at college. I hadn't been to my dorm room in so long it was like visiting my first room as a child. Only this room contained half-finished paintings, giant imitation Japanese symbols I'd painted in black on the walls, and a thick piece of foam for crashing. The paintings I'd been working on were collages that were triptychs. There were exact replicas of cartoon characters: Dagwood, Dondi, Doonesbury, Brenda Starr, Mary Worth, Archie—odd combinations I'd replicated exactly from newspapers and books. I'd torn up white T-shirts and lithographed prints of Native American kachina dolls, copied paintings of Hindu gods, and pages from the Torah. The sides of the canvases were lined with glossy primary colors on which I'd painted primitive fish, fruits, and dolls much like the outsider art from St. Lucia and Jamaica. Within thick gobs of paint I'd stuck some Cartier gold and diamonds. The paintings were exuberant and full of humor. Twisted metal stuffed with stolen goods from all the heists, over which I'd poured darker shades of red and amber, blues, greens, and gray stripes. Over all this I'd meticulously drawn faces in black. When you looked closely their expressions were terrified and ferocious. I didn't wonder what the artistic community would think of this totally different style in the "sculpture garden." The only person who saw it was David Sessions. He told me that it was diabolical genius and that if there were real gods I was probably provoking some kind of curse on this poor, mediocre liberal arts college.

After seeing Leonard I stretched a large canvas and began to paint, truly paint, which I hadn't done in a long time. I was elaborating on children's stick figures in odd combinations, from loving to pornographic to American families. The families were the most interesting because the mothers and fathers and children came out in very diverse colors, sizes, and energies. Family dynamics were bizarre. Dominant, abusive fathers and kind, maternal grandmothers. Delinquent children. Brilliant prodigies and psychopathic younger siblings. "Regular" families throwing plants at each other. Widows taken care of by overweight daughters. Fathers playing sports with sons. Mothers cooking with daughters. Catatonic, depraved, obese triplets in front of television sets. Love. Laughter. Violent fights. Some families dressed to the hilt. Some half-naked. Perfection. Tenderness. Incest. I was scribbling and moving at an uncharacteristic speed. The canvas seemed filled, with me as a Peeping Tom looking into the window of a whole apartment building. At the top of the canvas I wrote "American Dream."

I don't know for how long I painted. But luckily— God blessedly—this spurt of creativity coincided with the New Hampshire State Police arriving at our campus to interrogate the population concerning a series of pranks and robberies taking place in the New England area. These minor crimes had taken place very far apart and were most likely unrelated, but, nonetheless, the timing of it all was highly unusual and the style of the burglaries seemed to share a similar philosophy or game. The police in each state were starting at colleges, mainly at fraternities and sororities, to see if this might have its roots in hazing or initiations. But since my college had no Greeks, the police were conducting a very cursory sweep through the small student body. When they arrived at my studio I was covered in paint and freshly filled with coke, so I was fun and articulate. I spoke with them about what I felt was the oddness of their list and how hard it would be to put it together. They spoke to me about four of my friends who'd dropped out recently or transferred cross-country, but since the robberies had continued after their leaving, their names were virtually irrelevant. The police acknowledged that they knew I was a child prodigy and had a small fortune, but thought perhaps boredom and entitlement might lead me to become involved in crime. But when they saw me drenched in paint and practically glued to a new canvas they were embarrassed. They confided in me that, if the crimes were initiated from a college, they had their eye closely on Dartmouth because it had a reputation for drugs and wild parties, plus highly intellectual students. On the other hand they could be completely off track with colleges and were looking into communes and ashrams that had low supervision.

I called Miko immediately after they left and told him we had to abandon the Wolfmanns jewelry heist because the cops were investigating our earlier crimes.

"This is the perfect time, idiot," he laughed. "They're looking all over for pranksters and amateurs and we're the real thing. "We're going to do the job that makes criminals look like heroes."

He was probably correct, I thought to my stoned self. I was going to be a varmint-rat-Hells-Angel-girl

hero. Leonard's name sang in my head like the theme
song of a children's morning TV show. No. Guilt. No.
I just didn't feel it. I lost the urge to finish my painting and instead took out the Sunbeam Tiger with
the oversized racing engine that I was going to use
to knock the Wolfmanns' van off the road. The Tiger
looked like a sports car—an old Thunderbird, small
and harmless. But Miko and I had built its body with
the steel they use for army vehicles and attached tires
that they used in crash-car competitions. You could
fly over three trucks in a row, land with a boom, and
probably not even scuff the rubber. I never built anything like this before with Leonard. I loved this car.
And I was so ready to do damage. I'd shared some of
Miko's meth and it had given me a hungry curiosity
for violence, not necessarily the wish to do it. But
I took the Sunbeam out at dusk and drove up the
mountains to the most treacherous roads to see how
fast I could make the curves. We'd added a couple of
special gears to avoid skidding, but I didn't care if the
car went out of control. Life was interesting but not
the be-all and end-all. I had no fear of death. I had no
inner sensitivity toward how desperately trapped and
miserable I was.

By the way, *American Dream* is worth a fortune
now, and my parents aren't allowed to sell it or exhibit
it. If you ever find yourself in a rut . . . What am I saying? You wouldn't go near it would you? You'd rather
babysit preschoolers who go to fancy schools that
prepare them for Harvard.

47. The day of the heist came. Miko, through his connec-

tions, got the route for the Wolfmanns' jewelry van. I was staked out on my Kawasaki road bike. I'd chosen a driveway on a farm off Route 22, which connected from Route 7 in Vermont and was used by commercial traffic to get to the New York State Thruway. My plan was that, if I saw the van, I'd ride through the fields to a couple farms away where I'd stored the Sunbeam in an abandoned barn. I'd hop in my car as the van passed by, and begin the process of running it off the road. I'd approximated a quarter mile where I'd demobilize the van and then take off. Miko would be waiting in a souped-up VW van with a friend he'd commissioned for the gig named Jess Draper. I didn't know Jess except that he worked at the same car parts shop as Miko. He wore flannel shirts and chewed on toothpicks. I was annoyed. My criminality was ritualistic. It was my secret self. Miko had promised not to tell any other person about our robberies, much less bring some stranger to work with us. Miko reasoned he brought Jess because the van would be loaded with heavy boxes packed with layers of jewelry. He was afraid it would take too long to get the stuff into the new recreational vehicle he'd remade himself. No one was going to go after a camper thinking it was carrying stolen jewels. I mistrusted his whole plan, but he was a professional, rap sheet and all, and I had to respect him.

I sat on my small yellow road bike completely obscured. This was my second high-stakes crime—but my first crime with guns—and I was waiting to see if it would jazz me in a new way. Miko and Jess had the guns. The most violent weapon I'd used was pepper spray. At first, I was agitated. He said he'd only use them to scare the drivers if they got feisty. Most drivers were so out of it and shocked, they couldn't organize themselves to fight or get angry. I was really pissed off when the guy broke Miko's arm in the Cartier heist. I liked my work to come out the way I'd envisioned it. I needed to feel in control.

I saw the van speeding on toward Route 22. It was a big mother—a custom Cadillac truck—and it had solid wheels and rubber covering the rear bumper. I took off on my Kawasaki and had a blast getting to the designated barn. I jumped ditches and rocks, zoomed through cow turds, and zigzagged through cornfields. I had to clip one barbed-wire fence, which wasn't a problem for me because I used wire scissors constantly in steel sculpture and my hands were strong. I got to the barn with some thorns and nettles sticking into my jeans. The pain only upped the excitement.

When I revved up the Sunbeam it roared like the noble creature it was. It was a convertible and I was dying to put the top down, but couldn't. It would make an easier description for the police. I was about to take off when I glanced over at the passenger seat and saw Miko had put an open box wrapped in foam with a hefty black Magnum inside. The sight of the gun stopped me cold. I wasn't about to use it. I didn't know how. And I was the driver. I was always the driver. I never got near the real confrontations.

I bit back my anger, put the Sunbeam into gear, and tore onto Route 22 as soon as I saw the Wolfmanns' van pass by. I didn't want to play games, yet couldn't help having some fun. I drove up to its rear bumper and kept at the precise speed so I could follow it as closely as possible. The driver leaned on his horn, and I could see that he was signaling through one of his rearview mirrors that if I wanted to pass, I could pass. Then I began to bump him. Bump, bump. Luckily he was macho enough to speed up and not pull over right away. He thought he could really lose me, but I pulled up alongside him, gave him the finger, and started my maneuver to hit him sideways to squeeze him off his lane.

Then all of a sudden a blue car appeared coming from the other direction, so I just crossed lanes and went into whatever field was on the blue car's side. I downshifted so I wouldn't skid in the mud or dust and let a couple other cars pass until the van and I were alone again. The driver was still pissed off enough to try to match my speed, but there was no doubt he was utterly freaked by what I was doing. I'd crossed over the middle again and was banging the side of his van with the Sunbeam's special steel front, back, and sides. I was ready now to push the van off the road because I could see Miko's weird white camper waiting on a distant side road. I slammed one more time—hard—into the side of the van and the driver did the rest of the job for me. He began to slide around the gravel of the shoulder, and those vans aren't equipped for skidding. He swerved out of control and tipped over, did a full roll, and lurched to a stop in a wheat field. I took off. My job was done. I was exhilarated. But I didn't follow God's rule: "Ever wakefulness in the art of drag racing." I failed to see the car passing a pickup in the opposite lane. I smashed head-on into the Honda and literally threw it into the air. In my rearview mirror, I could see the car roll over the pickup it had been passing. It probably landed in a pile of metal and glass. The pickup did a whirly and landed on its side. For a second I didn't know which direction I was heading, but I got myself going south on Route 22, back in the direction I'd planned to go. My little armored vehicle had withstood the calamity. Then I realized my entire front window was shattered and shards of glass were all over my hands, face, and head. The dashboard seemed to be filling with blood and I could feel a tire dragging like a wounded soldier's leg, but I kept going. I knew I had to get rid of the car. When I finally stopped in the cow field of the farm I'd chosen for reconnaissance, I couldn't open my door. I was falling in and out of consciousness. I took the gun and put it in my lap though I didn't know against whom I was protecting myself. I sat there in my demolished treasure, unable to put my thoughts together. I was in a rush, but time was slipping by without anything happening. Miko didn't show up in his vehicle, and I knew it would be just like him to leave me to die. I didn't like the role of another dumb chick going down for her man.

Then, I don't know how much later, I heard sirens. Good, I thought, they'll pay attention to that accident with the car and pickup and not even notice me until I'm off toward Buffalo with Miko and the jewels. Where the fuck was Miko?

Treasure. When I was five years old, I'd dreamed of being a pirate. I didn't care about a black patch over an eye or a hook. I imagined a ship the size of the Empire State Building with sails made of black silk. I didn't fancy cannons. The image of shiny daggers and silver swords thrilled my love of color and shape. But most of all, there was a trunk located in the middle of the worn-down wooden bow. And the trunk was the size of a large cabinet. It had carved sides and gold and silver engraving on the edges, and the key that opened the brass lock was as big as the steering wheel of my father's car. The key was gold and carved with the names of the most famous, evil pirates of all time. On my pirate ship you opened the trunk and it overflowed with a bath of diamonds, rubies, gold nuggets, bracelets, necklaces, chains, and coins—so many coins from all over the world. It didn't matter to me what anything was worth. I was entranced by the color and the texture. Being the youngest and smallest pirate on the ship, I could crawl into the trunk and submerge myself in the cool metals and stones. I'd lift my arms through the trunk and swim through the pearls. I'd dive downward through the waves of shining emeralds.

A flashlight circled the interior of the Sunbeam. A spotlight blasted from the front through the broken window. Hollywood. Oscar night! The opening of a new Kmart! A circus—yes! A circus. I'd painted so many circuses. I could hear the ringmaster through his megaphone.

"I'm not saying this again, Ester Rosenthal. Toss the gun and then come out of the car an inch at a time."

What was an inch at a time?

Who was saying my name?

An inch in what time?

Inch and time and Ester.

You take as long as you want to do an inch. It depended on how many brushes. What was the shape? Sideways light or was it ashen?

"We're coming in."

The light blinded my eyes, but I grabbed Miko's gun and pointed it toward what blinded me.

"You're going to want to put that down, Miss. You're in a hell of a lot of trouble as is."

"I've been in a bad car accident. I was driving my car when a vehicle from the lane across from me attempted to pass and went right into my lane," I said calmly.

"Put down the gun."

"My car is especially well insulated or I'd be dead."

"What are you doing with that gun, ma'am? Just hand it over to me."

"'And who are you?' said the caterpillar. 'I don't know,' said Alice, 'for I'm not myself you see,'" I replied.

A club hit my already burning scalp and a gloved hand grabbed the Magnum. Some arms or legs or an octopus lifted me out of the car and threw me on the ground.

"Don't move," said a man's voice.

"I don't intend to," I replied.

"You don't want to end up like your friends," the voice threatened.

Now I saw red-and-blue lights flashing and white cars—perhaps eight of them in triangular positions. It was really quite pretty.

"I don't have any friends." I shook my head. "I'm an artist. We're lonely and narcissistic by nature."

"Well, I think it's more like this," said another voice. It was also male. It was scratchy. I didn't like its almost arrogant tone.

"All your friends are dead. Your friend Miko is dead. Your friend Jess is dead. That's why you don't have any friends."

My body went cold.

Many cartoon voices started screaming in my head. They didn't match or rhyme.

"Jess was not my friend," I shouted.

"Yeah, but Miko was your boy, right? And you and him were planning your cute little heist with the jewelry truck right? But we were waiting for him, and when he approached the Wolfmanns' van we told him to stop. They pulled out their firearms and killed two officers. We don't know about the third. Don't worry though, we gunned down your playmates, Ms. Jew-girl. They're dead as you're gonna be if you don't start realizing the godforsaken hell you're in."

I started screaming.

"What? Guns? Asshole! I told him not to bring guns! What was he doing with guns? You ask him. I said no guns. We never use guns. What're guns for, to rob a bunch of shiny jewels? Ask Shakespeare. That was in iambic pentameter."

"What about that gun you were waving around?"

"A water gun painted black," I pointed out what I thought was obvious.

A boot kicked me in the ribs.

"What're you on, bitch? You're swimming in chemicals."

The image of swimming in chemicals nauseated me. I threw up.

"You're in trouble, ma'am. You're an accessory to the murder of two police officers."

I tried to pull myself together.

"All right, I'll be completely honest," I replied. "I started the day with a joint. I've smoked maybe three pipes of crack cocaine. I've tooted I don't know how much coke on this run. I've had two hits of crystal and half a six-pack of beer. But I'm clear about what things I will and will not do in a moral sense. I'm always clear. Ask Miko. There's only so far I will go. And then he pushes me a little further. It's his eyes. I can't believe he finds me wild and attractive. He says I can take more shit in one day than anyone he knows and still stand upright."

"Ma'am. I've told you. Your buddy Miko gunned down two cops and must have a gun's worth of bullets in him. He's dead."

"This is Man Ray," I laughed. "None of this is real. Call Leonard in Denmark and he'll tell you what an imagination I have! I could work in one of those S&M clubs, you know where they stage scenes like maids and butlers and children's tea parties. I stage scenes. I staged this scene. Go to my forest. It's a sculpture. Ask David Sessions."

"She's lost it," an EMT said. "The drugs, the head injuries. She needs to go to a hospital. Now."

I felt myself lifted and put in a sluggish vehicle with a motor that wasn't capable of going as fast as they were trying to go.

"Take the engine out of my Sunbeam. It'll get us there in half the time as this piece of shit. I designed the Sunbeam myself. Mechanics is sculpture with function. That's why factories are so fuckin' beautiful. Construction sites too." My whole body was flashing stabbing pains and going numb. Stabbing pains. Ice-cold limbs.

"Help me," I screamed. "I'm the Fourth of July. I'm the Macy's display. I'm going off all over the place."

They cordoned off a section of a hospital somewhere in a chic town in New York. Police cars lined up across the front of it. Inside they began to examine too many parts of me at once and the pain was surprising. "Fuck you," I screamed, and passed out.

■   ■   ■

Dear Elisheva,

This is the accounting of all the crimes that I remember. I left out anything sexual for obvious reasons, but I'm afraid my rendition of events isn't as clean cut as you and Pony Batya Shulamit might want. Please feel free to edit out any commentary that is redundant or too much of an elaboration on "just the facts, ma'am." Also, any phrases or incidents that you think might traumatize an eleven-year-old girl—please, I beg you—cut, cut, cut. I will live with graphic details all my life—Pony doesn't have to. I swear I tried to be detailed and honest. I don't know how you'll choose to translate this into religious-looking Hebrew paragraphs but good luck. Maybe the whole thing is a scam. My fear about you knowing all this stuff is that you're a carrier, like a pigeon with a secret paper on its talon. Where are you really going with this story, and in whose calloused hands will it land? Yet I trust you, with your Cleopatra eyes. I don't want you to tell Pony that I'm sorry for who I was or what I did, or that I was sick and didn't know what I was doing. No commentary on your part. Just lots of cuts, and pick the right font and an objective translation. I doubt I will ever hear from either of you again. I've already told several authorities that I'm a sociopath and didn't care how any of it turned out. Sister Jean said that's my biggest lie, and when I break through that window to the truth I might drown from walled-up emotions. I thank you for your intervention. There's the possibility that you may decide not to show any of this to Pony at all, but if you do, here are the statistics:

Two cops died. One is paralyzed. Miko and Jess are dead. The two drivers of the Wolfmanns' truck escaped with minor injuries. I guess they built those trucks better than I thought. The truck and car involved in the accident contained two drivers and one passenger. They all died, but I was found innocent for negligent homicide because the truck came forward in a no-passing lane.

I don't know where Miko is buried. I never knew if he had a family or other friends. I think he might've just been an urban lowlife mobster who loved the mountains of New Hampshire and jumping road bikes over wrecked trucks.

In this story, at this point let the facts stand. If we continue, others will reveal themselves as time goes on. But time is not my friend.

Thank you for your attempt at a positive intervention, Elisheva. I wish I had the maternal instincts to relay my

saga to my little girl so she might forgive me. But I am
unforgivable. I am the monster under the bed.

Yours,

    Carleen Kepper (Ester Rosenthal)

When I finished my Homer-like list for the red-haired tyrant who would be my daughter, the chemical dawn was spreading its transparent, thin red-and-gray fingers across the Manhattan skyline.

I was in my room at the halfway house. I'd considered my writing time on the fishing boat sacred, but I'd become a robot when it came to rules and, without hesitation, had returned to the house at curfew.

I was cold, and sleep tried to pull me under a heavy white cloud. My arms tingled as if I'd suddenly contracted a nerve disease. It was as if my body was disappearing into smoke. I knew I'd outlined those years in too much detail with too many characters. The memories of the landscape of my criminal life put me in a trance. A list of drug-induced oldies. I was lying on the ground of an unknown desert. Then I slowly walked through a city with buildings as thin as needles, cars in postmodern geometric shapes, and absolutely no human inhabitants whatsoever. I was switching in and out of visual realities. My muscles cramped. My throat seemed to close up the way they describe a fatal allergy to nuts. I tried to breath, but I was inside of a tornado. My body was buckling under itself.

"Carleen," I screamed at myself. "Ester."

I punched at my arms and tried to scream, but what came out was like a psychotic cry for help, as though I were hallucinating an attack by an invisible killer. I dragged myself to the sink and let the cold faucet release a stream of water onto my face and then into my ears, nose, and mouth. At last I returned, and the weight of shame lay on my back like the rock of Sisyphus. I didn't think I'd stand straight again. I'd be condemned to be one of those old ladies who were bent parallel to the ground. The truth was, I had always been myself. I was this story. No other. No radical changes. No corruptors or predators or abusers. It was me. The legend of Carleen Kepper was her own doing. I was Yellowstone National Park. Bubbling gases. And devouring chemicals. I was poison. Why should an innocent little girl know that such chemical possibility could be mixed with her blood? I decided I'd never give the document to Elisheva. I thought about committing some new crime to put me behind bars for my remaining years. It was better to be an injured rabid animal than try to tame myself to coexist with others who had been born naturally decent. Leonard's genomes gave Pony a chance to live normally. Shit, I hope I hadn't wrecked that, too.

I began to pour sweat. I looked at the clock. It was time to pick up my first dog of the day. Should I call Hubb and wake him out of his drugged sleep and quit? Should I buy a Glock or a Magnum? Should I rip off my clothes and set myself on fire in front of Leonard's house? But I had no political passion, nor generosity. What good would I do? I was a Roy Orbison song—"Bad Boy."

CHESTER

How meek I was. I pulled on blue jeans, a flannel shirt, a jacket, and clogs, and dug out the key to my first gig. He was an old man with an old dog, and neither had much time left. Marty Trimbal at 645 Whatever Street. I couldn't remember. Maybe I didn't have much time left either. I checked out with the front guard and didn't say good morning. I hit the street.

"Well, that was dramatic," I said to myself. My panic attack (if that's what it was) felt exactly like detoxing, but I hadn't done those drugs for years. I switched my mind to Chester, Marty's dog. How strange that I could be so thoroughly nuked, and then set about my day. It was as if I were a child's ad for the postman. Maybe during a break I'd make a call to Sister Jean and tell her to go fuck herself. Maybe I'd throw myself in the East River like Spalding Gray. In the meantime, Chester was twelve and didn't hold his bladder well.

Marty was sixty-eight, not really old but he had emphysema. He was an insurance salesman and a low-stakes gambler, and he used to bet on dogs when he went to visit his mother in Florida. He told me that he'd lay down his bets and then cry when he watched the beautiful rail-thin dogs killing each other—for what? He knew that throwing greenbacks in the name of the half-bird-half-mammals as they were starved and tortured for snorting, beer-bellied ticket holders was wretched. But he did it.

Then, according to him, he went to one of those "left-wing, liberal, save-the-dolphins" places, and he saw this emaciated miniature disaster cowering in the corner of a wire pen.

"Okay, Chester," he said to the greyhound. And the dog got to its feet graceful as a stallion and limped over to him. He drove Chester back to New York in his Pontiac. The dog never made a sound or looked at him once. "Chester was worn out by life," Marty told me. "Just like—yeah, you knew I was gonna say it—me."

"But here's the thing," Marty continued. "He was bred to run. So he sort of had to run, even if he was fakin' it for his own benefit. Up until last year I could take him around the Village, ya know. He didn't need a leash or nothing. I fed him three times a day, but the spic in the bodega on Barrow called the ASPCA. He reported that Chester was 'thinner than he was supposed to be.' Some guy with greasy long hair and a mustache came by and checked my old dog out. Said I was doin' fine," Marty laughed. "I could grow a goiter the size of a tomato on my head, and no one would call about me. But dog people. They're fascists. I don't gamble anymore. Instead, I became a fascist searching neighborhoods for fucked-up dog-a-saurs."

Eventually Marty's breathing got bad enough that he could only go to the corner and back. He knew he had to hire a service. He called PetPals because he was living on social security and Medicare and we were the cheapest. Also, since I'd started at PetPals, they advertised, saying, "Also specializes in training and unique circumstances."

Chester and I took a cab to Central Park to arrive there

early enough that dogs could still be off leash. I admired him. At first he walked arthritically on the grass in crooked lines. He was my Giacometti beauty. My gray bone of driftwood. As he worked his kinks out his gait became smoother and his walk surer. Then he lifted into a tight canter and, though he couldn't go very fast, you could tell he was dreaming of a sprint around a ring. "That's Chester," I'd shout. "He's coming from behind. He's passing all the others. Watch him leap over the line! Yes, yes, it's Chester!" I opened my arms to him and he managed to place his front stick legs onto my shoulders. He panted and rubbed his prickly head against my cheek. He was old. I knew it, he knew it. But his dog dream created speed and victory. I felt less bombed-out myself, and I popped a dried-chicken treat into his gray mouth while I leashed him.

We walked a bit more through the park. I caught sight of a long line of mothers jogging and pushing strollers. Truthfully, at least to me, it looked ridiculous and a bit desperate. It was so pinkish and bouncy. Chester and I were like veterans from World War I compared to them. We had so many scars and fractures. He was gray. My hair was black, gray, and white. He had milky eyes. Mine were forever circled as if I'd lost round after round. And along came these pastel ice-cream pops in bright white sweaters pushing candy-cane vehicles. I preferred the broken-down, near-death version, and so did Chester. He refused to watch them and bumped up against my side with his bony rump.

Marty called Hubb every day to say, "She does real good by my greyhound. I don't want no one else. If I die you give him to her."

"She can't keep doing so much time for such chump change," Hubb would tell him. "She's got a tight schedule."

"You wanna put him down?" Marty'd growl. "Old animals can't laugh?"

"How about I put you down?" I once heard Hubb retort.

"That's up to me," he answered. "As long as Chester can make it, I'll keep wheezing away."

A VISITOR

After fifteen years in prison, the last eight at Clayton, I was told I was under orders to see a visitor. Up until then I'd been refused mail, phone calls, or communication of any kind. This was fine because I wouldn't have listened to or read it if I did. It was my prerogative as to whether or not I wanted to communicate with the outside world. I certainly wasn't making any effort in that regard.

I was surprised because I found myself in foot and hand shackles being led to Sister Jean's office. I'd only ever been there for counseling after a week in solitary or aggressive, strange behavior on my part. So, maybe ten or twelve times.

Sister Jean sat back in her overstuffed chair (she refused a desk) and signaled to the guards to unlock my restraints. Her office was colorful and comforting if you were ever in any shape to notice it. She didn't have gross metal crucifixes on the wall with Jesus draped like a zombie over the cross. All her crosses were gifts from Central and South America and Africa, where I imagined she'd served as a Maryknoll missionary. One of the inmates had made a table for her out of plaster of paris and bottle caps. I liked touching it as if I were blind. The texture was the closest thing to art in Clayton. For equality's sake she had a clay menorah, a wooden mezuzah given to her by some crazed Orthodox prisoner, several Indian gods such as Krishna, Shiva and Ganesh, as well as a big fat Buddha, and a tiny altar with carved candles and saints for the Latin girls who believed in Santeria. There was a prayer rug on the floor as well. There were photographs of indigenous people from all around the world. Clearly poor. Persecuted. Fighting for their rights and freedom.

Sister Jean sat in her chair concentrating on embroidering a piece of silk cloth. She raised her eyes and gave me a smile loaded with things to come.

"It's lovely to have you for something other than your usual bullshit," she said.

I shrugged. "I guess."

"You have a visitor we are going to leave you alone with. Given who he is, we trust you won't hurt him, but we've given him a Taser just in case. We're allowing him to visit on an off day because he isn't often in the US. It's my personal opinion, but a few hours with him may help ground you or help your sense of reality, which keeps switching on and off like a light-bulb in an interrogation room. I've allotted you cottage Sally 3 (cottages were named after inmates who'd died). You may do whatever you want—stare, have sex, argue, get reacquainted— but you may not hit him, nor he you. Guards will be posted outside." Sister Jean stood up.

"You may come in, Mr. Salin."

Leonard entered the room. He was a grown man now. Probably in his midthirties. Premature gray streaked his black curly hair. His glasses were rimless so his gray eyes were more exposed. His skin looked tan and he must've been going to the gym, because even though he was as thin as ever he didn't appear too fragile or weak. He burst into tears the moment he laid eyes on me. He sobbed quietly and Sister Jean patted him rather unsympathetically on his bony shoulder.

"He's here to divorce me," I stated plainly.

"Essie," he sobbed.

"Why didn't he just do it by phone or send a letter from a lawyer?"

"Leonard flew here from Israel to speak to you one-on-one, Carleen. I thought since he was your husband—*is* your husband—you both deserved to try to clear the mess that remained of your marriage."

"Israel? Have you joined a kibbutz?" I was snide.

Leonard laughed through his nose. Snot dripped to his chin. Sister Jean gave him a Kleenex. He was hiccuping slightly.

"No, I've been commissioned to build a playground around Jewish themes."

My laugh was a snort. I was conversing as if this were my best friend, my boyfriend, my lover, my husband . . . and it had been I didn't know how many years.

"So you make huge menorahs for jungle gyms and Jewish stars that go back and forth like seesaws and jungles with huge mezuzahs as trees?"

"Carleen, calm down," Sister Jean said in a quiet voice. "You're hyper." The tone of her voice shut me right up.

"Why did you come here now, Leonard?" I tried to keep my words in proper sentences that idiots and hypocrites could understand.

"Because they finally let me," Leonard sniffed. "I've been trying for three years."

"Bullshit, you weren't even around during my trial." I tried to keep what I thought was a level tone. Then I jumped him, knocked him over, and pulled at his thick, curly Jewish Afro.

Sister Jean grabbed my hair and practically yanked my head off my neck. Not your usual nun.

"This is not the kind of housecleaning I meant," she growled at me. She signaled the guards to relock my restraints.

"Sorry. Not very ladylike, Leonard," I said. His skin had gone gray with terror.

Sister Jean spoke again as if the current events hadn't just happened. "Take them to Sally 3 and only interfere if one of them calls for help or you hear distinct sounds of violence." She didn't look at me. "You go after him again—a week in solitary. Full restraints."

Sister Jean's voice meant business. I saw that the guards were curious and amused. Word would be out that I was alone with a Jew boy in Sally 3. The lifeblood of Clayton was gossip, speculation, and judgment.

Sally 3 was a small wood cabin like ones along a river for camping or fishing trips. The windows were small and covered with mosquito netting. There was a grungy double bed that honors women got to use for conjugal visits. I was a long way from that in my faded-orange uniform and leg and arm shackles, but being alone with Leonard drilled a hole in my armor. A vague memory of tenderness leaked through. He'd known me before I was Carleen, when I was just Ester.

"My God, what have they done to you?" he asked when the guards locked us in.

"You don't know me. You barely did. You're in Israel, but I'm farther away than any country you could find on a map and now you're pretending to pity me."

"Essie, please . . . Are you in pain?" Leonard continued.

"All the time, but in a way, not at all."

"This place looks at best civilized."

"It's a prison. I'm getting so worn out with useless talk,

Leonard. We're not at Elaine's. You've come to tell me you're divorcing me and your conscience will be clearer if you do it in person. " He coughed.

"I'll try to get us annulled first. If not there'll be divorce proceedings. You'll just have to sign the papers. That's all."

"You own nothing of mine. Not one canvas or paintbrush. And not one accidental drip on a canvas."

"I don't want anything, Essie. That'll be perfectly clear . . . Can I hold you one last time?"

"I'm in chains, Leonard."

"I'll work around them."

He put his arms around my shoulders and his smooth face against my cheek. I would've killed him if it weren't for Sister Jean's instruction. The tenderness was odd though. He'd never been there for me while I was in prison. And now he was leaving me. I was a teen comic-book cover with my bright-yellow hair in a flip and a turquoise tear drawn just below my eye.

"Let's try to fuck," I dared him.

He appeared to be slightly nauseated.

"I wash every day, Leonard. Being a killer doesn't mean you have crabs. Come on, one last time," I pushed him further.

I lifted my shackled hands above my head. He hesitated for a moment but then unzipped my prison-issue pants suit. It was impossible to spread my legs because I was chained at the ankles, but I managed to bend at the knees. With twists and turns we found an angle to get him inside me.

"Careful of the zippers," I said. "You might scrape yourself."

He was involved in some Hollywood end-of-the-world philosophical last fuck. For him, huge skyscrapers were falling and we were saying goodbye and all humanity on earth was doomed. I felt very little except that it was nice to be twisted up and not for punishment. A long time ago, Leonard had been really blah compared to Miko, but I was glad it wasn't Miko now. Miko was dead. And this had a sweetness some people called life.

When Leonard finished he began to weep again.

"Well, this is the weirdest S&M I've ever done," I said.

He smiled and we did the complicated do-si-do of straightening out my chains and overalls. His suit looked freshly ironed and untouched.

We sat in confused silence.

"Leonard, after this," I said. "Nothing."

He nodded.

"Like *Star Trek*, let's beam out of each other's lives. Not even memories. Particles."

"That's poetic."

"I haven't being reading a lot lately," I said. "And my memory is the back of a train yard. The tracks cross in fifty directions. Rarely do I end up where the thoughts are supposed to go."

He reached for my hand, but I'd become a statue.

"Essie," Leonard said. "I hope this nightmare ends. I hope you find creativity or peace in it."

"Leonard," I replied. "You're a hypocritical two-faced shit. Get the fuck out of here unless you want to use the Taser."

His face went white with shock.

"And you know in every square of every crossword puzzle what words I'm not saying. You could fill them all in. Go. *Now*. I mean it."

I'd morphed into a bitch because his kindness toward me had brought up all the years of need within me. I despised and mistrusted anyone who made me feel weak.

He stood very straight and knocked on the door for the guards.

"My lawyer will send the appropriate papers," he said.

I kept my thoughts to myself. They were too scrambled and paranoid, lost in voices. I watched him go. I sat on the bed and watched his body take on a proud but tentative posture. Essie the Jewish pygmy had shot him with her poison darts. Poison that lasts past the grave.

"Why now?" I asked him when he was far enough away. I knew he must be marrying another woman.

"You coming?" the other guard said to me. He had a smirk on his skinny face.

I stood up and slogged my way out of cabin Sally 3. "I think I'd like to go clean some toilets," I said.

I was surprised that Sister Jean didn't call me in to find out how well the reunion had gone. I wasn't surprised when I began missing my periods, so I waited three months to tell them. They didn't do abortions at Clayton anyway. They had their secret grants from the Catholic Church to protect human embryos. And most of the women found an odd hope or redemption in creating an innocent life inside a corrupt, demonized body. The ones who hated it were the eighteen- and nineteen-year-olds who'd be giving the newborns over to their parents only to get out after three years and have someone clinging to them just when they'd need freedom. That was the beginning of child abuse right there.

Clayton had an "experimental" maternity program. It was run by Samantha, who'd been there thirty years for multiple murders. She was white and Jewish but the wife of a martyred Black Panther leader. The crime was ridiculous. One night, the Feds got a little jumpy and by mistake raided a birthday party for her man, also a drug dealer, but who wasn't doing anything at the time except blowing out candles on a cake. There were so many radical suspects gathered in one house (it was a family enterprise) that, despite the fact the officers had no warrants, they broke into the party and discovered assault rifles, grenades, kilos of smack, and dynamite. There was "confusion," and the Feds gunned down three unarmed men and a woman who'd been pulling out steak knives. I think at least eight innocent people were killed. The scandal was out of control. The Feds had to steal evidence to mask their outrageous fuckup. The survivors escaped to the streets, but they'd lost precious loved ones.

Samantha, the wife of the gunned-down leader and a hotshot in her own Weather Underground–type troupe, found a safe house and plotted revenge. She knew the odds, but she refused to be blackmailed into testifying against her family. She decided to leave her mark in the name of the imprisoned, the poor, and her beloved martyr. So, after a night of planning and reaching out to her Panther and Weather connections, she called Cousin Brucie, the sixties rock jock, and told him to warn the FBI that Jesus was on his way. Then she blew up the FBI headquarters with grenades, dynamite, and firebombs. She got four agents in the blast, but the agents who illegally started the birthday debacle never saw jail. Sam was the queen of the Black Panther radicals, and the FBI hunted her down. She and two comrades were in for four life sentences.

Sam, unlike me, was a real political animal. She wrote lengthy polemics to the outside and marches were organized in her name. She thought Clayton was a neo-Nazi rattrap, so she tried unsuccessfully to radicalize the prisoners. Even as a newbie she'd had ideas for programs to make Clayton more livable. Jen Lee showed up around that time and agreed to negotiate. Together they set out to transform punishment and torture into real rehabilitation. Sister Jean was assigned to

Clayton shortly afterward. She had endured a horrendous spell in El Salvador, and she brought all kinds of anger and rebellion that nuns aren't supposed to have. She and Sam were sisters of righteousness, and Clayton gave the appearance of introducing change. Despite their power, of course, rapes by the guards, initiation beatings, gang rites, and underground black-market drug traffic continued as in every major American prison. There were a lot of newsletters and speeches exposing the corruption. To Sam's credit, she did initiate useful programs. One of them was a birthing center so fewer newborns died upon delivery in filthy cells.

Sam and I had a strained, sarcastic relationship. If there was any mutual respect, we didn't show it. Like most inmates, many versions of stories about my life and incarceration had spread and been reinvented over the years. Sam thought I was an upper-class dilettante who'd done nothing for the world (which was true). She'd heard rumors that I was severely mentally ill and suffered from post-traumatic stress syndrome, so she avoided confronting me directly. I thought she was a diva who disguised her megalomania by pretending to be furious with capitalism. This was also true, but she got things done.

"You never come to meetings," she said. "There are subjects that could interest you: the health center, polemic writing and graffiti, visitors sneaking visits to sisters in solitary, drawings for our children on the outside. You really could get attention from the media. Weren't you sort of the Michael Jackson of the upper-class art elite?"

"What would I want attention for?" I replied.

"The injustices in this place. The slavery of women. Do you know that over half the women in this place are here because they were committing crimes for their husbands or boyfriends?"

I paused. She was five foot five and had a runner's body and short, cropped hair like Annie Lennox or Laurie Anderson. I craved her dexterity and energy.

"Do you really believe in all these preachings you give, Madam Sam?" I asked quietly. "Did you believe in what you were doing when you blew up the FBI?"

She paused. She was holding her temper.

"Why do you ask that?"

"I just wondered what it would be like to believe in something," I said.

"Don't you believe in anything?" she asked.

My mind went blank.

"Color, maybe," I answered. "Yellow."

I was baiting her, but it was half-true.

"So, you just intend to waste your life getting nothing? Giving nothing?" She was disappointed.

"Try again later," I offered. "This is it for now."

"There's never a later," Sam said. "The time is now." I thought she was going to burst into song.

"You can kill me, but I don't care. In fact, I don't care if you blow me up," I said.

She shrugged. "I've never met anyone who takes being as cold as you. You've obviously never lost someone you loved or had your purpose in life taken from you."

I didn't answer. I simply wondered if my lack of feelings was a pretense, or if I was missing some vital wiring in my brain.

One of Sam's campaigns was to improve conditions for those prisoners who were mothers or who were going to be mothers, to stop them being treated as "field workers in a starving, occupied country." She had a son and daughter on the outside and was determined that their visits not continue to be censored conversations through phones or plexiglass. She designed a family visiting area on paper. There was a stretch of land that was nothing more than an unnecessary extension of the workers' parking lot. It stretched out about four thousand square feet. Sam came up with a visitor building that was made from simple wood and glass. Inside there was a modest playground for kids (better than one of Leonard's), magazines, and nonviolent computer games for teenagers. Families could gather on various donated sectional couches and, if they needed privacy, there were small rooms divided off where other chairs and couches let mothers be with their children in a nonfrightening atmosphere.

Sam applied for state funding to build her dream, and when they turned her down she wrote a letter to the governor telling him he would be directly responsible for:

> *bringing up a new generation of juvenile delinquents in this world. Mothers may make mistakes in society, but they still can be strong, loving mothers. Children need their real mothers, despite their crimes, for a sense of identity and connection. Mothers who are deeply flawed can be more nurturing than law-abiding men who care only for ambition, financial gain, and reputation. Fathers are experts in neglect. They have no natural instinct for kindness and no commitment to the future of their children or the children of the world.*

The letter was published in the *Village Voice*. Nonetheless, little attention was paid to it by the mainstream public because of Sam's criminal activities and her continued association with radical groups outside of Clayton.

So Sam got cadres of volunteers together from different gangs and religious sects, students and lifers, and went about building the thing herself. Several of the volunteers who worked at Clayton reached out to the community and to other townships and acquired wood, glass, steel, tools, and cons from the men's penitentiary several miles away to help with the heavy lifting, though I tell you these women were strong. The women set up a drop-off called, "No More Benches and Phones on Plexiglass," where the Salvation Army donated furniture, dishes, and decor.

I hadn't entered the underworld of motherhood yet, but I was told there was a committee headed up by several social workers who would work with Sam. They planned play sessions with moms and children to clear away some of the emotional dirt that built up over their separations. They were even in the process of planning sleepovers so a kid didn't have to spend intense, head-spinning visits with their moms only to return to empty beds in false homes: grandparents, foster homes, group homes. Sam had signs stuck up all over the prison that said, "Home Is Here with Mommy!" (I didn't agree.) Guards were strategically placed at several locations in the facility, but on busy visiting days their uniforms were khaki and casual and their firearms were concealed deep in their pants pockets. Sam's center didn't cool the rage among families in the grip of loss, but there was definitely more self-esteem in the women when they dealt with their kids.

Sam's other project was to provide doctors and advisors to the pregnant population of Clayton, which was made up of women who'd been pregnant or raped before they got there or by prison guards, but were too afraid to name names, as well as stupid idiots like myself who participated in conjugal visits without birth control. Sister Jean contributed to get Catholic funds to repurpose a part of the hospital into a maternity ward. Women worked through their off hours to sanitize the ward, whiten sheets, and do mailings to acquire medical birthing materials, and Clayton Volunteers Inc. traveled around the US collecting incubators, cribs, and blankets, as well as special gynecological tools needed for delivering babies in distress.

I was fed up with the maternity center aesthetically, and intellectually falling to pieces. I needed control so I made a decision. For the first time since I'd been in prison, I called my parents. I told them to sell two or three of my paintings and donate the purchase price directly to Clayton to Sam's maternity center and be as public about it as they wanted. I refused to say any more to them. Despite the fact that it would put the criminal carnival back in the spotlight again, my parents did their best to sell to my most loyal collectors. Soon word got out, and Mr. and Mrs. Rosenthal were harassed by calls from galleries and dealers for days after that. There was an editorial in the *Times* asking rhetorical questions about good deeds and bad acts. Can one balance out the other? Can there ever be forgiveness? The answer seemed to be no. Which was fine with me.

The paintings raised enough money to hire midwives and gynecologists who would make working visits whether we needed them or not. The emphasis went from simply treating STIs to concentrating on the health of an expectant mother and her future.

I told my parents to sell a fairly well-known sculpture so we could use the money to get a sonogram for the clinic. And I bought incubators and infant-health specialists. I added a program of renowned surgeons who would be on call if an infant was born with a deformed heart or craniofacial disorder.

I pretended to be asleep whenever Sam came by my cell. I'd been avoiding her in the cafeteria and when I had grounds duty on the playground. Other women were relentless in teasing me. "Buy me a Rolls, Mommy," one said. "Jew girl, why can't you get us a bowling alley?" I was trying to learn how to tune people out so I wouldn't attack them. I hated solitary, so I stayed as isolated as I could.

One day I was smoking a cigarette in the recreation yard and Sam stalked up to me and slapped me hard across the face.

"Don't burn your hand," I said mildly.

"What the fuck is it with you?" she yelled. "Did you need some publicity on the outside?" she sneered. "Afraid they were going to forget you?"

One look between us established the absurdity of that reasoning.

"You must've laid out over a million dollars," Sam said. "And you just had the money wired to me care of Sister. Why? You don't seem to be developing a conscience. You haven't taken part in any other activities. You don't like me, but you saved my project. What goes on in that head? Why did you put yourself through all that? Why did you do it?"

I looked down at my feet a long time. I tried like a coal miner to dig out emotions or motivations. After a while I lifted my heavy head and stared into her serious brown eyes.

"I don't know," I said. "I guess you were having all the fun."

"Don't fuck with me, Carleen," Sam snarled. "You don't know what I could do with your life in here."

Somehow I was tired of this. The whole charitable thing wore on me. Once Sam had cooled to a reasonable temperature and all our metaphors seemed genuinely insane, we sort of smiled. "The fetuses of the world salute you," she said.

After that rush of generosity, I quickly forgot about it and took to measuring up who were going to be my partners and posse in Clayton to keep me alive. My temporary institutional protection was coming to an end. I'd managed to keep to myself and challenge no one. But I'd also made no friends, and I could feel the growing rumors and annoyance that I had special privileges without earning them. There were extremely strong hierarchies and signals among the inmates far more complex than at Powell. A lack of "respect" was interpreted as "attitude." Mild dislike turned to suspicion. The challenges were subtle but difficult. Objects of mine were stolen or destroyed and the servings of my meals were cut in half. I was shaved or scratched accidentally. A storm was gathering around me.

The foreign whispers in my ear and slight insults started like days of light rain. But my real challenges and choices were postponed because I was pregnant. I didn't see the doctor immediately. I decided to take my time. I felt oppressed by the knowledge that there was another life inside me. I found it a little freaky. I'd seen *Alien* with Sigourney Weaver, and I carried myself with a sickly fear that a gooey little fist might punch through the skin of my belly and strangle me. I wondered if any woman had ever conceived a cannibal fetus and been eaten from the inside out. I was annoyed that, despite my myriad of beatings, stabbings, and injuries at Powell, I'd maintained the ability to conceive. Despite being big-boned and wearing less-than skintight uniforms, I still heard the rumors and mocking. More and more of the voices at Clayton were whispering, "Frankenstein's got her a baby." I rarely thought about Leonard. When I did, I visualized him traveling around the world building politically correct "We Are the World" playgrounds. I wondered if he was going to carve one out of ice in Antarctica, or make a series of slides and teeter-totters out of mud and straw in the refugee camps in Honduras. I wondered when the real Leonard would appear. At times, I wished the baby was Miko's because then there'd be a possibility that it would inherit those dark Samoan eyes and pitch-black hair. Miko was a maniac but he was the only person who caused me real pain. And pain was love. Not Leonard with that odd, slightly fake personality. Violence was what I understood as honest communication.

CELLO AND RASPUTIN

I maintained one Upper East Side client because I loved her dogs and she needed a cheap walker. Her name was Marianne Devonshire, and she had been a cellist with the New York Philharmonic. She was in her late seventies now, and arthritis had begun to cripple her strong, slim hands. She was of average height but still stood as straight as a ballet dancer. The tendons around her ankles were giving out, and the doctors told her that if she didn't wear orthopedic boots (they looked like astronaut shoes) when she took her walks, her arches would give out and she'd be a cripple. She found PetPals on her thick, old-fashioned computer. Marianne's pension was slim and she was very fastidious about her budget. She owned two black Bouviers named Cello and Rasputin. Bouviers are enormous in size and, unless well trained, wild in spirit. Her Waspish family had bred them and she'd owned them her whole life. Rasputin was seven and Cello was three and, until recently, she'd had no trouble walking or handling them. But with the weird boots and aching hands she'd lost control, and had taken a couple bad falls when Cello playfully leaped after other dogs in the street. Her children insisted she either get a full-time walker or get rid of the dogs. She'd never lived without dogs or an instrument so she found PetPals and called Hubb. He was going to explain that the service concentrated on downtown Manhattan, but I couldn't resist making my workload more complicated and difficult. So I traipsed up to Madison and the Sixties to take Rasputin and Cello to Central Park in the late afternoons four days a week. I was out of place in the neighborhood in my oversized man's shirt, ripped jeans, and high-topped Converse, but the dogs were so huge and glamorous I was rarely noticed.

One day, I think the season was fall, I was on Madison Avenue trying to wrangle Cello into discipline. I heard signals, looked across the street, and saw a group of girls around ten or twelve years old gathered in a clump. They wore uniforms. Short green dresses with pleated skirts and thin yellow-and-red stripes. They were accompanied by yellow knee socks. I was remarking to myself that these were some of the ugliest uniforms I'd ever seen when I noticed a girl with long red hair pulled back tightly in a headband. We both froze. The other girls zoomed across Madison to get closer to the dogs. (And me, I think. I was an odd uptown animal). Myriads of questions and *oohs* and *ahhs* were hitting me like stones.

"What kind of dogs are these?"

"Are they friendly?"

"Can I hug one?"

"Where did you get them?"

"They're so big."

There were seven or eight girls, but they might as well have been nonexistent and silent. My senses were concentrated on the redheaded girl whom I could see was desperately trying to decide whether to cross the street or not. If she did, I'd be too close to her according to the orders of the court. I could tell she was embarrassed by what I looked like. I know it would be impossible for us to pretend to exchange the spontaneous enthusiasm that was going on and on and on.

"Hey Batya," called one of her friends, "'fraid to cross the street?"

"These dogs are really cool. You could write a poem about them."

"Batya, you look stupid there by yourself."

The little girl didn't know where to focus. She caught my eye and immediately looked away.

"Batya, doesn't your dad let you talk to strangers?"

The teasing was a bit malicious and I could tell it wasn't new. I wondered if any of these girls sensed who I was and was using that to further torture her.

"Batya, are you allergic to dogs too?"

"Are you afraid?"

Cello and Rasputin were getting tired of all the attention and tried to hide behind my legs.

"Enough, friends," I said. "They're getting a little freaked."

"Will they bite?" a girl in sparkly lipstick and a chic Mohawk asked.

Immediately I imagined the dogs turning on the girls and viciously going for their throats. Or maybe I wanted to.

"Never," I answered. "But time to go."

"Batya!" one of the girls screamed. "Last chance, you little chickenshit."

Batya stood straight and shouted back.

"Those dogs are beasts. Filthy beasts. I hate them. You're all assholes. Dogs are for people who have nothing else to do."

She stalked off. I was proud. She'd stood up to them and managed to insult them, me, and the entire universe of dogs in the process.

As I walked away, I wondered how much bullying and teasing was directed at that snobby, intelligent little girl. I couldn't see her as on the edge of any popular clique. I wondered for a moment if all the mess around me made her stick out at a time when girls were best suited to move in anonymous herds. I thought to myself that my fiendish notoriety had been going on for so long that by now everyone was used to it or bored. Her problems were her own now, not brought about by anything having to do with me, except genetic inheritance or her immune system.

Later that week I told Hubb that if he kept me on the Upper East Side I'd quit. The old lady was getting demented, and it was too much of a commute. I thought he'd give me a hard time, but he just called Marianne and gave her the name of an outrageously expensive uptown service. He was such a sadist. I called her back and gave her some names of NYU students who'd posted cheap dog walking services around the supermarkets and dailies. She said Cello and Rasputin would miss me. I'd miss the big lugs, too.

I didn't have any goals to become a better person. It was that same mental thing as with Sam. I didn't like it when someone was conniving and getting away with bad stuff. I wondered if I had the same perversity to undo a competitor's good works, turn them into bad accidents or ruined plans. Hard to know the workings of Carleen's bashed mind.

A MEETING IS PLANNED

I got back to the halfway house after walking ten dogs, and Elisheva stood several feet away on the sidewalk. She had on very high heels and a black, clinging dress that went to her calves. Her silver necklaces made of mezuzahs, Jewish stars, tchotchkes, miniature scrolls of scripture, and rabbinic circles added to an exotic presence that reminded me of photographs of Moroccan Berber women I'd seen in coffee-table books in Rizzoli's. I'd gone there one day because I wanted to feel real books in my hands, books about art history, books about painters, outsider artists. But when I reached the bookstore that held all those colorful, thick, oversized, shimmery books, I couldn't touch them. I couldn't read the names or take in the covers, which almost always displayed the artists' most famous works. A hypermantra circled in my groggy inner ears: "I'm sorry, I'm sorry, I'm sorry." And for the first time, I experienced a remote ache having something to do with the colors, textures, and what might have been the soul I'd betrayed.

I pushed myself to the photography section and bent my head over all the African and Indian display books. "I'm sorry, I'm sorry, I'm sorry." The photography soothed me slightly because it was of all kinds of people who perhaps had faults too: chiefs, warriors, shamans, wives, grandmothers, farmers, workers. An array of human beings, and some must've ruined their lives as well. It was there that I saw the cover of a book about Middle Eastern jewelry and, on the cover, there was a Berber woman weighted down with silver, amber, and beads. Her eyes were lined with kohl. The picture was old so it was in black and white, but this made the woman's face more stark and mysterious. I also thought of the Russian poetess, Anna Akhmatova, who had the same strong, self-possessed profile.

Akhmatova had survived Stalin's purge after having lost her husband and son and had all her work censored, if not burned. When I was allowed to order books from the library at Clayton, I read her poems until I could paint the words. Ancient swirls, murderous storms, red hands of blood, and many, many profiles of strong women who had met with disaster but survived. And as I remembered Akhmatova, I thought to myself that Elisheva had the beauty, guts, and madness to rescue a generation. It was an exaggeration, but I felt moved when I looked at her half-mystic, half-tortured, bright young-woman presence. I wondered what it would be like to grow up in a world that was potentially good when my world had been measured by what could be stolen and who could get away.

I called out to Elisheva. She stopped and I noticed that, for a brief moment, she had trouble looking me in the eye. I could hardly blame her given what she'd read about me. Her smile was nervous, but genuine.

"Looking good, Carleen," she said. "You have a mountain climber's tan."

"And you look like a princess from the Sahara," I said.

Elisheva's grin grew, but I could tell she was still uncomfortable.

"Shall we walk?" I asked.

"Absolutely." Her voice had a false bravado.

"Or find somewhere to sit by the river?"

She sighed.

"A bench would restore my faith in God."

We flopped down as soon as we were in a slightly better neighborhood.

"Why do you wear those shoes?" I asked. "You're a tall woman as is."

Elisheva shrugged. "It's what's chic."

She did a phony French-model gesture with her arms. I think they call it *voguing*. "I have to convince my clients' rich parents that, not only do I know Torah, but I can also dress up to their Saks Fifth Avenue standards."

"You look like a French spy," I said. This pleased her.

We remained silent for quite a while.

"I had to edit the shit out of it," Elisheva finally said.

"I know, I got carried away," I replied.

"Maybe it was good to . . . write . . . all that down." My poised scholar couldn't find her usual glib phrases.

"No, it wasn't," I informed her. "I've had to write it down time after time for official psychiatrists. Talk it into tape recorders. Fill out forms. I didn't need journaling."

"I'm sorry," Elisheva looked down, "to have made you do it again."

"No, no," I said. "I'm just curious if anything comes of it."

Elisheva sat with her long white hands on her knees and bit her lip.

"Well, you know," she started, "translating even the minor crimes into Hebrew was a bitch. I tried to keep it simple without commentary. A list—just like she wanted. She wasn't so interested in the shoplifting, which I was afraid of her emulating. She wanted to know more about the "minyan" of the Terrartists. She couldn't understand, thank the dear Lord, why you chose Miko over Leonard. We had a lengthy discussion over whether, in fact, you were a murderer. What constituted killing someone and how responsible you might have been for the death of the policemen. I left out everything about Powell and your own physical torture. She'll learn enough about violence soon enough. She asked if you had a motorcycle now, and I told her you weren't allowed to drive. She asked if you still painted. I didn't know. I don't know. Do you?"

"I'm trying to regain flexibility in my fingers," I lied. I'd never stopped painting. It just took on different forms.

Elisheva remained stiff, somewhat afraid.

"She said you sounded like a very mixed-up person, and not very nice," Elisheva confessed quietly.

"She's not wrong," I admitted. "I'm a real criminal. But there are limits and I shocked myself. I'm attracted to destructive mischief. But truly I would kill myself a hundred times over rather than have those cops die, because I really didn't want those guns that day."

Elisheva listened intently.

"Here's the weird thing," I said. "I have rarely wished evil on anyone, but I've never wished anyone well."

Was that true?

Elisheva stared down at her nails. "If only I had a quote from the Talmud or a Yiddish joke." She tried her best.

"And you shouldn't talk to me anymore," I said firmly. "I don't want the responsibility of you getting in trouble and the blame landing on my back."

Elisheva grinned. "It's cool," she replied. "I think it's a mitzvah because Batya Shulamit wants another communication from you."

I felt an annoying lift in my spirits. It was a lift the size of a mosquito and I had to acknowledge it.

"She has two requests," Elisheva continued.

"I feel like I'm on some mythological quest," I said with a sigh. "You must cut off the head of the raptor, steal the belt of Hera, or buy Park Avenue."

"Like Monopoly," Elisheva joked. "My new boyfriend and his brothers play it all the time and I always win. I might go to business school because I'm really good at organizing, knowing when to save and then"—*skraa!* (she made the sounds and gestures of a tiger)—"knowing when to leap. He's such a bad sport. I don't think I can get serious with a man who won't speak to me because I beat him at Monopoly."

"Doesn't sound very feminist on his part," I said, trying to shift into her gear.

"Don't ask what's happened to feminism. It's been sucked up by a bog like in *Peer Gynt*, never to be seen again."

"Elisheva," I was anxious, "I'm sorry—but can we get started?"

She blushed. "No, I'm sorry. You're just the most adult person I've ever met. There's no child in you."

I didn't want to pursue it.

"The first thing is that Batya Shulamit wants to know everything that you stole. With specificity. Especially when you were young. And the second is she wants to make a date where you can sit on opposite benches somewhere and just look at each other from a safe distance without talking. Just for ten minutes or so. Nothing weird. I think she just wants to take more of you in without the obligation of conversing."

This was some strange girl, Pony Batya Shulamit. I shouldn't let her play games with me. I was wrong to let it go too far.

"Look," I said to Elisheva. "I hate this thing of you being Tiresias the messenger, and I'm ending it after this. So here goes: No—I will not tell her what I stole, and please explain why. They were my secrets. They were impulses. They have no meaning now, and, most importantly, my brain does tricks on me and I don't remember most of the cities or states I went to, much less the trinkets I pocketed. And if there's even one chance that she is getting intrigued by this little past hobby of mine, you tell her father. She can't take one step down my path. It's a sickness, you understand?"

Elisheva's face went white.

"Why are you so afraid of me?" I'd become frustrated and impatient.

"You're a convicted murderer for Christ's sake," Elisheva shot back. "I've never even known a jaywalker before."

She was smart. She had attitude. She could handle me.

"Now listen. I'll agree to this bizarre Shakespearian face-off at the OK Corral, but that's it. After this, I'm going to put in another petition to visit her, and if she and her father turn me down that's the end of it all."

"Look, it's not me," Elisheva was practically in tears. "Aliza Lavie's book of prayer says that a daughter and mother should cleave together like a flower, and as the petals of the elder dry up and fly away, the young one stands in her place with all the color of their joined roots."

"Are you like that with your mother?"

"Hell no," Elisheva snapped back. She reconsidered. "Really? At the bottom of things, yes. There's just a lot that gets in the way. A lot of missed signals. And we are two freight trains in opposite directions. We crash in the day-to-day shit. So that makes us totally drive each other insane."

She paused again.

"But only sometimes. You should see her," she said proudly. "She looks younger than you!"

I closed my eyes and tried to remember what I looked like at thirty, or even forty. I couldn't hold a picture in my brain.

Elisheva blushed. "But you look like genuine downtown."

"How are we going to pull off this staring contest?" I asked. "Are we going up to the Empire State Building like in some movie she saw?"

"Starbucks," Elisheva said. "She's allowed to drink coffee there and to study on her computer."

"She's eleven!" I shouted indignantly.

"It's right near her house. She's picked the one on Broadway near Bleecker and Great Jones Street."

"And I'm just supposed to sit there?"

"No, you can read or even sketch. Just find a seat and stay awhile."

"What if it's too crowded?" I found myself buying into their preteen *Law & Order* spy game.

"We'd like to do this Sunday afternoon. It's not so crowded, and sometimes if Leonard's screaming at some football game, we go there to study."

"Leonard watches sports?" I almost laughed.

"He loves football. He says it's modern dance."

"I'm glad he sees that much in it," I said. "He probably just likes football and is embarrassed by his middle-class distraction." I paused. We were both uncomfortable. "What time is my viewing to take place?" I asked.

"If you don't mind, at 3:00 p.m. Batya Shulamit has Hebrew school up until then."

"She has Hebrew school *and* you?" I asked. This was a bit too much Jewishness for me.

"I'm preparing her for bat mitzvah and teaching her the stories and meanings of the Talmud," Elisheva said proudly. "She wants a truly meaningful bat mitzvah. Not just a huge party and teen dancing."

I didn't see what was wrong with a party and dancing, but I kept my vow of silence when it came to Judaics.

"Are you going to be at Starbucks?"

"She's not allowed to go alone."

"So you're going to watch the two of us stare each other down. Should we bring binoculars?"

"You're not taking this seriously enough." I could sense Elisheva felt interrogated. She was nervous. "She has very deep instincts. She wants to get a sense of your aura."

"In Starbucks?" I laughed. I tried to understand. But who was I to judge an eleven-year-old girl born in a maximum security prison and brought up in a conservative upper-middle-class home, who wanted to respect her ancient roots as Batya, the Egyptian princess and sex goddess who saved babies from the Nile?

"It's a date," I said.

TAKING ON CHARLIE TIMMS

I got my second permission slip to leave Manhattan with the new ankle apparatus on. I decided to go back to Charlie Timms's rehab. I would be accompanied by Snuzzles the Wonder Dog. We'd breezed through the training for him to become an assistance dog, and this would be his first gig. He had his usual spiky spaniel Muppet appearance, only this time I had to wiggle him into a coat that was yellow and had the appropriate patches that verified he was a dog who could go anywhere under any circumstances, even the Condé Nast lunchroom, which Tina said had the best buffet in town. I knew Timms would curse and carry on when he saw Snuzzles, but I'd specifically trained the dog for hyper schizophrenics, angry homeless people, and wild kids. He'd fake a mellow, subservient mode and once the person calmed down he'd go into his ridiculous tricks. If things got too hot, we had signals. Either retreat or attack. Attack was against Snuzzles's philosophy, but we played a game where I'd hold a mirror in front of his face and teach him to snarl. My snarl was worse than his, but it would work to chill a hostile, aggressive creep.

I checked in at the desk at the VA facility, and they verified all Snuzzles's and my credentials. The woman at the reception rubbed him and took kisses and went through the *ooh* and *ahh* repertoire.

"He's so ugly," one woman said. "He's like a bunch of pillows and plants stuck together."

"I think he's beautiful," said another. She was heavyset and had a huge cross around her neck. "He's a little mixed up on the outside, but Jesus is in him."

I gave a signal and Snuzzles jumped up on his back legs and put his front paws together in a position of prayer.

"He's making fun of me." The woman sounded hurt. Snuzzles jumped into her lap, despite his fifty pounds, put his front legs around her neck, and licked her on the lips.

"That's the most action I've got in ages," she sighed.

My heart sped up when I went into the rec room. They said they'd call Charlie and see if he'd come out. I waited about twenty minutes and then, before I could focus, a wheelchair nearly ran me over. Snuzzles, to my surprise, snarled out of instinct, a regular threatened dog.

Charlie Timms appeared somewhat thinner than the first time we'd met. He still had strong muscles, but there were circles under his eyes and a yellowish tinge to his skin. He looked past me at Snuzzles.

"What is this?" he snarled. "The Salvation Army? Puppies for paraplegics? You really had the balls to come back here again? I told you, you'd have to suck my dick."

"And I told you I'd do it," I said.

"So what's with that deranged mutt?" Charlie asked.

"He's gonna film it," I replied.

"Come over here," he said to Snuzzles.

Snuzzles went into his not-too-perky-but-obedient mode.

Charlie used his good arm to mess up Snuzzles's fur.

"You sure are ugly," he said to the dog. Then he looked up at me. "But then so are you."

"Modeling has never been one of my ambitions," I remarked.

Charlie's whole body dove into a thick, heavy cough. It

went on for so long I thought I'd have to get the nurse. Then he stopped, and wheezed as if his lungs were pulling on a defective motor.

"Is it the dog?" I asked.

"Asshole," he hissed. "You nearly had me killed, but you get all soft about allergies. It's not allergies. I been sick. Pneumonia and shit. When the body don't have all its parts working you don't got the immune system. So you get a cold and then right away pneumonia or TB."

"Can I do anything?"

"You did it all already, sister. You can lick my ass."

Charlie seemed too tired to keep up with his discharge of curses. This troubled me. I needed his venom. I needed to fight against all that hate.

"Does this mutt do anything?" he asked. "Or just sit around looking like a giant mosquito. Otherwise I want you to get the fuck out of here and stop coming for your perverse NA 'I'm sorrys.'"

"He does tricks," I answered.

"Guys!" he shouted.

A bunch of young, old, beat-up, dying, healing vets trickled into the rec room. The wheelchairs and transfusion racks, the stumps, prostheses, scars, and blind eyes crowded around. Most of the guys sneered. I stood straight, but inside I blacked out.

"Hey bitch," I heard Charlie's voice. "Get your act on. Guys, this is the cunt who got Georgey and Luke killed, did what she did to me, and brought a dog to do some tricks to make it all go away." There was a chorus of "fuck yous" and "get outs," the usual.

Snuzzles lay down and put his paws over his ears.

"Hey, look," a voice said, "the mutt don't like our language."

"I got an idea," Charlie said. "Why don't you fuck the dog here and we'll watch."

There were lots of cheers.

Snuzzles got up, slunk over to me, sniffed my body, including my butt and between my legs, shook his head no, and walked away.

The vets cheered.

"There's a dog who knows a real hag-whore when he meets her," Charlie smirked.

There was a pause.

With minimal signals I took Snuzzles through a routine we'd planned for the guys. It included new flips and circles, and we'd added in some semblance of belly dancing and humping. The guys liked it, but Charlie started coughing again and it silenced the hilarity. Snuzzles went up to Charlie and lay his head on his lap. Charlie smacked him on the top of the head and said, "Get the fuck away." It took every lesson I'd learned in all my years of anger management not to run over and tip him out of his wheelchair and kick him in his broken back. Snuzzles lifted his paw as if to do a high five. The group began gently laughing again.

"Shut up!" Charlie yelled at the group.

"Listen, Carleen Kepper," he said. "This has been a very therapeutic visit and all, but what the fuck do you want from me?"

"I don't want anything," I said. "I just wanted to visit you."

"Hey, look at her ankle," someone said. "Get a screwdriver and get it off. Security will call the cops."

"Let the bitch go back to jail," a voice came from the dispersing crowd.

Charlie appeared tired, but in a different way. His rage had softened. That's what Snuzzles did.

"I'll go now," I said, and Snuzzles walked quickly to my side. I was halfway out when Charlie pulled up behind me.

"Look. Don't be coming here for forgiveness. There is no such thing. I don't forgive myself for living when the other guys had to die. I don't think their parents forgive me, either. My parents don't forgive me for becoming a cop instead of going to technical college. I don't forgive my wife 'cause she left me 'cause I wouldn't give her babies. If there's forgiveness from the grave, it's all a story you make up. There's no forgiveness. Did Adam forgive Eve? You bet your ass not. So stop thinking I'm going to forgive you because of dog tricks and shit."

He looked away from me. The speech had taken up valuable breaths. He was wheezing.

"I never came here expecting you to forgive me," I said.

"Then why the fuck did you come?" Charlie asked.

"I told you, I came to visit you," I said. And Snuzzles and I pushed our way out the heavy glass door to the waiting car.

PREGNANT AND IN PRISON

It became obvious that I was pregnant. Sam approached me several times to join her group for "mothers gonna be," and I told her I would. But in my head I was pregnant, not a mother to be.

I was still a questionable inmate. Now and then I got provoked by a quick punch out of the blue, but I was mostly heckled. This was because I never fought back or talked smart, and since everyone I'd known at Powell had died or been injured, I moved through life as if it were a battlefield. Everything could wait. I was there for life.

I was told by my floor mother that Sister Jean wanted to see me. I prayed she wasn't going to kick me out of Clayton. The bathrooms, floors, windows, and dishes smelled, and laundry was a long load to clean, but I kept doing what I could every hour I had. I took over kitchen jobs for women. I was beating myself down. I listened to odd electronic music in my brain and hallucinated my Southwestern landscapes, the apocalypse, and everything in between.

I sat down in the appointed chair in Sister Jean's office.

"It's been reported to me that you're keeping all stations very clean," she said. "You work from dawn till lights out."

"Yes, ma'am," I said.

"You're pregnant." It was no secret.

"Truthfully I don't know how it happened."

"Did you use protection?" Sister Jean asked.

"No."

"Well, there's your answer," she said.

"I just thought I was so broken and rearranged inside that there wasn't a chance in hell my ovaries would work."

"Funny thing about hell," Sister Jean said. "Have you thought about what you'll do if you don't kill the fetus? That seems to be exactly what you're trying to do."

"I'm not trying to kill anything," I replied. I'm trying to cause an accident. A fortunate accident.

Sister Jean stared at me.

"What do you plan to do with the infant if you don't kill the fetus?" she insisted again.

"I don't even want to hold it or look at it. Send it out to get adopted by some hopefully rich, law-abiding citizen."

"It's not that simple," Sister Jean said.

"Why not?" I asked. I'd figured out this plan the moment I knew I was pregnant. I'd originally thought about requesting to sell the baby, but I knew somewhere inside that that didn't demonstrate the proper amount of reform on my part. Once again Sister Jean ignored me.

"There's a father," she continued. "There's a living, healthy partner in this venture, and we believe he has a right to be notified and be part of the decision concerning the infant's future."

"I thought I'd never have to face my past again," I snarled at her. I was off-balance from an unexpected never-thought-about option.

"This isn't your past, Carleen. This is your child's future."

She pulled out a piece of Clayton Penitentiary stationery and a pen and handed them to me. The gesture was an order.

"Write him now," she commanded. "Write him so I can watch you and make sure you don't cheat."

"What is this, the SATs?" I asked. I'd begun to shiver.

"Breathe," Sister Jean said.

Dear Leonard,

I don't know what to say. When you performed your obligatory visit re: wanting a divorce, amid sobs and fucking, we conceived a child. I didn't do this on purpose. I can't think of anything I want less. But they want me to let you know about it. I'm all in favor of just putting it up for adoption. I'm sure the authorities here get rid of miscon-ceived infants with regularity, and therefore will place it with a family where it will have a decent chance to live out its life. If there is such a thing. I apologize for the inconve-nience, but it's the Maryknoll or feminist stuff that goes on here that requires I bring you into this. After this, you will not hear from me.

Okay,

Carleen

Sister Jean read what I wrote. She whistled. "That's as warm and generous a missive as I've ever read."

"Nothing from the past," I chanted. "Nothing from the past."

"Look at me, Carleen," Sister instructed. "You did this, and I think with conscious purpose. Writing this letter is one way of facing up to your actions. Giving a life to this world is no doubt complicated, but not a curse. Some women might see it as a second chance for a beautiful redemption.

"I know you struggle daily with the question of whether

you want to finish out your life, but you have no right to impose that depressive ambivalence on another. You will join all of Sam's groups. You will keep this future baby healthy. You will do your best to wish him or her Godspeed into a world where there is great natural beauty, adventure, potential, and even other extraordinary human beings."

"You're sounding awfully Catholic," I said with distaste.

"No, I am sounding like a decent woman, and it's time you act like one."

I slammed out of Sister Jean's office and ran as fast as my broken, bloated body could go. I ran around the huge campus. Up hills, on paths, workers' roads, between buildings. Exhausted and pouring sweat, I collapsed on the hill behind Sam's birth center and slammed my stomach with my fists, over and over.

Someone much stronger than me grabbed my arms and forced me to stop.

"You do that again," Sam hissed, "and I'll set you up for attempted murder. Put you in solitary with around-the-clock suicide watch and force food and drugs down your throat. I've got a few girls involved in that lovely procedure now and, believe me, it's misery, Carleen. Pull your fucking self together."

I was panting and tears covered my face—from pain, not grief. I thought I'd be strong enough to punch the little motherfucker out but, like a rock of soft lava, it held firm.

"I thought you'd be pro-choice—leftist, free the blacks, and all," I gasped.

"I'm for abortion, but not the insane torturing of a fetus."

Sam helped me up. She led me into a plain, one-story brick house. We went through a door into a ward of beds. There were about fifteen women in scattered locations with bellies from flat to full mounds. None of them greeted me, though they acknowledged Sam. Sam gave me a bed at the farthest end of the ward. The white walls were plastered with more bright posters like in the health center with clichés like, "Our bodies, ourselves," "We can make a difference," "Love is possible," and other catchphrases that embarrassed me. I was a criminal and a snob. I didn't believe in goofy sentiments.

Sam snapped one of my ankles into a thick restraint that attached to a ring on the wall.

"Until you can behave yourself," she said. Sam wore beaten-down farmer overalls and a T-shirt underneath. There was a tattoo of a fist on her forearm, but otherwise she was clean and purposely plain, though it looked like she'd just bought a pair of bright-white running shoes.

"Make up your bed," she ordered, throwing me sheets and a blanket. "Then rest yourself until lunch."

She handed me a thick packet stuffed with magazine articles and laminated Xerox papers that seemed to range from practical child-rearing to psychological treatises on how childhood relationships with our families influence us from the moment of conception until adulthood. There were articles on the emotional effects of giving babies over to family members or setting up infants for immediate adoption. There were forms to fill out, from medical history to current state of mind. I didn't understand what the forms were doing there since Clayton was like Big Brother and the staff knew what you were up to before you did. There were several articles in my booklet referring to the rights and needs of a woman's body and even a mimeographed sheet on masturbation. Another on lesbian sex. Sam was certainly thorough.

Over half of the women in the ward were eighteen or nineteen, which led me to believe that they'd been pregnant when they were arrested. They were hookers who'd assaulted or killed their tricks for their pimps. Or girls who'd muled for their boyfriends. Also, I'm sure there were more women who'd been raped inside Clayton than the place was willing to admit. Despite its high rankings and stellar reputation, Clayton stank of corruption. There were men in kitchen, mechanics, and landscaping jobs, not to mention the numbers of guards that patrolled the hallways, called out orders, executed discipline, conducted searches, and basically had free access to these women's bodies. There were surreal pamphlets in Sam's kit such as *Getting Past Rape*, *Avoiding Rape*, and *What to Do If You Are Raped*. There was a reporting system and a council. It was all very protective, honest, and stern, but none of it worked or was used.

There was also suicide watch, for which there was no pamphlet. Suicide watch was largely for those mothers threatened by the fathers who insisted on taking the newborns back into the filthy, violent, drug-dominated projects and would have treated the mothers cruelly if they'd had an abortion. Those of us being watched for suicide did shit like growing the vegetables for the oh-so-healthy mother meals. For weeks I had to go to Lamaze and birds-and-the-bees-for-adult-idiots classes, where the whole female body was laid out scientifically and revealed to be the mechanical miracle that it was. I wished I was back in the general population. Some of the women actually took pleasure in the idea that they'd be with their babies for several weeks before they were passed on to families or adopted. The breast took on the honor of being its own kind of phallus and learning how to squeeze milk into bottles was a class in and of itself.

I'd managed to settle down and had acquired enough pot so I'd stopped abusing my body and actually played little running games with my fingers over the lump. I sang stupid songs that made the other women laugh. "My, my," Sam said to me. "I'm surprised you'd be anyone's court jester."

"I feel like a stupid ass," I told her. "So I may as well act like one."

One day Sam approached me, looking grim. "Go see Sister Jean at dinnertime. She wants an appointment."

"It's my attitude again," I said.

"I can take care of your attitude," Sam said. "Sister Jean has other business."

I ignored Sam and walked into Sister Jean's office. Before I could even take a seat, Sister Jean started talking.

"Leonard Salin wants custody of the baby," Sister Jean said right out. "He called and said he'd pick it up when it's proper to take it to where he lives in Manhattan."

My head felt like a volcano erupted.

"He wants to be the father of this child?" I yelled.

"He is the father of this child," Sister Jean replied sharply. "Unless there's something you've hidden from me."

"No, no, no . . . it's him," I started pacing. "It's him. He's going to take this infant and bring it up with some sweet wife, but the kid is gonna turn out to be a bad seed anyway and somehow I'm gonna have to know about it. It'll never be over. It'll never get free from my past. It's got to have another identity. A foster place in West Virginia. A mother of three in Tucson. A gym teacher in Oregon. No, no, no. He can't have her, he can't talk about me. He can't explain me. I can't exist in its mind. It's got to end. The story's got to end. Stop him. Tell him that it's deformed. Tell him it died at birth. Oh God, no. This puts me over the line. Right over the line."

"You don't think he'll make a good father?"

"Will he make a good father? What's a good father? Yes, I suppose he'll be fine. Super. Tops. He's a good guy. He makes playgrounds for God's sakes."

"Then what's the problem, Carleen? SIT DOWN."

I flew into a chair and sat at attention.

"The story goes on. Someone will talk about me. I'll be talked about to someone else. Photographs will be taken. The baby will be a criminal. The blood. The DNA. The whacked-out brain cells.

"On a horse farm the kid would have a chance. Not in my exact environment. Not where my history is easy to find. They'll tease the kid. And I'll know when it gets teased, tortured, and then jumps off a bridge. The bastard thinks he can get all my money. He'll lock it in the basement and buy a souped-up Maserati."

"Carleen, you've got to calm down. You're panicked for no reason. We're simply talking about the rightful father of the child wanting his baby."

"I don't want to give it to him."

"You have no choice. We've looked into it. He's employed, perfectly fit—"

"What is this? The fucking CIA? We're getting a divorce! And I'm not allowed to know about all your little phone calls and investigations and meetings and decisions and strategies? Don't I have any say here?"

Sister Jean's voice went cold.

"Actually, no. You're a convicted murderer who has displayed uneven behavior and even less consistent good judgment. You have no choice."

I went for her with my teeth bared. My hands were clamped open. I wanted to pin her and kick her with my knees and bite her self-righteous, goody-two-shoes, apathetic, hypocritical face. I felt like some bear foaming at the mouth.

"Albert," I heard her shout, and then I was on the ground, hands cuffed behind my back. My head was pounding. What were they saying? More CIA? More conspiracies? More plans for their plans? More rearranging of the constellations? Nuclear missiles aimed at my bed? The story was going to go on. They were conspiring to create eternity. I was like Mia Farrow in that movie where she'd been conned into giving birth to Baby Satan.

PONY

I was on my bed in the birth ward. Of course in restraints. I had no idea what happened, why I was, where I was, or what I'd done. Vague images. Pinholes of emotions. Screams behind scrims. When I became fully conscious I saw that Sister Jean was sitting next to my bed. She was immersed in a mystery by Andrew Vachss, a gritty storyteller, but adamant about children's rights. People were always getting tortured and smashed up in his books. This was one weird man. Half-leftist. Half-Nazi. Why was she thinking of this now?

Sister Jean saw me staring at the cover. "An old pal," she said, closing the book. "A real son of a bitch, but a great antihero."

I was groggy.

"Did I . . . " A very unpleasant memory surfaced.

"You tried to eat me," Sister Jean said mildly. "We've got you on medication, which doesn't thrill me because of the baby. Your mood swings are wild. You're manic and self-destructive and God knows what else."

"When is the baby due?" I asked. "I'd almost forgotten about it."

"Any day now." Sister Jean got up from her chair and spoke quietly to one of the cons who was a helper. I didn't hear the words. The sister began to walk away.

"Forgive me," I said to her back.

She stopped, turned, and squinted at me as if she'd spotted a very interesting bird.

"You know, that's the first time I've ever heard you say anything remotely like that. We'll see if we can expand the spectrum of that phrase," she said. "In the years to come, perhaps you'll learn to apply it to yourself."

There wasn't going to be a second time.

I'd been beaten in the stomach and kicked in the back and kidneys so many times and had so many surgeries that I didn't register or differentiate between types of pain. I guess I went into labor because I was cramping more often than I usually did from my arthritis or stretching and contracting scars. At one point I felt the sheets turn into a warm pond, so I called out, as I'd been taught, "Hey, my water broke!" The prison midwives hustled on down to me and opened my legs like the trunk of a car and peered in.

"We can see it," one of them called out. "Push! Push!" So I did.

For whatever reason, this slithery alien poured out of me into the arms of one of the women. I heard a few of them talking as they washed me and the baby and changed my sheets. The group was more efficient than tender, which went perfectly with my physical state. I felt like I'd been turned inside out. They'd been warned because I heard a voice say, "We have to put the shackles back on."

"She has the reddest hair," a voice said. "I've never seen such red on a newborn! Like a little goddess."

"There's no reds in my family," I slurred. "He must've fucked someone else."

I paused.

"Put her on my stomach," I said. "Let me see her."

"We're not allowed to, Carleen," another voice replied.

I didn't have the energy to fight. Then I heard a familiar voice.

"Let her see her baby." It was Sister Jean. I peered down at my bloated, wet, smeared belly and there was this tiny turtle, a wormlike creature, with locks of golden-amber hair falling in all directions over her head.

"There's a name for that color red." I tried to remember. "It's—"

The creature squiggled on my deflated skin. Her warmth was that of a wet, curled-up cat.

"Let me hold her," I said.

"No," a woman said gently.

"I don't think so," Sister Jean said.

"Then let me name her. You tell Leonard what her name is."

There was silence.

"Call her Pony. I want her to trot and canter and gallop and jump. I want her to take in the world like a pony. Innocent, you know. Agile and strong. She'll leap. Not limp. New to the world every day. But never chased and never caught. And never ridden and never put in a fucking rodeo like me. A wild pony."

I fell asleep as the warm circle of life was lifted off my belly, leaving a light breeze.

THE STARBUCKS SHOWDOWN

Starbucks is an Edward Hopper painting turned inside out. Darkened booths and coffee-buffet flavors. The atmosphere of so-called privacy and isolation is destroyed by mismatched couches, chairs, and stools. The darkness and noise pull you inside yourself if you want to work. You could never carry out an affectionate bonding in Starbucks, so it was the perfect choice to meet someone from whom you wanted distance. Students in the Bleecker Street coffee shop huddled together and yelped and guffawed as if they were telling stories from partying the night before. At the other tables the laughter was quiet and sporadic. The long line for the various coffees was full of the poses of young people trying to give off the impression that they had no interest in making an impression.

I'd spent a ridiculous amount of time trying to decide what to wear for this silent movie. I didn't know whether I should dress more like a conservative mother and wear one of the two dresses I owned or just a blue jean skirt and simple V-neck T-shirt. What was the impression I wanted to make? "No, I am not a monster. I am hip." "I am not too street to go to temple." "I enjoy clothes." "Clothes are irrelevant." Why the fuck was I going through all this? Did I really care? This was a little girl. I knew absolutely nothing about what the species went for. She was, in words, "*my* little girl." But I knew nothing about how to know her. So the clothes took on all the importance. I decided on faded, but nicely fitting, blue jeans, a striped blue-and-white T-shirt, and a blue jean jacket that matched the pants, but not exactly. I also picked out the least beat-up cowboy boots I had. They were brown and blue and had a nice pattern woven through them. I didn't know if this little girl was against fur, leather, and killing animals, but my sneakers were filthy high-tops (from dog walking) and the prim and proper girl I'd met before wouldn't approve. I remembered she was a bit pudgy. My hair was impossible anyway because it was so thick. It went past my shoulders and did what it wanted. The gray-and-white stripes made me feel like a middle-aged drug addict, but I refused to cut it because I'd be reminded of prison.

I was more animal than human. The unexplained rages, attacks, seizures. How could I possibly look normal? Not in her eyes. My hands were permanently red and raw, and I never wore jewelry except for a charm necklace made for me at Clayton by one of my roommates as an award when I began to act civilized. She was "spiritual." She said it would protect me from the gods on earth disguised as humans who were trying to turn me into a wild animal. There was a Jewish star, an evil eye, a cross, a silver dog, an Islamic Hand of Fatima, two astrological signs, a fish, a skull from the Day of the Dead, and a tiny kachina doll. It wasn't a glamorous necklace, but it was all silver and each piece had its place in her list of spiritual cleaning devices. I was still unaccustomed to dressing for the seasons, so I alternated between sweating and experiencing a chill that was like an ache through my jeans, socks, and boots.

I'd arrived at the Starbucks an hour early. I'd brought an unpretentious medium sketchpad with me. Along with that, I had a box of charcoal and pastel pencils in a smaller purse inside a straw tote bag. I realized I'd forgotten to bring a bag of treats and a Pluto squeaky toy in case I ran into one of my dogs.

Shit, this kid was sabotaging me. I never let my dogs down. I hadn't forgotten the Swiss Army knife I used to untangle ropes and leashes and open difficult cans of food. This made me nervous. What if she saw it and it scared her? But she wasn't going to march into Starbucks and pat me down. She just wanted to look at me. This child, whose expertise was placing me in the middle of a tornado, was becoming more than just an object of my curiosity. I didn't know what I wanted from her, so how could she possibly know what she wanted from me? I almost left my chair a few times in self-disgust. I thought of all the women who were fucked over by a biological clock and took hormone shots and had eggs implanted in them as if they were an ultragourmet dish. Those women who flew hours to Russia, Romania, or China to pick up abandoned or outlawed babies just so they could have—what was it that they longed for so badly? What was this animalistic hunger women felt to have children growing parallel to their changing and softening lives? What was this love they described that was like no other? Carleen Kepper had no desires that carried that kind of passion. I barely kept up the fight to survive from day to day.

I thought I'd sketch at Starbucks. My wrist needed to loosen up. I couldn't draw nearly as precisely as I used to. I hadn't been able to for over ten years. Bringing the pads was a facade—as much for me as for her. I would be more than a woman who was a dog walker. I sat stiffly, aching for a cigarette, tightening up as each person came through the door. People resemble animals in how they creep or walk languidly, or step with false pride, or jump with protective impulse. Many are in an imaginary fashion show, so there's a subtle watchfulness to even the loosest, most clown-like moves. The kids that streamed in and out were all college age. I found myself actively leaning forward every time a girl came through the door. I was a human divining rod. Twenty or thirty minutes had passed since 3:00 p.m. and I realized she'd backed out, decided it wasn't worth it, and damned if I didn't feel a kind of humiliation. I was so new to the civilized world that I still took part in games that other people planned for me. I slowly gathered up my pads and drawing utensils. I almost kicked a chair.

And then I saw a small figure that was standing with the stillness of a ballet poster. She was perfectly placed outside in the middle of the Starbucks window. She was clearly and fearlessly looking in. Her long red hair was made greenish by the windows, but I could see she was wearing a maroon velvet dress with a white lace collar. She could've been created by one of the Brontë sisters. Her hair was pulled back so her whole face was exposed. She had a very high forehead and a widow's peak. I couldn't see the color of her eyes, but I remembered they were intelligent, sad, greenish blue. Large eyes. Not exactly symmetrical. She had a small nose and a slight overbite. I'd been through this before, but I felt I was fulfilling an assignment. Her braces made her self-conscious, and she kept lowering her upper lip as if trying to get something out of her teeth. She didn't change position and I didn't wave, thank God. I wondered what she thought of my quite battered (maybe still striking) Semitic face and the eyes that were so fearful and betrayed. We actually stared at each other until I thought I saw her make a move toward the door. I tried to get up from my chair to greet her, but she abruptly turned around and disappeared across the street. Before I could stand up completely I collapsed back into the chair and laughed to myself. The game was over. From now on it was normal communication or nothing at all. We were no longer in a mental institution or a futuristic video game where daughters kill their mothers with lasers beaming from betrayed eyes.

MEETINGS

I finally forced myself to attend another NA meeting. A balding man in his fifties spoke. He had a mustache and was a caricature of exactly what he'd been, a car salesman. Honda or Mitsubishi—I couldn't tell the difference, though it seemed very important to him. He'd been proud of the brand, and his pride shone through because he was a top salesman. The story went on and my favorite part was when he hit bottom.

At 2:00 a.m. one morning he was drunk out of his mind and he tumbled into his place of work and took the keys to all the cars off their hooks. He proceeded to get into each individual car, go as fast as he could, and smash it into another car on the lot. He explained that the air bags on these particular models were fabulous so he never got hurt. He just kept going until his drunken game of bumper cars had demolished twelve or fifteen cars. They found him passed out on a deflated air bag the next morning. He was arrested for malicious mischief and drunk driving, and I don't remember if he went to jail or not. Though he was still paying off the cars, I don't think his wife left him, and his boss suspended him for six months and gave him a desk job. White man's grief. My attention drifted in and out, but I empathized with him when he said he felt worse for what he'd done to the cars than any people involved. He loved those Hondas or Mitsubishis and was trying to forgive himself for what he'd done to their "sculptural" (my word) "magnificence" (his).

As I walked out of the meeting, David Sessions was sitting on the steps, speaking directly to the pigeons waiting for crumbs.

"You're no better than the legless vets on skateboards who claim they can't walk," he scolded them. "Buck up! Find jobs for yourself. I can't stand all this whining about unemployment."

I didn't have the energy to avoid him. I sat down next to him. He was wearing the usual Persian pants with the low crotch and a tie-dyed T-shirt with some kind of Romanian or Bulgarian vest. His bald head shone. Age had loosened the skin on his face a bit. I was sure he'd had a face-lift or used Botox.

"You look like Mr. Clean," I said.

"He's my idol. I think he's gay," David replied.

"Stop stalking me, David. I don't want to make up or talk it out or go over it or under it or around it." I felt my anger rising the more I talked. I stood up to walk away.

"I don't want you to forgive me," he said, "but I have valuable information." I stopped. He was full of shit.

"About what?"

"They're sending you to Afghanistan. They want you to carve huge heads of our forefathers on the rocks right where the Taliban is slaughtering our marines. They think it will be inspirational."

"Fuck you," I said.

He leaped up beside me. He was still very agile for a heavyset painter who never exercised and was always on the edge of being an alcoholic, but not quite making it.

"Stop punishing me, Carmine, Carleen, Camilla, whatever your name is. For ten years you've never answered one letter and you never came out when I visited. Nor have you acknowledged my appearance on talk shows on your behalf."

"You didn't do any of that," I said. "You dropped me, disappeared, became an artistic icon and forgot me. You're following me around now because you're curious about what jail's like. You're worried that I might tell all your worshippers that the great David Sessions is a selfish motherfucker."

"Well, everyone already knows that," David said. "But there's an obvious lack of vital information and communication going on here because, Carleen—Essie—I did everything I just said I did."

My body crumbled. David caught me.

He still had the same enormous loft. It must've been a whole floor of a factory. He put me down on his huge couch made for elegant decadence. It was white. New canvases, half-finished paintings, ladders, palettes, brushes, and tools lay in the otherwise empty space. A Japanese bedroom was visible in the back. David hated clutter in his personal life, and the same sensibility was reflected in his spare, abstract landscapes with his made-up languages done in precise, varied calligraphies across his seas, oceans, mountains, and flatlands. For years art critics had tried to translate or find the source or the meaning of the sentences on his paintings in pristine letters that were neither Asian nor Arabic nor Sanskrit. It was a combination and a negation of them all.

"Steal anyone's ideas lately?" I mumbled, but his news to me had made a sick kind of vertigo overtake my body, and I rushed to his bathroom and threw up. I kept throwing up until I'd emptied myself out.

"Shall I call the hospital or would you like a Tums?" David asked through the door.

"Water."

I jerked my way out of the bathroom, drank down a large bottle of Pellegrino, and lay back down on his couch.

"I take it you didn't know I was trying to find you all these years?"

"It didn't matter," I replied. "I hated the thought of you anyway."

"I wanted to explain," David said.

"No one came forward as a character witness. No one. It was as if I was the founder of this satanic cult and had no redeeming qualities whatsoever."

"The prosecution made the choice very difficult, darling. Testifying on your behalf could've ended up a nightmare."

I didn't trust him.

"Oh really, David? You couldn't tell them I enslaved myself to you, worshipped you, was your puppy, your fag hag?"

"Listen, if you *can* listen, you must LISTEN, Essie Carlene Carmine Brianna—what do you want me to call you?"

"I don't know anymore." I felt sick, but I held it in.

"Okay then, NAMELESS. The prosecution told me that if I testified on your behalf they'd question my integrity—my sexual integrity."

"Since when have you been in the closet? You always say, 'I swish with the best. I'm more flamboyant than Divine, and without a touch of lipstick.'"

"No, that wasn't it," David said. "They warned me they'd start looking for proof of rumors that I'd been seducing under-age students."

I said nothing.

"It wasn't true. There was nothing to prove. Besides, that kind of thing sells paintings. But oooh they were getting nasty. They made me take them to the tree house and saw all your crazy paintings and sculptures, and, being the refined art critics they are, they came to the conclusion that this work could only be done under the influence of drugs."

"That's probably true," I said.

"But darling, they planted bags of weed right in front of my eyes, and they said that if I spoke on your behalf they'd have to bring up my knowledge of your drug use, and how good would it sound if I admitted you were a drug addict. They implied they'd nail me as your dealer."

I felt no pity.

"They said I'd be a disaster as a character witness in a small town in New York. A swish with a drug habit. Then they threatened to arrest me and put me in a penitentiary where fags rarely came out alive."

"That's possible," I replied, longing for champagne, "but I didn't know shit about this."

"Well how could you, darling? No one would let me near you. They said you told them to tell me to die. And the Feds began auditing my taxes for every penny. They still do."

"Stupid pigs," I mumbled.

"You're hardly a Mensa candidate, Essie. Murdering state troopers is like killing Jesus and painting Jewish stars all over his martyred body."

"I didn't murder anyone." I was back in time. Denying. Rejecting. Refusing. Defending.

"Do you think I didn't know that? It was that stupid-ass Malaysian stud of yours, Miro or Milkman."

"Miko."

"You're the stupid ass for teaming up with him."

"I don't want to do this, David." And I really didn't.

"Though he was stunning."

"I can't do this, David," I urged him.

"Then let me provide you with knowledge you can process

when your mechanisms are in working order, darling. None of your prisons allowed communication with you. No one could speak, visit, write, skywrite, send blimps. You were to be cut off from all communication. I asked a lawyer—a very expensive lawyer, by the way—if that wasn't somehow unconstitutional under the 'cruel and unusual punishment' label, and he said I had no idea how easily federal penitentiaries could manipulate the law. Later he found out that the FBI—can you imagine, it would be sexy if it wasn't ludicrous and sadistic—suspected that you were connected to an international drug corporation, manufacturing and distributing crystal meth all around the world. A murderous corporation. One that makes Mexico and Colombia look like Club Med for toddlers.

"Why on earth would they pick me?"

"Why on earth, my darling?"

"They were suspicious of me even at Clayton?" I felt like I had a virus. I was shaking. I couldn't see.

"You mean the 'Gloria Steinem Reformatory for Women Who Did Bad Things because this is a Misogynist Society'? Yes, they were under orders to be quite cautious. And maybe that place does arts and crafts, but they use ECT like cable and experiment with loopy psychiatric drugs. You know the ones with side effects like death. God, how I prayed they didn't put you there."

"They did," I said, quietly.

David held out his arms to me.

"I don't touch people," I said stiffly. "Plus, I was nuts. Really nuts. I had brain damage and stuff and the drugs screwed my perceptions and I kept doing weird shit and being put back and punished for it. It was Dante's Ferris Wheel. Around and around. It never stopped."

We sat silently for quite a while. For once there were no

flashbacks, just quiet waves as if I were in a swimming pool on one of those posh vinyl floats.

I could tell that David was going over something in his overly educated, quite corrupt mind. He was making checks and balances, weighing and measuring what to say or not to say.

"I'm an Amazon now," I said. "I'm Wonder Woman, or more like the Hulk."

"I was thinking of making a movie about superheroes that meet daily at a table at the Algonquin," he said. "They drink martinis and discuss poetry, philosophy, and music. At night they throw babies into burning buildings and bulldoze graveyards. Purely evil intellectuals."

"I have to go," I said. "I'm on a strict schedule."

David took my hand. I tried to pull away, but he held on. It was like being gripped by the paw of a panda bear.

"So what do you think of me now?" He tried to catch my eyes, but I avoided him.

"I understand more," I replied.

"Can you love me again?" he asked.

"The question is more will I remember you when I leave this house. Or will I remember you but forget what to believe. Or care. Does it matter if I remember, believe, or care?" David stood up. He was crying.

"You were so young," he said. "Such a unique delinquent." When I didn't answer he went on. "When you want them, I have all your paintings from college. Unfortunately the authorities still have the sculptures from the woods."

I let out a sound like a laugh. "The idea of Sheriff Rex Waddles of Duchess County, NY, owning an original Ester Rosenthal sculpture thrills me. Remember I called that the Dorian Gray masterpiece?"

"I'm worried you'll walk out this door and that'll be it. What do I have to do to break through that Patty Hearst rage? How do I get you back in my life? Somehow a dinner party doesn't seem like the choice. What do I have to do?"

"Get a dog," I said, and left David Sessions's historic loft.

A LETTER FROM BATYA SHULAMIT

Dear Carleen Kepper née Ester Rosenthal,

Thank you for maintaining your side of the deal. I hope you saw that I kept mine. I will give you my impressions. I don't know what blue jeans and a matching jacket means, but I think you were trying to dress neatly, and I appreciate your effort. I hope you are in good health. I perhaps was too dressed up, but I was in my favorite color—maroon. Actually, my favorite color is purple, but I thought a purple dress would look stupid, so I chose maroon. Here are three things about myself:

1) I ride horses.

2) I write poetry.

3) I loathe the smell of brussels sprouts.

Please write back no more than three things about yourself, and do not suggest meeting in person because in my brain that is utterly impossible.

Oh, and I like your hair, but it scares me.

Shalom,
Batya Shulamit

The letter had come by mail and not through Elisheva, so I wondered if she was out of the picture. I hoped not. She was the closest thing to a friend I had. Of course, I didn't know if I should absolutely trust her either, given what David had told me. She could've been an agent of Leonard's keeping the information between me and Pony somewhat fluid while reporting on my activities to the FBI. The Russian poet Osip Mandelstam wrote a teeth-gritting, funny poem about Stalin. Mandelstam was a neurotic, nervous, but beloved man. His friends said of him that "most people are paranoid and have no reason to be. Osip, however, is right. The God of Artist Executions is watching him."

I could no longer trust my roommate, Seña, because I often smelled liquor on her breath and she had two demerits already for breaking curfew. I sensed she was hanging out with her pimp again, and drugs were not too far down the road. He would get her kicked out of the halfway house and back on the street again. As for me, I was enjoying the role of goody-goody, but I was beginning to get the urge to confront my parole officer for being a lying, two-faced Polack. I was sure he knew things he wasn't telling me.

As far as Batya Shulamit went, I decided to wait two weeks before I wrote a return letter. I didn't want to seem too anxious and, also, I didn't feel particularly anxious. I didn't have any wish to seek David out, and I doubted I'd ever paint again. As usual I had to force emotions to the surface like the geysers at Yellowstone. If I didn't work at it I'd function at a perpetual float, a blimp with no energy or direction. Then the eruptions would occur. Violent attacks of loss and self-hatred that resulted in punching myself and pulling my hair. I had to attach specific feelings to the free hours of my day or I'd get out of control. Dogs were the only things that focused me, so in spite of illness and exhaustion, I took every job. I covered for everyone. Lucinda accused me of taking amphetamines. I offered to take a blood test. But would she? There was a feeling in the office like the dark air before a downpour. Hubb mostly slept.

Dear Batya Shulamit,

I will tell you six things about myself because, although I am no longer a criminal, I don't always follow rules. I have had to follow very strict unjust disciplines for years. It was dangerous to break them. So I hope you won't get indignant if my list is somewhat mediocre.

1) I love dogs.

2) I'm slightly pigeon-toed.

3) I read comic books.

4) I am horrendous at math.

5) Tugboats soothe me.

6) Garbage of any kind makes me want to throw up.

Your hair is a golden-amber waterfall. I wonder if you know it is not just one color. So far I have counted seven shades of blond, red, and brown in it.

Be healthy,

Carleen Kepper née Ester Rosenthal

POSTPARTUM

After they gave Pony to Leonard Salin, I had, I guess, a breakdown. I was reassigned to the Mental Disorder Ward. Curses and death wishes spun in my head. The ward was a psychotic washing machine. Hate caused a bitter taste in my mouth, and I had to brush my teeth six or seven times a day. I was terrified of being given electroshock treatment again so I spent most days lying under my bed.

Then an East Indian psychiatrist whose name I couldn't pronounce said something to me like:

"Ms. Kepper, you are having mild postpartum depression. I will be prescribing medications to go with your other medications and we will see if we can lift you up."

"I think I need surgery, doctor," I said to him.

"But whatever for?" he asked.

"I have terrible butterflies in my stomach. They flutter all day long."

"Well, we must have you x-rayed for that," he said, and I couldn't tell if he was serious or not. "How would it happen that you would swallow caterpillars? Please do not be eating insects. You will become very ill."

I pulled myself together.

"I'm anxious, you asshole," I said. "It was a joke."

The doctor retreated.

There was no room at Clayton for two separate wards, so they mixed the criminally insane with the bipolar, the schizophrenic, and the women just stressed out or depressed. Bad cooking. Horrific color combinations. Certain death. One of my acquaintances had shot and killed eight of her coworkers the day after she was fired.

There were the usual Jesus Christs, fuck-me-fuck-mes, alien communicators, and even a woman who claimed they'd manufactured capsules and "think liquids" specifically to prepare her to be the first black leader of the Ku Klux Klan. There were two women who'd killed their kids. One who, like me, was being put together piece by piece, only she'd jumped in front of a subway doing her "teamwork with Eddie Murphy" in a cop movie. There was snake lady who had tattoos all over her body. She refused to keep her clothes on and hissed at everyone who came near her. There were more elderly women with dementia than I chose to count. Every week someone was being brought in for detox or to come off a hallucination that went wrong. There was a Whitney Houston (a junkie) and a Miriam Stubbs, though no one knew who Miriam Stubbs was. There was the person who never stopped walking to-and-fro and to-and-fro unless someone knocked her out. There was one woman who screamed at the top of her lungs in a tongue that she claimed was given to her by African gods. There were two former serial killers, both charming in an eerie way, both ready and eager to talk about their kills: how many, where, when, what methods, and so on. Most women, including me, were in restraints, and the clang of chains and the screech of metal beds being dragged across the floor was constant. There was a self-mutilator who was horrible to look at and had to be strapped into a collar because she bit herself whenever she could. There were the women who crossed the line from normal murder, assault, and robbery to insane, and they were so drugged they lived like zombies. But if a drug wore off the whole ward was in danger.

One night I felt a weight on my mattress and immediately went into a defensive mode in case one of the real killers had gotten loose. But when I sat up, it was just a beautiful young woman, twenty-three or four, who was emaciated, impeccably groomed, and had wide, lustrous, happy eyes.

"Hi," she said, "I'm Marcella Histrionics. I don't eat. It's out of habit. I was a famous fashion model in Germany, and so I had to be rail thin to maintain prominence in display fashion. I am not mad, really."

"Why are you here then?" I asked.

"Well, I am in the Clayton Correctional Facility because I set fire to the warehouse of a designer whose clothes did not please me. I burned up his fall and winter line. I would've burned him to ashes too, but the firemen got him out. I also burned down a tent on Seventh Avenue during fashion week because I had not been invited to model in their particular show. And oh how I love fire. Don't you just love flames?"

"It depends where they're flaming," I said. "Or who's flaming."

"You don't belong here," Marcella announced to me. "I heard them say you had a mood and thinking disorder that could be treated quite successfully with the right cocktail of mood stabilizers, antianxiety pills, and uppers. Actually, I'm thrilled for you. There's no cure for anorexia." She looked at herself.

"Friendship," I said cautiously. It seemed like a harmless enough reply. "You eat your friend's food off your friend's plate and then you're not eating your own food."

"That's a somewhat false metaphor, and a little sneaky," Marcella noted. "But I like the sentiment behind it."

"I've had enough conversation," I said. "The cameras are aimed on me and microphones are planted everywhere."

"But I was going to tell you the story of my life," Marcella explained. "Don't you want to know? I was adopted from Sudan by two guilty Jewish liberals. They sent me to a fine psychiatrist once I started setting fires to my toys. I actually stopped for a while and had a year or so in middle school of a fairly normal Sudanese Jewish life. But I was so exquisitely beautiful a famous manager saw me at Peace Arab/Israel, a special camp for refugees in Aspen, Colorado, and asked my parents if he could book me. My parents, of course, thought modeling was superficial and that it contributed to the consumer addiction in the USA. But I told them I wanted to send half of the money I earned to the Sudanese family from which they'd stolen me. What could they say to that? So I divided my time between schooling, modeling, and setting small baskets of trash on fire. I had to go back to the psychiatrist, but we all have had our problems to get through, no? Ford Models picked me up and I became a sort of minor superstar. I was in *Vogue* and *Elle*, which wasn't bad for sixteen. By then I'd stopped eating, set some neighborhood backyards on fire, as I explained before, and they dumped me in a delinquent home. Well this went on for two years, in and out, and finally I was out long enough to set fire to a bridal shop. I've always wanted to see bridal gowns go up like toupees. But then I literally began to suffer from heart failure. Hospital, hospital, hospital. I was sent here for arson."

"Don't fires bore you after a while?" I asked.

"One would think so," Marcella said. Tears came into her

enormous round eyes. "I certainly would like to get out of here and transfer to the B building. It's so crappy with all these murderers and their foul hygiene. Why are you here?"

"Oh, honey." I let out a sigh.

"That's what I like about you." Marcella smiled a radiant, batty, luminous smile for some invisible camera. "You're so modest. Models are so narcissistic. Talk, talk, talk: body, thighs, skin cycle, lashes, workout, yoga, bulimia, agent, no sex drive, and so on. You don't care about any of that, do you?"

"Not at the moment," I replied.

"That's what I respect about you." Marcella's smile widened. "You care about the deeper things. The profound things. The existential stuff. How do your thoughts go, specifically? Two at a time? In religious choirs? African drum ensembles?"

"I hate to disappoint you," I answered her, "but I don't care about much."

"Aw, that's just your heart being modest. I'm a sensitive, you know. And I have you psyched. You don't care about much because you are caring in *itself*. The fish-in-the-bowl syndrome."

"If you're a sensitive then why don't your powers tell you to eat?"

"Because I have to keep my receptacles open for messages. They can't get clogged with food." She paused. "I have a favor."

"What is it?"

"When we get out of here and graduate to C building, will you be my husband-dyke-protector? We can protect each other's weaknesses."

I shivered and suppressed what might have been a laugh.

"I don't do that shit, Marcella," I said. "My brain isn't organized for trained defense."

"But you have to strengthen yourself here and now," Marcella whispered. "You're not a newbie anymore. This is a couples and gang penitentiary. If you're not taken, you're free meat. And you being white, the Aryans will try to recruit you, and they are simply boring, with hate and uncombed hair. And if you and I were a couple, the bull dykes wouldn't fight over me because of my obvious beauty and we could avoid all kinds of mess in the cafeteria and rec room. One still has to be as sharp as a cat every minute, but it helps if you're married. We might survive."

I thought about survival and Pony for a moment. Marcella was right in her slightly demented logic. The bartering at Clayton was subtler, but loyalty oaths and protective relationships were a strong part of the society.

After a while, and before they released me back to the general population, I was assigned to an advanced convict named Nora Lasheen. Her primary job was to explain the system and make sure that most of the inmates were assigned to appropriate ranks, cells, and workloads.

"You been here I don't know how long and you don't know shit, baby," Nora said to me. "Whole time you been locked up in solitary, in the hospital having a baby, in the loony bin." She genuinely laughed. "A real model prisoner. Maybe you'll last in the general population this time," she said. "But I doubt it. I'd pray for you if I prayed, but I don't want to waste it.

"Clayton, if y'all let me explain, is run exactly like a military camp. You got your ranks and you got who's superior to you. You don't fuck with a superior or your rank gets dropped a number. You do your jobs, keep your hands clean, stay outta the underground, and you get promoted. Sometimes you get promoted and you don't know the fuck why. Sometimes you get demoted. It usually means someone's out for your ass, you pissed someone off, or you broke a rule. There's a committee made up of honors convicts, administrators, Sister Jean, the warden, Sam, and highly regarded guards (they're the ones who can stab your back). They all decide on promotions or demotions. With a promotion comes a pinch of more permissions and a squeeze of more respect from the other inmates. Or jealousy—that can get you bad cuts on your skin. It's all about politics and power, right?

"You'll be starting in the B building with no privileges. The cells are overcrowded and there's fights on the hour. There's guards up the wazoo and they be mean. Meaner to you 'cause you're crazy and famous. It's your video game, Carleen Kepper—get yourself transferred outta there soon as can be. You need advice or whatnot, you can look around for me, but I won't be much help. I got where I am through bribery, getting my GED, and sleeping with one of the married administrator's ladies. Your path to redemption will be part sensible behavior and part quick feet."

I moved into a cell made for two that held five women. They had corners staked out, and I took whatever space was left. They were a tight-knit gang—sisters of the Crips and I was the only white. They shoved me whenever possible and stole everything, even my toothbrush. I prayed that Marcella would be released from the loony bin. I was certain women were cautious of her because she was mad as a hatter and would set fire to the possessions of anyone who displeased her. But until that day, I had to use my experience to survive.

I started out making my roommates' cots every morning before they even ordered me. I washed our bathroom area, did their laundry, and changed their towels and washcloths weekly. I never spoke unless spoken to. I thought I was doing pretty well until one night, one of the women, Rashina, asked me, "Don't you care about sex, white girl? You had your baby months ago. Ain't it time for the drive to be coming back?"

"I haven't thought about it," I said quietly.

"I hadn't thought about it, *ma'am*," Rashina said, and the others laughed.

"Ma'am," I whispered.

"Which one of us you want to fuck?" Another woman, Celia, chimed in.

"None of you," I answered honestly.

Mean smiles filled the room like a nest full of Cheshire Cats.

"Ma'ams, if I may explain," I practically begged. "I came from Powell and they tore me up there. Then I went and had this baby after my husband raped me. The baby had to be pulled out with forceps and I bled for two days. Now I'm healed up, but I'm all scarred and sometimes the scars get infected and the medicine for the scars gives you this thing like herpes— not herpes, but worse. And I hurt all the time. So, worse than being raped, I could get my lover infected or sick and then I'd get the shit beat out of me and put back in the loony bin, and I don't want that."

"Don't you come near any of us then," Celia said, and I felt a special relief because I'd succeeded in talking myself out of the inevitable initiation. I dared to go a step further.

"Besides, my wife's in the loony bin," I said. "And she'd give me hell if I cheated."

"As if that matters—who?" Rashina asked.

"Marcella Histrionics," I replied.

"She's plain nuts," Celia shouted. "She's beauty itself when she ain't a twig. But she gonna burn us down."

I was pleased by the reaction. It proved what I'd hoped for. I'd have good protection married to an arsonist. I just had to make sure she ate.

Marcella Histrionics was eventually released from the hospital. She was still rail thin, but she didn't look like a Tim Burton skeleton. We were moved into a C-level double, which she proceeded to decorate like a bordello in a Western movie. She pushed the beds together and designed a canopy out of extra sheets she'd taken from the hospital. She went to the hospital junkyard and found anything velvet or velveteen left over from other prison construction or deconstruction. She restored a child's rocking horse and made it our centerpiece. For a dining room table, she bribed one of the guards to give her two benches. The room was so crowded with her furnishings I didn't have room to walk.

"Hop, squeeze-bitch. Dontcha love it?" I admired the energy of a girl who was so thin and sick. But I knew she was manic, and I lived in fear of her setting the place on fire during a "vision" or tantrum.

"Marcella, how did you get us into C? Neither of us earned it."

"*Ah*," she replied. "I made a deal with the doctors. I said, 'I gain five pounds and keep them on, and you let me outta here. I gain ten? You put me in C with my-painter-protector-husband."

"You gained ten pounds for this?" I was flattered and appalled.

"Ate ice cream, rice pudding, cheese grits, mac and cheese—no problem. I love all the food. It's just a sacrilege to eat it."

She pulled out packages of Ex-Lax and danced around where there was space in our country-western whorehouse.

"I *also* copped this," she said, and shook a full box of kitchen matches like maracas.

I felt like Alice through the Looking Glass living with a wired black queen.

POOKIE IN CRISIS

Hubbs called me on my cheap cell.

"You got two queens in hysterics. Get your ass to West Chelsea Vet when you finish with Socks. But don't cut his time off—y'hear?"

I ran west, caught a cab, and dashed into West Chelsea Vet. Ralph and Evan were seated together holding each other's hands. Ralph was openly sobbing, and Evan was biting his lower lip so hard I was afraid it would bleed. I hadn't talked to them much since I'd botched our dinner, but Pookie remained a regular rambunctious client who jumped like a circus entertainer and chewed on precious antiques. We'd been making progress, however, by putting tiny sprinkles of red pepper on the most valuable furniture, and I'd become strong enough to catch her midair when she jumped and swung me around in a circle. She loved it while it was happening but became extremely disoriented and dizzy when I lowered her to the floor. She'd lurch around like Buster Keaton and sometimes vomit, but it was cutting her back on her antics. Evan put together delicious care packages for me and fed me foods whose names I was glad I didn't know, but these delicate clients had become sensitive enough to refrain from asking me to stay for even a glass of wine.

Evan patted Ralph on the shoulder.

"Carleen's here, darling. Carleen's here."

I cornered one of the vet assistants and asked her about Pookie.

"Pookie's in surgery. She swallowed one of those glass paperweights and it's stuck in her intestine. You know, one of those things you shake and they make snow. Ralph said it's over one hundred years old. So Pookie's what, collecting antiques?"

"How bad is it?" I asked.

"Dr. Fabor's the best," she reassured me. "But if it breaks through the intestine or gets stuck in her bowels . . . I thought poodles were supposed to be smart."

"I don't know, maybe she thought it was an egg," Ralph sobbed. "I have over twenty of them. This has never happened before."

"You know Pookie's made for trouble," I told them. "She just had to find a new way to torture you."

I only had a half hour until it was time for my next client, but I knew I couldn't leave these two desperate men. I didn't know what to do about Pookie. She was just such a bad girl. That was her virtue. Ecstatic, sweet, yet satanic disobedience. I called my next client, a banker with a Spinone, and told him I had an emergency and might not make it. He said he was on a conference call and asked me what the hell he was supposed to do. I guaranteed I'd get there. He told me that if Pano (his dog) went on his new floors, he'd call my boss and have me fired. I was sweating when he slammed down the phone. I hoped Pano would pee on the new floor—have diarrhea even. Luckily he had been my last client before my dinner break, but I stayed with Ralph and Evan through my dinner break and my two night appointments. I rushed to get substitutes to fill in for me. Finally, an exhausted Dr. Fabor walked into the waiting room holding a beautiful, clean glass Cartier egg with a miniature town and snow inside it. I rushed up to him. Ralph and Evan were too terrified to move.

"Did she make it in one piece?" I asked.

"Barely," he replied. "What kind of dog eats a glass egg? I opened her up and got it out with a spoon and a spatula. But we decided not to boil the glass egg to disinfect since that would destroy it. Pookie's intestines are sewed up and she'll be in pain and weak. Unless she gets infected, she'll be okay."

I told Ralph and Evan to keep Pookie at the hospital for at least a week or she'd roll in something or steal something and hurt herself.

"No, no, I'll sit by her day and night and watch her every move," Evan said.

"I'll store all the small objects in appropriate containers so she can't get at them. Let us take her. We'll hire a private nurse to watch over her."

Dr. Fabor raised his eyebrows at me. He shrugged.

"We're hysterical queens," Ralph said. "Evan, let's go home and disinfect her room and the bathroom and the kitchen." He sniffed and his posture regained its dignity. "When may we see her?"

"She's still sleeping," Dr. Fabor said. "Why don't you drop by this time tomorrow. I have to keep her sedated so she doesn't tear her stitches."

Evan and Ralph went home shaken but resolute. Dr. Fabor let me peek in on the patient. There was a large bandage covering her whole belly and she was attached to various tubes.

"Pooks, you're an idiot," I whispered, and headed out for my next job.

Hubb called my cell. He sounded high.

"Who the fuck said you could put in subs and babysit with those faggots?"

"It was a mess here, Hubb, and they pay above our highest rates."

"You better make sure they pay for every penny of that extra hand-holding shit," he snarled. "And Carleen, I decide *when* to call subs and I decide *who* subs. You don't own this place, you hear me, bitch?"

"They were hysterical. I'd have called you but there was too much drama going on."

"Just remember what I said, Carleen. No private deals with my clients or you're on your ass. I want to see the cash from this extra two-hour thumb-sucking."

"Got it, Hubb."

He'd never see it.

SAM

Sam rarely came to visit me. I had the usual mixed feelings about her. She was nearly ten years my elder. She was an intellectual and supposed feminist. She created programs for Clayton that clearly helped the women. I'd given her programs two million dollars. We had a commonality that few other prisoners shared, and yet she treated me exactly like I was the lowest rank in her system. In her system, As represented rich, two-faced, lazy, criminal goody-goodies; Bs were newbies who deserved some training; Cs were either stupid or purposely clueless; Ds were on the hunt for personal injury; Es were excellent effort.

Sometimes it seemed like she used this system to purposely mock me. She made me take an English class that was clearly for women who were illiterate. I spent hours xeroxing legal papers that came through every day having to do with appeals, legal technicalities, and reports from prison associations. She forced me to attend humiliating activities like chapel choir and math class, where everyone sat around like zombies and no one listened to the terrified, inadequate instructor. But at least she realized that if she'd sent me to art therapy or arts and crafts, I'd have gone after her despite the consequences. Even so, there were times I refused to work. There was no reason for my strikes. More often than not if someone reprimanded me I froze deeper. The con who was head of the library kicked me one day, and I went after her with my whole self. When I'd knocked her out, I tried to rip up as many books as I could in the library. A small array of guards and inmates had to beat me down and I got thrown into solitary for three weeks.

When I was let out, Sam was waiting for me.

"Fuck you," I mumbled. I was too tired to fight her.

"Shhh," I heard her say. "Calm down. Walk with me."

We went to a nearby place called Big Lawn where advanced convicts were allowed to play soccer one hour a week. We sat on the lawn side by side, and she didn't say anything for an annoyingly long amount of time. Then she sighed.

"If I'd treated you like an equal from the start I'd have lost years and years of work. The women would've seen me as favoring a rich white murderer over thieves or mules of darker colors. But I don't take any joy in watching you be pushed around the way you are"—I didn't believe her, not for a second—"and it's not the trip I thought it'd be to have you do all those shitty, worthless classes. I have to do it though."

She was a liar, like a boss from hell.

Sam went on with her bullshit, "Politically speaking, this place is a feudal system. It's a corrupt hellhole with a centrist, middle-aged board of directors trying to manipulate the federal system so they get to keep their profits. I do what I feel is in the realm of the possible. I try to prevent the usual schisms that the white right-wing powers set up and use to tear apart the population. I try to get the women educated for their own self-esteem and future. I try to prevent the injured and sick from dying when they don't have to. I try to keep even the lifers from giving up hope. You show them, with the possibility of success they work harder. In all honesty, I do fail, but once in a while . . . " She smiled at this. "And then there are those who would assassinate me. Who are you, Carleen Kepper? I can't figure out what you want for yourself."

"I have nothing to say about it."

"Why?" Sam asked.

"Because I'm permanently lost," I replied. "I can't get out of Daedalus's maze. I just turn corners and follow lines without trying to get anywhere."

"That's very selfish," Sam was impatient. This heart-to-heart wasn't going the way she expected.

"Artists are selfish."

"Art is a luxury, isn't it?" Sam sang the old leftist song. "When there's poverty and torture and famine . . . "

"Just stop," I blurted out. "Order me around, but don't lay your humiliation shit on me. You compromise every one of your left-wing congresswoman's do-goods every time you have some poor shell-shocked lowlife clean a toilet."

"That's not me," she said quietly.

"Really? I thought you were the president of the United States."

"I could get you put in solitary for how you're talking to me," Sam threatened. "But I came here because once you get strong after solitary, there are jobs for you. The birth center looks like an ASPCA building from the outside. Drab yellow walls surrounded by a filthy fence. It looks like we keep sick animals inside, and this depresses and scares our pregnant convicts. Furthermore, I think it adds to the resistance and hostility we get from the women when they are scheduled for examinations or counseling."

"Space defines intention," I repeated from some drunken discussion I'd had with David Sessions years ago.

"Yeah, like a cell for two crowded with five. Corrupt action defies good intentions. I started just like you. I was from the white upper class. Back then, *we* were at fault for everything. I got beaten up every day. I purposely acted out so they'd put me in solitary. But I told myself that the stuff I was experiencing, those women had endured every day of their lives, and I made it political not personal. Gradually, they accepted me. It helped that my old man was a Black Panther. Though not much. Most of the women here have such screwed relationships with men, but they go back to them when they get out of here.

"Look, Carleen, we want you to paint a mural around the whole birth center. I want every inch of those walls covered with positive images of women. I don't care if it's Amazons or pilots or Harriet Tubman or fictional explorers. I want landscapes, too. From all over the world, so the women can dream of other places. Of getting out of here. Of taking their kids to mysterious hideouts. You get what I'm saying."

"I get that the birth center is enormous. It's at least a three-year project if I work every day. Hours every day. Seven days a week."

"Where else do you have to go?" Sam sneered.

I was raging inside. I thought of Fits and the last time I was imprisoned by art.

"Why don't you make it one of those team projects?" I suggested. "Get twenty or thirty women to do it all at once. They'll learn about art and working together."

"Your sudden political generosity is transparent, Carleen," Sam replied. "It's the project the board has chosen for you alone."

"I'm not Michelangelo. I won't live to finish it."

Sam was not sympathetic. "You'll pace yourself. Abigail Woods is cutting down that forest over there and planting a vegetable garden to feed two hundred prisoners. You're *so* not victimized."

"But this isn't liberal or advanced." I was shaking. "It's its own form of slavery. It's torture."

Sam got up and brushed off her jeans. Honors and double honors convicts were allowed to wear their own clothes.

"I'm not going to do it," I protested quietly. "Put me in solitary."

"You don't want that," Sam warned me. "You just got out. Solitary is extremely dangerous to your mental state. You don't want to start all over again, do you?"

"I won't be your slave. I won't build your pyramids. Put me in solitary."

Sam spoke into her radio and two guards came and led me toward the bleakest building of all. Sam walked off without looking behind her.

Back in solitary, I experienced flashbacks and hallucinations. Fits was in the room with me. There were empty notebooks tossed about the cold floor. "Fill them all tonight," she demanded. "Fill them with real art because I'll know the difference. This time if you fail I'll cut off all your fingerprints. You won't exist, Carleen Kepper. I'll poke out your eyes and lead your nameless self from darkness to darkness. You better get painting. Fill those books. *Fill every inch.*" I didn't have any paint. I used my raw, bloody fingers to draw on the cement floor of my cell. When I finally got out, I learned that most of the women gossiped and said I was trying to avoid work. Some thought I was possessed and stayed far away from me. It got to the point where one morning before dawn I broke open most of my fingernails and painted my face with blood.

I ended up in the psychiatric wing of the hospital with my hands and forearms bandaged to my elbows. But the humiliation of my return to the ward was more painful than any self-mutilation. Also, I saw my "wife" Marcella. She'd set fire to our cell when I hadn't come home. Only her feet seemed burned and she was swinging around on crutches. "Aren't we the pair?" she said. "Whitney Houston and Kurt Cobain have twins."

"Why did you do that?" I snapped at her.

"You were gone, my heart was broken, and I knew I'd never trust a living soul again."

I could barely look at my sweet arsonist. My protector. Now I could see burns on her from head to toe. I wondered if this place was any better than Powell. The whole prison system was fucked. We were radioactive trash hidden from civilization so they didn't get diseases from us. Eventually, we'd spread all over.

"They say I'm to die if I keep these kinds of games up," Marcella said very dramatically. "If I must do so, let it be on my own terms. Find me some matches, my husband, so I can blow up my oxygen tank."

"Why don't you stop it, Marcella?" I asked. "With you I think it's a choice. You could have me back and see the sky."

"I can see the sky from the windows," she noted. "I can see the barbed wire, too. I think the barbed wire is prettier. More like the sculptures they do at Soho fashion shows."

"You'll never do another fashion show if you don't save yourself."

"I am now starving myself in the name of the children of Sudan," Marcella said. "Only I don't know where Sudan is. Actually, Carleen, you know I'm not starving myself. God's semen is filling me up more and more."

"Oh, don't give me that shit." I shook my head. She giggled and kissed me on the lips. Her breath was rancid.

"I need you," I said. "I want us to have a home."

Marcella giggled and sat on my lap. "I want pet gerbils."

It took only five days for my hands and arms to heal to the point where I could be released from the hospital. It took considerably longer to be let out of the psychiatric ward. I spent those days with Marcella, watching as her breathing became more and more labored. After a while she couldn't walk around carrying her glucose transfusion on its pole so I sat by her bed. I don't know what they were feeding her intravenously, but it didn't seem to be doing much good. Her beautiful face seemed to sink into itself, her eyes surrounded by black circles, her thick lips dry and cracked. She refused to swallow even water, so I wet her lips regularly with Q-tips and gauze. Her gums bled. Her eyes turned yellow. I'd never seen anyone die so slowly before. I wanted to shake her and blow life back into her.

"I'll let you set a fire if you'll just start eating," I begged her. "I'll find some really valuable, beautiful, glossy book and we'll watch it go up in flames. I'll paint a masterpiece and you can dip it in glowing coals whenever you get a jones for fire."

She laughed with a wheeze. "You'd do that?"

"I'm your husband," I smiled. She smelled of dried blood and dung.

"The psychiatrists said all this is about my daddy doing me as a child, but half the women here got diddled by some man and they're fat. I am just permanently unhungry."

"Don't you want to live?" I asked her.

"On some other planet where the food comes out of silver tubes and balloons and you have to try to catch it with your tongue."

"What's wrong with earth food?"

"I told you, darling. It blocks the passageways for the gods to send their beams to me, which contain their prophecies."

She slept more as the days went on. I had nothing to say to the other patients, who were shouting and carrying on like they were in a cheap, abusive zoo.

Eventually, they took a layer of bandages off, and I could feel the scabs and stitches on my fingers, hands, and wrists. It hurt like hell to move, but I was in some desert, in the Serengeti or the Sahara, and the pain was both excruciating and very far away.

Soon after, Sister Jean visited me.

"Long time no see, Sis," I said, mocking a high five.

"You've been worthless to me," she replied. I laughed. I liked that.

"The doctors say that none of the damage is any worse than what was inflicted on you at Powell. A few tiny broken bones. They're healing along with the abrasions and cuts."

"I'll go back to solitary," I replied.

Sister Jean leaned forward. Her expression was fed up, but for the first time kind of real. Even so, her "realness" seemed fake.

"Listen to me. Listen to me very carefully. Here is why I think you refuse to settle in at Clayton. Not because it insults your aesthetic, which it does. Not because you are in psychic agony, which you are. And not because you're afraid you'll disappear into the crowd, even though you might. The reason you won't take to these orders and rhythms is because it will open up a wide space that will cause you to confront the extraordinary amount of time you have as a convict. Years. You will finally have to admit to yourself that you're going to be in this prison for life. That might mean many, many years, Carleen. You can't tolerate the idea that you may have to live in a routine that goes on and on. You'll do the menial tasks that you do, live your life as it finds its rhythm, and most likely die on the grounds. The more violent interruptions you make, the less inevitable this time seems. These are distractions and minisuicides. You're trying to live in squares like a comic book. Small stories in a giant book. Sectional time. But after a while even that won't work. Time is not your friend. It holds you down. It mocks you. However you choose to spend your time here, Carleen, you will be doing it for most of your life and not out of choice. You have to give yourself over to this horrifying isolated reality. You will give up. You are here for the rest of your life. Time is going to pass no matter how hard you try to stop it. You are a true prisoner. In every aspect of your life."

The truth of what Sister Jean had said caused a grief, a yearning, for life that I only imagine people felt when they knew they were going to die. For the first time at Clayton I let out a sob and began to cry. Not a lot. But I knew how arid my real life was. How dirty. How sick. It was a long road. An empty, ugly desert, not mystical but full of shrubs and dried-out plants. No colors. Sister Jean put her arm around me. None of the women stopped or stared. They knew it. They knew what I hadn't actually known until that hour when I realized I was in a boat on my own and never coming home.

Soon after that conversation Marcella died. I knew then that they had completely broken me down. But I didn't know what was going to change or, as if in the twilight zone, I'd wake every morning to the same day, weather, and food. The same number of steps to work, same exact conversations, same lies, same brown dreamless sleep, same wish for death, same cowardice to carry it out with dignity. I was alone.

JUDAICA

I got a message from Elisheva. She picked a time for us to meet when she knew I had a break and named a restaurant called Bread. The place was on Church Street in Tribeca, very *ooh la la*. She was fifteen minutes late and wearing a black dress and white tuxedo jacket. Her charm necklace of mitzvahs and menorahs and stars and charms hung heavier on her neck. She'd added several new charms. She had a new, bright red string around her wrist. Her eyes were lined with kohl.

"I'm sorry it's been so long," she said. "Hey, you look good. It's all that walking. I should walk more. All I do is spin cycle. I've missed you. I really have, but personal crisis—my crazy sister broke up with her fiancé and threw her $20,000 wedding dress out our window. Luckily, it landed on the balcony. Can you imagine? Children dying of starvation and she throws a cheesy wedding dress that could feed a whole refugee group out a window. What kind of crazy family do I come from? Then she makes up with him. Also, I've applied to Hebrew Union College to become a rabbi. How exciting! And as far as Batya Shulamit goes, we had a small but fascinating catastrophe. She woke up one morning and decided she was an atheist. She also got her period. Not on the same day, but our straight-laced little angel is showing a few kinks. She likes you slightly more than before, by the way, but thought she detected the tiniest bit of unnecessarily generalized annoyance. Like you were getting fed up at following her rules. 'Too bad,' she wants me to tell you. You're a convicted murderess and she's just protecting herself. Anyway, I think her theological meltdown was almost moot. If there's no God there can be no bat mitzvah. Leonard was pissing in his pants, forgive me. I don't know what tilted her philosophically, but suddenly our girl discovered that evil and good weren't well organized or equally distributed in the world and therefore how could there be a God? It's my job to take care of this mess. So first I tell her about Tampax, which practically mortified her to death. She showed me the passage in Leviticus: 'When any woman makes a running issue out of her flesh she is unclean . . . ' Why is God so nauseated by women's periods? Is he really? And if he is, why? Batya Shulamit and I are beginning to worry about God and women."

Elisheva stopped suddenly and took a breath.

"I'm totally talking my head off," she said with a laugh. "Don't worry. I'm just a little manic because my own life is like a rowboat on the Niagara River headed for the Falls. But I'm really glad to see you. How are you?"

I wished I could smile at her and reassure her, but the fact was, I did think she was a little nuts. For some reason, I had a jones for a Ziploc of weed like I hadn't had in months. For the smell of it. For the feeling of that whistlelike sucking. Cigarettes. Weed. I wondered if I was losing my grip on self-reform . . . if all this obedient behavior was really transporting me to a better place in life at all.

"I don't change much, Elisheva," I told her.

"Do you believe in God?" she asked.

This question irritated me. "Can we just get back to Pony? What happened with her relationship with God?"

Elisheva blushed. Almost as if she had that condition rosacea. "I've really blown it here. I don't know why I get so nervous."

"Because you still believe I'm a criminal. And you're probably right. And you're breaking your word all over the place. And if you're going to be a rabbi, your promises to Leonard probably seem more sacred. So tell me what you're here for, and then you don't have to see me again."

She bowed her head as if I'd scolded her and she was ashamed. "Here's the news," she said. "Batya Shulamit asked Leonard how there could possibly be a God if he wasn't letting her follow the Ten Commandments. Honor thy mother and father. How could it be if she honored him, he wouldn't let her honor you by inviting you to the bat mitzvah?"

I liked this. I leaned closer toward my mortified messenger. "And how did he answer her?"

"He said because her mother—you—had committed many terrible sins and she wasn't required to honor you."

"That's bullshit," I mumbled. "Is that even correct religiously or whatever?"

"No, Leonard was punting," Elisheva said. "But I wasn't going on that little family trip with them. Anyway, a couple weeks later Batya Shulamit found God again. Whew—just in time, too. She has her most arduous work ahead of her: midterms and the Haftorah."

"Did she say what caused her," I asked, "to throw years of painful belief out into the stormy weather on one particular day?"

"No, that's the weird thing," Elisheva replied in a rush of emotional turmoil, because she was gossiping and enjoying it.

"A twelve-year-old girl wakes up to a godless world and dis-avows her religious commitments. We have a collective heart attack and then—get this, get this—a week later she has a pri-vate conversation with her father wherein she tells him she really wants to return to her Hebraic studies double-time. And she wants to have a family meeting with the rabbi so they can construct a truly holy, traditional, folkloric, prayerful, mystical ceremony. So much for her chilling out. She wants everyone to speak Hebrew. The only English is when she gives her inter-pretation of the passage. The girl's bouncing off the walls. I per-sonally think it's hormones."

I didn't want to mix my feelings into these reports. I kept a nonrelieving silence for five minutes or so and then, in a voice that showed some annoyance, said, "So why are we meeting, Elisheva? You know I can't get off schedule. And you're taking a greater risk than usual."

Elisheva let out a dramatic groan. "Because she wanted me to give you this."

She dug through her huge bag and finally came out with a medium-sized lump wrapped perfectly in newspaper and duct tape. The girl obviously wanted no one to get his or her hands on the content.

"I don't have a clue as to what it is. And I'm not supposed to be here when you open it. There is a note attached. You have to admit we're making progress here," Elisheva said.

"Unless it blows up in my face," I replied.

"Have you ever had anything blow up like that?" Elisheva asked, trying to mask her greedy curiosity.

"I've been the object of a couple small explosions and fires," I admitted. "But mostly tear gas—one time, though . . . "

"One time what?" Elisheva asked.

"I'm not going to regale you with prison stories, Elisheva,"

I said. "You can read millions of first-person narratives crazier than mine."

"Why do you want to go to rabbinical school?" I asked her. "I thought you were . . . ambivalent."

I could see her engine rev for a long, speedy answer, but she caught herself.

"I don't know," she said quietly. "I just know I'm in love. This time for real."

I wanted to punch her. I wanted my bitterness to turn to envy. But it didn't. I could find amusement in the idiocy of adolescents hurting. But humans seemed to be without variety in their wishes, smells, and dreams, and without stamina to keep their dramas going over obvious finish lines.

"Do you believe in God, Elisheva?" I asked.

"Yes. Absolutely." No hesitation.

"Then don't you think God will sort all this stuff out for you and drop you down on the right runway?"

"I don't think God takes direct actions. I think he gives us our humanity. We direct our own lives, and he gives us the faith and guidance to live a life the best we can hack it. But it's hard to be truly truthful and good."

"Time to go, kiddo," I replied.

Elisheva stood up. She took a long pause and asked, "Are you mad at me?"

"I'm mad at everything."

"We'll work on that." Her old grin came back.

"No, we won't," I replied. "Go." I wanted to read Pony's note.

Dear Carleen Kepper née Ester Rosenthal,

I am working on Batya with Elisheva, and I was only wondering that if you saw a baby in a cradle made of twigs floating down the river, and you knew the baby was meant to drown, you knew if you were caught you would be executed and you weren't even Jewish, would you save the baby? Please answer honestly and with thoughts.

My Best,
 Batya Shulamit

P.S. Please don't think the gift means I want to do one of those TV reconciliations.

I put the note on my bedside table and decided not to think about it. I wanted to see what she'd sent me.

It took forever to unwrap Pony's object. The tape was so tight I had to find scissors to cut through the skintight layers. But since we weren't allowed any sharp objects in the halfway house, I had to go to the reception desk. The security lady watched my every move until I'd cut through the layers of tape and newspaper. In the middle was a small china horse. It was a fairly ugly looking thing. A pink china statue as if made by Hallmark, but it was a horse— a pony.

"I need to look at that," the security lady said. "All that wrapping was suspicious."

"It's just a toy," I said. I could hear the edge in my voice.

"I'm sorry, I have to see it," she said. She was one of those square security types with orange-yellow bleached hair, bangs, no makeup, and no sense of humor. I handed her the pony.

"Cute," she said gruffly. She shook it a little to see if any weed or powder would pour out.

"Who's it from?"

I had to answer quickly. I couldn't get into a whole conversation.

"Just a little girl I know," I said.

I went to a jewelry maker off Canal and asked him if they could drill a hole in the pony without breaking it apart. I wanted to wear it around my neck. The bald-headed Jewish man with thick bifocals looked at me like, "Lady, have I been doing this my whole life or not?" But to his humiliation and my fury, he did crack the pony in several pieces as he was drilling. "It vasn't made for dis," he said depressively. Then we began the dance that he'd buy me a new one, but I said it only had to be this one, and finally we came to a creative solution where we managed to drill a hole in one of the bigger shards and fit a delicate chain through it. Then we took epoxy glue and fit the pony back together again. It was a cracked but complete pony necklace, and I was going to ask him to help me clasp the hook so I could wear it around my neck. But I stopped myself short and wrapped the drying pieces in newspaper and put it in the large breast pocket of the men's dress shirt I was wearing instead.

I rushed back to the halfway house and thought I'd put a nail in the wall by my bed and hang up the broken pony. Of course the symbolism didn't escape me. But that was too much like a crucifix, and besides, it would provoke questions I wasn't prepared to answer or lie about. So I put it in the drawer of my crummy bedside table where I kept Pony's notes. Aesthetically, I really liked how the too-pink Hallmark tourist gift had turned out with its cracks and bumps and mismatching silver chain, and I wished I could figure out something more creative to do with it.

On Sunday I went to midtown in the Forties somewhere and found a Judaica store. I took Doorbell with me and put his yellow "dog assistant" coat on in case they didn't allow animals in the store. He was so huge and tragic looking he reminded me a little of a more sympathetic version of a Golem. My Jewish Frankenstein. It was impossible not to be infatuated by his smashed-in face and mournful eyes of the ages. Even the somewhat uptight lady in a wig and thick glasses at the register took to him after her initial panic.

"What can I help you with?" she asked not unkindly, her eyes glued to Doorbell. He sat in a "stay" position and barely blinked.

"There's a bat mitzvah coming up and I want to get the little girl a special charm."

"Ach!" The woman gestured as if this was what life was made for. She took me to the back of the store and pulled out three trays of all kinds of mezuzahs, charms, stone circles with Hebrew script on them, Jewish stars of all sizes, miniature scrolls, and several beautiful Jewish symbols I didn't recognize.

"There's antiques for a fortune and silver and silver-plated for more reasonable," she explained. I stared at the trays for a long time. Doorbell lay down and chewed on a plastic monkey I'd brought for him.

"He's very well behaved," the woman noted.

"He's trained to work in children's hospitals," I half lied.

"Well, you look," the woman said. "I have to keep my eye up front. Let me know if you need anything."

I saw an antique mezuzah that was a cylinder instead of a rectangle, and it was made out of some kind of stone lacquered in an amber color with a Hebrew Chai on the front. I also saw a 14 karat gold circle with a Jewish star engraved in the middle. All around the edges of the circle were tiny lacquered, multicolored doves, and I knew that was Pony's kind of thing. I took both to the register as Doorbell lumbered beside me.

"He walks like a horse," the woman grinned admiringly.

"He weighs 180 pounds," I said.

"Gentle as a lamb," the woman sighed.

"It just goes to show you," I said, "God's animals are here to teach humans, not the other way around."

The woman nodded earnestly, but she didn't quite agree.

"Did you find anything?" she asked politely.

"So much to choose from," I replied. I laid down the gold circle with the Jewish star and doves.

"Oh, one of my favorite pieces," she chirped. "But quite expensive."

"How much?" I asked.

"Two hundred thirty-eight before taxes," she bit her lip, almost fearful of my reaction.

"I'll take it," I nodded.

The woman brightened up as only that kind of slightly morose, monotone woman could.

"Cash or charge?"

"Personal check?" I asked. I wasn't allowed a credit card yet. I signaled Doorbell to retreat into his bored, lying-down "stay" position and dropped the antique mezuzah into my jeans pocket. What a rush I felt—and then a terrible crash that I was still connected to that style of stimulation. So close to suicide, Sister Jean.

I pulled a wrinkled blank check from another pocket and filled it out. The woman wrapped Pony's gift in tissue paper with "mazel tov" splattered in primary colors all over it and placed it in a jewelry box.

We shook hands and I left the store. It would be a long time before she'd figure out the mezuzah was missing. The piece was definitely valuable.

"You're an accessory to a crime," I told Doorbell. He wagged his long sloppy tail. I bought a silver chain down the block and put the mezuzah around my neck. I hadn't ever worn a freshly stolen item in the open. But it made me feel close to Elisheva and Batya Shulamit. Not necessarily to Beth or Pony.

The next time we met, Elisheva was calmer as we sat on a bench overlooking the Hudson. I was beginning to recognize seasons again and, if I had to take a guess, I would say it was early spring, though I wasn't sure. Calendars meant nothing to me. I was an alien. I lived in my own time zones created to survive at Clayton.

"I'm sorry I was so hyper the last time I saw you," Elisheva blushed. She bit her thumbnail.

"Sorry is a word that hardly ever needs to be said to me," I replied. "It's meaningless. In so many different ways. Empty. You don't have to deal with the past with me."

She was relieved and confused simultaneously. I had that effect on her, two to three reactions at the same time.

"She'll have to tell Leonard that the gift is from you, Elisheva. She'll have to learn to lie. You're rewarding her for conquering a difficult passage that she was struggling to get through," I explained.

"That's feasible," Elisheva said. "I've given her gifts many times."

"But does she lie well?"

"I don't know. She's never had to lie to me. But she's handled this whole communication with you as a deadpan poker player. Can I see what you got her?"

I pulled out the package.

"For God's sake, take that nauseous mazel tov wrapping paper off. She's too cool for that. Just give her the bag."

Elisheva took great pleasure in unwrapping the tissue paper. When she opened the box she looked at the necklace for a long time before saying anything. I was afraid I'd missed the point completely.

"This is perfect," she said finally. Her voice was raspy as if she was going to cry. "I mean, I'd never wear it, but for Batya Shulamit it's a combination of really cool, religious, and not gushy, which would scare her away." Elisheva practically hugged herself.

"Oh, what a mitzvah I've done." I thought of the smashed pony in my drawer and the stolen mezuzah on my neck and decided that Hashem had an unpredictable sense of humor.

"You're wearing a mezuzah!" she practically shrieked.

"I was fascinated by the structure, Elisheva, not the belief behind it."

"Can I see it?"

I quickly unhooked it rather than have her touch my neck. She held it reverently in her palm.

"This is truly spiritual," she mumbled quietly. "It's very old and was crafted with great love. It will protect you well."

"Do you want it?" I asked her.

"Oh, no!" Elisheva handed it back to me. "It's yours. It has your spirit all over it."

"I don't go with any of that spiritual shit." I shook my head.

Elisheva laughed. "Do you have a note to go with our little girl's charm?"

I did.

Dear Batya Shulamit,

If I were working by the river then I would most likely be a slave. I would have no food or housing for a floating baby. So I have to admit to you I'd think twice before saving it. But I believe strongly that innocent creatures of

any kind should not be mistreated or put in danger. It's
not their fault, and they're helpless. So yes, I would fish
the baby out of the water, but I would immediately pass
it on to another woman. Perhaps to a slave higher up on
the ladder, or a slave who believed her love could save the
child. I would not be strong enough to keep it after hours
and hours of labor and bear the anxiety of getting caught. I
hope you like the charm.

Sincerely,
    Carleen Kepper née Ester Rosenthal

After Elisheva left with my package, I went to the nearby CVS
and bought hospital gloves, a package of white envelopes, and
stamps. I returned to my room at the halfway house, put on the
gloves, wiped off the mezuzah for fingerprints, and wrapped it
safely in newspaper. I left the gloves on and put the mezuzah
in an envelope and inserted the folded envelope into another
envelope. I looked up the address to the Judaica store and
wrote it on the envelope using letters that looked nothing like
my handwriting. I put many, many stamps on the envelope to
cover how much the mezuzah might weigh. And then my heart
sped up, and I knew I had to get to a mailbox very quickly. I
practically ran down the street until I found one. I dropped
the envelope in the mailbox and opened and closed the little
door on top so many times I was like a locked-up obsessive
compulsive. I figured it would arrive in a couple days, and until
then I'd feel uncomfortable in my stomach and anxious. I recognized that I'd been unusually jittery lately and I had a hole in
my center like a Henry Moore statue.

THE MURAL

It took me close to six years to finish the mural at Clayton. First I had to cover the whole building with a base. Art supplies were essential, but, in order to do anything, I had to write a ten-page document listing all the brushes, scrapers, types of paint, ladders, papers, and platforms I'd need. Everything I needed was locked up in a wooden toolshed with three thick locks on it. Only certain guards were allowed to have keys, and I was to meet one of them at first light so they'd open the shed and again at sunset so they could lock it up. If I changed my mind, needed new brushes or turpentine, or wanted to add a color, I had to submit my requests in writing. The materials cost a fortune. There was no way they'd get the money if not from my estate. But some of the inmates treated me differently. In fact, worse. "Take a look at the Jewish debutante building herself a playground." Joseph Heller would've enjoyed the irony.

They brought me my meals in paper bags and gave me an hour for lunch. It was no better than working for Fits. Guards patrolled me regularly to see if I was painting. I was utterly uninspired, so I decided that during my lunch walk I'd cover as much territory on the grounds as I could. I'd memorize the faces of every woman I saw. My memory was good enough to hold on to the civilization of pain and struggle and even pride that I saw in the eyes, jaws, and broken or straight noses. Laying down the base seemed to be work enough, but then I started with the faces. I began the mission at the top of the wall and worked down like window washers. The building was ten stories high. I used acrylic and oil for my faces and decided to go with realism because I hated murals that looked like outsider art, and if I was condemned to do this, I'd decided to commit suicide doing it. After a while I went totally manic. I didn't stop. I didn't eat. I'd work away all day and find I'd only covered one small corner. I worked in miniscule detail, and I attached the faces to every kind of activity imaginable from surfing to burying the dead. I painted African princesses, Texas society ladies, Amazons—all with the faces of the women of Clayton Correctional Facility.

I knew nothing of what was going on in the prison. I had no friends. Many women would wander by and look at what I was doing, but they gave me no comments. I was mad with loneliness. I'd just as well be in solitary. By the time I reached my room for break, the women were returning from dinner and ignored me. "You stink all the time," they'd say. I rarely showered, and when I did, I couldn't get the layers of paint, turpentine, and sweat off my body.

Months went by. At least I thought so. If I finished a significant section I could be sure that night someone would come along and spray-paint the finished yard or two with FUCK YOU or STUPID CUNT or PAINT THIS. At first I tried to wipe the words and gang symbols off and paint the sections again, but then I began to like the mixture of my detailed, proud Carleen Diego Rivera Memorial pictures and the rage of the letters and secret signatures. I heard that the warden announced that whoever was carrying out the destruction of the work would be arrested, taken to court, and charged with malicious mischief. They'd have the months added on to their sentence and would be dropped to the B newbie level. I told Warden Jen not to do it, that the swirls and scribbles added layers of passion to my stories. She obviously didn't listen. I saw a bunch of women being taken to court, and more than one of them gave me the finger. The loss of the graffiti brought me into feelings of deeper isolation.

The new rule didn't increase my popularity. Guards had to be posted by the birth building at night, and I was handcuffed to a guard wherever I went for protection. I liked the graffiti better than my own work. It had real rage and mischief. I was affected when one of the artists was caught, an eighteen-year-old gang member from Peekskill, NY, who'd killed a rival for an initiation test. I admired the guts it took to sneak in and attack my walls. And where'd she get the spray paint? When she was caught I heard that she said, "I'm ten times better than that bitch anyway." It was hard not to agree with her. Art had lost its meaning for me. It wasn't any different than scraping difficult stains off dishes. Painting had become terribly painful. My hands swelled again. My knuckles were paws. I suffered from arthritis, stiffening bones and tendons. The fumes and chemicals from the paints produced headaches. The mural was absolutely a fitting punishment. An annihilation of who I'd been. I was self-mutilating the girl from New Hampshire who heard colors and rhymed circle and square. More months passed. More months. It burned to breathe and my whole face broke out in infected cysts from the chemicals.

My relationship to the birth center project was empty of thought or feeling. I was painting snapshots of whatever popped into my often feverish head. Except for the constant prevalence of the ever-growing number of inmate faces, the rest was free association and automatic, without any involvement. Maybe in the long run some critic from the space age would view it as a great ruin with secrets to our culture, the way we look at cave drawings in dark magical caverns in France. Horses. That would be a good joke. Anthropologists would draw conclusions about the symbols of society from a half-brain-dead, crippled criminal who'd painted this very revealing classic so she could go from dorm B to C and have her own room.

Sam didn't drop by very often. Though she said she liked the "beauty" of the faces of the women of Clayton, she thought it was degrading that I had them involved in activities that had no relevance to their plight, the pain of their lives, or the society which had brought them so low. One day she called me off the ladder and stared silently for a pretentious amount of time, examining what must've been months of my labors.

"It's almost like you're making fun of us in some sections," she said. "Degrading us by putting us in ridiculous scenarios."

I didn't want to get punished so I made up some bullshit that I knew she'd relate to.

"You don't get it do you?" I asked her. "I'm showing dreams that have been stolen. I'm speaking out for possibility. There's plenty of history I've already done. A slave ship. A starving village. Can't you see the torture sections and the soldiers and the rapes? That's what you want. But without contrast—without showing the humanity of the women—how can we know the injustices of the punishments? Don't worry, you'll get more torture than you want, and besides, why can't I include cartoons and stupid jokes? Aren't the women allowed to laugh?" I spoke so passionately, I almost believed myself. I didn't know where this voice was coming from. A new neighbor at a cocktail party.

"I guess I believe you," Sam replied. "Just don't make any

enemies with your jokes. You have no protection. Since you have to spend all your time here, this is the only way we know you."

"I thought you were trying to get the women to work together," I said. "You know, break up the gangs, the underground mafias, the territorial disputes . . . I thought that was one of your campaigns."

"I wish the government really gave a shit," Sam sighed. "The American prison system makes it almost impossible to form any positive programs. They'd rather make a maximum security facility than try to educate or teach bitches who are mostly victims."

She was so smart but utterly humorless.

We were silent.

"Two girls just hanging around in purgatory having a swell time," I said.

I thought I caught Sam almost smile.

"I don't understand why Jen Lee doesn't give you a day off," she said.

"Because this is jail and she has her own logic. She probably thinks this is easy on me. No one believes artists really work." I showed her my calloused, blistered hands and my face with scars over scars from the chemicals. "Stand on the ladder for hours a time," I said. "You'll see how much fun it is."

"White girl problems," Sam said dismissively.

An anonymous year passed and at some undramatic point I noticed the building was finished. From the distance it looked like a crowd of over a thousand women heaped together for no coherent reason whatsoever. It was a town put together with the remnants of several bombings. It was a protest march for thousands of different issues. It was a mural of a ton of criminals doing completely incoherent actions. By then I could barely feel the back of my neck or my arms. My legs held me up like wooden posts. I felt like I had lung cancer. But I marched into Jen Lee's office, ill and hating her, and laid a brush on her desk. She looked exactly the same. A squarish, small lady with short gray hair and thick glasses. But she'd definitely aged a few years. I wondered what power trip made her want to stay a warden. I pointed at the brush.

"I take it you've completed your task."

"Yes, ma'am." I said.

Jen Lee slapped me hard with the back of her hand. A school ring she was wearing made a cut on my cheek.

"You don't ever talk to your warden like that. Not ever. I thought you'd learned some boundaries. Some control."

"Warden," I said. "Every cell of my body knows its boundaries. I'm ill. I'm emptied, and the last years have been unrelenting hell. I have only talked to hecklers and guards, so I don't have words." I didn't apologize. She obviously thought I had.

"That's more like it," she said. "Let's go see the masterpiece."

We walked slowly toward the birth building because of my difficulty breathing. Looking at the mural through her eyes, for the first time, was spectacular. It wasn't necessarily good art. But there was so much art that there was something for everyone. It was the criminal's Sistine Chapel. Six years of my life—every day, every hour.

"Carleen, this is spectacular," Jen Lee gasped. "It's a true piece of art. The trustees will be satisfied that our prison is growing in sophistication. It's a shame you couldn't include every woman, but you did your job. It shows the local government what we can do to make female prisoners useful and creative. If we push our women, like we did with you, if we are unrelenting, maybe we can break through the innate negativity brought on by racial strife and poverty. There's a religious thing about it that has no specific god, but there's the possibility of finding a personal god who can forgive anyone, from those souls headed toward death row to teenage drug smugglers."

I wanted so badly to knock her out and claw her face off and sign my name in her blood. There wasn't an inch of anybody's god within a mile's distance of the mural. I didn't have a fucking clue what she was talking about. Truly not a fucking clue. I looked at the mural and I hallucinated it exploding and collapsing, poor half-naked women dying and holding their babies and children out to laughing cops. The wounds of the trapped women spilled a variety of colors. The smoke swirled like a tornado, and my stick thin Marcella was suddenly holding a fistful of sparklers, which she had just set on fire with an antique lighter. And then suddenly there was a beautiful explosion of light. I collapsed.

I knew the hospital so well. But this wasn't the mental ward. Many women were sleeping, and I had the distinct feeling they were dying. A doctor pulled my curtain open with a flourish as if a show was about to begin. He was wearing a surgeon's mask and glasses. His name was Peter Collins.

"You have Hepatitis C," he said, "malnutrition, and a nice list of other viruses and injuries. But the medicines are doing their work, and in a few weeks we'll know if you're out of danger. You tried to kill yourself in slow motion. I'm sorry, but it's my vocation to bring you back."

"Please don't," I begged. "Be incompetent."

CUSTODY REVISITED

The courtroom was smaller this time. I wore a denim skirt, white blouse, and blue-and-white striped jacket, in which I felt actually decent. My hair was longer, and the white Susan Sontag stripe had grown more prevalent and even whiter. Tina had given me some Kiehl's face cream a few months back, and, although I refused to wear makeup, my skin seemed smoother. I had acquired a pair of Toms, simple canvas shoes. In other words, I'd done the best I could to appear clean and normal.

"I don't know why you're doing this," Harry said. "It hasn't even been a year. What can change in a year? Wait. Don't tell me. Everything. Everything can change in a year. But petitions like this—"

The judge began to speak.

"On the matter of Carleen Kepper/Ester Rosenthal and her petition to gain visitation rights to see her birth daughter, Batya Shulamit Salin, we have heard the petition. She plans to be released from the halfway house and is in search of an appropriate apartment. Her employment is steady and she pays all her expenses. There are several letters here that say she has an unusually loving relationship with her animals and that she works overtime for free to get them properly trained. She has had no difficulties with the law and carries no debt. She attends NA meetings regularly and is on her way to establishing a life as a solid citizen of this city. At the very least, Ms. Kepper Rosenthal would like to have supervised visits with her daughter and obtain permission to attend her bat mitzvah, which will be taking place within the next three months. She would like to buy her daughter a present and personally congratulate her."

The judge looked at Harry.

"Anything else?"

"Not at this time, Your Honor," he replied.

"May I hear from the other side?" the judge asked.

Leonard's fancy lawyer was much younger this time. He looked like an associate, clean cut, frisky, and wearing an expensive suit. He smiled.

"Batya Shulamit's family is very pleased to hear of Carleen Kepper's progress, but there are several items that prevent us from going along with the petition. We can't overlook the severity of her crime nor the length of her time in prison in comparison to her time in the civilized world. Eighteen months or so as a member of our city is really very little, and she has only been released from supervised living in the last week. That her first act was to file this petition reflects what might be an unhealthy obsession to get what is not legally hers—a pattern that has been prevalent throughout her whole life. Furthermore, her employment is dog walking. The defense would hardly call this a skilled, reliable, or steady job. It is a transitional job, and we see no evidence of what Ms. Kepper plans on doing next. If she plans on being a serious trainer, she is not registered with any legitimate company.

"We'd also like to say on behalf of Batya Shulamit, the little girl in question, that she is now on the verge of a sensitive time in her life, puberty. Due to Ms. Kepper's tough years in prison, we are afraid she might speak too coarsely or be unintentionally provocative at a time when the child's parents report moodiness. She doesn't need a mother's notoriously ugly past to figure into her calculations as she begins the journey of finding herself.

"Finally, the bat mitzvah itself is a celebration for which Batya Shulamit has been preparing for three years. This precious, essential ritual should not be marred by the girl worrying if her irresponsible mother will show up or not. And if she does, will she behave properly in the synagogue and not draw attention away from Batya Shulamit? Carleen Kepper's notoriety could overwhelm the peaceful—indeed holy—atmosphere. When a young girl passes into womanhood, it should be celebrated in the purest, most religious, most joyous atmosphere.

"Once again, as in the last session, I will read a statement from Batya Shulamit herself which makes her feelings on the subject clear:

"To the court, I don't care how much Carleen Kepper née Ester Rosenthal has reformed. She is still a stranger to me. My feelings about her grow more and more complicated, and I need my life to be simple so I can concentrate on Torah, Haftorah, and the day of reckoning. I do not want her at my bat mitzvah, nor should she contact me in any way about it. And I ask that she stop petitioning the court because it causes me extreme agitation. I would like the court to tell her not to send me presents or notes. When push comes to shove, I never want to hear of this woman again."

The judge sat for several moments and then rubbed his forehead.

"Well, all middle school kids hate their parents, so I don't take this letter too seriously. And I think an ex-convict with over a year of good behavior deserves a break. I'm concerned about the mental health history of the plaintiff, however, and whether she's ready to keep control of her emotions in stressful situations. I also think she needs to settle in and prove to the court that her current job is truly a serious long-term vocation that she plans to make her life's work. She might attach herself to an established city- or state-certified organization to help the court take her accomplishments more seriously. The bat mitzvah is out of the question. It is a day too loaded with meaning for Batya Shulamit to have any major psychological distractions. However, in three months' time after the bat mitzvah, I am going to allow for a supervised visitation between the girl and her mother to see how it goes. We will have a social worker present, and her observations will determine whether any further contact is desirable or detrimental. I am canceling the writ of protection in that there is no evidence that Ms. Kepper has made any effort to contact the girl. And as my colleague said before me, it would be to the child's advantage not to denigrate the mother any further. Let the girl make up her own mind."

Court was dismissed.

Harry knew by now not to hug me, but he shook my hand.

"We moved an inch forward? Or I didn't help you with shit."

I pulled my hand away.

"It's not you, Harry. Your loyalty, despite my insane wishes, is very real. I won't forget. I can pay you now, and I want you to quote me billing hours that a top family lawyer would lay on the client."

"I'm not giving up." Harry shook his head. I moved slowly through the courtroom. I didn't know what I'd expected. Suddenly I decided to can it with Pony, permanently. I was exhausted from her jerking my chain. I was angry at myself for this odd masochism, and once again I asked myself what my motivation was. What would be accomplished by building a relationship with a kid who really didn't want me? What did *I* want? Zip. Nothing. Let it go. But, still, it was difficult.

Why was I trying to be a mother? The itchy ache of it made me jones for a distraction. I missed my scams. How to acquire good, cheap stuff at the seaports, airports, train stations, truck stops. New faces, new names, new ways of hiding, new ways of pacing back and forth. The rides. The speed of vehicles. The love of an engine like a beating heart. I missed always wondering if I was going to get caught. Those feelings would be more real than some kind of worthless visit three months away with a PhD observing my body language. She'd probably be the kind with glasses hung around her neck and a clipboard. I saw the Henry Moore statue in my head again. Why couldn't I crawl permanently into one of his holes and disappear?

THE HONORS COTTAGES

After a two-month stay in the hospital wing at Clayton after finishing the mural, I was released to an honors cottage. The honors cottages were tiny, but each was its own small house made of brick and had a bed, a dresser, a kitchen sink, enough room for a table, a hot plate, a minimum of cooking utensils, a bookshelf, and most importantly, its own toilet.

There were the honors cottages and the double honors cottages—two- and three-star hotels. I think there were about twenty little houses in all. They were set apart from the rest of the prison on an acre with grass and sporadic trees. There was a volleyball court and a tetherball pole. The area reminded me of a run-down, abandoned prep school campus. The women who occupied the cottages were prisoners of all types. There were lifers who were too elderly to cause trouble but were still sharp, functioning, and in charge of various aspects of prison life—groundskeeping, garbage disposal, food delivery, funerals. They shared a pay phone to take care of their diverse chores. There were a bunch of women who'd shown themselves to be exemplary by honestly reforming, changing from vicious criminals to strange, repentant women who counseled both newbies and long-timers in trouble. Some of them were up for parole, close to leaving, but some would never leave. I thought my years of terrors and mental illness could find their end here. I wasn't necessarily correct, but it seemed that way in the beginning.

Twelve women—all honors prisoners—and Sam, Sister Jean, and Warden Jen Lee made up the jury that met several times a month. Normally I would've gone in front of them to make a plea to be moved to an honors cottage. I would've prepared a portfolio of my accomplishments and gotten signed letters from monitors and supervisors speaking to my improved behavior. I had none of that.

The committee sat behind a line of tables like at a court-martial, and there was a single chair where I was to sit and face them.

"You haven't gone through the required regimen to be living in an honors cottage," one lady said, picking her teeth with a toothpick. "Someone wanna tell me why she's taken up some deserving black woman's space on the waiting list? Did her color give her advantage?"

"You know that's not true," Sam said. "I'm the only white in the honors cottages."

"So what'd she do that's so special?" This came from a tall Latina named Beet who helped many women with gender issues in prison.

"She's a psycho," exclaimed a tiny woman named Midge. "She'll blow up our corner."

"She's not *that* crazy," Sister Jean said. "Like all of you, she has serious problems. However, we don't believe she is a danger to anyone but herself. If she misbehaves, she'll be returned directly to the general population."

"So if we find her hanging from a light fixture she goes to solitary right?" Midge asked. A couple of women laughed.

Warden Jen Lee's gruff voice cut in.

"Let's cut the shit, okay? Carleen has been approved for an honors cottage not because of what she did, but because she's going to need the room." The committee looked puzzled and shuffled through their papers.

"What the fuck?" I heard someone say under her breath.

"That's correct," the warden said. "The Association for the Blind has asked if we would experiment in training Seeing Eye dogs. We are starting with one dog. It's a rigorous day-and-night training and requires the kind of extreme commitment Carleen has proved capable of displaying."

"What're they, pit bulls?" a woman named Amanda chimed in. "My cousin, he used to fight pit bulls for a living. They'll rip your throat out."

"If the committee approves, Carleen will receive a puppy tomorrow, and for the next year and a half she will train it to comply to strict commands. The dog will become a more than suitable companion to a handicapped person. There are hundreds of signals and skills the dog will have to learn."

"Why Carleen?" Sam asked. "She has demonstrated no facility for bonding or getting along with anyone."

"Could be a good fit," Midge suggested. "Lots of people say she's an animal."

"I want a puppy," chirped a young member of the committee. "I created the whole toddlers program at the birth center. I could love a puppy, too."

"Love isn't the point. Training is. Carleen's detachment is exactly what the association says is necessary for the process of building a proper dog. It's a mutual development of trust and affection. Not smothering."

I tried hard not to laugh. I felt as if I were standing before the pearly gates and the angels were discussing whether I should go to hell or purgatory.

"What about your temper?" Sister Jean asked me in a firm tone. "We can't have any abuse or physical punishment because an innocent animal isn't learning fast enough."

"I'd be much more likely to go after a person hurting an animal than any animal itself," I said with a smirk. "They are creatures. They're more like me than humans. That's why you want me—you even admitted it. That's why you brought me here. This wasn't my idea."

"Are you even interested?" Sam asked.

"When has that ever made a difference for any of us?" I replied. "But truth is, I wouldn't mind living with a dog. I wouldn't have to make conversation."

"Let's try for a few months with Carleen and see how it goes," the warden said. "If the training works out, we'll let her continue and see if it's an appropriate match between inmates and dogs. The techniques for training are strict, complicated, and time-consuming. There are books to read, and Phyllis Gelb, a woman from the Dogs for the Blind Association, will bring the dog and talk to you about techniques and attitude. She will visit regularly to check in on your progress."

There was a silence, a shuffling of papers.

"How do you feel?" asked a blond-haired, suburban social worker. She tried to sound kind, but she was the most scared of me of all.

"Not there yet," I said.

The first woman I met in the new cottage was Amanda, a large woman like myself, in her fifties, who played the viola. An aunt of hers had bought it at a yard sale and no one knew what to do with it, so Amanda's mother brought it up when she came for a visitation.

"I thought that was a mighty big fiddle," she told me, but

Amanda had been in a church choir before her downfall and had an ear for music. She said about twenty years ago she got permission to go to the gym on off hours and "squeak her heart out." She developed a self-made repertoire of gospel and blues on the viola that was, to my ears, like listening to the ocean—low, melodic, and complete. Her confidence grew and she began to sing again. And through music she evidently found the forgiveness of God. Over the years as she scuffled and scammed through the general population, she convinced another administrator, Laura Phillips (a charitable tennis-playing WASP), and Sister Jean to find organizations that would contribute instruments. Many of the instruments were unplayable, but some could be restored over at the male penitentiary a few miles away. I discovered that with my past mechanical abilities, I could weld a cap or two on a saxophone and stretch a drumhead over some toms, keeping the tension without ripping the material.

She said God had given her joyful music to drown out the voices of her husband, Justin, and brother whom she'd shot in cold blood after they stole three thousand dollars she'd been saving for years. She'd planned a long and loving visit to Georgia where her mother and the rest of her family lived. Her dream was destroyed when they stole her savings.

"I just took Justin's gun. They begged: 'Amanda, baby, baby, don't. Amanda, I'll get your money back.' Then I shot them both in the head." When she imitated them her voice was mocking. "Some things turn you to ice," she said. But the Clayton Family Band and Choir was her "Christian" redemption, and she made sure they were good.

Another woman who caught my attention was that tiny, fast-moving insect of a lady named Midge. Midge was an impatient little woman and had no tolerance for litter, windows without screens, lights left on, or unarmed guards. She was always in a rush and one could rarely have a conversation with her. She was a cranky old bitch, but she showed generosity in strange ways. She'd been an English teacher in some other life and was appalled by the lack of literacy in prison. "They're gonna say Negroes are stupid and they're gonna be right," she'd growl. I heard that she'd made it her goal to read every book in the prison's paltry library. But she decided she'd read them out loud. You could walk by the library anytime, day or night, and hear Midge reading *The Invisible Man*, *Uncle Tom's Cabin*, *The Sun Also Rises*, *The Encyclopedia Britannica*—whatever was her fancy—in a low, nasal voice. Her sense of drama was keen, however, and she somehow made all the descriptions and characters talk out the windows of the library, ringing down stairways and bouncing off ceilings. It was as if a loudspeaker were reciting *Moby Dick*.

Women began to gather. At first it was to laugh at this tiny, crazy black woman reading out loud a mile a minute, as if nothing mattered but the stories she told with grizzly drama. Then the listeners began to get caught up in the stories. And after six months or so she would have fifty or sixty women gathering at the library on their free hours to hear Midge's rendition of worlds they knew nothing about, not even how to get to them.

One day Midge called out, "I've got a permanent sore throat. I refuse to share my books with you anymore. You want stories, you learn to read!"

Thus began Midge's reading classes. From what I was told, she taught as if she was constantly annoyed and aggravated. She treated every student as if she were an idiot. She slammed her chalk against the blackboard, threw erasers at students, and insisted on quiet and absolute discipline. Fights broke out between her attackers and protectors. She spent time in solitary, but knew a great deal of poetry and books by heart and would screech them out in a scratchy bird voice from within her cell. Nothing seemed to faze her.

"You're the psycho" was the first thing she said to me at the cottage.

"I hope not anymore," I said.

"Once a psycho, always a psycho," she said. "It just gets rearranged, but it stays psycho."

On my doorstep the next morning I found copies of Sylvia Plath's *The Bell Jar* and *Ariel*, and a thick book about African art and sculpture filled with brilliantly colored photographs.

As a thank you, I left a thick book on her doorstep called *Politics as Poetry and Prose: The Fist with a Pen*. It contained sermons, polemics, poems, and satires from all around the world dating back to the ancient Greeks and finishing with writers like Ginsberg and that ilk. I'd bought it once when the Salvation Army visited the prison with books and clothes for the inmates. I got a pair of overalls that I still wear and black clogs. I picked up several books that day, and the poems and short polemics actually taught me something. I'd never thought about suffering other than my own. The book showed me there were worse prisons than Powell, women who'd committed terrible crimes and yet struggled to make sense of it all through writing. Despite the rapes. The beatings. The painful, demanding, menial cleaning-lady work. The boot camp. The random searches. The fact that they arrived at Clayton as low as a woman could be to begin with. Sam told me that most of the women at Clayton were there because of the abuse of men—what they did for men, what men drove them to do. I often didn't appreciate Sam's politics, but when I thought about this I came to a definite conclusion: I had been my own man. I did all my crimes for myself. Not Miko. He got me high.

But I was my own hungry animal. I was the man who made me do what I did.

But *The Fist with the Pen* turned me on to men and women who risked their lives to scribble their opinions on leaves or the pages of other books. And the famous voices, too, whose books were burned in the streets. Care! I yelled at myself inside my head. Care about this! All this shit! All this injustice! This pain! This death! Care, you bitch. *Feel* it. And I almost did. But not enough. I needed to build up my empathy muscles.

Midge returned it a week later with a note. Her penmanship was as small and precise as she was.

> *Yes. Fairly good book. But remember, Ms. Kepper, good causes do not always make good writing. There are many selections in here, however, that one might say meet in the middle. Top rate writing. Worthy of the oppressed.*
>
> *Thank you.*
> M.
>
> *P.S. I don't know what you thought of the Plath, but I find indulging certain mental illnesses rather raw and unattractive, don't you?*

When I moved in, Midge came immediately to visit me. "You just keep the dog away from me, you hear me?"

"It's just gonna be a puppy," I said.

"I don't give a damn what the hell it is—it's a dog and they bother me to death," she practically shouted.

"Okay, calm down," I said. "I'll absolutely avoid you. If we cross paths it'll be by accident."

"No accidents," Midge said through clenched teeth. "Out of my sight." She rolled up her sleeve and showed me an embroidery of scars that covered an entire arm. "You went to Powell, I went to Georgia Federal Detention. If they thought you had an attitude, those fuckin' Southern state troopers took you to a field, fucked you, and then used you to train their dogs. They really liked me because I was so little that the shepherds could carry me around. I got patterns and patterns of teeth all over me. Don't make me kill the dog and ruin my life."

"Take it easy," I said. "I'll make sure you're safe."

"I'll never be safe," Midge grunted.

PHYLLIS

Phyllis Gelb greeted me with a hug. I almost threw up in her embrace. We met in a private room in the warden's quarters. She sat down in a folding chair and patted another one for me to join her. The puppy was lying asleep next to her in an iron crate. I could hardly see what it looked like. Phyllis Gelb, however, was obese, and wore an alligator T-shirt and khaki capri pants. She was fair skinned with blondish hair and in her forties. I didn't want to be unfair, because it was clear that she loved dogs and wanted all of life to be perfect. She just talked a lot. She talked so much. She talked as if she knew the definitive answers for everything from household tips to why guns were not necessarily bad if you locked them up. I knew all about dog breeding and training philosophies and her family history and theories about the president before she remembered to ask my name.

"Carleen, believe me, I'm psychic in matters like these, and I can tell you have real dog sense. Dog people *know* dog people, and you *are* a dog person. I'm going to be giving you a pamphlet the association put together. It tells you everything from what your puppy should eat, to the correct toys, to the voices you use to talk to him, to the training techniques, to when he should poop. Please read it thoroughly and not like we're just some weird cult who lives for animals. We've been training dogs for the blind for over seventeen years. Hasn't always worked out perfect, but we have an 87 percent success rate and that's because people like you pay attention and are devoted. This is the first time we're trying out at a prison like this, Carleen. Dogs can't read your records. They only know your heart."

Phyllis then bent over to pull the sleeping puppy out of his crate. He opened his eyes and wagged his tail and went back to sleep on her lap.

"Long trips tire 'em out till they're trained otherwise. We've got dogs now that travel with businessmen all over the world. In private jets even. Seventeen-hour flights. You wouldn't believe." I was trying to get a look at the puppy, but all I could see was a mound of reddish-brown curls and big feet.

"The standard dogs for guiding and protecting tend to be Labs, golden retrievers, and German shepherds. This one here's a hybrid. Don't know what in the hell he is. We found him in a litter of retrievers, but he was clearly stuck in there by somebody because he has no resemblance to those who would be his brothers and sisters. I just hate dishonest breeders, don't you? Also, he's not typical because we think he's going to be larger than most. We're starting a program with strays to see if they respond as well to puppy trainings as the ones bred for the task. So you're new. He's new. The experiment is new. New. New. New. I believe change and experimenting is all there is in this world." Phyllis Gelb shifted in her seat again. But the puppy stayed out cold.

She paused and appeared to be sad for a brief moment. She tried not to glance at my somewhat sickly thinness.

"You strong enough for this, Carleen Kepper?"

"Yes, ma'am," I said.

"Then take him. Just pick him up and look in his eyes."

So I carefully took the curly, dead-to-the-world, gangly creature off her lap. My hands felt big and calloused. He awoke immediately, and I held him out in front of me so I could get a good view of his face.

All I remember are his brown eyes. They were the first eyes I'd ever seen in my life that instantly, without thought, trusted me. With no knowledge of the past. No fear of the future. And I experienced a loosening inside myself that I'd never felt before. It was as if a breeze blew through me. There was no instinctive pulling back, like a child used to being beaten. I leaned forward a little bit at a time until he put his head on my shoulder and snored.

BAT MITZVAH TALK: ANOTHER LETTER TO BATYA SHULAMIT

Dear Batya Shulamit,

I know more now about your chosen name. Please forgive me for parroting back stupid details when you are a vessel of biblical facts and subtleties. I simply had an urge to tell you why I find the name so fascinating and perhaps inspiring for me. Batya wouldn't worship any idols, which I personally find an admirable trait. It seems to me that an idol can often be given unearned power and will allow its source to abuse people. I don't like the word "idol" because it promotes a kind of easy stardom—like that show American Idol, which seems to me to be a lot of yodeling, crying, and creating hysterical pseudostars before anyone's even proven that they're a pseudosuperstar. I just really don't like the word "idol." It sounds like the word that means doing nothing. Revving, but in place.

Also, I am very intrigued by the version of the story that says the angel Gabriel slew all Batya's handmaidens because they wouldn't retrieve Moses's basket and, in place of them, by magic, he made her arm and hand grow so she could reach into the water herself. The image of a long, reaching arm is so beautiful to me. I think of a swan, or

blue heron. I can even see the Loch Ness Monster rising
out of the lake, not as a hideous creature, but as a glowing
white hand with a tiny basket made from brush and twigs.
What an arm!

And finally, among many other variations I like, I find
that papyrus, which surrounded Batya and Moses, can be
made into paper. So appropriate considering your ambi-
tions to be a writer.

I further admire Batya because she was rebellious, but I
will say no more on the subject.

I hope you remain and shall always be well.

Carleen Kepper née Ester Rosenthal

I showed the letter to Elisheva. "I can't cry, I can't cry. I'm
gonna drip. God, I cry so easily and I wear too much makeup.
It's so stupid." She dabbed expertly around her eyes. We were
sitting in the Leroy Street dog run right off the river.

"Will you give it to her?"

"Give it to her? I'll shove it down the little brat's throat. I'm
telling you, puberty—she's worse than some child soldier in
the Congo . . . No, no, I didn't mean that. Really, I didn't mean
it. I'm not racist. Well, maybe unconsciously—but not overtly.
No, I just mean she's turning into a viper, a vampire. She's still
Miss Goody-Goody most of the time, but so full of herself—so
judgmental. Do you know she got sent home from school for
refusing to change into her gym clothes in front of the other
girls? Refused. Told me they'd make fun of her. Because she
has a belly."

"Does she?" I asked.

"She's still got some remnants of the little girl, and that part
of her hasn't smoothed out yet."

"Good thing she doesn't have to eat what they served us in prison: Meat. Cheese. Salisbury steak. Thick mystery stews. Jello pudding pies. Mac and cheese.

Elisheva eyed me competitively for a minute. "You're pretty fit," she muttered.

"Manual labor—the best workout," I mumbled.

"Anyway, Batya was in hysterics and Anna, who is cool, Danish, gorgeous, and about as psychologically adept as Judge Judy, called me. Leonard was beside himself because, you know, any hint of anger or distress and Batya goes straight to the shrink on the Upper East Side lest she become . . . ," Elisheva stuck her tongue out at me, "'a psychotic.' Leonard's very quiet lately. Softer. Not so many lectures on the environment and self-serving stories about playgrounds in Cambodia. He also used to make her laugh, but he's not as funny as usual. Maybe business is bad. That's freaking her out, too, I think."

"What did you say to her?" I asked quickly.

"I tried to find a comforting passage in the Song of Songs about sexy, fleshy women, but she wouldn't have any of it. I told her that all her friends were too worried about their bodies to notice her. And, finally, I just said, 'Stop being such a Jewish princess,' and *that* got to her."

"I'm glad she's on the right moral path. Concerned with the future of mankind."

"You're not," Elisheva said with a laugh.

APARTMENT HUNTING

I'd spent every day for two months trying to find an apartment. Something strange was going on. I'd find a modest studio in the Lower East Side, put down a deposit, and the landlord said he'd check my references. The next week I'd get my deposit back and a firm *no*. This happened over ten times. I called Joe Kasakowski and asked him if he'd changed his opinion about me. He said he'd given the okay to anyone who called.

"Clayton's giving you an A+, too, Ms. Kepper, so I don't know what's going on. I'll make some calls."

I gave him the number of some of the landlords who had recently rejected me and in ten minutes he had the answer.

"It's your so-called employers. They're saying that you won't be working there after next week, so they can't guarantee you'll have a job. Did you fuck up?"

"I swear no, Joe. They said I was their best walker."

"Go talk to them and get back to me. It's time for a visit anyway. 'Specially if you're getting canned."

Neither Hubb nor Lucinda would look me in the eye. Lucinda looked jazzed on some speed. Hubb swished papers around on the desk as if he was working, but he wasn't.

"What the fuck?" I said.

"Watch your language," Lucinda said. "Show some respect. You always act as if you own the place."

"You want good manners?" I was weirded out. "And I can't find a place to live?"

"Sorry 'bout that," Hubb said, "but we're terminating you."

"But why?" I asked. "I haven't broken one rule. I've brought in over three-fourths of your new clients. I thought we even liked each other." I could see that they'd both fallen off whatever rickety wagon they'd been riding. I had to watch it because they were in a dark high.

"We was talking," Lucinda said, "and we figured out that you was planning a coup." She pronounced it *coop*.

"You're gonna try to worm your way in with some of your ex-con friends and take over our business. We're all criminals, Carleen. We know how you think. But me and Lucinda, we made something here. You're a jackal," Hubb explained.

"I've been completely loyal," I said. "I didn't have any plans like that at all."

I suddenly realized it was ridiculous to have a rational conversation. They were heavily back into their drugs and booze, the perfect cocktail for paranoia. I saw the future. Their business was going to fry, and they'd end up in their separate jails. There were so many reasons I had to get out of there, I didn't say goodbye.

Instead of sinking into despair, I went into a fury. I got wired. The first person I called was Elisheva. She met me later that day, and we sat near the fountain at Washington Square Park.

"I'm waiting for the day when we can meet inside and stop playing *Mission: Impossible*," she said cheerfully. But she noticed I was jumpy. And I was smoking a cigarette, which I rarely did anymore. I was grateful to her for not becoming afraid of me.

"Look," I said. "I know you're in over your head, but could you help me start a business?"

"I'm all about business," Elisheva said excitedly.

I told her the story of what had transpired.

"Those bastards!" she yelled. "Let's get right on our phones and call every single one of your clients, tell them exactly what's been going down, and you'll just start your own agency."

"No, we can't do that," I said. "I can't be associated with any drugs or junkies. Not even if I'm out. Me and anything negative and illegal brings up associations, you know? One person talks to one cop. One word gets out, and I'll be the one to go down."

"Then what do we do?"

"You be my business partner. You'll call the clients who like me best in your cultivated, college-tone voice and tell them I've decided to branch out and try to start my own business. We'll buy a cheap cell phone and we'll give them the number. You'll be sure to say that, of course, they probably want to stay with Hubb and Lucinda, but if they know of anyone new looking for walkers, Carleen is available, as she has always been, to provide all services. If they ask why she's not working at Pet-Pals anymore, you just say that I want to try and make it on my own. Let them make the decision. Don't coax or hint."

Elisheva's hands were dancing with excitement as she took notes, wrote little scripts for herself, and copied down my twenty-five or so names and numbers.

She looked at me, a wide grin showing perfect orthodontist teeth.

"What're we calling it?" Her enthusiasm wasn't helping my anxiety. I was already worried about involving her.

"You name it. But don't make it Jewish," I said.

"I know you'll melt and die if we put your name in it, so let's just call it We Love Dogs."

"Yeah," I said mildly. But Elisheva was hesitant.

"Your daughter objected to the 'love.' Batya said, 'Stop

using *that*. *That* has been overused, trivialized, and made absolutely improbable. It takes years and years to achieve the truly holy status of that word. And Hallmark and *Grey's Anatomy* and *Sesame Street* have all blasphemed it!'"

"Wow."

"She's been a little intense lately."

"I personally have little feeling about the word," I said. I was nervous and desperate. "We Love Dogs."

"Yes!" she said, and shot her fist into the air.

"Elisheva, calm down. Let's get the clients first."

"I'm on it," she said, and was tapping away on her phone as I left her at the fountain.

My young partner was a rabbinic dynamo. By the end of the week I had fifteen of my original clients and three new ones. Soon, five more of my old clients had come over to me. I was still living at the halfway house, and the counselors kept reminding me that there were women getting out of Clayton and Bedford and Reed that needed beds more than me. But I was still a middle-aged ex-con with no steady work I could guarantee. I absolutely refused to use my fortune or reveal anything about it. It would change the delicate balance I was beginning to find.

WALKING THE DOG

I had dropped off my last dog and was taking my time as I headed back toward the halfway house. I was more and more uncomfortable there. It felt like kindergarten, with rules, crying, and cautious voices surrounding my nun's cell in uneven bursts and waves. I was trying to count in my head if I had enough plastic doggy bags for the morning rounds. Very deep. A sudden, sharp pain jammed into my lower back and then another. Prison experience taught me immediately that it was a knee and I was being jumped. Unfortunately, they didn't offer martial arts classes in Clayton, but I knew what to do. I sat down. I did it because I figured if there was an attacker behind me there'd also be one in front of me. Or, if not, it would at least give my mugger pause. But I was correct, and a fist shot up under my chin. Someone yanked me up and held me from behind as another fist slammed me in the face and stomach. The pain was excruciating, but my thoughts were strange. Either they're going to kill me—which wasn't complicated—or they'd leave me there, in which case someone would call 911. When the cops arrived and looked up my record, they wouldn't think for a second that I was a victim, and after some stitches or a night in the hospital, I'd be brought into the precinct or thrown in jail. My parole would be put into question. The inner voices shouted, Not now. Not now when life was throwing some chances at me. These thoughts floated and zoomed at different weights and speeds like a dream, and I didn't fight back at all. I barely tried to protect myself. "Enough," I kept saying. "Enough." But the blows kept hitting me like a storm of rocks.

"Okay, I think we've made our point," I heard Hubb say. "I told you to stay out of my business, Carleen." He leaned down into my face.

"What is this—*The Godfather*?" I managed to say.

He spit in my face.

"You shut down your business this week, bitch. Or you won't have such a sense of humor. We'll go after your teenage lover."

I froze. I'd long stopped caring about my life, but I hadn't considered Elisheva.

"Give me a couple days, Hubb," I said. "Let me do it right. I'll shut it down. Completely. Just don't go near her."

"Deal," he smirked. And with one last, vicious kick, he and his friends took off.

I was badly beaten, but not worse than before, and I tried to get through the streets without stumbling. I found the doorbell I was looking for and practically fell on it. Finally, David came to his entrance and opened the door. He caught me and laid me down on one of his $10,000 couches.

"So you've finally come to visit," he said.

"Watch the blood," I mumbled. "It stains."

"I'm calling an ambulance," he said.

"No!" I shouted. "You can't. David, don't. That's why I came here. Don't you have some rich buyer who's secretly in love with you but also a doctor?"

"You're very chatty for someone who's at death's door," he replied, but seemed less panicked.

The shock wore off and I writhed in pain.

"Those sons of bitches," I moaned.

"Who? What sons of bitches?" David's voice sounded far away. They'd probably broken one of my eardrums.

"I'm calling the cops," David said.

"No, no, no," I yelled, or I thought I did. "Think. Think."

David held my hand until I heard his doorbell ring, and then I blacked out.

When I woke, a woman with very black hair and thick, large black glasses was looking down at me. I felt bandaged, taped, stitched, and stoned from some painkiller. Her expression was kind, but a little shaken.

"So, this is the criminal genius you're always talking about," she said. "She surely earned her reputation tonight."

I looked at her. "Thank you."

"I'm a gynecologist," she explained, "but we always fondly remember our internships in the ER. Nothing's broken. But you're bruised like hell, and someone cut your head badly enough for fourteen extremely clumsy stitches. You might have a cracked rib."

"Thank you," I said again, and fell back asleep.

An hour or so later I woke up in a panic. I was conscious enough to tell David the story in its entirety.

"Things like this don't really happen," he said in awe. "Why, darling, no wonder they're so many movies with the same plot lines. They're derived from actual reality. Essie, I've never seen tears. Those are actual tears."

"Elisheva," I remembered. "I can't screw another person in this lifetime. At least not a good one."

David clapped his hands together joyfully. I wasn't sharing his fun.

"I can't believe I'm doing this," he smiled. "But I actually have a solution. This is *so* Mario Puzo."

"David, calm yourself."

"No, seriously. Essie, listen—and shut up. I'm very famous in Russia these days. I think it's the new mixtures of browns in the backgrounds. But I have some major collectors."

"Russian mafia," I tried to laugh. "You're playing Clue. David, this is crazy serious."

"I'm telling you. They're rich, these men. So don't they all know each other somehow? Listen, I've wanted to help you so badly since all that's gone down . . . Let me make a few phone calls."

I was in deep despair by now. Scared for Elisheva. I had no hope. David had no sense of reality. Old suicidal images were blowing past me like dark dust storms. But what was far worse was the image of Elisheva's face. She deserved freedom. My life was a black train and every track led to a worse connection. Elisheva had done nothing but play a business game with me.

I must've been moaning and hallucinating for quite a while.

I was in bed. David sat at the edge of it. He seemed very serious and a little scared.

"I think I've taken care of it," he said. "I'm frightened and just a bit titillated."

"Don't have anyone killed, if this is really you, not just playing Sherlock Holmes. Please. Enough death."

"No, it's not worth it," he said. "I said exactly the same thing. We bartered. Yossi and I have been haggling over the commission for this massive canvas for his dining room wall. He said he'd find a way to scare them so badly you'd never see or hear of them ever again. And he said no violence, no revenge. Just relocation. Your Hubb has been given the finances to start a new drug dealing and dog walking cover in Philadelphia where business is thriving. However, if he comes near you or your Elisheva—instant execution. I trust Yossi. You're safe. The word, shall we say, is *out*."

"Shut up," I groaned. "You're enjoying this way too much."

"I lowered the commission," David added, "but not by much. Some gangsters have a strange sense of honor. Yossi owns three Rhodesian ridgebacks and a miniature dachshund and makes borscht to die for."

ANDROCLES

"Whatcha name him?" asked Phyllis Gelb. It was Phyllis's first visit since she'd given me the puppy.

"Androcles," I answered immediately. I didn't know why, the name just came to me. But there he was. Phyllis Gelb was confused.

"Oh, that might make it difficult to make urgent commands. We usually recommend two syllables or less."

He was Androcles to me and would be no other, but to please my earnest mentor I said, "Okay, how about Buff?"

She happily clapped her hands together and said, "Right on—absolutely right on. He'll be strong and quick like on those infomercials on the E! channel. They have all those machines. You pull, you twist, you straighten your legs out, you pull 'em in. You do some ab stuff and some butt stuff. And they always say, 'You get buff!' Do you think the men shave their chests?"

"Wax them. Definitely wax them."

"Ouch," whined Phyllis Gelb. She breathed out a long sigh. "Now, Carleen, if I may call you so," she spoke sternly. "Don't train Buff with too many snacks. It disconnects them, and they'll do their commands for the wrong reasons. Buff will be a working dog. He has to learn his job because that's what he does. Is that clear?"

"Absolutely," I said. Meanwhile, Androcles had put his head in my armpit.

"He likes your smell," she said proudly. "I just knew you were made for this, Carleen, and, believe me, I've trained over a hundred people for this over the years."

I believed her.

Phyllis Gelb hefted her considerable weight onto thick, wobbly legs. I'd felt secure in her noisy presence. The space and silence she'd leave behind made me anxious.

"You're leaving?" I tried to sound buddy-buddy to disguise the nerves. "Don't you have more you want me to know?"

She smiled. I noticed she had beautiful teeth.

She tapped them.

"You just read my book page by page. Be as patient as Mother Teresa, and you'll be fine. I'll be back in a month."

A whole month.

"I made Sister Jean and that mannish woman—"

"Sam," I reminded her.

"Sam," she said distastefully. "Anyway, I told them to give you special phone privileges so you can call me day or night."

I prayed she wasn't going to hug me. What if she picked up right away on my resistance to being touched? Then she'd take Androcles away. But she held out her hand and tried to avert her eyes from the scars and bumps all over mine.

"It's going to be beyond fine," she said.

Later that day I lifted Androcles out of the crate and carried him to the grass. He peed instantly. I was supposed to cheer him with glee to show what a good dog he was, but cheering wasn't exactly my style, so I leaned down next to him and whispered, "Righteous Androcles. Righteous hero." He got the idea and licked my nose. We stayed outside another ten minutes or so, enough for me to have a cigarette and see if anything else was coming. Phyllis Gelb's book said that, with guide dogs, it was important to teach them when they should go on a regular schedule and not wait for them to ask. But the bowel movement wasn't happening, so we went inside.

According to the book, if you bring a service dog up right, the first months are as exhausting as having an infant. When we got inside he shit on the floor. No punishment. I just said, "Wrongo, boy, not the behavior of a future service dog." He tipped his head to one side, but didn't wag his tail.

I took him out every three hours with varying degrees of success. I was outside so much a woman named Flax walked past me and said, "You gonna get skin cancer, girl." But she never said hello to the dog. Amanda, who had town shopping privileges, brought me back these special plastic bags in bright blue made especially for picking up dog shit. They were much better than toilet paper.

"Just wash your hands all the time," she warned me. "You wash them so much you be like those crazy folks with that thing Jack Nicholson had in that movie with Helen Hunt. I don't want to get no tapeworm from your door handle."

Phyllis Gelb's book said to play with the dog all the time. And when you played, you also taught obedience. I didn't like the idea of teaching anybody or anything obedience, so I faked it. He had this rubber ball that was his favorite toy. I'd roll it around on the floor and he'd swat at it with his enormous paws. I could watch him forever. Now and then he'd catch it in his mouth and I'd say, "Righteous Androcles, righteous hero." He didn't quite get what he'd gotten right, but enjoyed what he'd come to recognize as my pleasure. I told him that he was going to have to learn some stuff so the big lady would let me keep him. I talked to him a lot, which soothed us both.

"I guess dogs have to learn all this shit," I said, "because of the A dog B dog principle. One of us is boss. I ask you to do things for me and vice versa, but neither of us has to make a power trip out of it because it's really stupid stuff—way below what the righteous Androcles can do." So I taught him to sit, lie down, stay, come, fetch—the usual repertoire—and I tried to do the same for him. He didn't have the words I did, so when he wanted me to sit he'd tap his paw on the ground. I always told him, "Righteous Androcles, righteous hero," when he did a command correctly. He'd lick my face when I obeyed him. We got home training down in about two weeks and basic institutional-type commands in a month. We were both sitting, lying down, staying, coming when called, and the rest of it so quickly it got a little boring.

The only obstacle was how to get him to do similar commands to two different names. Then I realized that when he was Androcles, he was mine and when he was Buff, he was the temporary property of others. So before I'd call him Buff, I'd just whisper "showtime" in his ear. He liked performing. His growing body would go into this alert, straight position, and I could see he was just ready for tap shoes and a top hat. It was a strict rule that he sleep in his crate, but he soon learned to open the contraption and get into bed with me. We had to negotiate this point, so I took the crate apart and made it more of a fence. When he was Androcles I let him sleep with me, but when he was Buff I crawled on the floor and slept next to him on the stinky linoleum. After a time I left him alone half the night, then three quarters, then the whole night. Neither of us found this situation terrifically comfortable, but I knew he'd have to do the crate trick sooner or later, and I didn't want him crying or barking when he was left alone.

He was more a physical dog than a noisy one. He didn't whine, cry, or bark much, and when he did I'd tell him he really didn't have a very pleasant voice and to keep it down or my sisters would get me kicked out of the compound. I explained to him that they were animals like me that had bratty, gruff personalities.

Whenever we had these talks, we'd sit across from each other, and I'd teach him commands like "shush," "keep it down," and "lower the volume, please." Over time he got the idea. In the beginning Flax would shout, "Shut that animal up!" and Androcles would bark back at her in the exact same rhythm and then shut up. He had a remarkable ear. One of his favorite pastimes was to go to Amanda's cottage and listen to her play the viola. He'd lay his head on her feet so he could feel the vibrations. Once in a while he'd grab the bow in his mouth and try to chew it. I lost considerable money buying new bows. Then we figured out we'd give him his own bow. We took out one of the ones he hadn't completely destroyed, I restrung it, and Amanda taught him to pull it across the strings. It produced a squeaky, cavity-hurting, nasal sound. The *squannch* scared him so much he stayed away after that.

He knew Flax and Midge hated him. Dog cops had sniffed Flax out at a crack house and she was cornered by three German shepherds. It was terror transformed into hostility. Androcles always let her pass and gave her lots of room, but one day she'd either done badly on a physics exam or maybe it was another visiting day and she, like me, had zero visitors. She was in a foul state of mind and deliberately kicked him in a hallway. I lunged at her and held her down and slapped her over and over again across her face until her nose began to bleed. Androcles sat up very straight and did his best to bare his teeth, though they hadn't fully grown in yet. Flax and I got pulled apart and I was sent to solitary. I told the guard that the rules were that Buff and I were not to be separated. So the growing puppy and I spent a week in a small cell with a hole for a toilet and an iron cot.

Androcles's height preceded his coordination. When we were reinstalled in our room, it was too small for a tall, big-boned woman and a growing Labrador-poodle-setter mix with long legs and huge feet. I knew Phyllis would be disappointed, but I got rid of the crate. Instead, I dug though the trash and found an ugly but usable square of rug. I washed and vacuumed it thoroughly and laid it out in the corner of my room. When Androcles curled up on it to sleep, he fit perfectly, but he didn't like it because I wouldn't join him. Buff had to sleep there when I said so, and Androcles could sleep on the bed as a treat after an especially vigorous day.

When Phyllis arrived for my evaluation I was nervous. I wanted to please her, and resented it. Androcles was as casual as he could be. I was certain that all Phyllis lived for was the dogs, and she was not going to be lenient if I fucked up.

Phyllis wobbled toward me, and this time she did hug me. A wave of blackness went through me like I was going to faint. I didn't get the urge to throw up again at least. Maybe it was a sign I was getting used to Phyllis. Androcles sat obediently beside me during the greeting. I'd whispered "showtime" just as she was heading over.

"Well, look at Buff. What a gentleman he is already. I'm telling you, Carleen—he's going to be *hu-mon-gous*."

He sat like a soldier as she squatted down and went over his body with her hands. It reminded me of the Westminster Kennel Club Dog Shows you'd catch on TV before immediately turning them off. I always wondered what those judges were feeling for anyway. What did it have to do with winning or losing?

"He's filling out terrific," she said. "I think he's definitely one of those chic breeding experiments. Everything for a buck, right? But sure makes him a stud. He is a beautiful creature." I looked down at Androcles, and he was sitting as straight as a china doll. He liked the compliments. And he liked Phyllis, too.

Phyllis became businesslike, yanked herself up, and said, "May I see you do your commands now, Carleen—as far as you've gone? But first, is he house trained?"

"Completely."

"Fine," she said. "Now proceed."

"Showtime," I whispered again. I hoped she didn't hear. Buff lay prone as I told him to. He sat. He offered a paw. We walked a complete circle together. He came as called. Walked toward me with civility. Ran with athleticism. Stopped dead on command. Rolled over on his back. Walked gently toward Phyllis and sat beside her staring straight ahead. Phyllis was checking boxes on a form and watching straight-faced and studiously. I called him back and he lay at my feet.

"You may release him," Phyllis said.

"Righteous Androcles, righteous hero," I mumbled under my breath, and he leaped up as if he were a dolphin careening out of a pool. He darted around the space and raced through my legs. I took out his ball, and he did his best to retrieve it, though for some reason he'd gotten it into his head that he could catch it with his paws. He missed and rolled over. Panting, he zoomed over to me, and I scratched him behind his ears and on his neck as objectively as I possibly could. I let him drink from his water bowl, and had a notion of what was coming next.

"Now, if I may take him through his commands," Phyllis said.

"Showtime," I whispered again, pretending to fix his collar.

Phyllis worked with him for quite a while, calling him Buff

the whole time. I could see her skill and ease, and she was very strict in a sweet way. She did commands in changing orders and held him longer in positions. She praised him after every correct action and corrected certain positions when he sat and lay down. I watched and realized he was a handsome dog. He might even grow to be uniquely stunning. He had his own stripes of reds and browns. He'd have great posture, but not at all elegant and prissy.

"Go to Carleen," I heard Phyllis say, and obliging, but a little too eagerly, he headed in my direction. "You can release him," she said.

I knelt down as if to pat and scratch him and whispered, "Righteous Androcles, righteous hero—but chill." He licked my face, stood up, shook himself out, and his tail went bat-shit. He pranced up to Phyllis and rubbed against her, and the woman plopped herself down and sat with him, put her arms around his neck, tickled his ears, rolled with him, laughed, and pulled a strip of something that looked like beef jerky from her pocket and fed it to him bit by bit. Androcles was stoned. I'd never given him a treat before.

"Now you sit, Buff, and let your Aunt Phyllis get herself up."

I held my breath, but Androcles sat attentively, still in won-der from the treat.

"I might need a crane," she joked to me.

I took her arms and, like a Russian Olympic weight lifter, I pulled her to her feet. We both almost lost our balance, and Androcles, who'd been watching this Three Stooges event, let out two barks praising us both for our hard work. I knew I should quit anthropomorphizing him, but he often surprised me with his instincts.

I led Phyllis to a bench nearby, worried about what was next. Androcles followed behind, carefree.

"No, sweetie," Phyllis started. "He must always lead." She

snapped her fingers a certain way and made some clicking sounds, and Androcles immediately picked up his speed and walked just about two paces ahead of us. I was impressed with this woman. I had cheated her as I cheated everyone else, but she was still the boss.

We sat on the bench quietly and then she spoke.

"What is that whispering you do with him?" she asked.

The pathological liar slipped right into place.

"It's just a signal I give him to let him know we mean business. Just sounds."

"Well, some day you'll have to teach that to his future owner, you know. Can't be any secrets between you and him that his family won't be privy to. It'll confuse the training."

"Absolutely," I said. "I'm sorry."

"*Sorry?*" Phyllis practically yelled. "Sorry?" She slapped my thigh. "This is the best-trained, most well-adjusted puppy I've ever seen. You're a natural, Carleen. I'm damn impressed. Beyond impressed. I'm dreamy."

"Thanks," I said.

"You got to keep drilling and drilling and drilling. No slacking off because he's doing good. These fellas ain't lazy or bad intentioned, but sneaky habits set in when they're young and then you could lose his absolute respect and priority of mind to be a hard worker. I'll be back in six weeks to check where you are on agility and socialization."

I had to test out Phyllis on the subject of socialization.

"I'd like to speak to you confidentially," I said.

Phyllis sat up like a midwestern housewife watching a reality show.

"Cross my heart," she said. "Or whatever."

"Agility will be no problem once he grows a little more into his body. I'm also good at building, so I can fashion the course from your book exactly. No problem. It's the socialization I'm concerned about."

Phyllis was intrigued. "I don't see any signs of aggression. In fact, he has a happy-go-lucky nature and—what do you call it—his stillness, well, it's almost Zen. Am I missing something? Is there a nervosity or fear reaction?"

"No," I said. "The problem's not him. It's the environment. I don't know how I can socialize him with other dogs when there are no other dogs here. And I don't know how I'm going to get him to work in a basically hostile environment. I was wondering if you could ask the warden if I could take him to an obedience class once a week to meet other puppies and walk him around the town so he gets used to less agitated people."

Phyllis had been listening intently. "Well, I hadn't honestly taken this into consideration so it's both our problem. I have a meeting with the warden to tell her of your progress, so you sit here and let me see what I can negotiate."

I watched her walk off toward the main building. I was apprehensive and wondered if I was making too big a deal about it. I knew part of it was the criminal trying to get a pass to the outside. Androcles put his head on my lap and we waited for our verdict.

An hour later Phyllis Gelb came out of the warden's office and seemed to be having a hard time making the distance to the bench. "Showtime, Buff," I said, and he lay in the proper position at my feet. Phyllis finally plopped down and took a deep breath.

"The news isn't good, but it's not the end of the world either. First of all, your warden congratulates you on a job well done and is pleased you'll be able to continue. She might have even smiled. But she said you are a prisoner who could have absolutely no privileges to leave the penitentiary. You are never to leave the premises. Wowie zowie. But she came up with several solutions. She said she would authorize a daily program where Buff could work with different groups of your choosing, and he would learn about normal people just fine." *Normal?* I wanted to scream in the realm between laughter and terror. "She said Buff could eat meals in the cafeteria under your strict supervision, go to classes, and partake in all activities. She and I agreed that if there was some unwarranted resistance from time to time, that as long as you kept your cool it could possibly be good for Buff and prepare him for future unpleasantries. It could determine the neighborhood or type of owner with which we place him, and that's fine.

"The puppy problem wasn't so easy. There's lots of workers who have dogs, and we'll have to set up special weekly sessions. One of the authorities will determine when and where these socializations will take place. Since no other prisoners have a dog, the prison will contact the staff and relatives of the staff to volunteer and bring their dogs to an enclosed area. You will then see if Buff is aggressive or timid with other dogs and if he is obedient around distraction. Next visit I personally will take him into town to begin street and sidewalk training."

There was a silence.

"Wow," she shook her head. "You must have done something awful bad not to be allowed a breath of fresh air. Or they must be doing something real bad to you girls."

I patted Phyllis Gelb's thigh.

"Both," I said.

I concentrated on building a simple agility course that I'd expand in difficulty as Androcles got older. It consisted of low hurdles, tubes to crawl through, a slide, a hoop, a bunch of stairs going up one side and down the other, and a simple maze.

Agility was not his strong point. Whereas when he ran free he was astonishingly like a deer or TV pictures I'd seen of tigers or antelopes, his tricks were earnest but clumsy. I took him through each section of the course separately, showing him how to do it myself. Anyone who walked by laughed at me, but I figured if I did it he'd do it.

We both made our way through the course, gradually but not brilliantly. Then I realized what was wrong. This was the most boring, unchallenging agility course a person could put together. I kept it up so Buff could use it with Phyllis, but in another location I designed my own Olympic Coney Island that was much more up to Androcles's speed. He was a klutz, but was having a blast, so he learned faster. I designed treadmills and turnstiles and ditches and limbo bars and revolving wheels. I made cages to open and close, long running tracks with borders on each side, difficult-size windows to jump through, and whatever I could get my hands on kept adding devices as they came to me, and Androcles got better and better at the jumps, leaps, rolls, and crawling. We'd warm up on his private agility carnival and then walk over to the course that followed Phyllis's exact blueprint. He became more coordinated and was able to execute the more simple angles and heights.

Socialization started with my own honors coven. We met in our tiny recreation cottage, and these women, aside from Flax and Midge, couldn't wait to get their hands on him. His hair was soft like a baby poodle, and Amanda put her big, fat arms around him and drew him to her bosom. Androcles softened, wagged his tail, and licked her without jumping all over her. Midge, to my surprise, at one point rolled around on the floor with him wrestling. Each woman had her turn petting him and holding him, and I saw that each member of the coven was hungry for a baby. A baby they'd left back home or never had a chance to have. Androcles always returned to me, put his paw on my knee, and then leaped up and licked me. Flax sometimes stood in the doorway with her arms folded and a disgusted look on her face. Mostly she didn't show up at all.

I asked to have a large table at the far end of the cafeteria, and when I brought Androcles in for my first breakfast, there was almost a riot.

"Don't you bring an animal in here."

"My family's starving. You gonna feed him our own food?"

"He's filth, he'll contaminate the food."

"Fleas, bugs, worms!"

"I think he's sweet. C'mere, poochie."

"Who said he could be here? He could go wild."

"He's gonna bite."

"Call the guards."

"Throw Carleen and her twin outta here."

A couple guards stood by the table and Buff took a "stay" position and didn't move. He was shaking a little. He'd never encountered so much hostility. I kept him in position and went up in line to get my food. A few women tried to push me, and the cook refused to serve me. Finally I reached over the counter and grabbed some eggs and bacon for myself. "Demerits," hissed one of the servers. "You can be sure you'll get demerits."

"So will you, bitch," I said. "You can't refuse to serve me."

"I can when you bring filth into the cafeteria with you," she shouted back. I almost threw my steaming eggs in her face, but I didn't want to spend more time with Androcles in solitary. He needed fresh air and light.

I got back to the table and Androcles was still shaking rather badly. "Easy," I whispered gently. I'd never used that word as a command before. But there would probably be situations like this where Buff would be sorely tested. I took off my shoe and rubbed his neck with my foot, being careful not to use my hands with so many phobic prisoners looking out for bugs and fleas. Androcles licked my foot and rested his head on it and he calmed down. Five women came over to the table to sit with me. I recognized one from the pants factory and four from the fields.

"He don't beg," said a woman with a shaved head and a tattoo of a bull's-eye on her scalp. She had on overalls and had grubby hands. "That's a virtue." I remembered her name was Teresa, a gentle name for such a tough-looking woman. "I had a hound—we hunted birds together. Great beast. But at the table he'd walk around as if we were starving him."

"Buff's not allowed to eat human food. Strict rules."

"He's a convict like us," said an uptight woman at the edge of the table. She was showing her sisters somewhere in the room that she was brave, but still shook when Androcles made any move whatsoever.

There was a slender woman who worked in the gardens. I think her name was Tashi, but she reminded me of Marcella Histrionics. I tried to glance casually at her plate. She'd finished her eggs, so I relaxed. I saw, however, that her eyes were pitch-black, and I realized she was stoned into dreams with quaaludes and barbiturates.

"Can I touch him?" she asked slowly.

"Buff, up," I ordered. He stood, immediately joyous to be released from lying down. The ten or so women who'd joined the table all twitched or jumped.

"It's all right," I said, to the dog and the table.

"That's Tashi—go to her," I instructed.

He loped slowly in the direction I pointed and sat down next to Tashi. She held out her hand above his head.

"Go ahead," I told her.

She stroked him timidly, and then with more courage. He wagged his tail.

"He's a sucker for a touch." I smiled.

Then she put her arms around him, and he burrowed his head into her hair and behind her ears.

"He's my teddy bear," she shouted. Longings for childhood dolls or stuffed animals or soft-haired babies must've opened up in the women because they started asking almost all at once if they could hug him and touch him. Phyllis Gelb's book said that the dog couldn't go up to anyone without permission. So Androcles went from woman to woman when I gave permission, and I could see how he filled in a physical gap I'd never thought about. Not that the women didn't have sex. They had visitors, were lesbians, or forced into being lesbians. But it was a much more childlike need. He and I were in constant physical contact during training, so he probably filled a void without me knowing it.

After a few weeks different women would visit my table, and one day I made the leap of having Androcles stand in line with me. When the cooks saw he didn't jump up and grab food, they calmed down too. Word got passed around the prison, and though there were still angry words and unsettling groans, Androcles and I ended up being accepted or at least tolerated as we entered and exited more and more classrooms, recreation areas, and cells.

When the time came for Androcles to socialize with the other dogs, the workers and guards, confused and annoyed, showed up at the appointed time. There were dirty squares of grass near the staff parking lot. A wide variety of men with dogs showed up, but the majority of their pets were guard dogs, a lot of pit bulls, shepherds, Dobermans, and large mutts. The owners had been told what the meeting was for, but they didn't really understand at all and used the occasion to have a few beers and laugh at me. A young guard with a baton had been sent along to make sure I wouldn't make this an excuse to run off.

By the book, Buff was to be instructed not to approach a dog on his own, and to be friendly and accepting when a dog came by, but not to initiate play. The guard dogs were also well disciplined, but little by little they sniffed Buff and formed a small pack and began to roughhouse with each other. At a certain point I said, "Release," and Androcles joined in with the roughhousing. He got along much better with the mutts with whom he chased and tumbled. Then he made the mistake of approaching the guard gang and got humped by a Doberman and snapped at by a particularly quick-moving German shepherd. But I didn't realize how fast Androcles the Hero was, and he got away from the aggressive dogs easily. He zoomed to my side the second I called him and lay down.

"Not bad," said one of the men. He had a crew cut, plaid shirt, and potbelly. I think he owned a fairly mellow pit bull. He stood next to a younger guy, dressed similarly, but with a strong upper body and long dark sideburns. He had a white shepherd on a chain leash who seemed ill tempered and restless. The others were gathered around their trucks and cars, dealing with their dogs, and getting ready to go.

"Are you as well trained as your puff puff?" asked the guy with the pit bull.

I didn't say anything.

"Yeah, it looks like your puff will do whatever you tell it to," said the smaller man.

"The bitch ain't the expressive type," snickered the other. "She needs to be trained slow, more passion. Has to listen to commands."

"I like that type," smirked the small one. "And I know a lot of commands."

Now the other men started getting interested. It was obvious they'd drunk a lot of beer.

I could feel my guard tensing up.

"Has your puppy had his balls cut off yet?" asked another man. He was tall and wearing an undershirt and baseball cap.

"I bet he has," grunted the fat man. "She looks like one of those lady murderers who cut her hubby's penis off."

"Naw, she ain't never seen a cock," the little guy chimed in. "She's a dyke. Wishes she had one."

A very big drunk guy in jeans and a jacket roared with laughter for no reason I could tell.

I sank inside myself, ready for whatever was next, when I heard an ear-splitting whistle. Everything stopped. It had come from the woman guard. She was medium sized, black, and appeared fearless. She held up a can and showed it to the stumbling, confused men.

"You know what this is, cocksuckers?" she yelled. "This is pepper spray. You know how it burns, assholes? It burns like little tacks and coals and stingrays all over your body. It can blind you for days. So back up on the count of three, babies, or I'm gonna start spraying like you're mosquitoes."

She counted off, and though the men spit at her and pretended to take their time, none of them tried to hit her or come closer. My male guard had his baton halfheartedly in the air, but he was the type who would easily sympathize with the men and let happen whatever they had in mind. He was the type who'd be raping newbies or crazy women in solitary.

When the last of the vehicles had taken off, I said to the female guard, "You saved me and I won't forget it. I wish I had something to give you."

"Can I play with your dog?" she asked. "I know he's being trained for the blind and all . . . "

Androcles had been panting with agitation, and so when I said, "Release, Androcles," he jumped up and put his legs on my shoulders in a hug. "She saved me," I said to him. "Kiss." He jumped up and gave the guard a similar hug and then did his dashing, bounding, and leaping routine to let off the tension. "Come play," I shouted. He bounded back, and he and the guard wrestled and chased and tumbled. She played tug-of-war with her glove, and the two of them kept going until the guard was out of energy.

As we walked back to my cottage, my lackluster male guard trailing a few feet behind, she said, "I have a Maltese, but I've been thinking about getting a bigger dog too. What breed is this one?"

"No breed," I replied. "Just a fancy mutt."

"Yeah, I've been thinking about a rescue," she continued. "But I spend so much time around, well . . . "

"Damaged goods," I looked over at her. "You want something without scars or a temper or craziness."

"Well, yeah," she was embarrassed. "Sorry."

"I don't blame you," I replied.

The male guard snorted. "Damaged goods ain't the half of it."

"Good morning, Buddy," said the woman guard, turning to face him. "And thanks for all your help back there."

"Whole thing's stupid," he grumbled. "This place is 'sposed to be a prison. You know, lock up murderers? Not make us a petting zoo. You're all fuckin' nuts."

He trailed off in another direction.

"I hate this place," she muttered. "Guards as evil as the inmates. They got so much drug business goin' on back and forth you'd think it was South America. Everybody's got somethin' on everyone else, too. Blackmail city."

I didn't ask her about herself. We reached my cottage.

"Made it out alive," she smirked. "Next time we get some of them rich, bored housewives and their dogs with bows on their butts."

"Listen," I looked her in the eye. "You saved me. Thanks. You did. You saved me."

"Nice to do the job for once," she said.

She headed toward the main house to make her report. Then she turned around to look at Androcles.

"You give me a kiss," she said.

"Go," I whispered.

Androcles ran up to her and nearly knocked her over. He licked her face and put his nose on her neck. She laughed, got up, and headed out.

"I think he's a person," she smiled at me.

I realized I didn't know her name. I guessed she didn't want me to. She probably knew mine. That night Androcles slept in my bed.

It was months and some seasons later when, after visits and tests, one day Phyllis just showed up. I saw her pull up in a van, which was odd. Androcles was massacring a stuffed rabbit Phyllis had bought him that played a squeaky outer-space version of "America the Beautiful" until he destroyed the little music box inside. Thank God. Phyllis called it imaginary aggression and said it was fine for this dog, who had one of the best temperaments she'd come across.

We went out to our bench. I don't remember if it was cold or hot. I was uncomfortable. My body felt bigger than itself and ached. "Down," I said to Androcles. "Down, Buff." He lay in front of me, but put his head on my feet.

"You know better than that," I said to him.

"Let it be," Phyllis said. She was trying to get comfortable on the bench, but she was trying to settle another discomfort as well.

"We all have our instincts," Phyllis sighed. "Buff's leaving today. He's more than ready to go join us at the school for guide dogs. It'll be another eight to ten months for training, and then I'll match him with his owner. I don't give my puppy trainers advance notice because a lot of good work can get undone in two days of sentimentality, just letting the dog become a pet because you're sad."

"Sad," I said emptily.

"I hope you'll forgive me, but I have one of my workers clearing out his stuff from your cottage. We take it for the first period of adjustment to the new place, and then, when he's settled, we start him in an entirely alien environment. These creatures have to learn to adjust to changes very fast. The only constant can be none."

"Yes, you've told me that," I said.

"Now Carleen, darling—I have a question and you must answer honestly. What is the other name you use for Buff? For the forbidden 'pet' relationship. I've known all along he has one name for you and Buff for everyone else. We can't take him further if we don't know every cheat and tiny bending of the rules."

I was genuinely shocked that she'd figured this out, and it relieved me a bit to admire her professional side again.

"Androcles." I looked down at him.

"You wanted to name him that first off," she remembered. "What's it mean?"

I told her as best I could about the lion and the thorn and the paw.

"I do love those ancient fairy tales," she said. "I wish I was better educated."

I wished I knew nothing.

"So, did he pull the thorn from your paw?"

"Don't know," I mumbled. I didn't want to talk anymore. "It's in pretty deep and there may be more than one."

"Like I said, you've done a hell of a job." Phyllis couldn't look at me. "I'm going to suggest to the warden that we set up a regular puppy school here. You'd run it. Show me the agility track—the one you invented."

I took her to my secret park, and she took a maddeningly long time examining my jumps and turns and tunnels. She whistled.

"And he can do all this?"

"Flawlessly," I answered.

"I'm going to take some of the ideas if you don't mind."

"Could you go now?" I asked. I saw her van in the distance.

"He's gonna walk to my van with me and he's not allowed to look behind. So say your goodbyes now."

"We don't have hellos and goodbyes," I said. "Just go."

She grunted and picked a harness out of her pocket. It reminded me of the type ancient slaves wore in pictures in history books when they carried rocks on their backs. He sat in his military position as she expertly snapped the halter on him.

"You'll be hearing from me. You have a gift. We'll see if we can get that warden to set up something."

"One way or another," I said.

I watched her lead Androcles toward the van, and he turned

his head and stared at me for a long time, but Phyllis didn't seem to notice.

"Phyllis," I called out. "Phyllis Gelb." She stopped. My shouting shook her up a bit.

"He broke training," I said so she could hear. "He turned around. He looked at me. That's not the proper conduct. You have to start again."

Breathing a bit hard, she brought him back to exactly where I was standing.

"Go again," I said to Buff. "You know what you did. Do it like you're supposed to."

He lay down and Phyllis did some of her own sounds and harsh commands. This time Androcles walked properly by her side and made no effort to turn around.

I headed back to my cottage before I could see her load him into the van. I don't remember what I was wearing, but I didn't take it off. My room was cleared of the rug, the dish, and his rabbit. I got into bed with my clothes on—maybe even my coat. I fell into a thick gray sleep. When I woke up I had no will to even sit up. I pulled the covers tighter over my head. For the next week, ten days, or two weeks, who knows, I stayed that way. I only got up to go to the bathroom, and that moment alone was so sickening and exhausting that I was propelled by a deep terror to get back into bed immediately. I had closed myself in so I wasn't surprised, and I didn't care, when I heard the guard breaking through my lock with his gun.

I stank. I felt the familiar shackles around my arms and legs. The mumbling and crying and whispering of the psych ward was memorized music. I knew when they were wheeling me toward ECT. Nothing helped. I had no longings, no fights. It would have been convenient to build up the energy to attempt suicide, but I appreciated being invisible and didn't want to draw attention to myself. The female guards finally forced me into a shower and, when I washed myself, my skin felt like it was wailing. I asked them to cut off all my hair since brushing was unbearably painful.

I squatted on my bed and held my knees to my chest. I rocked back and forth, the autistic savant they always thought I was. The rest of the time I slept.

Sister Jean came to visit once or twice but I had nothing to say to her.

"You're grieving," she said. "And because you're Carleen Kepper, your insides are acting out a Cecil B. DeMille movie. You're very dry on the outside, Carleen, but you have monsoons and tsunamis that crest up inside and take over. Stop now, or sooner or later we won't be able to pull you out."

I didn't know what she was talking about, and I thought the poetry was trite. I just wanted to sleep. I didn't have any inner dialogue. It was almost silent inside. I was a stone.

Phyllis Gelb was brave enough to visit me. She glanced around as if she were in a pen of dogs way past trainable. Her hands trembled.

"We'll go to my bed," I managed to say, and she wheeled me into the dorm, which wasn't much better, but at least you could pull a circular plastic curtain around the bed, which allowed a bit of privacy and kept out the noise. I stayed in the wheelchair—I was chained—and she sat on my bed. I wouldn't look at her.

"Wow, you've really lost it," Phyllis said in wonder. "But you'll come back. We always do. Oh yes, Carleen, do you think a woman can look like this and not suffer constant humiliation? But you'll bounce back."

She didn't know me.

"Do you want to hear about Buff?" she asked casually.

I tried to yank myself from my wheelchair and go for her. She pulled out a little pink gun from her cleavage and aimed it at me.

"They didn't check deep enough," she said. "I thought I might need this. They said you had moments of aggressive behavior."

"Pink." I was amused.

"Yes, my husband bought it for me for my birthday. I think it's adorable. But don't think it doesn't hit dead on at target practice."

For the first time I really looked at her.

"Yes, there's a lot you don't know about me and vice versa, Carleen. We're complicated women both locked in prisons. Part of why you're here is my fault, you know," she said. "I didn't prepare you thoroughly enough for the loss you'd feel when we took Buff. If you break the rule and fall too much in love, it's like a death. You fooled me. I thought you'd figured that one out. I didn't take into account that you're a lunatic."

I smiled. Then I held back screams or sobs or whatever were being let loose in my throat.

"I had a long talk with Sister Jean and the warden. You're the best damn trainer I've ever laid eyes on. Your basic skills are A+. I think it's 'cause, aside from Buff, you have a kind of distant passion. You don't get caught up with humans. You don't need them very much. Also, Carleen, because of whatever is in your head, repetition soothes you. You can go for hours. I read something somewhere that repetition is what they call Zen. It gives you faith. Maybe your life, like mine, has had its disasters. But you can really take pleasure, real pleasure, out of small technical accomplishments. We thought when you get outta the hospital that I'd bring up two dogs, ones with great potential, but troublemakers. You'll get a bigger space and you'll start over."

"Never," I muttered.

"Bullshit," Phyllis shot back. "Here's what else we've got planned. Sister Jean, the warden, that Sam woman, and the board will choose a group of ten women and we're going to train them to raise puppies. Then I'll interview the women, and if I like 'em I'll match them both with a puppy."

"Good luck."

"You'd be surprised about human nature. Our best trainers are certified nutcases, but real kind and a lot more interesting than menopausal socialites."

"Well, well, well," I snickered. "I never took you for a bitch."

Phyllis leaned closer to me. I thought for sure the springs would break.

"My first dog they took from me. Afterward I quit. Just quit. But what brings you back is not praising yourself for the good you did. The truth is, honey, what else is there to do? You could die. I guess. So go ahead. But training dogs beats the hell out of a factory life or a coal mine and you're cooped up here for—"

The ice and quiet began to take over again.

"It's the preferred way to live out this friggin' life. Right, Carleen Kepper? And they want you to teach the women how to train the dogs."

"I don't teach," I grumbled quickly. "I won't teach."

"Why?"

I didn't answer. I couldn't say that it was too much contact with too many people. And that I didn't have enough words. I'd run out of them.

"I won't raise police dogs," I said suddenly.

"You'll raise whoever the hell I order you to," Phyllis retorted lightly.

She couldn't get off the bed by herself and I was shackled and helpless. I called and a couple nurses lugged her up.

"I'm gonna have that operation and get as skinny as you," Phyllis huffed. "And you're gonna stop the fruitcake routine and train me an army of dogs unlike any other. You hear that? You don't want to live in the godforsaken Day of the Dead zombie hotel, which is where they'll keep you by the way. I just blabbed my head off telling 'em stories about people who gave up their first dogs. Made people more insane than you, if that's possible."

"Thank you, Phyllis Gelb," I said as she started to leave.

"I want you to give it a go," she answered.

"I'll think about it," I looked at her.

"You don't think," Phyllis said, "you just do."

I did as she told me to. And during the remaining years, we made a school for training dogs, and most of the inmates pulled it off fine. We worked every day, no days off, and I did well, though I don't remember any of my students' names. I only ended up in solitary two times and the hospital twice more. I stayed in the motion of dogs, and I found a permanent boundary between my hellish impulses and what was good for animals.

I don't know how it came up that I got parole. There were crisscrossing stories, and I didn't care enough to try to untangle them. Part of it had to do with a group of liberal lawyer types who took it upon themselves to review what they called "cold cases." Work was devoted to murder convictions with insufficient proof, even though mine was an open-and-shut conviction. But somehow my record fell into some young, overexcited feminist's hands, and she researched every second of my life from high school through Clayton and got some sleepy judge to agree that, contrary to four life sentences, my trial had been an unjust circus show. I was underage, I'd been set up, I'd suffered cruel and unjust punishment, and, most of all, I was severely unstable and that hadn't been taken into account.

That little spitfire, who was just out of law school, did all of this without even meeting me, but she got my sentence reduced. My treatment in prison was also taken into account, with pictures and statements primarily from doctors at Powell and Clayton. This was also the time when Powell went under investigation. As all this was going on, a long ago billionaire collector of mine offered to contribute toward a full workout area and nutrition program at Clayton. And there was another story that *People* magazine was going to do a cover feature on the dog training camp, which I'd built up. We produced up to fifty dogs a year. I remember some reporters and photographers. Another magazine story featured my murals on the cover, calling them "masterpieces as locked up as the woman who painted them." Inside, a special foldout showed the walls and walls I'd painted during that psychotic six years. Which story was true? Did it matter? And then one day Jen Lee called me for a meeting and informed me that there was a possibility that in one years' time I might be released into the civilized population and I'd better watch my ass. She didn't look at me, played furiously with her swizzle sticks, and spoke tightly and quietly as if she didn't want to hear herself.

By the time parole happened (two years later? three?), no one seemed to have much of a problem, except they were worried about the dog school. By then it was a self-functioning institution connected to the National Association for the Blind with civilian supervisors and ten to twelve expert convict trainers, even a waiting list. Phyllis Gelb was president. She flew in regularly and no one fucked with her. No one had anything to worry about. I was a founding member, but it had grown so much bigger than me.

A MYRIAD OF TEMPTATIONS

Job placement was impossible. No small towns had programs and the larger cities, like Albany or Syracuse, wouldn't go near me. I couldn't work for Phyllis because I wasn't allowed out of state. Word was, sections of the population at Clayton were furious I'd been paroled and the administration was dealing with a lot of attitude problems. Finally, under bureaucratic pressures, Jen Lee came up with the halfway house and the exemplary Lucinda and Hubb. I think she was testing me as hard as she could. Sister Jean showed almost no confidence in me. If I turned out to be a repeater, then it proved I was hopeless and not some kind of misunderstood head case. She believed I had it good at Clayton and should live out my time there. She believed that outside Clayton I'd revert to my destructive habits: stealing, speed, and violence.

"New York will have a myriad of temptations," warned Sister Jean.

"I don't get tempted. It was about the voices and engines inside me that made me do things," I said.

"That's probably bullshit," she smirked. "But I'll give you the benefit of the doubt."

"They're gone now," I lied.

Sister Jean stared at me. "No, they're not. *If* they existed."

"They bore me. They're stupid. And I don't need that rush anymore," I said.

"That's more the truth," Jen Lee nodded in approval. "I think I believe that. That's why you'll have to live in a high-security halfway house."

"I know."

"Do you think you can learn to make some friends?" Sister Jean asked.

"When I learn what one is," I replied.

"You'll be vigilant about medication and probation."

"You know I'm the one who follows orders," I answered solemnly. "I've bought a notebook and made a list."

"And if you start to slip . . ."

"I have my probation officer, the name of a doctor, and your phone number."

We paused.

"You look worried," I noted.

"I'm always worried," said Sister Jean.

"Because I'll always be a criminal," I replied.

"No, because you have the fragments of a criminal, Carleen," Sister Jean explained. "And it's your choice whether to glue them together again or throw them away."

"Weak metaphor," I mumbled. She ignored me.

"So, we found a job for you in New York with ex-junkies. It's about as far from ideal as I'd want. The warden gave you the details. And you know I'm utterly against this."

She stood up abruptly and reached out her white, freckled hand to shake. I was frightened to touch her, to let go of her. Maybe jail was the only home I could handle.

"Get going, Carleen," Sister Jean said. I was released.

"Goodbye," I said, and walked out of her door. I didn't say thank you because I realized I didn't like the way she'd shown up when she decided it was right and was unavailable when I was in need. I felt a drift of anger about her so-called straight-forward way of helping me, with insults hidden in her advice. "People are complicated," she once said to me. "And no more so than you. In some ways you're scarier than a run-of-the-mill killer."

I tried to forgive her sarcasms and her complicity—in the painting of the birth house that nearly killed me, in my days in solitary and the psych ward, in the ECT, in the guards sneak-ing in and beating me and the others without reprimand. The unreported rapes. Instead, I tried to remember the hundreds of things that she'd said that had saved my sanity. But there was a sadistic coldness to her that prevented me from quoting her wise words in my head. I didn't say thank you because, in the end, I'm not sure she was a good person. Maybe she'd had an Androcles who had broken her heart.

On my way out, I took a route that went by the birthing house and family condos. The living conditions for visiting families had vastly improved but could so easily be taken away, too. Anything positive that got added to Clayton was to the advantage of the warden, Sister Jean, and other authorities, and was used as bait for improved behavior or as prizes denied because of the wrong attitude.

"Hey," I heard a voice that made me stand at attention and want to take off at the same time. It was Sam. She always man-aged to hurt me one way or another. I cringed. Her cold, blue eyes were coated with tears. "I can't believe you're getting to go and I'm stuck here," she said. "It really doesn't speak well of the justice system. But then you've always put on a good show."

"You'll be out soon," I said. "You've started all the programs. You practically educated every woman in the place."

Sam's hands became fists. She gave the loudest scream I'd

ever heard. She was a hurricane of rage. "IT SHOULD BE ME!" she yelled. She leaped at me and slapped me hard across the face. I did nothing. She slapped me again.

"You can kill me so I'm not able to leave," I told her, "but even in dying I'd be leaving. I'm leaving. You didn't win." She punched me in my chest and stomach. I caught her arms and twisted one behind her back. "You're nuts with jealousy," I grunted. "But you can't change it. Not with programs, lectures, book contracts, or honors power."

I walked away from her.

WHAT IS NORMAL?

David Sessions's loft had a winding staircase to another full loft above it. This top floor must've been four thousand square feet and held the canvases he was currently working on. His paintings were so large that I could feel and hear the colors he'd chosen for his backgrounds. They were a light blue with pink, like the edges of a dawn in a chemical city. I didn't know what he planned to paint on them, but he usually did large groups of people in different situations on the same canvas: Shopping at Target. Swimming with sharks. Race-car drivers. Meth manufacturers. Ballet recitals. There had to be close to a hundred activities going on in each painting. And the detail was stunning, and ranged from realist to bombastic cartoon. In fact, our styles had often been compared. His canvases could at first seem like collages, but after a while a person who examined the painting could see the disparate pieces were oddly and inextricably connected. Were these people related? Was this a town? Was the whole scene being watched through a telescope? It was his mystery. His damning incoherence became one solid, beautiful world. In this way, he was truly a master and I couldn't touch him

Behind David's canvases were three offices. One for Rosita Perlman, his dealer and manager, one for himself, and a third office that his last lover, a nineteen-year-old video-game designer, had helped set up. When the boy left him, David gave him all the equipment and left the office with wires sticking out and dust gathering on the desks. The empty office would be perfect for We Love Dogs.

"I'm going to ask him," Elisheva said to me. Within the week she'd set up a full office for We Love Dogs. I said nothing. Nor asked anything. Nor thanked anyone. Favors were a curse to me. I was afraid to ask for them because the debt would grow and I wouldn't be able to pay it back, to return the volume of my needs, and I'd start to do what I loved—steal. I insisted on paying $400 a week, which was what was left after deducting Elisheva's half of our earnings, the $300 for dog supplies and food, and $100 for my living expenses. I didn't need to eat much, nor did I like to. I had enough clothes since I wore mostly jeans and long-sleeved T-shirts to cover the multiple scars on my arms. I liked converse high-tops, but Elisheva said I was too old for them and they made me look dykey. As if I cared. But she took me to buy some soft, fashionable Nikes that were good enough for walking the dogs while also fulfilling my obligations toward downtown fashion.

I was alone most of the time, but this didn't bother me because my days were filled with dogs and their owners. And David started forcing me to go to Perry Street NA meetings with him, where he relished seeing and hearing the rehabilitation pseudoartist crowd. They were well dressed and self-righteous. I preferred lying, noninsightful criminals. I worked late into the night writing filing cards by hand. Each had the name of the client and dog, the address, how many times a week, how many hours, whether it was a walk or training or specialty exercise, and any idiosyncrasies about each dog or client I should watch out for. I had a bulletin board with holes and hooks from which I hung keys and special leashes for particularly aggressive dogs or dogs that pulled me too hard. And on one tiny hook hung a pink, unexplained, broken-and-glued-together china pony.

Elisheva handled the phone and schmoozed the new clients. She'd bought one of those Barnes & Noble calendars sporting photos of purebred dogs dressed in high fashion and filled it with my schedule. Simultaneously, she was tutoring a whole slew of bar- and bat-mitzvah students, but her energy was high and being with me was her idea of an adventure. Truth be told, I didn't even know if she had any kind of emotional connection to dogs. But she did know business. And she was a master hustler. She worked hard to get word of mouth going for We Love Dogs.

I asked her if Batya had received my last letter, and she paused for a minute and said she didn't really know. She told me that Batya Shulamit was in the adolescent phase of finding her father stupid and ridiculous, so, out of spite, the little girl had told him about the letters and Elisheva's part in the espionage of connecting with me. Leonard fired Elisheva on the spot, but didn't call the Jewish, pre–bar mitzvah parents of uptown New York. Batya Shulamit was clearly exquisitely prepared and told her father that if he caused anyone trouble, she'd tell her teachers he beat her.

Elisheva found the whole thing hilarious, but I, on the other hand, was stricken by fear. I wasn't sure how vindictive Leonard would be. If he'd call the cops, a lawyer, the police, child protective services. I didn't know what could come down on my head from a legal point of view and ruin any chances of a positive outcome of my next petition. Sure, Batya Shulamit threatened Leonard with telling lies about child abuse. But was she protecting me as well, or just Elisheva? I felt strangely lost because now I had no real way to get to Batya Shulamit except through letters that would probably be thrown out before they reached her.

"When did this happen?" I asked Elisheva. I held back a reaction of betrayal that I knew would scare the shit out of her. "When were you fired?"

"Oh my God," Elisheva said. "Months ago. So many months ago. I didn't tell you because We Love Dogs was just taking off and I didn't want to stress you out more. I miss Batya terribly, though, because she understood the true meaning. I'm choking on Hebrew, Carleen. It tastes like gefilte fish in my throat. These rich parents. The bar mitzvahs with dinosaur themes. Or waitresses dressed like SWAT squads. The millions of dollars spent on the parties. I am sick and I am ashamed. It has nothing to do with the reason for the ritual. It has no relation to the beauty of Judaism. To community. To family. Ancestry. Keeping our faith though generations destroyed by madness. It no longer has anything to do with the beauty of the language and the metaphors for a truthful and moral life that appear in each passage. But Batya truly understood."

"Understood what?" I asked.

"The search for true goodness. For God's light in a dark world. Don't you go cynic on me. Listen. She understood that her bat mitzvah was her welcoming into a world full of charlatans. Sure, she was having her teenage psychosis, but she never stopped studying, and quietly, when she wasn't worried about being popular, she continued to write and read poetry. She never stopped praying."

"You never told me that. You never told me any of this."

"She told me when Leonard fired me that it was better for me to disappear because the dishonesty of her talking to you through me was beginning to stress her out. Stress *her* out, mind you. She said she'd get in touch before the bat mitz-vah and we'd study in the last days. That I'd given her more than any teacher would dare. How can you stay mad at a kid like that?"

"You say this was months ago?" I probed.

"If there was going to be any trouble, it would've happened already," Elisheva assured me. "I was so worried. But Batya told Leonard to ground her and leave you out of it. Like I said, if he got you in trouble, she'd tell the police he'd been abusing her. Poor Leonard. He's not a bad man at all. No father was blessed with the equipment to go to war with a smart teenage daugh-ter. I think it's as hopeless as Afghanistan."

"So this happened months ago?" I knew I was asking the same question over and over again. I just couldn't wrap my head around it.

"Oh, yes," Elisheva said. "If Leonard was planning some conspiracy or if he was going to have us taken in for child endangerment, it would've happened already. I still tutor all of Batya's best friends, so there's not even an embargo."

"Months ago," I repeated. Batya Shulamit hadn't contacted me at all.

MAURICE

David was in a frenzy of pacing back and forth upstairs. He paced constantly, and I found the continuous movement comforting. We saluted in passing but barely talked. He had a highly published show of new works at MoMA and was drastically behind. He kept saying he couldn't get the textures he wanted for his backgrounds and it was destroying him. Nonetheless, he'd go out all night carrying on with young and old lovers and friends. He had a yearning for late nights at tiny, new Village and Soho restaurants that would only seat twelve or fifteen people. He adored exploring the architecture of the run-down, impoverished Lower East Side apartments of his very young lovers, and the minimalist, oriental, massive loft spaces of his choreographer and musician friends who'd made it in the art world. He went to do the samba at SOB's and went to see post-modern dance concerts and performance art after midnight in small, nameless theaters and site-specific living rooms and kitchens. He was avoiding his painting. He was destroying himself, because without his backgrounds he was nothing.

As for me, the chaos of a dog walking day usually ended by 10:00 or 10:30 p.m. I'd have a sandwich and walk the streets, or I'd go home and go to sleep. Elisheva was ingenious at building out business. She said this was her calling, along with producing Broadway shows, falling in love, and having babies. She had built our practice to the point where we needed another walker, but I trusted no one. My health was better but it would never be prime, so I didn't mind hanging around David's at night to compensate for my twelve-to-fifteen hour days.

One night at 1:00 or 1:30 a.m., I was particularly edgy and I found myself pacing like David in between his canvases. He was gone for the night, as usual. I looked down on the paintings as if I were scaling a rock face outside Jackson Hole. I suddenly knew what he'd been searching for in his backgrounds and that, for some self-destructive reason, he was blind to it. I pulled out cans of paint and poured them on his half-done canvases and brushed in the colors and laid on the textures. I used up all the paint in the studio and finished the backgrounds for the two biggest canvases that had been torturing him. He'd simply wanted a thicker cover. He'd needed his own planetary surface. I drifted into a kind of chemical sleep on the floor next to a canvas. I breathed in the smell of paint. I was covered in the muted blues, grays, and reds he'd been searching for. I knew those were the colors of his planet. As it dried on me I became a reptile, with hard but flexible skin. I was pleased with my work.

"Get in here!" he screamed from his office. "I mean *now*," he wailed.

I was sticky with paint and sick from taking too much of it in my lungs. My arthritis was stiff from all the activity the night before. I panicked, but I realized it was still dark. I hadn't missed any dog pick-ups. Then I remembered what I had done. I'd gone on a binge.

David was sitting in a revolving desk chair in a bathrobe he'd stolen from a luxury hotel in St. Barts (he had a collection of stolen bathrobes). His large face was very severe, and he wore his glasses, which made him look old and powerful. I sat down on the floor in front of him.

"Sit in a fucking chair," he said coldly.

I began to shiver. I was afraid of myself. That I had done something or would do something to blow apart my carefully structured routine. I seemed incapable of a settled life.

"You broke the boundaries, Essie. You broke the most sacrosanct, profound boundary. You invaded my painting. You painted *on* my canvases."

"They were empty," I said helplessly.

"Not really, and you know that. I was getting ready to commence work."

"No you weren't," I replied. "You were stuck. You were panicked. You were empty." David stared at me with what he hoped was hatred.

"You trespassed on the most personal territory. It's as if your monstrous journey has taught you nothing. You used up all my materials. You're a sick, ungrateful bitch."

I was shaking with fear.

"You still can't control your strange impulses. You don't know anything about giving back."

"I was giving back," I said. "Now you can start painting."

David was silent for a long time.

"I should have you pack up your things and get out of here. I should commit you to Payne Whitney. My loft is transformed."

"Yes, it is," I tried. "I found it necessary to do so or you'd wreck your career."

"It's absolutely none of your business," he shook his head.

"I'm trying to learn about friendship, David."

"But you weren't thinking of me when you slobbered on

these canvases. You were only thinking of you. It's too good. It's too deep. It's the work of passion and commitments. Your body is in that paint."

"That was my way of thinking of you. I became you. I haven't painted anything worthwhile in years. I'm a dog walker."

"Get out of here." David was exhausted. "When you're done tonight start packing up. Why do I always love the psychos?"

I had my day ahead. I didn't want to be late for my 6:00 a.m. call. I showered with my clothes on since they were covered with paint. Then I changed and dashed out. As I left I could see David pacing unsteadily near a canvas. He had a paintbrush in each hand.

I went through my day with no major incidents. I had one dog, a mutt named Maurice, who was the size and shape of a French bulldog but with a hairy, long face—like a small, fat walrus. He had a bad habit of going after much bigger dogs on the street. He'd bare his teeth and jump toward the dog's neck, and usually a ruckus would ensue. The owner of the other dog would get offended and check his dog for bloody nicks. I'd get lectured, yelled at, and each walk was a minute war. Maurice's owners, Ellen and Clarence, were perfectly nice people who'd rescued him from Bideawee, where Ellen would make an annual contribution following a clear mammogram. One time she saw Maurice and he took her heart. She lugged him into a cab and introduced him to her husband, Clarence, and he too fell in love. But Maurice must've been badly abused because he'd go after Clarence for no reason. He'd bitten him twice out of the blue. And his behavior on the street caused them great distress. They'd had to pay vet bills for three other dogs. Otherwise, Maurice was obedient, loving, and playful. And his ugliness was so beautiful. Ellen and Clarence were heartbroken, but the vet said it would be best to put him to sleep before he really hurt someone or killed a dog, so they hired me as a last resort.

I'd started working with Maurice back when I was still with Hubb. I had a reputation for cooling out difficult dogs, and of course Hubb laid him on me without any warning whatsoever. I got bitten repeatedly and had to pull his chunky body off enough big bruisers before I got the picture. Mr. Pugnacious was scared to death of anything bigger than him that was male. So I started out by keeping him in the office and having some heart-to-hearts. "Look," I told Maurice, "they're gonna kill you and here's why." I bit him really hard on the neck—not enough to draw blood—and he was so shocked he didn't retaliate. He backed off. I did this several times and then slapped myself lightly, saying, "Stop." So I stopped myself and Maurice was relieved. I also found a large stuffed camel, and Maurice went insane when he saw him. I let him do what he wanted and he ripped the camel to shreds. The guy really could be a killer. The second camel I soaked in the hottest Tabasco sauce I could find. Maurice went after the camel and it burned his tongue so much he panted and whined and ran in circles and drank up three bowls of water. But this didn't stop him from going after the camel again because it was bigger than him. I told Clarence to wear old clothes around the house, to pour as much Tabasco sauce on himself as possible, and to carry a bottle in his pocket. Maurice became confused and withdrawn. But I bought him several balls, sticks, and bones made of really tough but chewable rawhide, and little by little I had Clarence feed him those toys from hand to mouth. I also kissed him all over and talked to him about what a good life he could have as I scratched his favorite spots.

Now, months later, the attacks were definitely taking place less and less, but he was still on dog probation so I took him as much as I could for training. I used a spiked chain collar, which stopped him. Phyllis would not have approved of this negative technique, but some dogs had been reared in pain and could only be reconditioned with another kind of pain. I understood that. I was rooting for the little walrus. I didn't want him killed. I was rooting for myself too. I didn't want to be homeless and have to resort to the trust fund of the shit person I'd abandoned years ago. I didn't want to ask Ester for money.

I knew I had to relocate my office, but I had other things to think about. This was what I called boot-camp day. There was a two-hour period when I was asked by the owners to simply walk their dogs with others, have them do their business, and bring them home. I looked like one of those Upper East Side walkers with arms full of leashes, leading bored, snooty dogs of all sizes who were spoiled and didn't get enough exercise. Many of them had T-shirts or coats despite the weather, and politically correct collars supposedly beaded by women in Kenya.

I couldn't stand the pack walking, and I felt useless and stupid. So I came up with a routine. We'd all walk, but we were a troop and we had formations. I taught the dogs, including Pomeranians and toy poodles, to start on the same foot and walk in unison. "Left, right, left," I'd call out. I had them in formation from the smallest in the front to the Bernese mountain dogs in the back. They marched, and when I called out "Halt!" the whole gang screeched simultaneously to a stop whether we were at a crosswalk or not. They sat on "sit down, doggies," and lay flat on "down ya go." They ran when I yelled "hep, hep," and they stayed in formation, no dog butting in front of the other.

This wasn't hard to do, and made the walk more interesting for me and certainly more athletic for them. I had plans for them to sit and drag their butts on the ground, hop on their back legs and then their front legs, and I wanted them to make concentric circles. All of this in good time. I never did any of the group stuff when people pointed at us or started to gather. I knew it looked insufferably cute and the dogs would know it, too, and I wasn't in the business of creating a dog show for birthday parties.

Later that night when I returned to David's loft, he was dashing from canvas to canvas with two or three brushes in each hand. He had five interns from the School of Visual Arts outlining figures from his sketches that were hanging from all the walls. He was wearing flip-flops and calling out demands in a happy drawl.

"Oh no, darling. I made that a curve. A simple curve. Like a contact lens, not a pregnant woman. Add red—no, brick—no, red. Darling, add 50 percent red 2.0 and brick 3.0, and I'll kill you later."

He saw me and motioned that I go into his office, which was now covered with patches of color, sticky notes, pads, telephone numbers written on the walls, and piles of smaller paintings—exquisite paintings of cartoon characters and ultrarealistic people involved in activities that superficially had no relation to each other, but they all subliminally danced.

"Are you satisfied with yourself?" he asked in a snotty tone.

"I'll be packing up, but I haven't had time to find another space," I replied.

"I was a guilt-ridden yenta this morning," he said.

"You were right. It was criminal behavior. I can't stop myself. I have to confine myself to a small space and do my job. I slipped. It scared me. What if I start lifting things from clients' homes?"

"No," David said. His voice dipped low. He sounded like a favorite aunt. "You have been doing *so* well, Carleen Kepper Ester Rosenthal Jim Jones, whatever your name is. I was narrow and cruel. I was humiliated. You'd found what I'd been unable to produce. You took the risk a friend takes."

"It wasn't my world to explore. I was like a squatter. I broke rules. I had a breakdown."

"I don't think so," David continued. "I think you were saving a dog from being put down. I was absolutely paralyzed and you knew it. You also knew the backgrounds I'd been screaming for inside. It was a gift. You were right. I see that now. It's just that you're so strange. Essie, one doesn't even know when your punches are coming. Help me finish the paintings. Otherwise I'll never make it. I promise not to give you credit."

"I'll pack up. I'll get on that Craigslist thing you showed me."

"Let's not do a 1940s 'I'm going, you're staying, I'm going, you're staying' scam. Neither of us has the time—and, well, I have the drama, but it doesn't go with your absolute lack of affect. Stay until the business really gets off its feet and then maybe, who knows, maybe we'll open a spa for dogs. Walking, training, massage, yoga, drumming, aromatherapy . . . "

"I hate that shit," I said. "Dogs are animals. Can I go to sleep?"

"No. Help me finish these paintings. You know exactly what to do."

I sighed. "If you hint that I helped you . . . "

"Are you going to agree to keep your office here?"

"Yes," I said immediately. "I'm too scared not to."

"Maybe you'll paint your own inner mind."

"Maybe I'll do neurosurgery and botany."

"The backgrounds were brilliant and perfect," David gushed.

"You use hyperbole too much," I said. "Or do all gay men do that?"

"The gods have not left you," David grinned wider.

I lay down on my rug next to Elisheva's desk and didn't bother about pajamas that night. I took in several breaths to calm me and prepared for extreme forgery. The bright light seemed more like the flicker of a castle of candles, and the active interns, as they learned, mixed, and painted, were nothing more than shadow puppets. The room had an old smell of paint and turpentine, which agitated me. But soon the stink of the dogs prevailed from the rug and the blanket. It was like a bizarre, somewhat foul bakery. I breathed in its scent. My night was brick and red colored. I worked on David's paintings in half the time of anyone else. But I stayed out of the master's way when he'd step in and conjure his final touches. His greatness was still apparent. And so was mine.

AN UNEXPECTED VISITOR

I was taking my lunch hour inside the *Queen Mary* fish boat on the Hudson. I'd been watching tugboats and freighters, when I heard footsteps. I turned and was surprised to see Batya. I couldn't help but feel my lips spreading into a small smile. But then I noticed she was by herself.

"What are you doing here?" I asked with anxiety. Maybe my maternal instincts had finally kicked in.

"Elisheva said this is where you ate lunch on Tuesdays, so I decided to try."

"Are you alone? It's not good if we're alone, Batya. Social services, the court, your father, my parole officer . . . "

She stayed on her feet.

"God, it's like you're in kindergarten. Jethro is going to tell Mr. Black and he'll tell the vice principal and she'll tell the Board of Education. I thought you were braver than that."

I sighed. She'd lost some of her pudginess and was becoming a lovely shape. Her long, straight red hair fell down her back and she parted it down the middle, each side held back with a barrette. Each barrette was a turquoise plastic bird. Her green eyes were brighter. I think she was wearing eye shadow. Her teeth hadn't quite straightened out yet, and I liked the silver of her braces. It made her look simultaneously fearsome and vulnerable. She was wearing a simple flowered dress, white with light purple flowers, and a cotton sweater that matched the flowers, and ballet slippers on her feet. She stood very straight, her hands in fists.

"Sit down." I sighed.

She tried to find one of the metal benches on the boat that wasn't too rusty. I could tell she was worried about her dress. Finally, she gingerly sat herself down on a ledge.

"Do you get seasick?" I asked her. The boat rocked heavily with the wind and tide. She let out a sigh.

"*Lawls,*" she said.

"Lawls . . . what?" I asked.

She rolled her eyes. "It's just a figure of speech."

I was quiet.

"Well, don't you want to ask me any questions?" Batya challenged.

"You're a minefield, lady," I answered. "Anywhere I step could blow up."

She liked that.

"Do you want to know why I'm here?" She was petulant.

"I figured we'd get around to it," I replied. "But keep in mind, I'm never late for my clients, so if I cut you off it's nothing personal."

"You're so confusing." She was annoyed.

"The fact that you find that confusing is confusing to me."

Batya looked down at her feet and swung them a little.

"I'm here to tell you that I know you've been really trying. But I don't want you to come to my bat mitzvah." She spoke fast and nervously.

"Here's why. If people see you, they'll know it's you and it'll be, whoa, this big deal. Dad'll freak, but he'll work really hard not to show it, and there'll be this whole subtext going on in the room that'll take away from the holiness of the occasion. And the whole thing will become about you when the day is meant to be completely focused on me."

"You've conveyed all this once already," I said, "and I shall obey."

Her face was red and she was slightly breathless.

"Does that hurt your feelings?"

I thought about it.

"I don't know," I answered truthfully.

"You don't *know*?" she asked angrily. "Your own daughter bans you from the most important day in her life and *you don't know* if it bothers you?"

"You've never pulled that card before," I said with surprise.

"What card?" Batya was sulking.

"The 'daughter' word. I'm a little taken aback that you consider yourself my daughter. Isn't that tall, blond Danish—"

"*Swedish*," Batya practically spit. "She's kind. She's a housewife. She likes fashion. She does meals and goes to dinner parties. She's told me stories about Europe. She knows nothing about art, literature, music, or writing. She designs children's clothes. How spiritual is that?"

"She seemed to do until recently."

"She left me alone," Batya scoffed. "I think she's scared of me because I'm smart. She's always left Leonard to deal with the heavy stuff. With me, I'm much more complicated than bunny suits and tiny winter caps with attached earmuffs."

"But she'll be up on the bema with you. She'll read a passage in Hebrew. She'll kiss you."

"I hate when she kisses me. She sticks to me like chapstick. How do you know about the bema and the reading?" Batya asked defensively.

"I'm learning to google," I replied.

"So you do care or 'are interested.'" There was a slight mocking tone.

I was quiet.

"I don't know," I answered.

Her face turned red and her nose began to run, but I have to give her credit, there were no tears.

"You're like some zombie!" she yelled. "You don't get your feelings hurt. You don't know if you care about anything."

She shuffled as if ready to storm out on me, but I could tell she wasn't ready yet. When she tried to get up, the boat rocked more.

"Sit down," I said rather firmly, and her face took on a frozen look. "Still scared of me?" I questioned.

"You *are* a serious criminal," she replied snottily.

"Good thinking," I said. "So you probably didn't come alone."

"No."

"Someone's waiting for you outside."

Batya was embarrassed.

"Actually, yes," she said. "Do you want to know who?"

"Not particularly," I said. "As long as it's not a cop."

"Hardly," she smiled her silver smile.

"Whatever," I said. "But this person has been waiting."

"He said he'll wait as long as I want."

I registered the "he" but didn't say anything. I made a difficult decision and became slightly anxious.

"Can you come a little closer?" I asked. "I promise I won't touch you. I want to tell you some confidential facts."

Reluctantly, she moved to my bench, but the far side from me.

"When I was in jail, I got beat up a lot. I might have some brain damage." A moment passed. "No . . . what—" I tried to start over. "No, I think I was born this way. I'm like a clock that's set wrong. Or I have lifelong jet lag. I don't react to things too much when they happen. Sometimes before. Sometimes after. Sometimes even weeks or months after. Time is not my friend. It keeps me from people. I don't have emotions when I should. But I do know that this isn't normal and my actions do affect others who are normal and have regular emotions. And sometimes those actions are enough and they satisfy me. Like I know this visit will have a very big impact on me. I just don't know when or how or what it will feel like."

Batya Shulamit was fascinated, but dubious. "So, what are you, autistic? Or that Asperger's thing?"

"I don't know. I'm going to google it and see."

"So you think that's an excuse?" Batya went nasty again. "An excuse for your whole fucked-up life?"

"I don't believe in excuses," I heard myself saying.

"I think you're just rationalizing because you never say you're sorry and you never *are* sorry."

"I may be somewhat pathological," I agreed.

Batya stood up and held on to the rocking boat.

"Be careful," I said.

"See?" she hissed. "You said *that* on time."

"It's not a regular phenomenon." I tried to get the facts straight.

"I'm really glad you're not coming to my bat mitzvah because, according to you, maybe something that happened to you ten years ago will just pop up and, *oh*, you'll start taking your clothes off and singing a chant from Hare Krishna."

"It's not like that," I said tightly. "You're smart. You know it's not like that."

Batya bowed her head.

"Well, I'm not sorry you're not invited to my bat mitzvah. You're mentally unbalanced and selfish."

"You could be right," I agreed again.

"God, I hate you," she grumbled.

"I have something for you," I replied. I held out the antique mezuzah with the amber stone. I'd gone back and bought it.

Batya Shulamit gasped.

"It's, like, the most beautiful thing I've ever seen. I love jewelry and this is so cool. It's so spiritual and ancient . . . but it doesn't change anything!"

I helped her put it on. When I touched her I felt the beginning of a kind of weeping in my throat. The boat rocked and she fell into me. I kept completely still.

"You'd let me fall and not catch me?" she asked.

"I don't know," I said. "I don't think you'd get hurt."

Batya held the mezuzah as it hung around her neck as if she couldn't tell if the shape gave her strength or weakness. Then she spit at me. Actually spit.

"Just don't come," she shouted. "Make sure you don't come."

"I don't even know the date," I told her. "Or the place. Or the time."

She started climbing out of the boat. She looked at me. It was as if she wanted me to say something else, to say I was coming.

"Goodbye, bag lady, dog woman, psycho, never-ever mother."

"Batya Shulamit," I called out, but she didn't stop.

I spoke quietly, but loud enough so she could hear if she chose.

"I came to New York City with no hope I'd ever talk to you. Or even see you. Even from a distance. You've given me so much more. A powder keg of mixed blessings."

THE SAVIOR'S ARM

I arrived at my office to find the area surrounded by ten or twelve tall piles of old cardboard boxes. Elisheva and David sat on the floor trying to gather the massive amounts of bubble wrap that had been ripped from inside them. I saw a corner of a twenty-year-old sketchbook. It set me into a flashback. I wanted to kick David and Elisheva in the head for uncovering them. I could feel in my legs the urge to lunge at them and the boxes. I heard screaming voices and the creaking of bars from above my head. Ugly laughter. Mocking words. Pain burned my joints. Fear and anger brought vomit to my throat. I struggled to the bathroom and sat down next to the toilet. I stood up and poured cold water on my face and hair. I resisted the urge to smash the face I saw in the mirror. A younger version of myself covered with bruises and scars. I was boxed in. It was an amusement-park ride. The walls were pushing in closer and closer—the floor lifting, the ceiling coming down. I was going to be crushed. But I couldn't call for help. I looked for an empty notebook. If I could fill it I might avert the physical abuse that was surely coming my way. I'd do bright colors, shapes, vehicles. Fits loved 18-wheelers. She'd open up the room but there were no sketchbooks. No paint. The room was closing in. I was suffocating. I blacked out.

I woke up later with my head on the toilet seat. I'd thrown up and cracked my forehead against David's expensive porcelain. Blood dripped down my face. David and Elisheva stood hopelessly in the doorway.

"Essie?" David asked. "Should I call a doctor?"

"I'm Carleen Kepper," I hissed at him. "I don't need a doctor."

"Well, I'm calling one," Elisheva said, her voice mixed with panic, efficiency, and disgust.

"I'll give you the name of my gynecologist friend," David said. "Don't make funny faces—just call."

I was so dizzy. Vertigo gripped my feet and swung me around in violent circles. But I was returning to the present tense. David pressed a towel filled with ice to my forehead. I grabbed it from him and pressed it hard myself. The pain pushed me closer to wakefulness.

"How in fucking hell's name did those boxes get here?" I moaned.

"I don't think you should talk now." He ignored my question.

We sat in silence for a long time.

My injury throbbed at an even beat. Rappers sang to the constant drum. Electric whines played descants. Gilbert and Sullivan joined in. A marching band. I was passing out again.

When I opened my eyes I was sitting up on my bed, and the gynecologist with severe black hair and large glasses was finishing stitches on my forehead.

"David," I heard her say. "This woman belongs in a hospital. She could have a serious concussion. She's obviously unstable. She's trouble for you."

"I'll take care of it," I heard him reply. "Write down what you're supposed to do for concussions."

"David . . . "

"I'd like to pay you. And I must pay you for silence. Please, pick a watercolor."

"But David they're worth . . . ," the doctor stammered.

"Luckily I'm not Georgia O'Keeffe, so you're not stuck with something that looks like a vagina. Pick one that soothes you. I know this is all a little unsettling."

The doctor picked a painting that was about eight by ten and quietly went toward the door.

"Lots of fluids." She gaped at me through her thick-framed black glasses.

Elisheva was cleaning the bloody gauze and towels and changing the pillowcase. She appeared completely unruffled, but I think at that moment she was reconsidering the entire direction of her life.

"Elisheva, come here, please," I said. I patted the bed. She sat down cautiously, more for my sake than hers.

"I'm starting to be able to explain some things, so let me tell you what you just saw. It was a flashback. Like you see on TV when all those vets have flashes about Vietnam and go berserk. I am learning to control them as well as possible."

"I've never seen a look on your face like when you saw those boxes." She shivered.

"They have dark memories for me. They represent a time I have to forget. In my subconscious. Think about me like I'm a vet. I'm back from a firefight where all my friends were killed. Like an Oliver Stone movie, okay?"

She still looked freaked out.

"Tell me how these got here," I slurred. Elisheva snuggled a little more into the bed. She always liked to tell a good story.

"So the doorbell rings," she started, "and it's FedEx, and I'm busy working on this month's billing so I let them in, and it's these kind of musty cardboard boxes. And they keep coming and coming and coming. It's like those clowns that come out of a little car in the circus. They just don't stop coming! I always wondered how they did that. Trap door? So I have the deliverymen pile them in the hallway by the offices like you see, and I sign for them. And bam! The door doesn't close and about fifteen guys come in wearing bulletproof vests and shit, holding those *Hawaii Five-0* rifles, and I'm thinking, 'Please, dear God, I don't want to die before having at least four children and a career as a star,' and then I'm so afraid I stop thinking. It's like I'm sweating on the inside and I say, 'Wait, wait you guys—wait I'm twenty-six years old. I work for a dog walking service and I teach Hebrew. Can I see a paper or something?'"

"Good for you," I said.

"So this bald guy comes up and he's holding a folder that's as thick as *Vogue*'s fall fashion issue, and he says, 'Lady, I got papers and papers,' and he pulls out a badge, 'but why waste everyone's time?' So I'm sorry I didn't make them wait. I really thought I was going to throw up like you. I'm not good with conflict. The man told me some old lady in Ohio died and left instructions that these had to be transported to Carleen Kepper at whatever cost—directly with no interference. The local post office called FedEx and FedEx was nervous about those boxes. They looked at who they're being sent to and they recognized the name and called the FBI. So the FBI picked up the boxes at Kennedy and took them to their office in case they were bombs or drugs. There they searched out where you live. So the FBI put together this SWAT team to deliver the boxes to a terrorist cell or something. But it's this millionaire famous painter's loft with all the furniture so white that it makes them more suspicious. Then they check every inch of those boxes for drugs or illegal arms.

"I thought I'd plotz. But I wanted to be there to represent you when they opened the boxes. God knows why. They were so disappointed, man, when it was only sketchpads. 'Specially since each pad was wrapped like something dangerous in bubble wrap and masking tape. Whoever wrapped those notebooks was totally anal. Even with scissors and knives it took forever to open each one. And there had to be, like, I don't know, four hundred sketchpads. They flipped through all the pages to see if there were names or codes or telephone numbers or threatening letters or proofs of crimes and they took pictures and then at some point they just gave up, pissed as hell, and just left. David came home and found me in the middle of this resounding mess, and then you. Neither of us, I swear, looked long at the paintings. First of all, there are like four million of them and, second, someone should respect your privacy."

"Elisheva," I began. "You did right. Absolutely right. But I don't think you should be around me so much anymore. It's too much fear and drama. I can do my billing and appointments. You come in every month or two and check out that I'm not doing anything to get myself arrested."

Elisheva picked at her skirt and looked both sad and relieved.

"I think you're right."

"Good," I said. My head was starting to send pain messages throughout my whole body.

"Here's the other part of the barter."

"What barter?" Elisheva asked tearfully.

"You did more than your half already. Are you going to rabbinical school?"

Elisheva turned away a bit as if ashamed to look at me.

"Yes," she said. "Because of my grades and work, I am starting as a second year at Hebrew Union College rather than a first."

"I thought so. Okay, so you know I'm rich? Right?"

Elisheva nodded. "But you've never touched a penny of it."

"Because I have to live out more years of building back from the crook I was," I explained.

"I don't disagree," Elisheva said.

"Okay, so when you're a fully fledged rabbi—anointed, plowed, endowed, whatever—you call me on the day of your embalming or whatever it's called."

"Why?" Elisheva's expression was slightly suspicious and worried, like I might do something to embarrass her.

"Because I'm going to build you a temple," I said. "We'll find the right spot overlooking the river and I'll buy the land. Then I'm going to design it and draw it from my own visions. I'll collaborate with you, and I'll hire young carpenters with strong hands that you can go out with after they're done working for the day."

"That's a dream," Elisheva said with a sad and hopeful smile. Deep inside she thought I was mentally ill. Deeper still, she knew I wasn't.

"I rarely dream," I told her. "It's not very practical and it doesn't get things done."

"You'd do that for me?" she asked.

"I'd do it now except you don't have the proper beatification or coronation papers or whatever they are."

"Why did you decide this now?" she asked, still thinking I was jabbering from my head injury or shocked at seeing the sketches.

"Lately I've been thinking . . . and I think this woman named Phyllis saved my life, though I don't know for how long or if it was for any good reason. I know I'm alive when I make things.

I know I'm alive when I walk dogs. I feel my feet on the grass or cement and the slight pull on the leash. And I know that, like me, they don't know why they're headed forward with this force behind, guiding their direction. Aside from necessary practical acts. Your temple tugs at me like a good dog. Like Doorbell, one of my favorites. That simplicity keeps me going. And you are the unusual person like Phyllis who deserves a pulpit. Don't ask me anything else. Just graduate. I want to walk dogs, build you a temple, and do a couple other things that aren't any of your business. In your world, you might call it gratitude."

Nights later, I caught David leafing through the sketchbooks.

"If I wasn't medicated I'd take you in a choke hold," I grumbled.

He jumped. Everyone will always remain slightly scared of me.

"What *are* these?" He couldn't take his eyes off the pictures.

I told him the story of Fits. My big, jowly, gay friend sat with his mouth open the whole time.

"Catching flies," I said at one point. He closed it.

"There's so much going on here. It's an encyclopedia of psychosis." He opened it again. "But in this whole bunch there must be fifty absolute masterpieces or more. I need more time."

"I want to give you all my money except the dog walking profits, David. Tomorrow I'm going to contact my schmo lawyer Harry and move all my accounts and trusts and bonds over to you."

"But, Essie," he looked over at me, "I'm already rich. I certainly don't need it."

"That's why," I answered simply.

"Let's do it this way," he said playfully. "It's our money. I'll put in all of mine too, and we'll have joint bank accounts and estates and all that."

"Sounds like fun," I nodded.

"But I spend and you don't. You have to start spending."

"I have plans."

"Legal?" he asked nervously.

"Yes," I snapped back.

"Well, I have to protect myself from your craziness."

"Oh, absolutely," I agreed. "Protect yourself away."

"Where is all of this coming from?" he asked.

"My soul was locked in those sketchbooks. I want to see if there's any possibility of breathing better when they're out in the open. Pandora's box. The opposite of Pandora's box. Once the box is empty the mythological flies and gnats and maggots can be gone. That time of my life can recede from my nightmares."

"But no happiness?" David questioned.

"I don't live in a country that has that word. It is not even a term that applies to my kind of creature."

"And what is that?"

"Subhuman. Unfeeling. Criminal. I have one thing I want to do though, if you're interested."

"Are you going to paint again?" David asked with too much hope. It grated me.

"Fuck no," I answered. "I walk dogs."

David was laughing and I liked to watch his face. He was like a traffic light or a stop sign in a big windstorm.

I made sure I was a half hour late. I hid in the back in the darkness of one of those corners or curves that large synagogues have. I'd brought Doorbell, all decked out in his jacket with the yellow training cape and stickers and stenciled letters so no one would question us. I'd even attached him to a blind person's halter, though I made no effort to pretend I couldn't see. He looked ridiculous. I wore one of the flowered dresses Tina had picked out for me and a silk shawl. My colors were shades of blue. I wore ballet flats so I wouldn't make myself any taller than I already was. She couldn't see me during the service. I didn't like the tableau up on the bema, with Pony wrapped in a shiny embroidered cloth and a white yarmulke on her red head. Leonard stood behind like a modest hippie who was only now adopting the faith. A young rabbi with a Bruce Springsteen beard stood next to Pony, and on the other side stood Elisheva, dressed in a chic black dress, high heels, and an even more embroidered shawl than Pony's. Her yarmulke was more Muslim than Jewish and beaded from top to bottom in bright colors and Hebrew letters. "Go girl," I said to myself. At least she was fighting the mortuary setting. I also saw Leonard's wife in basic parental black. This was the first time I'd looked at her and she was not unlikeable. She seemed to be completely out of place in her tall, slim model's body and platinum-blond hair. But she was making a go of it. They all chanted various Hebrew passages in varying bad accents, and Pony Batya Shulamit was the star.

She held a long silver claw and whipped through the Torah portion like a pro. I could see Elisheva mouthing all the words by heart. She pushed my daughter into womanhood with her true heart. The rabbi invited grandparents onto the platform and my parents crawled up, so old. They assisted each other. They both had problems walking. I found this interesting but not moving. I was relieved when they left the bema because they'd made the picture too crowded. I noticed for the first time that the synagogue was old and Byzantine with a round, stained-glass roof. Audience members packed the pews and I began to sweat. Who were all these people? Doorbell sensed my nerves and sat up. The light on the bema was very well focused, and the family looked like a Jewish version of the nativity scene. The room began to contract, expand, vibrate, and my hands went cold and numb. I slipped myself a Klonopin. Now Batya Shulamit sang and read by herself and it actually sounded like the first song a bird would sing very early in the morning. It reminded me of the one or two sparrows I could make out when I lay in my bed in the honors cottage at Clayton looking forward to the day with Androcles. Not a pretty sound, but earnest and dutiful. Then Batya began to read a speech in English, but I couldn't understand it because it was like the ocean rushing in my ears.

I held on tight to Doorbell's harness and he leaned into me. I wished I could've heard my daughter's style of writing, but I knew the content too well. The princess. The prodigious infant floating in the woven basket by the bulrushes. The leaves growing from the water that could be dried into paper. The unexpected cry from the usually silent baby that alerted the princess to the existence of the basket. The blessed elongated arm of the princess as it reached to retrieve the basket from the murderous Nile. The non-Jewish princess unknowingly loving the prince who would free the Jews from her tyrant of a father. She brought him up as her own son. Mothers and children. Blood ties and bonds of blind love. The irony. The fairy tale. The future of the Jewish faith in the long arm of a woman who smashed her father's idols.

The story was beginning to go out of sequence in my head. The beautiful little girl on the bema called out her interpretations as if running for office. Confident. A seeker. A lover of stories and their real meanings, what she thought might be the truth. Her small hands gesturing in the air like sad and beautiful torn flags left after a war. She finished. Applause.

Then the rabbi mumbled some conclusive Hebrew and kissed her on the forehead. The congregation cheered and sharp objects began to fly through the air. My first instinct was to drop to the floor. The snipers were breaking up a fight in the courtyard. Then I remembered that Elisheva told me how, at the end, the community throws hard candies at the young woman to welcome her and wish her a sweet life. But then why did one hit me just above my eye?

I looked up and Batya Shulamit Rosenthal Kepper Salin was grinning at me. A mouth of silver. She'd nailed me. She threw another and it hit my hair. I gave her a thumbs-up. Batya's concentration went back to the cheering crowd. She became engulfed in a group hug of those who were strangers to me.

I slipped out past middle-aged Jewish men in tuxedos, carnations in the button holes and lapels. They regarded me suspiciously, and Doorbell and I picked up our pace. Limos lined up for the landslide of people who would descend the steps.

I had a moment to myself and felt an emptiness that was not unpleasant. It was like when you're high up in an airplane and you look out the window and the sky creates flat blue spaces in between unpredictable white clouds that have nothing to do with rain. Then I noticed that my forehead gently stung. I put my fingers to the spot and the impact of the candy had broken the skin. There was just the littlest spot of blood. Batya Shulamit had quite a strong arm. And, despite the bobbing heads and flutters of hats, she'd reached a long arm and found her mark. Her aim was flawless.

AFTERWORD

The singular book you hold in your hands is the final work of Liz Swados—a trusted girlfriend, a whirlwind of ideas who always took my imagination past all previous boundaries, a wood sprite who was some timeless and mysterious force of nature, and a very practical organizer working hard to get her next project done. Since her ideas had no precedent and were somewhere between street theater, opera, a consciousness-raising group, and a homeless shelter—not to mention books of words and images for children and grownups, including one that made depression un-depressing—this was never easy. Yet when her projects happened, no one exited the theater or put the book down as the same person they were before.

I always left her with a feeling that my sense of color and texture had been heightened, as if no one else's hair was that shade of red, and no one else's tweeds and sweaters had the same feeling, and no one else's vibrations were as tuned as the guitar she played. I used to worry about her high level of energy—she was just on a faster timeline than the rest of us, and I feared she might burn out.

I don't know if that's what happened. I do know that it is

wrong that such energy and talent and kindness and creativity should have left the world—especially when she was a decade and a half younger than I am. It's not right.

I can only suggest that each of us who loved her try to take on an echo of what we saw and felt in her, and keep it alive at our dinners together and in our books and in our theaters and in our activism and in the world.

Then she will be with us always, now and forever more.

—GLORIA STEINEM
New York, New York
February 2016

© *Mike Coppola*

ELIZABETH SWADOS is most well-known for her Broadway hit *Runaways* and her graphic memoir, *My Depression: A Picture Book*, which received the Ken Book Award as well as a New York Public Library Award and was adapted into an HBO documentary starring Sigourney Weaver and Fred Armisen. She is a five-time Tony nominee and the recipient of three Obie Awards, a Guggenheim Fellowship, and a Ford grant, among numerous other honors.

Swados died on January 5, 2016, soon after completing this novel.

The Feminist Press is a nonprofit educational organization founded to amplify feminist voices. FP publishes classic and new writing from around the world, creates cutting-edge programs, and elevates silenced and marginalized voices in order to support personal transformation and social justice for all people.

See our complete list of books at
feministpress.org

THE FEMINIST PRESS
AT THE CITY UNIVERSITY OF NEW YORK
FEMINISTPRESS.ORG